MW01609350

The Alien Mate Index

Book 3: Descended

Evangeline Anderson

PUBLISHED BY:

Evangeline Anderson Books

The Alien Mate Index

Book 3: Descended

Copyright © August 2016 by Evangeline Anderson

License Notes

This book is licensed for your personal enjoyment only. This book may not be re-sold or given away to other people. If you would like to share this book with another person, please purchase an additional copy for each person you share it with. If you're reading this book and did not purchase it, or it was not purchased for your use only, then you should purchase your own copy. Thank you for respecting the author's work.

Dedication

With love to all my Kindred readers. If you like *Kindred,* I think you'll love *Alien Mate Index* as well. I write these books with all of you in mind. I feel very blessed to have such awesome people to pretend with me.

Hugs and Happy Reading to you all!

Evangeline

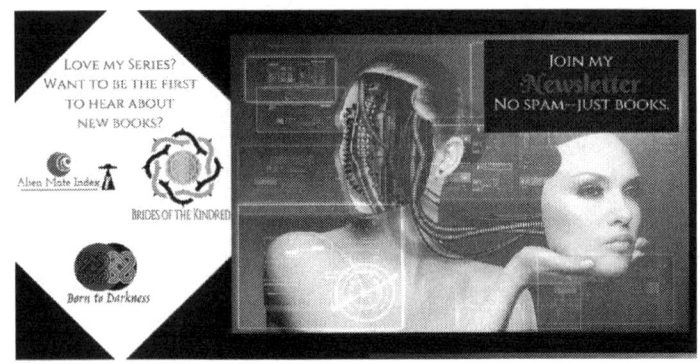

To be the first to find out about new releases join my newsletter at www.EvangelineAnderson.com.

Table of Contents

The Alien Mate Index

Book 3: Descended

Evangeline Anderson

Prologue

Location: Aboard Assimilation ship EOC-2789, the private vessel of Count Doloroso. In orbit around the planet humans call "Mars".

Time: Several solar days following the death of Doloroso's human host body and the subsequent acquisition of his new Majoran host body.

The new body was working out splendidly. Count Doloroso— for so he still preferred to refer to himself, despite his numerous recent physical changes— stretched his muscular arms with delight. He still couldn't get over how much *better* he felt in the Majoran host than he had in the human one.

This body was young and strong and virile and best of all, it wasn't orange. Well, not unless he *wanted* it to be. For Majorans were chromatacromes, able to change their hair and skin and eye color at will. It was the perfect disguise—really, he couldn't understand why he hadn't taken a Majoran as a host before.

It had been extremely lucky, his old host body dying just as a perfect new host was available right on his own ship. The little silver drone that carried his essence and injected it into new sentient host bodies had only had to fly a few feet to sting one of the Imperial Guards on the neck. No one had even noticed when he took over—the transition had been exceedingly smooth.

As for the other Imperial Guards, he had managed to lure them down to the stasis booths in the belly of the ship. One by one he had tricked them into entering the empty booths and one by one he had frozen them in suspended animation. Now he had enough hosts to last him for years! Count Doloroso felt positively rich.

Of course there was still one problem, Doloroso admitted as he paced back and forth in the control area of his ship—he still lacked a

La-ti-zal to utilize in his new breeding program. How could he begin production of a whole new race of Organic Assimilated if he couldn't get a *La-ti-zal* female to impregnate?

There was the one, of course—the last one of Zoe's friends who was one of those females blessed by the Ancient Ones. But how could he get to her? Especially now that the *Majoran* captain of the Imperial Guard was watching over her? That was the question that had been occupying him for days as he orbited Mars, out of range of detection from his enemies.

A sudden thought made him stop pacing.

Then again, who said he had to get to her and take her away from Earth himself?

A slow smile curved his new lips. The *Majoran* captain would do that for him. Because he believed that Charlotte—that was her name, correct?—was the new incarnation of the Goddess-Empress. And so he would take her away from Earth and head for Femme One, where the throne and palace of the Empress was located.

Doloroso had a long history with the Empress—the old one, that was. She had been a *La-ti-zal* and a Seer—one who was granted visions of the future by the meddling Goddess of the Twelve Peoples.

Due to her unfair advantage, the old Empress had been able to wipe out his entire race. He alone had survived to try and propagate his species, that of sentient machines inhabiting living hosts. The Assimilation had once been a mighty force to be reckoned with and yet the Goddess-Empress had brought them low and all but wiped them out.

What if he returned the favor?

Doloroso's smile became a wide, evil grin. If he could get his hands on the new Empress, what amazing things could he accomplish? He could impregnate her with his seed, yes, but the possibilities went far beyond a single pregnancy. He could hold her for ransom and demand anything he wanted—he could even demand that every *La-ti-zal* in the galaxy be brought to him for his personal use and delectation. He could have a whole *harem* of *La-ti-zal* brood mares—all impregnated with his seed—all incubating Organic Assimilated fetuses!

Doloroso rubbed his new, strong hands together in delight. Oh yes, he had plans for the new Empress. And he wouldn't even have to go to the trouble of going down to Earth to find her. Captain Verrai would bring her right to him…on Femme One.

Quickly, he went to set a course for the Majoran capital planet. He would have to make excuses, of course, for his delay and the "loss" of the other Imperial Guards, but those little details could easily be explained. There was much to put into place, many preparations to make in order to be ready.

He was determined that this time, he would not fail. The Assimilation would rise again and every sentient being in the galaxy would speak its name with fear and awe and wonder.

The Last Day would become the First.

Chapter One

Charlotte

I slipped into a supply closet at the North Florida Regional Medical Center hospital where I was doing my surgical rotation, and crammed myself into a corner, breathing hard.

He'll never find me here! I'll be safe here, I told myself. Yet how many other times had I told myself the same thing, only to find that I was wrong?

I took a quick scan of the closet and breathed a sigh of relief. Stacks and stacks of fresh sheets and towels, sterile, plastic wrapped trays for various procedures, bags of saline—it was all good. I didn't see any shiny, reflective surfaces here. There was no way he could find me.

That is, until I had to go out again.

Which would be as soon as any of the dozen or so patients under my direct supervision had a problem and one of their nurses paged me. And that could be at any moment. So I needed to take a moment to enjoy my sense of peace and safety now.

Then I heard it—that high, squeaky voice that had been haunting me for weeks.

"Attention, Charlotte Walker," it said, coming from somewhere overhead. "I have a message that I must deliver to you."

Looking up, I saw that the light fixture in the supply closet had a curving, silver metal side which was shiny enough to reflect light. Only instead of the dull glint of the light bulb, it was showing a strange, blue worm-like creature with multiple arms and eyes that were mounted on stalks.

It was the same creature I had been seeing for weeks. It appeared *everywhere*—the bowl of my metal spoon when I was eating oatmeal or yogurt, the side of the toaster when I was making toast, even the shiny metal surgical instruments laid out on the tray in the operating theater where I was supposed to be assisting.

The other day it had appeared in the middle of a splenectomy, speaking to me from the blade of a scalpel in its tiny, high voice that only I could hear.

The blue worm creature had startled me so badly I had dropped the scalpel I had been handing to the surgeon right into the patient's open body cavity! Luckily, the scalpel had fallen handle first, so it hadn't severed any major blood vessels or punctured any organs, but the surgeon had been livid. I had been dismissed from the surgery with a black mark on my record.

Thanks a lot, you little blue bastard!

Day and night the worm followed me—unless I slept in a completely dark room with no reflective surfaces. But have you heard when medical interns get to sleep? That's right—almost never. We're constantly on call, constantly on the move. And we almost never get a good night's sleep—or any sleep at all, for that matter.

It was awful and also, the main reason I was convinced I was going crazy.

"Charlotte Walker," the blue worm said again. "I have accepted payment to deliver a message to you regarding—"

"No! *NO!*" I screamed, finally "losing my shit" as my best friend Zoe would say.

Zoe. God, I missed her—she had disappeared months ago and nobody knew what had happened to her. When my other friend, Leah, and I had finally made the painful decision to stop looking for her, I had decided to go to med school and drown my sorrows in work. And because I was already a PA, I'd been allowed to jump right into the third year which meant clinical rotations at the hospital and plenty of action to distract me.

At first, everything had been fine—well, as fine as it could be after losing my friend. But then the blue worm had started stalking me. And now, after weeks of constant harassment, I couldn't stand it anymore.

"Charlotte Walker—"

"No, no, no!" I shouted. "Leave me alone!"

I pulled off one of my comfortable clogs, stood on a plastic stool which was obviously used for reaching the higher shelves, and began banging on the light fixture as hard as I could.

"Leave me alone!" I screamed at the weird blue worm. *"Leave me the fuck alone!"*

"What's the matter, Walker—pager driving you bugshit?"

I looked over to see my friend and fellow intern, Sebastian Trent, leaning against the door jam with his arms crossed and a sarcastic little smile playing around the corners of his mouth.

"Shut up," I said, climbing off the stool and quickly replacing my clog. "I just, uh, thought I saw a worm up there."

"A worm?" He frowned. "What would a worm be doing on the ceiling?"

"Uh, spider, I mean. I thought I saw a *spider*," I said quickly. "And I *hate* spiders."

"Oh. I thought maybe your pager was going off when you were trying to catch a nap." He smiled sympathetically. "I know how *that* feels."

"I don't nap on duty," I said. "Especially not when I'm covering the Pit."

The "Pit" was what we called the ER, which was generally jammed almost all the time. Tonight, however, it had been strangely quiet, which was why I had dared to duck into the supply closet to try and get five minutes of peace and quiet.

So much for that.

"Well ex*cuse* me for interrupting your 'me time' your royal highness," Sebastian snapped bitchily. "I just thought you might like to know you have a new triage."

"In the Pit?" I asked. "What is it? MVA? Gunshot wound?"

"Knife fight victim." Sebastian grinned. "We think anyway— there's blood coming from somewhere but we can't get to the wound. Anyway, just *wait* 'till you see him."

"Why? Is he in bad shape?" I was already moving down the hall with Sebastian jogging to keep up with me. "You think he'll need surgery?"

It may sound ghoulish but I was kind of hoping he would. We interns are always trying to get more cases under our belt. What's bad for the patient is often good for us. Not that I want anyone to die—I just kind of hope they're in *danger* of dying and that I can save them.

Wow, that sounds crazy, right? But that's the life of an intern—rushing from emergency to emergency, trying to save as many people as possible and soak up as much knowledge and experience as you can along the way.

If I hadn't had that damn blue worm following me and popping up everywhere to yell at me in his high, Disney-character voice, I would have been having the time of my life. As it was, I was miserable—though the idea of a stab wound so bad it needed surgery *did* cheer me up considerably.

But Sebastian was shaking his head.

"No, I'm not talking about his trauma—I'm talking about his *ass*," he gushed. "You should *see* this guy. He's got to be over seven feet tall and every inch of him is pure *muscle*. Not to mention he has this incredible blue-black hair and these amazing eyes—"

"Sebastian..." I sighed and shook my head. "What am I going to do with you?"

"Get me this guy's number and ask if he swings both ways," my friend said promptly.

"If he's so hot, why didn't you take him yourself?" I demanded. "You're on Pit duty too."

"Believe me, I *tried*." Sebastian opened his eyes wide and made a helpless gesture with both hands. "But he only wants you—he asked for you by name."

"He *what?*" I frowned at him. "What are you talking about? Is he from Tampa or something?"

Tampa, Florida is my hometown and the city I had been living in until I decided to go back to medical school in Gainesville, which is a couple of hours to the north. But even in Tampa, I hadn't known any seven foot tall guys with black hair and amazing eyes.

Of course, Sebastian was probably exaggerating on at least one, if not all counts. He was perpetually horny and had already worked his way through most of the male nurses at North Florida Regional, as well as a good number of the young male doctors.

"I don't know *where* he's from," Sebastian said, as we rounded the corner and went through the automatic doors that led to the ER triage area. "I just know he's *gorgeous* and he's asking for you. You lucky girl."

"Shut up," I said under my breath as we came to a curtained area. There was some kind of commotion taking place inside— someone was yelling and then I heard the clang of instruments being thrown on the floor.

"I told you," a deep male voice shouted. "I will speak only to Charlotte Walker. She is the *only* person I will allow to treat my wounds!"

"Sir if you'll just—" came the voice of a nurse from the other side of the curtain.

"Charlotte Walker! I must see her *now!*" he bellowed, loudly enough to hurt my ears.

"See what I mean?" Sebastian whispered. "He wouldn't let me touch him either and believe me, honey, *I tried.*"

"Well he can't be *that* bad off if he's yelling like that," I muttered back.

He shook his head. "Actually, I'm afraid he's got a really nasty slice up the right side of his abdomen. You better get in there and see what you can do for him."

I glared at him. "You're enjoying this."

"Of course I am! Girl, this is better than an episode of Grey's Anatomy!" He grinned and gave me a nudge towards the curtained area. "Go on—have fun."

Putting on my *I am a serious doctor* face, I squared my shoulders and pulled back the light blue curtain.

Sebastian hadn't been lying.

Lying on the hospital gurney was the biggest man I had ever seen in my life. Even flat on his back, I could see that he was more than seven feet tall and, as Sebastian had said, every inch of him appeared to be covered in muscle.

I don't mean that he was grossly over-muscled in a roided-out body-builder kind of way—it was just that his entire frame was pumped in all the right places. He had kind of a swimmer's build—long and lean and muscular with broad shoulders and narrow hips.

I bet myself that he had less than two percent body fat. Must be nice—as a plus sized girl, I have considerably more than two percent myself.

But back to my patient.

He also had curly black hair and eyes like nothing I had ever seen before. As I watched, they seemed to change color from sky blue to pale, leaf green, to iridescent silver. Wait—silver? Nobody had silver eyes. And how were they changing like that?

"Get away from me!" the huge patient was storming at the nurse—a girl named Gloria—who was trying to take his vitals. "I told you, I will have none other than Charlotte Walker as my healer!"

"Honey, I'm just trying to take your blood pressure." Gloria held up the extra-large cuff. "Come on now, why don't you be a sweetheart and settle down?"

"It's okay, Gloria, I said, coming into the curtained triage area. "I'll take it from here."

"Fine." She threw up her hands and let the BP cuff drop. "You handle him, Dr. Walker. You're the only one he seems to want, anyway. Just be careful, I don't know *what* he's on but it must be some wild stuff. You see those eyes?"

As a matter of fact, I did. At the sound of my voice, the patient's incredible eyes had fixed on me and he was practically staring laser beams right through me.

"Charlotte Walker," he breathed, reaching for me with one catcher's mitt-sized hand. "I have come for you. I must warn you— you are in danger!"

And then his eyes rolled back in his head, his head thumped back on the pillow, and he was out like a light.

Chapter Two

Charlotte

"Okay, let's see—what have we got?" I bustled forward, pulling on a pair of gloves to examine the patient. Sebastian came with me, obviously eager to get a closer look at the big guy.

"What *is* this he's wearing?" he asked under his breath. "Looks like some kind of weird costume from a Roman soldier movie or something!"

I had to admit he was right. My new patient had on a molded golden breastplate which buckled at the sides and a short kilt made of many leather straps that ended above his knees. There was an undergarment—an under-kilt I supposed—beneath it that had been pure white, which was now bloodstained and ragged. High black boots with golden metal greaves over the shins encased his feet—which had to be a size sixteen at least—and matching golden vambraces covered his forearms.

In case you're wondering how I knew all the names of this stuff, it was from playing waaay too much Diablo III with my friend Zoe, back in college. I'm not exactly a gaming geek—I don't have time to be—but I know my way around an RPG. Still, I had never expected a guy who looked like a fortieth level Paladin to land in my ER.

"That is one fancy gladiator outfit," Gloria remarked. She had come back to do the blood pressure now that the patient was out for the count. "You know he has a sword too?"

"You're kidding!" Sebastian exclaimed.

"Uh-uh. Look under the gurney."

Sebastian flipped up the trailing sheet and gave a long, low whistle.

"Oh my *Gawd*. It's as long as he is! I wonder what his *other* sword looks like—huh?"

He grinned at me but I was barely paying attention. I had finally managed to unbuckle the golden breastplate on both sides but it was really heavy — somewhere in the neighborhood of forty or fifty pounds. This was no cheap Halloween gladiator outfit — it was the real deal. Why was he wearing it and how did he walk around with this stuff on? Added all together the breastplate, vambraces, greaves, and sword, must weigh a ton!

Also, how had he known my name? But that question would have to wait until I figured out what was wrong with him.

"Help me lift this over his head," I told Sebastian, who was happy to oblige. We lifted the breastplate carefully, sliding it over the patient's head, and leaving the heavy front plate dangling down over the top of the gurney.

The white wife-beater type undershirt was also bloodstained. But I couldn't see a wound — only evidence of one by the way the white shirt was rapidly turning crimson.

"Scissors," I said and Sebastian handed them over. Starting at the bottom of the shirt, I slid the sharp blades up, careful not to touch his skin, which seemed to have a slightly jaundiced hue. Only it wasn't yellow so much as a shimmering of gold — very strange. I wondered if he had something wrong with his liver. But what liver disease turned your skin gold?

When I peeled back the sodden undershirt, Sebastian gave a long, low whistle.

"Oh my God — would you look at that!" he exclaimed.

I frowned. "It's a nasty slice, all right. Give me some gauze — let's try and stop that bleeding."

"No — I wasn't talking about the knife wound!" Sebastian threw me an incredulous look as he passed the supplies I was asking for. "I'm talking about the way his chest and abs are even *more* muscular than that molded breastplate he was wearing! Forget a six pack, he's got like...an *eight* pack."

"I'm only interested in knowing if any of his fabulous abs got cut up in this fight," I snapped. "*Not* how hot they look. Speaking of which, look under his kilt and see if there are any wounds there."

Sebastian's eyes lit up like a kid at Christmas.

"Yes, Ma'am!"

I sighed and shook my head, going back to the matter at hand. My new patient had a long slice that started at the top of his right pectoral region, just under the clavicle, and ran all the way down to the top of his groin. It was shallow but nasty and it looked like he had already lost a lot of blood. He might not need surgery but he sure as hell was going to need a whole crap-load of stitches.

"He's hypotensive," Gloria announced, pulling off the blood pressure cuff.

Damn — I had been right about the blood loss.

"Does he have any ID?" I asked the nurse. "Is he in the system? Do we know his blood type?"

"No to all three." She shrugged. "He just stumbled in the ER door asking for you and collapsed."

"Great," I muttered. Just *great.*"

"No lacerations around the groin but he clearly needs a transfusion," Sebastian said. "Let's hang some O neg."

Of course, this would normally be the right course of treatment. We didn't know the patient's blood type but O negative is the universal donor. Still, something made me hesitate.

"I *said* we need O neg up here. And a suture kit." Sebastian can be really bossy sometimes.

"Wait." I held up a hand to stop him.

"Charlotte —"

"Just *wait,* I said!" I snapped at him. "This is my triage, Sebastian — he asked for me personally. So I'm going to determine the course of treatment."

"But —" He began, but I ignored him. Instead I took off my glove.

Now this is something a medical professional should *never* do — especially around an open wound in a patient with an unknown medical history. There are so many blood-borne pathogens on the loose out there it's not even funny. But I had a feeling about this strange patient with his bizarre outfit and his golden-sheened skin — and I always listen to my feelings.

Taking a deep breath, I placed my ungloved hand on his face, cupping his cheek carefully.

I felt a strange tingle run between us that almost made me pull my hand away. It was like a low-level electrical shock. What in the world could it mean?

And then my sixth sense kicked in and I *knew*.

What did I know from a simple touch? Well, all kinds of things. I knew that O negative blood would sicken or perhaps even kill this man. I knew he had been recently fighting for his life. And I knew something else—but it was something so strange and disturbing that I immediately pushed it to the back of my mind and concentrated on the important stuff instead.

How did I know all these things? Well, I have a sixth sense—a gift that I really don't talk about. An *impossible* gift, most people would say. When I touch someone, I pick up information about them. Not everything, just...bits and pieces. Don't ask me how or why it works—I don't understand it myself. But I've had it all my life and lately, it seemed to be getting stronger. This time the certainty was so strong, I didn't even try to fight it.

"O neg is no good," I said. "We'll have to do a cross-match."

"What?" Sebastian frowned at me incredulously. "If O neg is no good then what blood are we cross matching him with?"

I took a deep breath.

"Mine," I said.

"Yours?" He looked like he couldn't believe it. "Charlotte—"

"Just do it," I said. "Get a cross-matching kit."

Like my mysterious gift for knowing things when I touch people—my *touch-sense* I call it—my rare blood type is something I almost never talk about. Even my best friends Zoe and Leah didn't know these things about me. They just had a vague idea that I had a rare blood type and thought I was a good judge of character.

I don't know why I keep the truly important things about me from the ones I love the most. Maybe because I've always felt different—like I don't belong. Of course, being adopted could have something to do with that. Even as a young child, I remember trying to hide my touch-sense from my adopted mom and dad. I think I was afraid I would drive them away with my weirdness.

For whatever reason, I saw no need to reveal to anyone that I could tell the minute I touched someone if he or she would make a good friend or would probably turn out to be an enemy. Or that they were fighting with their parents. Or that they were having an affair with a married man, or that cheesecake was their favorite food…or any of the hundred other little incidental tidbits I'd gotten from people over the years when I touched them.

And in the case of men that I touched there was something extra. Another dimension of knowing that was both troubling and provocative. I always knew the moment I touched a man if he —

"Here's the kit *and* I brought a sample of O neg," Sebastian said, breaking my train of thought. He handed me the kit and the sample with a sullen look on his face. "Just for your edification, *your majesty.*"

"Fine," I said, ignoring his sarcasm as I peeled the plastic sterile wrapping off the tray and set it up.

In cross-matching blood, you take a small sample of your patient's blood and mix it with a small sample of the blood you want to transfuse them with. If the blood starts to clump up, you know it's not a viable match and it wouldn't be safe to give to your patient. We were in a hurry but the patient wasn't crashing — yet, anyway. So I decided to prove Sebastian's incredulity wrong with a demonstration.

Taking a small plastic pipette from the kit, I sucked up a small sample of the patient's blood. His wound had mostly stopped bleeding by now but there was still plenty to go around. I deposited the sample into the small plastic tray. Using another pipette, I put a small sample of the O neg on top, letting the patient's blood and the O neg mix.

The result was immediate and dramatic.

Big clumps began to form in the small plastic tray like curdled milk. In under a minute, the tray didn't hold liquid blood at all — it was just a big, nasty looking blood clot.

"Holy God," I heard Gloria, who had been watching over Sebastian's shoulder murmur. "I've never seen *anything* like that before."

"It's really weird," Sebastian agreed in hushed tones. "Now what?"

"Now this," I said. I took another sample of the patient's blood and put it in another one of the plastic trays. Then I pulled down the right sleeve of my white lab coat, baring my arm in my short-sleeved scrub top. "Gloria," I said to the nurse. "Would you mind using a sterile needle to stick me for a sample?"

I have a really good vein on the inside of my left elbow and Gloria was a pro. In no time she had a small sample of my rare blood in yet another of the plastic pipettes and Sebastian was slapping a band-aid on my arm.

I put back on my lab coat and squirted a few drops of my own blood into the tray containing the patient's. Then, we waited.

As I had expected, nothing happened. Which in this case, was a very good thing. No clumping or clotting—I was a clear match with this strange man who I had never met before in my life.

"All right—I don't know how you knew, but you were right." Sebastian was already frowning in concentration. "So what are you going to do—pump out a pint for him right now?"

"No need," I said. "I have several bags saved here at the hospital. Gloria, if you could go get one…no, better make it two." I told her where to find them and she nodded and went at once.

In case you're wondering why I happened to have several bags of my own blood lying around, it's for a very good reason. When you have an extremely rare blood type, you often can't accept donated blood from anyone else—at least, unless their blood exactly matches yours. So it's better to bag some up for emergencies like car injuries or unexpected surgeries. I had never had either one of those but I'm a person who believes in keeping two steps ahead and being prepared.

The Boy Scouts have nothing on me.

As it was, it was damn lucky for my patient that I was so anal retentive, as Zoe used to like to call me. Otherwise, he would have been in big trouble with no possible donor.

"All right," Sebastian said, putting a hand on his hip as I got the suture kit and began to stitch up the long gash across my patient's chest and abdomen. "How did you know? And what blood type are you, anyway?"

I shrugged uncomfortably and answered the easier question.

"I'm just a rare type, that's all."

"Bullshit!' Sebastian exclaimed. "There's rare and then there's *rare*. What type are you?"

"All right, I'll tell you but you have to keep it to yourself." I sighed and looked up from my stitches. The patient was stirring uncomfortably but he wasn't waking up—not yet anyway. I didn't like to give him any medication for pain while he was unconscious *and* hypotensive so I tried to be quick.

"All right, all right—I promise," Sebastian said eagerly. "Now *give.*"

"I'm...Rh null," I said reluctantly.

"What?" Sebastian exploded, his eyebrows raising almost to his hairline. "You have *the golden blood?*"

"Shhh!" I glared at him. "You promised to keep it to yourself!"

"Yes, but...hell, Charlotte—that's the rarest type in the whole freaking *world!* I did a paper on it last year—I think there are only something like ten or twelve registered donors anywhere on the planet."

"Nine," I said, still stitching. "Could you start a line on him and give him some fluids while we wait for Gloria?"

Sebastian did as I asked, but he couldn't stop talking about my rare blood type. There's a lengthy, boring, scientific explanation that goes with it but to make a long story short, Rh null blood has no Rh antibodies or any traces of the Rh factor that most people have at all. Which means that it can be given to anyone—even people with extremely rare blood types. Hence the nickname, "the golden blood." Rh null is the true universal donor but it's so incredibly rare that the blood is usually hoarded for extreme cases.

I knew all this because I had been donating blood twice a month since I turned eighteen and my rare type was discovered by my doctor's office.

My blood had saved a lot of lives but if *I* got sick and needed a transfusion, the nearest donor with my blood type lived in Australia. Which again, was why I always kept a couple of bags on hand for myself.

Just in case.

Gloria came bustling back soon enough with several bags of my blood. She hung one from the IV pole and connected it to the drip already in the patient's arm. I was halfway done with the stitches by then, and hoping to be finished before the patient woke up. But the minute my blood hit his arm, his eyes flew open and he tried to sit up.

"Whoa! Whoa, there big guy!" I put a hand on his arm and urged him to lie back down. "Just settle down and let us take care of you."

He frowned, gazing at me blearily with unfocussed eyes.

"Goddess?"

"It's just me—Doctor Walker," I said and added, "Charlotte Walker. Remember, you asked for me?" Although I still didn't know how he knew me.

"Goddess," he whispered again but his eyes seemed to focus more. "I feel strange. What...what are you doing to me?"

"Stitching you up," I said matter-of-factly. "This is a nasty wound you have here. How in the world did you get it with that big, heavy breastplate you were wearing in the way?"

"Assassin droid," he muttered, his eyelids beginning to drift down again. "They have...armor penetrating weapons. Nano-blades. Caught me...unawares. Inexcusable lapse."

"Um...okay. Sure, those sound bad," I said, wondering if it was the blood-loss talking or if the guy was just out of his head. I mean, assassin droids? Nano-blades? Really?

"What else are you doing to me?" he murmured drowsily.

"Well, you need a transfusion." I kept stitching since he wasn't complaining and nodded at the bag of my blood hanging from the IV stand over his head.

"What?" His eyes opened all the way and widened, cycling through a strange rainbow of colors again. Blue, green, pale yellow, silver...what was going *on* with him? Was this some kind of rare mutation? If so, I had never seen anything even remotely like it.

He looked worried about the transfusion so I hastened to reassure him.

"Don't worry—I know you have an extremely rare blood type."

"It goes beyond rare," he said. His voice was deep but melodious — like someone playing a cello. It was rich and somehow utterly masculine. "No one on this planet could give me blood except..." His rainbow eyes widened and he stared at me. "No," he whispered. "Please, my Lady...tell me you did not give me your own sacred blood."

"How did he know?" Sebastian demanded. "I thought he was completely out of it when we hung the fluids and blood."

"Sebastian!" I hissed in frustration. I had been going to give the patient a little disclaimer about how all transfusion blood is carefully checked and completely anonymous but my big-mouthed friend had ruined that.

"Goddess...my Lady, you *cannot!*"

My patient reached for the line in his arm, about to yank it out. I dropped my curving suture needle and grabbed for his big hand instead.

"Stop!" I put as much command as I could into my voice and stared him right in his rainbow-shifting eyes. "You stop that right now Mr...." I had to trail off there, because I didn't know his name.

"Verrai. Captain Kristoff Verrai of her majesty's Imperial Guard of Femme One."

"Okay, Kristoff," I said. "That's quite a title and I bet there's a long story behind it. But I've got a short story for you right now — you try to rip that line out of your arm and I'll have you in restraints so fast your head will spin."

"But..." He shook his head helplessly. "You have the rainbow aura. I am not worthy to receive the sacred blood. My mother was only a lesser noble — I have no royal lineage."

"Uh, well that's okay," I said, patting his arm. Now he was just spouting nonsense but at least he didn't seem inclined to pull the line out anymore. "I don't care about your, uh, lineage," I told him. "It's my blood and I say you can have it. All right?"

He looked deeply troubled but I held his eyes with my own until, at last, he nodded and sank back on the gurney.

"Very well. But I fear there will be grave repercussions when we get to Court. Or perhaps even before."

"Well, we'll cross that bridge when we come to it, all right?" I said, using one of my dad's favorite expressions. "For right now, just leave the line alone and let me finish stitching you up."

He nodded, his eyes still fixed on my face.

"I knew you were a *La-ti-zal* but I never thought you'd be a Healer. The old Goddess-Empress—she whom I still mourn—was a Seer. And so was the Incarnation before her and the Incarnation before her. I thought all of them had the gift of Sight or Knowing in some way."

"Uh...sure," I said, nodding again. Behind me I heard Sebastian whisper to Gloria,

"Are you *hearing* this stuff? Better check his blood alcohol level."

"On it," she whispered back.

I had thought that my patient was settling down again, but then he started shifting on the bed, his hips moving from side to side uncomfortably.

"What's wrong, Kristoff?" I asked, frowning at him. "Are you experiencing discomfort? Do you have another wound we should know about?"

"A wound? No. But discomfort..." He shifted again, one big hand coming to cover his groin. My eyes were drawn to his pelvis and behind me I heard Sebastian give a long, low whistle.

"Oh my *Gawd*," he muttered. "It's fucking *huge*."

That was when I saw what the patient was trying to hide—a perfectly enormous erection. Seriously, it looked like something out of a porno. The leather kilt was flipped up from Sebastian's earlier search for another wound and the white under-kilt didn't hide much. The thin fabric was stretched tight over the patient's burgeoning member, which he tried vainly to hide with one big hand.

"Forgive me," he muttered, his face turning crimson. "It is the effect of your blood, Goddess. I cannot help it."

"You can stop calling me that. Dr. Walker will do just fine," I said, trying to ignore his obvious "problem."

"But you *are* a Goddess—or most believe that you are," he said, looking at me earnestly. "It is a title of respect."

Behind us, Sebastian snorted.

"Right. The Goddess of Trauma, maybe. You better stop or Miss Goddess's head will swell too big to fit in the door of the hospital."

The patient glared at him.

"Be still, commoner. I know you cannot see it, but this female has the rainbow aura—she is in fact the true Incarnation of the Goddess-Empress. You are not fit to stand upright in her presence. Better you should grovel on your knees before her and beg her forgiveness for daring to speak so disrespectfully in her presence."

"Hey!" Sebastian put a hand on his hip and frowned. "Look, we're going to just pass that kind of talk off as blood loss. But for your information, Dr. Walker here is just an intern. A very good intern and apparently one with an incredibly rare blood type…" He gave me a speculative look. "But just an intern all the same."

"Sebastian…" I glared at him in exasperation. Never knowing when to shut up was my friend's defining personality trait. Discussing me with a patient was extremely unprofessional and probably broke all kinds of Hippa laws. Not to mention that it was also kind of insulting.

"Well, it's *true*," he said airily. "Sorry to burst your royal bubble, *Goddess*, but—"

The last word ended in a choked gurgle. My patient had sat straight up on the gurney and reached one long arm out to grab Sebastian by the throat. Without any apparent effort, he raised the intern with one hand and glared at him.

"You do not speak so to the Goddess-Empress," he said, his deep voice a menacing growl. "It is disrespectful and rude. Were you on Femme One it would be grounds for immediate execution and I would gladly swing the axe myself."

"Shit!" I shot to my feet as Sebastian's sneakered feet kicked a good twelve inches off the floor. "Gloria—give me ten of Haldol *now*."

"Yes, doctor!" Gloria could move fast and she was back with a syringe almost before I could blink. I darted around the side of the bed and injected directly into the patient's left deltoid. It was twice the dose I would have given anyone else but Kristoff was so *big* and from the way Sebastian's face was turning the color of a ripe eggplant, he was strong too.

The meds kicked in quickly. Kristoff's muscular arm sagged and Gloria and I were able to get Sebastian away from him.

My friend coughed and choked, his hand going to his throat to explore for injuries. I thought he might have some bruising but I doubted there was any permanent damage—I hoped not, anyway. Sebastian could be an annoying, arrogant prick at times but he was still the closest thing I had to a friend now that Zoe had disappeared and Leah had moved to Virginia with her jerk of a fiancé who was now her husband.

Kristoff's eyelids fluttered over those amazing, rainbow eyes and he seemed to realize what had happened.

"What is this…this feeling? This lethargy?" he demanded, his deep voice starting to slur. "Wha…what have you done?"

"I've given you something to help you calm down," I said firmly. "It's for your own good." I tried to help guide him back down to the gurney but he resisted.

"But…how…how can I protect you if I'm…if I can't…" His eyelids were drooping and his broad shoulders started to sag.

"Look," I said, "I don't know how you know my name but you have a wrong idea. I'm not any kind of Goddess or Empress or anything like that. I'm just a medical intern and you *don't* have to protect me."

"Yes, I…I do," he protested. "I…" Suddenly his eyes snapped open and he lifted a wavering arm, pointing to something beyond the pale blue curtain which was still hanging open. His lips moved but for a moment it seemed like he couldn't speak.

"What? What is it?" I asked, frowning. Outside the curtain it was just business as usual in the ER. I could see that we were starting to get busier. Interns and attending moved around the beds as well as nurses, techs, and other support staff.

But one person in particular seemed to bother my patient.

"D-danger," he stuttered hoarsely, his wavering arm still outstretched.

I frowned at what he was pointing at. It was just Carlos, our elderly janitor, emptying the trash. He was a nice old guy with gray hair—probably in his late sixties with a slightly hunched back. He never complained about cleaning up when a patient was sick or incontinent and he was always there to lend a hand when we needed lifting help.

"Who, Carlos?" I asked, frowning at Kristoff. "Don't worry about him—he's one of the sweetest guys you'll ever meet."

"No...danger!" he insisted. Clearly he was fighting to stay awake. I couldn't believe it—I had never seen anyone fight off that amount of medication. "Please..." He grabbed my arm, his eyes swirling so many colors now I couldn't count them. "Give me...help me...wake up. Have to...have to...protect..."

If he hadn't looked so serious and desperate I would have laughed at the idea that I needed protection from Carlos. He was such a sweetheart—I would have sworn on a stack of Bibles he wouldn't hurt a fly.

Still, I couldn't help feeling touched at the fiercely protective look in Kristoff's strangely gorgeous eyes. After he woke up I would have to have someone who specialized in ophthalmologic disorders come take a look at him. But in the meantime, I wanted to reassure him.

"It's all right," I told him gently. "Carlos is a good guy. He would never hurt me."

"Not...who you think," he insisted. He was still fighting the meds but it was a losing battle. His eyelids were fluttering closed and I saw that he had incredibly long lashes for a man. "Assassin...droid..."

"*Annnd* we're back to the delusional fantasies," Sebastian's voice was hoarse but still snarky.

"I'm glad you're recovered enough to be sarcastic," I said as Kristoff finally sank back down on the gurney. "I was worried there for a moment."

"Oh, I'm fine. Just *peachy*." He massaged his red throat gingerly. "You think that's the first time I've been choked by a hot guy?"

"Can we *please* not get into your sex life right now?" I asked in an undertone as Kristoff's big body finally slumped into drugged unconsciousness.

"Just because *you* don't have a sex life to discuss—" he began but I waved him off and went to check on Kristoff now that he was out.

Where *had* this strange man come from? And what was the deal with his weird skin and eye coloration? How did he know my name? And how did he have my blood type—or at least a type so rare that it was only compatible with mine?

There were so many unanswerable questions it made my head spin. But there was no way of getting answers now. I had gotten everything I could from him with my touch-sense earlier, and I had given him enough Haldol to put him out for hours—probably until sometime tomorrow afternoon at least.

"Come on." Sebastian tugged at my arm. "They're bringing in a multi-trauma MVA. Some idiots who were texting and driving plowed into each other—we've got more triage to do."

"Okay, you're right. Go ahead and I'll be there in a minute." I nodded at him to go on and turned back to Gloria. "I want this guy put in a room on the psych floor and be sure he's restrained," I told her. "I don't want him hurting anyone when he wakes up."

"Well, with ten of Haldol on board, that's going to be a while," she said. "But sure, I'll get the ball rolling, Dr. Walker."

"Thanks." I gave her a grateful smile and took one last look at Kristoff Verrai. There was something special about him—my touch-sense told me so. I wanted to get to the bottom of it, but for now, I had business to attend to.

I turned to go and from the corner of my eye, saw that Carlos the janitor was watching me. He turned away as soon as he saw me looking, but there was something in his expression—a coldness—that sent a shiver down my spine. Suddenly I wondered what I would *know* if I walked up to him and grabbed his arm.

"*Assassin-droid,*" murmured Kristoff's deep voice in my head. "*Danger!*"

It was crazy, right? But was it any crazier than what I had been experiencing lately?

Suddenly it occurred to me that I was putting him on the psych floor in restraints when I myself had been seeing visions of a blue space worm trying to contact me through shiny surfaces for weeks now. Talk about hypocritical!

But that's different, I argued to myself. *I'm probably just having those visions because I'm tired. Plus, I don't go around dressed in a Roman gladiator's outfit, grabbing people by the throat.*

Of course Kristoff had only done that because he felt that Sebastian was disrespecting me but still...

"Goddess..." he had called me. And he had seemed to think I was in danger.

Don't be stupid, Charlotte!

With an effort, I shrugged off the sense of dread that had somehow settled over me like a cold, clammy coat. I had patients to treat, a night in the Pit to get through, and morning rounds to do before I could even think about getting some rest.

It was time to get back to business as usual—I could worry about my strange new patient later.

Chapter Three

Kristoff

I swam through drugged nightmares, fighting my way to the surface, only to be dragged down again and again. Over and over I saw my Empress in danger...over and over I saw her slain, the assassin-droid killing her in a hundred, a *thousand* different, awful ways.

Her face...the young one of the new Incarnation and the old one of the female I had served all of my adult life mixed and melded, melting and flowing into one another until I couldn't tell which was which.

"Save me!" the old Goddess-Empress cried but when I turned to shield her, it was the new one I saw—her lovely face and sharp green eyes so like the ones of my former mistress.

"I'm coming, my Lady!" I cried but I could never quite reach her. Always the Assassin-droid got there before me. Always I was left holding her broken, bleeding body in my arms, her lovely blonde hair matted with crimson.

The dream reset itself over and over, I know not how many times. And all the time I prayed—not to the Goddess-Empress but to the Goddess of Mercy, she who made us all through the Ancient Ones.

"Goddess, please—let me reach her on time! Let me serve my Lady and keep her safe. Protect her while I am not able. Please, Goddess—help me to save her!"

I do not know if she who made us all heard me or not. I only know I struggled in the nightmare, longing to wake and shield my new mistress. But I was unable because of the drug flowing through my veins.

And yet—that was not the only thing in my veins. The Empress's own blood was in me. Though the Council of Wisdom would call it blasphemy, it gave me strength. Somehow, I knew I would reach her.

I just hoped it wouldn't be too late.

Charlotte

"Come on, Charlotte, this is a *good* thing. We actually get to go *home* to sleep." Sebastian prodded me with one sharp finger. "Come *on*. Don't tell me you don't like that."

I didn't like it, though I couldn't say why. I ought to be beyond grateful, after the night I had had.

Not long after my mysterious patient, the ER had been slammed with a ten car pileup and then several gunshot wounds and a heart-attack that turned out to be an aortic dissection.

By morning rounds Sebastian and I had been dragging. Even *before* the craziness in the Pit, we had been up for eighteen hours straight. So by the time morning rounds rolled around, we had both gone well over twenty-four hours without sleep. Even black coffee can only do so much and the two of us were yawning so much so that our attending, Dr. Calgary, had ordered us home for at least eight hours of uninterrupted sleep. I had tried to protest but he wasn't having it.

"I appreciate that you interns think you have something to prove and normally I'd let you prove it," he'd said sharply when I protested that I still had patients to see. "But you two are so tired you're falling asleep on your feet—that's no good for anyone. Especially not your patients. Go home, turn off your phones, and get some sleep. That's an order."

"Yes, Sir," I had muttered. But I couldn't help the sense of foreboding that filled me, even as Sebastian and I trudged out to the employee parking lot.

"You're not still thinking about *him* are you?" Sebastian asked me. "You know—tall, gold, and grabby?"

I shrugged irritably.

"He only grabbed you because you were being a dick. And no—I wasn't thinking of him."

Which was a lie, of course.

It had been a crazy night — so crazy I could almost forget about Kristoff. But somehow, even after such an exhausting shift, I found he was still at the back of my mind like a piece of music I couldn't forget.

"He'll probably wake up and wonder where the hell he is," Sebastian said, grinning tiredly. "Picture this — he's actually a high-stakes attorney and he was at a fancy dress party last night. Some girl who wanted to hump him and dump him slipped something psychotic into his appletini, had her way with him, and then dumped him outside the ER when he started getting too wild to handle. Now, this morning, he opens his eyes and he's strapped to a hospital bed and he has no idea how he got there."

"You should have been a romance writer," I said, shaking my head. "That's a hell of a story."

"Thank you." Sebastian made an elaborate bow which almost ended with him face-planting onto the concrete because he was so tired.

I laughed at him. "You need to stop before you fall over and need stitches. I'm in no shape to sew up your pretty face right now."

"I'm fine," he declared, opening his eyes wide to show how awake he was. "Although I *do* appreciate you acknowledging my beauty."

I barely held back a snort of laughter.

"Seriously Sebastian, do *not* make me laugh right now — I don't know if I could stop. Okay, this is me." We had stopped in front of my little blue Spark.

"I don't know why you even bother to drive to work," Sebastian grumbled. "You only live a few blocks away."

"I drive to work because on the off-chance that I get to go home and sleep, I don't want to spend half my time walking there," I said. "You've got a lot further to drive than I do, though. You want to crash at my place? You can have the couch."

Sebastian considered it for a minute, then shook his head.

"No, I'm going home. I might be able to get Lalo, that hot Latin guy I met at the club the other night, to come over."

"Sebastian!" I exclaimed, frowning at him. "We're supposed to be going home to sleep – not get laid."

"Who said anything about getting laid – I just want to cuddle," he said coyly. Then, when I continued to glare at him he shrugged his shoulders. "Fine, so I want to get some. So what? You know, you wouldn't be so judgmental if you ever got laid yourself."

"Leave me out of this," I said.

"No, seriously." He put a hand on my shoulder. "You're pretty, Charlotte – hell, you're *gorgeous.* And I can say that without things getting weird between us because you know I have absolutely no urge to be with you."

"Oh, thanks," I said dryly. "You're right – zero weirdness."

"No, I mean it," he insisted. "You're gorgeous – so why aren't you with anyone?"

"With the life we lead?" I said, raising my eyebrows. "Crazy-busy morning, noon, and night? Who would have me?"

"Any number of the guys at the hospital," Sebastian said quietly. "Like Dr. Hunter, who I heard you turned down last week. Seriously, you can't use our schedule as an excuse. Anybody who works here would understand."

"Well maybe I don't want to date anyone where I work," I said crisply. "Besides, Drake Hunter is a predatory jerk."

"Maybe you just don't want to date anyone at all," my friend said quietly.

"Maybe it's none of your business," I snapped back.

"All right. Okay." Sebastian put up both hands in a 'don't shoot' gesture. "Wasn't trying to piss you off. I'm just saying – you should get some once in a while. It really helps to take the edge off."

"I don't *want* to lose my edge," I said. "Which is why I'm going home to sleep – not get laid."

"Geeze, I'm *sorry*, Charlotte, I was just trying to be a friend." He looked really offended now. "Forget I said anything."

I knew I had gone too far and I felt bad about it. But still, my romantic life – or lack thereof – was a sore subject with me. Leah and Zoe had always assumed I almost never dated anyone because I was attacked once in college and it put me off men in general.

I let them think that—and that was part of it, I admit. It was also why I carried a taser in my purse everywhere I went. But there was more to the story than just a drunken frat guy and an attempted rape. There was also that fact that I had never been sexually turned on by any guy I'd ever met and that included Dr. Drake Hunter, who every other single woman (and some that weren't so single) in the hospital, was panting after.

I don't mean I'm gay—in the past I had often wished that I was. How much easier it would have been! But women didn't attract me either. No one attracted me and no one would—that was the thing I always knew through my touch-sense when I was touching a man—whether he could turn me on or not. And I had never found anyone who could. Until...

"Look, I'd better just go," Sebastian said, breaking my dismal train of thought.

"Sebastian, I'm sorry," I said lamely. "I just...don't like talking about that kind of stuff."

"Fine. I'll remember that," he said frostily. "Bye, Charlotte. Have a good time *sleeping.*"

Before I could say anything else, he had turned and was trudging down the rows of parked cars, looking for his Jeep. I thought about calling him back, but what else could I say?

Reluctantly, I unlocked my little Spark and got inside. It was stifling already thanks to the Florida weather. I cranked up the AC and headed for home which was an apartment complex just a few blocks from the hospital.

Well, even if my only remaining friend was mad at me, at least I could get some sleep, I told myself. After a good eight hours in bed, I would wake up feeling like a new woman. Everything would be better soon.

I had no idea how wrong I was.

Chapter Four

Kristoff

I don't know what time I woke—sometime after dawn, I think. There was a warm, golden light pouring in through the nearby window which was quite different from the pinkish light of Femme One. The Majoran solar system has a red giant star at its center so even at noon, our day looks much like an Earth sunset.

I would have gone to look out the window but when I tried, I found that someone had tied my wrists and ankles to the strange, metal-framed sleeping platform I was on. Not only that, but they had taken my armor and sword. I was wearing a thin, short shift-type garment which ended well above my knees, probably because it had been sewn for one of the inhabitants of Earth.

I had been on the small green and blue planet for a number of days and the first thing I had noticed was how *small* they all were here. They might well be Pure Ones, with rare DNA, but it didn't seem to have done them any good—at least none that I could tell. Even the new Incarnation of the Goddess-Empress, whom I had been watching over, was smaller than her predecessors. Though tall for an Earth female, she would still only come half-way up to my shoulder if we stood side by side.

The Goddess-Empress! Charlotte Walker!

Suddenly, my activities of the night before came back in a flood. I had been watching over Charlotte, waiting to reveal myself until I could first identify the threat I was certain was stalking her. Why was I certain? Because of the Court politics on Femme One. There was always someone seeking to gain power and the Ascension of a new Empress to the throne was a perfect time to gain it.

The moment the news spread that the old Goddess-Empress, Sundalla the 999th, had Ascended to the Heavens, the race had begun to find and crown her new Incarnation. Of course, there could be only one true Goddess-Empress, but that wouldn't stop ruthless power mongers like Prince Morbain—a male I particularly loathed—from trying to put their own imposters on the throne. Morbain and others like him would seek to put a weak, easily controlled female in the place of ultimate power—that way they could rule through her and twist the galaxy to their own will.

Sure enough, someone—probably Morbain—had sent an assassin-droid after Charlotte. I had been waiting, hidden by *Nicean* stealth technology that essentially rendered me invisible, and watching the entrance to her place of work where she was apparently a Healer. From my vantage point, I had seen the droid appear, stepping from mid-air to make a grab for a young male wearing the same long white coat many of the attendants at this House of Healing wore. So, apparently I wasn't the only one with stealth tech—it was an unwelcome surprise but good to know.

I had grabbed for the droid—which was faceless and silver at the time—and kept it from taking its intended victim. Who just happened to be the same male that had insulted the new Empress in my presence later that night. The one I had felt compelled to punish for his insolence. At the time, however, I only knew I had to stop the assassin from finding its target.

I knew what the droid was trying to do—the moment it snatched some helpless, unsuspecting idiot, it could suck out their life-force and assume their identity. And by choosing someone who was already emotionally close to Charlotte Walker—someone she considered harmless and not a threat—it could kill her quickly and easily, the moment it got her alone.

I had dragged the struggling droid around to the abandoned side of the building, trying to disable it. But the sleek, silver killing machine had another surprise for me—nano-tech.

My armor is incredibly strong—made of the best alloys the galaxy can produce. But it's not meant to repel a weapon so small it can seep through any chink or crevice. As I struggled with the droid, I felt them working on me—thousands, perhaps millions, burrowing into my skin to make the long, jagged wound which Charlotte had sewn up last night.

Though I fought with all my might, the nanites had taken me down, ripping into my flesh, seeping inwards to attack my vital organs. In fact, I had no doubt that without the transfusion of sacred blood the new Empress had given me, I would have died of their damage.

The blood—why had she given me her blood? My mind swirled with the memory of her essence entering my body. It was forbidden for any save the Consort candidates to have the Empress's own blood, and even they only imbibed a tiny bit of it during the Culling Ceremony. To have it pumped directly into my veins—it was worse than wrong—it was *sacrilege.*

I had tried to stop it but Charlotte had ordered me to allow the transfusion to go on. Why? Was it simply to save my life—the life of a male she had never even met before? If so, maybe she truly *was* worthy of my devotion, as my old mistress, Sundalla the 999th had insisted she would be.

No. I hardened my heart against such a thought. Though our relationship had never been physical, I had loved and served my old mistress with my whole being. I had promised to protect her successor but I knew I could never give myself as wholly to another mistress as I had to Sundalla the 999th. Most probably, Charlotte Walker had given me her blood because she had no idea of the consequences of her actions.

As she had no idea that an assassin-droid was stalking her, intent on taking her life before she could ascend to the throne.

It shall not happen! I swore to myself. Charlotte Walker was the true incarnation of the Goddess-Empress—I knew it because I had the Vision—the ability to see the gorgeously-hued rainbow aura that radiated from her like a cloak of pure energy. But the Vision was rare—in fact, I might well be the only male with the gift left in the Majoran system. Which meant that Charlotte would have to pass several tests to prove herself as the true Incarnation, since I doubted the Council would take my word alone on such an important matter.

But she had to survive the inevitable assassination attempts first—and how could she survive them without me to protect her?

I knew what victim the assassin droid had taken—the older male with stooped shoulders and graying hair. He didn't look threatening in any way but I had seen the gleam of silver deep in his eyes when he looked at Charlotte...I had to get to her before the droid did.

If it hadn't gotten to her already.

No — can't think like that. Have to get out of here and find her!

I tugged experimentally at the soft but strong restraints that bound me to the metal bed. I could tell that they would hold a lesser male easily — probably even a large Earth male. But I am Majoran — the Captain of the Imperial Guards. No restraints could hold me from honoring and protecting my new Empress. Though my heart had been given to my old mistress, still my loyalty belonged to her new Incarnation.

I tugged again but the restraints were at the wrong angle for ripping. Soon I concluded that it would be easier to tear away the part of the bed I was bound to. Of course, I didn't know how much noise it would make or when someone might come into my room. I would have to be quick — I couldn't risk getting injected with another dose of sleeping medication.

Gripping the railing with my right hand, I gave a quick, hard jerk. There was a sound like tearing metal and the entire long bar came off in my hand. Then I was able to reach across my body and untie my other wrist. The process was somewhat awkward because I was still tied to the metal railing, even if it was free of the sleeping platform, but I managed.

I had gotten myself free of both wrist restraints and one ankle restraint as well, when I heard voices outside my door.

"...haven't got a bed for him yet, so we put him in here and just left him on the gurney," one — an older sounding female said. "He's supposed to go to the psych ward and be evaluated."

"Why?" asked the other — a lighter, younger female voice.

"Apparently he came in dressed in a Roman gladiator outfit with a huge sword and everything."

My ears perked up at that, even as I worked fast to get the last restraint untied. My armor had my stealth tech and weapons, as well as the remote that would call a shuttle from my ship, which was orbiting invisibly around the Earth's moon. I needed it if I was ever going to get the new Empress off this ridiculous little planet and back to Femme One where she belonged. I wondered what the

Earthlings had done with it.

"He was all cut up from some kind of a knife-fight and he was asking for Dr. Walker," the older voice said.

"Who's that? The blonde intern? She's really pretty," the younger one said.

"Yeah, but she's as cold as they come. I heard Dr. Hunter asked her out and she turned him down flat. Can you *imagine?*"

"She turned down Dr. Hunter?" the younger voice squealed in obvious disbelief. "Is she *crazy?*"

"Probably just frigid—you know, married to the work."

The other voice snorted. "Hell, I'd leave this place in a heartbeat if someone like Dr. Hunter offered to sweep me off my feet. Wouldn't hesitate a *second.*"

The door opened, as I had been hoping it wouldn't, and both females came in, still talking. Their conversation stopped abruptly, however, when they saw me standing there, out of my restraints and towering over them with a scowl on my face. Of course I was scowling—how not? They had stripped me of my weapons and armor and tied me to a sleeping platform when I should have been protecting my new mistress.

"I...uh..." one of the females stuttered, staring up at me.

"Where is my armor?" I demanded, getting right to the point. "What have you done with it? I need it."

"I...I..." the younger female stammered. Apparently she was too shocked to speak. Unfortunately, the older female had no problem speaking—or shouting as it turned out.

"Help!" she yelled, backing away. "Security—*Security!*"

I didn't like the sound of that. I had to find my armor and get out of here! Then I felt something strange—almost a tug, somewhere in my midsection. I looked down at myself but couldn't see anything. The tug came again—were there still some nanites inside me, doing damage?

Hastily, I ripped the flimsy garment I was wearing off—which wasn't hard since it tied in the back with little strings—and stared down at myself. My flat, muscular abdomen looked the same as always but I could still feel it—that tiny but unmistakable tug just behind my navel. What could it be?

"Oh my God," whispered the younger female, her eyes glued to the area between my legs.

Belatedly, I realized that ripping away the thin garment had left me naked. Not only that, but for some reason my shaft was standing at attention, hard as a rock. I felt the tug again and my cock hardened even more. What in the Frozen Hells was going on?

The older female had already turned and fled but the younger one was still backing away, a look of horror on her face as she stared at my erection. From the expression on her face, I guessed she thought I was going to attempt to molest her.

"I have no intention of harming you sexually or any other way," I said, taking a step towards her. "I have sworn my chastity to the Empress. I just need my armor."

"No..." she moaned, dissolving into tears. "Please, don't...*please.*"

I heard voices and shouting in the hallway outside the room and realized that the older female had run to get help. I had no time to get my armor now—I had to leave the House of Healing before I was captured and sedated again.

Pushing past the weeping female, who had now fallen to her knees and was crouching on the floor, I ran down the long hallway, in the opposite direction of the shouting voices.

Feet were pounding down the hallway behind me but thankfully, there weren't many people in my way. I saw a few startled glances as I flashed past but no one tried to stop me—I think they were too surprised to see a large male running past them in the nude. My erection bobbed in front of me indecorously with every step but I couldn't help it—the damn thing wouldn't go down!

Running down the halls of the House of Healing nude, with my shaft waving like a flag wasn't my finest hour, I'll admit that. But at the moment, I was just intent on escaping to find Charlotte.

I turned a corner and then another. I wanted to find a safe place to hide until the pursuit died down and I could find a way out of the House of Healing. There were any number of rooms up and down the long hallways but most of them appeared to contain sick pilgrims who had journeyed there to be healed. I needed to find someplace that was unoccupied.

At last I saw a sign that said, *Supply Closet. Employees Only*. I blessed the foresight that had prompted me to take an injection containing strands of translation virus that facilitated not only the understanding of spoken language, but of written words as well, and ducked inside.

Inside the closet there were stacks and stacks of white linen and lots of other Earth implements I didn't recognize. I was just about to examine them when I heard a voice outside the door shouting,

"In there! I thought I saw him go in the supply closet!"

The knob started to turn and I knew I was trapped.

In any other situation, I would have fought my way out. Even unarmed I was larger and stronger than any of the Earth males I had seen and I had been trained in the arts of hand-to-hand combat since I was a boy.

But I do not like to kill innocents and several of the voices were female—I had no wish to hurt them. They were chasing me because they thought I was crazed—out of my senses. And I couldn't say that I blamed them—in their situation, I would have thought the same. So I did the only other thing I could do...

I stepped back against the solid wall of white linens and concentrated on blending in.

Majorans are chromatachromes—meaning we are able to change the color of our hair, skin, and eyes at will. By the time the door swung open, revealing two beefy males in blue and gray uniforms, I was the exact some color from head to toe as the linens. Even my eyes were white and I didn't move a muscle—didn't so much as twitch as they stalked around the small storage area, blank frowns on their pudgy faces.

"Is he in there?" asked a quavering female voice—I thought it belonged to the younger female who had feared I would force her sexually. As if I would do such a thing! Even if I had not sworn my chastity to the service of my Empress, the very idea of taking a female against her will was repugnant to me.

"Don't see him," one of the males said at last and the other grunted in agreement.

"But I was so *sure*," she insisted. "I *saw* him go in!"

"Sorry, Darleen—he must have gone in a different room," the first male said dismissively. "Now look, why don't you go back to the nurses' station and let Bill and me hunt him? It's not safe for you to be looking for him."

The female gave a miffed-sounding reply but I didn't catch it— they had already closed the door and moved on.

I held my new color for a few minutes and then, with a sigh of relief, I let myself revert to my normal dark tan. In the presence of the new Empress, of course, I would automatically take on the gold skin-tone that only the Imperial Guards are permitted to use and when I began to serve her, my skin color would match her mood— but only in private. Out in public what the Empress was thinking and feeling must be kept secret—so my skin would remain gold at those times.

But just now, I wasn't with my new mistress and so I could relax and let myself be the color I had been born with.

Speaking of the new Empress, I had to get out of this closet to find and protect her. But how could I do that with everyone in the House of Healing looking for me?

My question was answered when my eyes fell on another stack of fabric—this one light green. It looked like the color of the strange, baggy clothing Charlotte and her colleague had been wearing the night before.

Unfolding one of the stacked garments, I saw that it was so. The shirt I found was much too small for me but after rummaging around in the pile, I finally located one that fit—albeit tightly—over my chest. The trousers were a different problem—none of them were long enough for my legs and the thin material showed my continued erection embarrassingly.

Because I was *still* hard. I didn't know why—I wasn't full of desire, not the way I had been the night before when the new Empress's blood had begun to work on me and I felt her cool touch on my fevered skin. So why...?

I felt that tug behind my navel again and suddenly made a connection. The Goddess-Empress was said to have sacred blood because it called her people to her. Of course, it was just a saying but what if there was some truth in it? What if the tug I felt was leading me in the direction of my new mistress?

The minute the thought occurred to me, I knew it to be true. The tug was leading me to Charlotte—maybe even because she was in danger! I *had* to get to her.

I found another stack of linens—this one of the white coats so many of the staff wore here. Most were too small but there was one labeled XXXL that finally fit. Shoes were a problem—they had taken my boots. Then I saw a small, rectangular box marked, *Shoe Covers.* Inside I found pale blue ovals of thin cloth that were clearly meant to stretch over the feet. They were a tight fit for me, even without shoes on, but I made do. After all, they only had to get me out of the House of Healing and on my way to find Charlotte. I felt instinctively that she had left the area and was on the move.

At last, I looked almost Earth normal—well, except for my size. Crouching a little to disguise my height, I ducked my head out the door. No one was watching so I stepped out, keeping the too-tight white coat wrapped firmly around myself to hide my continued erection. Gods, I wished it would go down! It was extremely uncomfortable to be sporting such an obvious mark of desire, not to mention the discomfort of trying to walk with the rigid shaft between my legs.

There was a sign at the end of the hallway marked *Exit* with an arrow beneath it. The tug behind my navel told me to follow it. In fact, it tugged so urgently I had to fight the desire to run. Was the new Empress in danger? I had to find her soon! But I knew if I went racing down the halls again, I would only attract attention to myself. Trying to look as though I belonged there, I strode confidently down the hallway at a brisk pace.

Hang on, my new mistress, I thought as I followed the urgent pull that guided me forward. *I am coming for you – I swear I am!*

Chapter Five

Charlotte

I had an uneasy sense of being watched as I pulled into my assigned parking space in front of building 4 in the Sunshine apartments. It was actually a retirement community which wasn't supposed to admit anyone under sixty-five. But I reminded the landlady of her granddaughter and I had explained my situation—lowly intern who barely gets any time off—and how hard it was to find someplace decent to stay near the hospital.

She had taken pity on me and I after I had practically sworn on a stack of bibles that I wouldn't bring home strange men or have any wild parties, she had rented me a small one bedroom ground floor apartment with faded blue carpet and a shower that sometimes went ice-cold when one of the upstairs tenants flushed.

It wasn't the nicest place in the world, but that hardly mattered because I almost never saw it. I lived at the hospital for the most part, only dashing home occasionally to pick up a few things and take intermittently icy cold showers.

As I got out of my Spark and clicked the alarm key, I told myself I was being foolish and paranoid. There was no one around to watch me but Mr. Peterson—the old man who liked to feed all the stray cats in the apartment complex. He was my next-door neighbor and the scent of cat urine frequently wafted from his open door when he came out to put down food for the "outside babies" as he called the strays.

"Well, howdy there, Doc," he said, smiling jovially at me as ten or twelve cats of all shapes and sizes twined around his skinny legs. "Haven't seen you in a coon's age. You been busy down to that hospital of yours?"

I smothered a small smile. Mr. Peterson might smell of cat pee but I liked his folksy way of talking. He'd told me once he was "born and bred" in Texas and though you could take the man out of hospital cafeteria food which isn't exactly the most nutritious stuff—at least, not in my hospital—and I always gained weight in my boobs first. Not to say that my hips and ass were far behind, it's just that I've always been kind of top-heavy and anytime I put on a significant amount of weight, I can tell because I gain a bra size.

There were no panties to go with the black teddy but I didn't mind—after all, I was going to be sleeping alone so why bother?

I walked to the oval mirror I had hung on the wall and twitched the towel I had draped over it carefully to one side. I was half afraid I would summon the blue worm just by looking in it, but all I saw was myself. Just a blonde girl in her late twenties with a little too much flesh stuffed into her black lace teddy. Okay—more like a *lot* too much.

I bet myself that if the handsome (and unbearably self-satisfied) Dr. Drake Hunter could see me now, he would take back his dinner invitation in a heartbeat. Without my baggy scrubs and lab coat to hide it, it was clear I was quite a bit more than "pleasingly plump." Well, what else could you except from one of the Plus-Sized Musketeers, as Zoe always liked to call herself and Leah and me?

"Time to lay off the cafeteria cheeseburgers, Charlotte," I muttered to my reflection. "Maybe try the salad bar for a change."

And then my image flickered and was replaced by the damn blue worm again.

"Greetings, Charlotte Walker," it began.

"No!" I shouted, before it could go into its spiel again. "No, just *leave me alone!*"

I put the towel back in place hurriedly, but that only muffled the worm's voice.

"I have a message for you," it started saying.

"No message!" I shouted. "I'm *not* interested!"

There was silence for a moment, and then the worm started talking again. Only this time I couldn't hear him because on the other side of the paper-thin wall I heard a sharp *click* and a newscaster's voice started up loud and clear.

"...continued speculation about what happened to the famous billionaire politician who disappeared completely a few weeks ago," it said, sounding pompous and self-important. "Some have speculated that it was a plot hatched by Democrats. However, they have strenuously denied any involvement. Today we have breaking news on that story—a statement from one of his aides who is just now coming forward. Mr. Kyle—can you tell us and our viewers what you saw?"

"This is going to sound crazy," a nervous male voice said. "But, well...he was sucked away into...into an espresso machine."

"I'm sorry—what?" the reporter asked, sounding incredulous. "It sounded like you said he was sucked into an espresso machine."

"He *was*," the aide insisted. "I was there—I saw it! This strange music began to play and then he said, 'What the Hell is that racket? Make it stop!' We had a stainless steel espresso machine with silver sides and the music seemed to be coming from there. He walked up to it and said something like...well, I shouldn't say what he said on TV." The aide cleared his throat. "But anyway, the next thing I knew, he was getting sucked into the shiny silver side of the machine. Just...sucked in like it was suddenly a black hole or something. And then...then he was gone."

"Well, Mr. Kyle, you'll forgive me if I say that sounds kind of far-fetched." The news reporter sounded like he was trying not to smile.

I certainly wasn't smiling. Sucked into a shiny surface? Strange music playing? That sounded like what had happened to Zoe. Or what *might* have happened to her, anyway. Leah and I had been on a three way call with her when she disappeared. The last thing Leah and I had heard was weird music that sounded kind of like a trumpet or a bugle. Then Zoe screaming. Then...nothing.

Could all this be connected somehow? The worm in the mirror? The weird music that played right before someone disappeared?

I sank down on the side of the bed and put my head in my hands. What did it all mean?

And then I heard a pounding on the door.

With a sigh, I got up and looked for my robe. So much for a quiet eight hours of rest—I'd be lucky to get *any* with all the racket going on, both inside and outside my head.

My robe was dirty—not just a little bit either. I had spilled canned tomato soup on it the last time I'd had a minute to relax and eat dinner at home. I make a mean grilled cheese sandwich but it needs the soup to go with it. Only I had been so tired, I had dumped the entire bowl in my lap, I remembered as I surveyed the now-crunchy red stain on the pink terrycloth.

Luckily, the black lace teddy had a robe that went with it. It wasn't nearly as substantial as my pink terrycloth one, but it came down to my knees and wasn't see-through so I decided it would have to do.

Whoever it was pounded on the door again, the TV in Mr. Peterson's apartment blared, and the blue worm went on and on in a muffled voice from my oval mirror, demanding to give me a message.

God, what a mess.

Sighing, I left the bedroom and took a few short steps to the hallway — the apartment wasn't very large. It was probably just the UPS man trying to deliver to the wrong address again. Mrs. Nader in the apartment above me, was always ordering toys for her little dog and the apartments weren't very clearly marked. I couldn't count the number of times I'd had to direct someone up the stairs to her place so she could get her dog toys and treats.

Speaking of the dog — which was a Jack Russell terrier mix — I could now hear it starting to yap and bark frantically just above my head. Well, great — one more noise to add to the cacophony. I really should have stolen some earplugs from the MRI suite before I came home to try and sleep.

Without looking through the peephole, I opened my front door.

"Look, you want the apartment upstairs," I was already saying when I saw that my visitor wasn't the UPS man or the FedEx guy at all. Instead, it was Carlos, the kindly old janitor from the hospital.

"Excuse me, Dr. Walker," he said, bobbing his graying head humbly. "But I just got a flat tire not too far from here. Could I use your phone to call? I don't have no cell phone — my wife, she kept it today."

"Oh, uh..." For a moment I had a really strong impulse to slam the door in his face. I remembered Kristoff's whirling rainbow eyes and his deep voice warning, *Danger!*

But that was crazy, I told myself. Carlos was a sweet old guy — nobody to be afraid of. And Kristoff had also called me "Goddess" and warned about assassin-bots or something like that which sounded like it was straight out of a science fiction novel. So who was I going to believe? The kind, grandfatherly coworker I'd known for months, or the crazy patient I'd seen for just a few minutes last night?

When I put it like that, it seemed there was no contest.

"All right, Carlos," I said, stepping aside to usher him through the door. "Let me just get my phone."

Chapter Six

Kristoff

The tugging pulled me away from the House of Healing, as I had known it would, down several residential streets lined with the odd-looking Earth houses. The paved streets were already hot even though judging by the position of the sun, it wasn't even mid-morning yet. The blue shoe covers I was wearing on my feet were already in shreds and tatters, causing me to long for my heavy black uniform boots.

Even more than the boots, I missed my weapons. The assassin droid had very few weak spots and I had nothing but my bare hands to put it out of commission. That would have to be enough— I just hoped I reached it before it got to Charlotte.

Because if it touched her and injected her with nanites from the receptors in its palms...

I couldn't even think about it. Following the incessant tugging, I ran, praying I wouldn't be too late.

Charlotte

"So how did you know I lived here?" I asked, as I rummaged around in my purse for my cell phone. "I mean—"

I turned my head and my sentence ended in a startled gasp. Instead of staying in the living room area while I went through to the tiny kitchen to dig in my purse, Carlos had come up right behind me. And he had moved so quietly I hadn't heard a thing.

"Uh, I mean..." I took a step back, my hand still in my purse. "I didn't think anyone but my friend Sebastian, the other intern, knew where I lived. Did you ask him?"

But of course he couldn't have asked Sebastian, I suddenly

remembered. He had been sent home to sleep the same time I was. Also, how would Carlos ask *anyone* from the hospital where I lived since he was driving home when he had his flat tire? There should have been no way he knew where my apartment was. So how had he found me? Had he been...following me?

"Sure, I asked him," he said, nodding agreeably and taking another step toward me. "He told me just where to find you."

I took another step back, my polite smile frozen on my face and my hand still in my purse.

"Um, if you don't mind, it's kind of a mess in here," I said, my voice coming out high and tight. "If you, uh, want to wait in the living room, I'll bring you the phone when I find it. I know it's in here somewhere." I gestured at my overstuffed purse and tried to laugh but it came out sounding nervous and fake.

Carlos shrugged and smiled, not actually answering. He didn't move either—he just stood there, staring at me. His eyes were brown but when he moved his head, I saw a flash of silver in them which was...weird. *Really* weird.

"Um..." My searching hand finally found something but it wasn't my phone—it was the taser I had bought after I was attacked in college. A Vipertek VTS (in black—not pink because screw the companies that think everything a woman uses has to be pink and girly.) It looked a little like a small, black flashlight and it fit right in the palm of my hand. I gripped it now, my fingers sweaty with anxiety.

Carlos—was it really Carlos?—took another step towards me. He was close now—too close. Well inside my personal space.

"Carlos," I said, trying to make my voice firmer. "If you could just go back to the living room I would really appreciate it. I'm not comfortable having you in this part of my home."

Instead of backing off, he took another step forward and grinned. It was a terrifying expression because it didn't reach his eyes at all. They were cold and emotionless and...and silver. They were pure silver now!

I gasped and took a step back, bringing the taser out of my purse with one swift gesture. I pointed at the person I was pretty sure wasn't actually Carlos and waved it menacingly.

"Get back," I said, wishing my voice didn't sound so high and frightened. "Get away from me."

"Empress," it whispered and its voice sounded nothing like the kindly old janitor's now. "Goddess..."

The words sent a shiver down my back. Goddess—that was what Kristoff had called me! What did it mean? What the Hell was going on?

The Carlos-thing took another step towards me and I couldn't take it anymore. I thrust the taser right in its face and pressed the trigger button.

Often just firing the taser off into the air is enough to back down a would-be attacker. I knew because I had used it once or twice on dates that tried to get too handsy—(this was before I gave up on dating in favor of practicing medicine and not thinking about how I couldn't get sexually excited, of course.)

The taser is supposed to emit a bright surge of electric charge and make a loud, intimidating crackling that sounds like the world's biggest bug zapper frying the world's biggest bug. Lots of guys run for the hills when they see it, so there's no need to even actually use it on them.

To my dismay, instead of the bright bluish-white crackle of electrical current between the two test prongs, all I got was a slight, sputtering sizzle. Oh no—when was the last time I had charged the damn thing? I usually plugged it up and charged it every night religiously but lately my schedule at the hospital had been so topsy-turvy I must have forgotten to do it.

I tried again with the same effect—the weak, sparking sizzle—not very scary at all. At least, not to the Carlos-thing, which just kept coming.

"Goddess," it said again and put out its hands to grab me.

"Get back!" I shouted, jumping back myself. Just then a movement behind the Carlos-thing's back caught my eye. My heart stuttered in my chest as I recognized Kristoff, my patient of the night before. His skin was a normal deep tan now and he was wearing scrubs and a lab jacket which he must have stolen from the hospital. But it wasn't what he looked like or what he was wearing that interested me—it was the fact that he was somehow in my home and he appeared to be stalking the thing that was stalking me.

Catching my eye, he gave a slight shake of his head and put a finger to his lips. The message was clear — don't say a word and just keep the thing's attention.

"Who *are* you?" I demanded of the Carlos thing, still backing slowly away, just out of reach of its grasping hands. "Who sent you? What do you want with me?"

To my surprise, it answered me — well, sort of.

"I am not programmed to answer such questions," it said in a stilted, mechanical voice, all traces of Carlos' soft accent completely gone now.

"Well, what *are* you programmed to do?" I asked it.

Behind it, Kristoff was closing in. There was a knife block sitting on my kitchen counter — it had been my mother's and she gave it to me when I left for college, even though I had never had much interest in cooking. Kristoff grabbed the hilt of the biggest knife and slid it silently out of its sheath.

"I am programmed to *kill,*" the Carlos-thing said and rushed at me.

Everything seemed to happen at once.

I screamed and ducked to one side, just barely managing to get out of the way of the charging Carlos-thing

At the same time, Kristoff stepped smoothly forward and buried the knife to the hilt in the back of its neck.

There was a popping, grinding sound and suddenly the thing's silver eyes started blinking and glowing, emitting beams of colored light that flashed off and on like some kind of demented disco ball. At the same time it jerked and writhed, as though it was inventing a new dance. And then, from behind the paper thin wall that separated my apartment from Mr. Peterson's, a car commercial came on playing the song, *Funky Town. "Gotta make a move to a town that's right for me..."*the commercial crooned while the assassin-droid flashed and jerked.

It was freaking surreal.

Oh my God — this is crazy! This can't be happening, can it? I thought, trying to get as far as I could from my would-be killer's flailing limbs while the car commercial invited me to go to Funky Town. *This has to be some kind of a dream.*

But it was no dream. Despite my evasive maneuvers, the Carlos-thing still managed to brush my cheek with the fingers of one flailing hand. The place where it touched me burned like fire and I gave a cry and grabbed for my face.

"Goddess-damn it!" Kristoff growled. He made a ruthless gesture, twisting the knife hard.

Suddenly, the lights stopped and the Carlos-thing went completely limp, sagging like a marionette whose strings had been cut. The image of Carlos—stooped shoulders, gray hair, kindly wrinkled face—flickered and was gone. In its place was a smooth, glossy silver figure. It was vaguely man-shaped—it had two arms, two legs, a torso and head, anyway. But it had no face at all—it was just smooth, blank silver.

"Oh my God," I whispered but Kristoff didn't waste any time looking at the now-limp silver figure. He dropped it to the floor and strode over to me, stepping over the fallen ex-Carlos as though it wasn't even there.

I looked up at him, wide-eyed.

"What are you—" I began but before I could finish, he was already taking my face in his big, warm hands and examining my cheek. "Hey!" I protested, as he turned my chin from side to side, as though looking for something. "What the Hell do you think you're doing?"

"The droid brushed your cheek with its hand. I saw it." His deep voice was grim. "I have to be certain it didn't inject you with nanites. If it did—"

"Nanites? What the hell are you talking about?"

"Your face—your cheek is red. Do you have a portable magnetic field?" he demanded.

"Do I have a *what?* No—of course not! You think I keep an MRI machine in my pocket or something?" I demanded. "And why would I need one, anyway?"

"To corrupt their memory and short out their circuitry, of course," he said, sounding impatient, as though I ought to know this stuff already. "Look, if the nanites reach your brain, or even your mucus membranes, you're going to be in big trouble."

I wanted to brush him off and tell myself he was talking crazy — the things he was saying certainly *sounded* crazy, anyway. Then I remembered that he had tried to warn me about Carlos — or the thing that had *looked* like Carlos, anyway. *That* hadn't turned out to be so crazy, now had it?

Also, my cheek was still burning like fire where the thing had touched me which seemed like a really bad sign. So I supposed I had better take him seriously.

"Microwave rays will work too," he said urgently. "Or an electromagnetic pulse."

"I don't have either of those," I said blankly. "I mean, I have a microwave but I'm not going to stick my head inside it. Even if I wanted to, it won't turn on unless the door is shut."

"You must have *something* I can use." He sounded frustrated beyond belief. "Think, my Lady! Though some have named you a Goddess, you are all too mortal and easy to kill."

"Well, short of running back to the hospital and walking into the MRI room..." I started but then my eyes fell on my refrigerator which was right behind him.

I don't go for knick-knacks much, but I do like to get souvenirs when I travel or do something memorable. Fridge magnets are small, cheap, and easy to transport — I have a pretty good collection of them. In fact, they cover the whole front of my refrigerator.

"Would one of those smaller magnets do?" I asked, pointing at my crowded fridge. I had one from San Francisco that was rainbow colored and one from London that was shaped like Big Ben. Another — a gift from Zoe — had a picture of a happy 50's housewife standing in front of the stove saying, "Make your own damn dinner."

"These are magnetic?" Kristoff turned to my fridge and grabbed a white phantom mask from the time Zoe and Leah and I had splurged and gone to see The Phantom of the Opera at the Straz — the Tampa Performing Arts center.

"Well, yes — weakly magnetic," I said. "They —"

But he was already rubbing the magnetic side of the phantom mask over my cheek. His other large hand was buried in the hair at the nape of my neck to hold me still and there was a look of intense concentration on his finely chiseled features that somehow kept me from complaining.

At last he stopped and dropped the magnet on the counter. Taking my face in both hands, he examined me again, his eyes whirling rainbows.

"How are you?" he demanded. "How do you feel?"

"Fine, I think." I took a deep breath and reached up to touch my cheek. It didn't burn anymore, so that was good. "Did you, uh, get them out?"

"I incapacitated them," he said. "Disrupted their functions. As long as you don't feel a burning sensation you should be fine."

"I don't." I touched my cheek again. "I feel normal." Well, as normal as I could with a seven-foot tall muscular giant looming over me and cupping my face in his hands.

"Good." He breathed a sigh of relief. "I was almost too late. You should not have incapacitated me with drugs last night, my Lady. How can I protect you if I am unable to stand by your side and fight?"

"I didn't know you were sent to protect me from that...that *thing*." I nodded at the collapsed silver figure and shivered. "I thought you were just some crazy guy—you grabbed my friend, Sebastian by the neck!"

"He was disrespecting you," Kristoff said, as though that excused nearly strangling someone to death. "He got off lightly by Ma*jor*an standards. No one dares to act or speak so disrespectfully in the presence of the Goddess-Empress on Femme One, lest they lose their head."

"What? Why do you keep calling me that?" I demanded. "And who are you, anyway?"

Kristoff took a deep breath and ran a hand through his blue-black hair. Then he looked at me directly.

"My Lady," he rumbled. "A better question might be *who* are *you* and what is your true identity?"

Chapter Seven

Kristoff

I could see by the expression in her wide green eyes—half frightened and half defiant—that my words had shaken her to the core.

"What...what do you mean?" she whispered.

"I mean," I said. "That you are the true Incarnation of the Goddess-Empress. You are Sundalla the 1000th, she who is the rightful ruler of the Goddess's Cloak."

I dropped to my knees before her, prepared to make my vow of fealty. I was glad, at least, that my erection had gone down—the fight with the assassin-droid had taken all my concentration which had helped. But I felt it stirring again when I looked at her—she was wearing a short lacy black robe which hugged her lush curves and showed her long, lovely legs. It was enough to give me blasphemous thoughts—thoughts which I pushed quickly out of my mind.

"My Lady," I began but Charlotte was shaking her head.

"The Goddess's Cloak? What's that?" She was still looking at me uncertainly. I reminded myself that she came from a closed world and so was ignorant of much of the workings of our galaxy. But surely she had gotten *some* information from the message her friend Leah had sent to her via the Commercians? The little bastards were mercenary but they were also thorough—they wouldn't have stopped communicating with her until she understood.

"The Goddess's Cloak is what most of the Twelve Peoples call the galaxy we all live in," I told her. "What do your people call it?"

"The Milky Way," she said, sounding distracted. "I'm sorry, but did you just tell me I'm supposed to be the *ruler* of the entire *galaxy?*"

"You will be if I can get you back to Femme One to undergo the trials and prove to the Council you are the true Incarnation," I said grimly. "Unfortunately, there are already those who would rather see you dead than sitting in your rightful place on the Golden Throne."

"Oh my God..." Charlotte shook her head, backing away from me. "I...I can't believe this. This is *crazy.*"

"I know it seems overwhelming." I rose from the floor and went to her, moving carefully so as not to frighten her even more. Already I was attuned to her, though I had yet to give her my vow. I could feel her fear and disbelief in the air between us. Without conscious effort on my part, my skin turned a deep purplish blue to reflect her emotion.

"Oh!" Charlotte jumped and put a hand to her mouth, her green eyes getting wide.

Again, my body responded unbidden, my skin giving a bright flash of yellow in response to her fear and surprise.

"Why are you doing that?" she asked in a wavering voice. "What does that mean?"

"You mean my skin color?" I could have asked the same thing. It seemed strange to me that I was already so attuned to her that my body changed my skin tone without conscious effort on my part. But then I remembered the blood she had given me—that must be the cause.

"*Yes*, I mean your freaking *skin color*!" Charlotte exclaimed. "Why does it keep changing?"

"My body is simply reacting to your moods—reflecting your emotions as you have them," I explained.

"What? That...that's bizarre! *Why?*" she demanded.

"Because I am yours, Goddess," I told her simply.

It was what every Majoran male says to the female he chooses to give his life to and acknowledge as his own personal goddess but my words seemed to bother Charlotte deeply.

"You're *mine?* What does that mean?" she demanded. "I don't even *know* you!"

"No, but you will. Come..." I led her to the small, padded couch she had behind her food-prep area. Once she was settled, I went to my knees before her once more.

"What are you doing?" She looked at me nervously. "Why do I get the feeling you're about to propose?"

"Propose?" I frowned at her. "You fear I am asking you to be my bonded mate?"

"Um...I guess that's one way to put it." She nibbled her full lower lip nervously and I had to fight to keep my body from flashing orange in response to her emotion.

"Please don't fear that," I told her. "Though my life and my chastity are sworn to your service, I would never be a candidate for Royal Consort—my blood is not exalted enough. As I told you before, my mother was only a lesser noble."

"Um..." She still seemed not to understand. "So then...why are you on your knees in front of me like that? It's kind of, uh, making me nervous."

"I know," I said. "I can tell."

Feeling the emotions of the Empress, even though none of us is her fated mate, is one of the unique attributes of the Imperial Guards. Most other males of the Twelve Peoples only feel the emotions of their chosen females *after* they bond. But for us, the ties of loyalty run so deep, we are intimately connected to she who sits upon the Golden Throne.

"Kristoff," she began but I took her hands in mine, sending a charged tingle through both of us.

I knew well enough what that tingle meant—that the new Empress was a *La-ti-zal*, a female specially blessed with gifts from the Ancient Ones—and that we were sexually compatible.

I had never felt that tingle with my old mistress but then, she was forty years my senior and desired no one after her Consort had died. It was a shock to feel it when I touched my new mistress, but I refused to let it show on my face, even though Charlotte gave a little gasp.

"My Empress...my Goddess," I began formally, looking into her lovely green eyes. "I, Kristoff Xander Verrai, am yours to command. My body shall be your shield. My blood is yours to spill, my shoulders shall carry your burdens, and my lips shall keep your secrets. My heart shall beat only for you. I will never leave you or forsake you — I will follow and protect you until the end of my days. Unswerving Loyalty, Unquestioning Devotion, Unremitting Obedience, and…" I paused for a moment, my throat working. "And Unending Love," I said, though I hadn't meant to say it. "These are the code and the credo of the Imperial Guard. Until I die, my Lady, *I am yours.*"

As I said the last words, a mighty surge ran between us — a rush of electrifying power — of a vow given and received. It was a sign that the Goddess of Mercy had heard and acknowledged my oath to my new mistress.

Charlotte must have felt it too because her eyes got wide and she tried to pull her hands out of mine.

"What was *that?*" she whispered in an awed voice.

"That was me tying myself to your service for life," I said simply.

Although I still wasn't certain why I had added the "Unending Love" part, which was not actually supposed to be part of the vow. I had added it when I gave my oath to my old mistress, Sundalla the 999th because I felt very strongly for her.

I never expected to have such strong feelings for my new mistress — my heart was in the grave with the last Goddess-Empress and though my loyalty was the new Empress's to command, my love was dead. Yet somehow the words had come to my lips and I had uttered them anyway. Why?

Before I could answer the question, Charlotte was yanking her hands out of mine and edging away from me.

"This can't be right — I mean, you don't think you're going to stay here, do you?"

"Of course not," I said. "We will be going to Femme One as soon as I can get my armor back and call my ship to come to us."

"What? I'm not going anywhere with you!" she exclaimed. She got up and started pacing back and forth. "I never met you before last night! I have a life here — an internship! Do you know how hard it is to get into one of these programs? And…and I have sick people depending on me. I can't just leave them!"

I considered rising to go to her but I could feel her fear and trepidation — though I was careful not to let my skin display those emotions. Instead I stayed on my knees, motionless, to avoid causing her more distress.

"You want to devote yourself to the service of others," I said calmly. "That is the defining characteristic of the Goddess-Empress. But if you stay here you can help what—hundreds? Perhaps thousands? If you come with me, you will be able to help *trillions.* My Lady-Goddess, so many will be touched by your divine hand—"

"Stop calling me that! I'm *not* a goddess!" she exclaimed. "And…and get up off the floor. Stop kneeling to me like that—it's crazy!"

"It is a sign of respect," I said gravely, staying where I was.

"Well, it's freaking me out." She ran a hand through her hair distractedly. "This whole conversation is insane. I can't believe I'm even talking to you instead of just telling you to leave. None of what you're saying can possibly be true."

"Are you calling me a liar, my Lady?" I asked, my voice deepening towards a growl. "After what you have seen?" I nodded at the sleek, silver form of the assassin-droid, jumbled in a heap on her floor.

"I…I can't…It's just, this is the first I'm hearing about *any* of this." She put a hand on her hip and glared at me. "You can't blame me for saying it sounds crazy!"

This time, I did rise to stand before her.

"I know you come from a closed planet which has no knowledge of the outside universe," I said. "But did the Commercians tell you nothing when they gave you the message from your friend, the Lady Leah?"

"What message? She shook her head. "What are you talking about? Leah called me a couple of times but I was too busy to talk."

"No, the message should have come through the Commercians," I said, frowning. "Char'noth the head of the Alien Mate Index took payment in exchange for reaching you to tell you the details of your friend's disappearance and ask you to relay the information to her family."

"Who is Char'noth?" she demanded. "And Leah hasn't disappeared—she just moved to Virginia with that asshole fiancé of hers."

I felt a surge of anger.

"So you never heard from the Commercians? Those little blue bastards! Gravex told me they took payment from him in full. They're avaricious but it's not like them to defraud a paying customer."

"Wait..." Her face had gone pale. "Did you say...blue?"

"Yes, blue. They are long and thin with eyes on stalks. They stand about so high..." I showed a measurement with my hand not too far from the ground. "They make contact through shiny objects such as viewers or..."

I trailed off because Charlotte had sunk back down to the padded seating area with her head in her hands.

"Oh my God," she was murmuring. "Oh my God...*Oh my God!*"

"Mistress?" I knelt before her, feeling her distress so clearly it roused my protective instincts. But there was no outside foe to fight for her — the source of her suffering was internal.

"The worm," she said at last, looking up at me, her eyes filled with a strange mixture of relief and regret. "That damn blue worm! He's been trying to talk to me for *weeks.* Every time I looked in the mirror or the side of the toaster or even a metal spoon...I mean, I couldn't even use the bathroom without him yelling at me from the reflective water in the toilet!"

So the Commercians *had* tried to contact her.

"You never listened to what he had to say?" I asked, frowning.

"You don't understand — I'm a practical person. I don't believe in things like ghost stories or fairy tales or aliens. I..." She put her face in her hands, her voice coming out muffled. "I thought I was going *crazy.*"

At last I understood the source of her tangled emotions — she had feared for her sanity.

"Mistress," I said as gently as I could. "You're not insane and neither am I. There is another world outside your own small planet — a vast one that needs you. Needs you *desperately.*"

"I can't." She sat up, shaking her head, her lovely face set. "I can't just pick up and go. I told you—I have a life here. I, uh, appreciate that you came all this way and that you saved my life…" She looked at the remains of the droid and shivered. "But you'll have to go back to that…that other world without me. I'm staying here."

"Then I am staying with you," I said, though my heart was heavy. "I have pledged myself to you for life, my Lady. I will never leave your side."

Charlotte

"What?" I stared at him blankly. "What are you talking about? You can't just *move in.*" I thought about how I had promised my landlady not to have strange men over. And a seven-foot tall, muscular alien with rainbow eyes and skin that could change colors was about as strange as it got.

But Kristoff had a stubborn look on his chiseled features.

"My Lady, I have pledged my life to you," he said, frowning. "My place is at your side. I will not abandon you."

"Well then you'll have to rent your own apartment," I said, crossing my arms over my chest. "Because there's no room for you here. I only have, uh, one bed." I could feel my cheeks heating as I said it but I went on anyway. "And I'm not letting some strange man sleep with me. Also, you won't fit on the couch." I indicated my little loveseat which was barely big enough for one normal sized person to stretch out on—there was no way a seven-foot tall alien would fit.

He frowned. "I will sleep on the floor at the foot of your bed, if necessary, but I will not leave you alone. That would not be safe."

"Why not?" I demanded. "You killed the, uh, assassin-bot thing." I gestured at the shiny silver jumble on my carpet.

Kristoff's strange eyes narrowed.

"Assassin-*droid.* And do you really think that is the only attempt your enemies will make on your life? As long as you live, you're a threat to those who want power—power which should rightfully be *yours.*"

"I don't *want* that much power!" I exclaimed. "I just want to be left alone!"

He shook his head. "That is one thing you will never be again. The Goddess-Empress must be warded at all times for her own safety and protection."

"Look here," I said, glaring at him. "You can't just decide to move into my home and never leave!"

"Which is why you must come with me to Femme One," he said. "Only there can you be adequately guarded."

"I told you, I'm not—"

Our argument was interrupted by a loud knocking at the door.

"Wait. Just wait a minute," I said to Kristoff. "I have to see who this is."

"Are you mad?" He stepped in front of me when I would have gone to get the door.

"No, I'm thinking I have someone at the door," I said. "Now will you please get out of the way and let me answer it?"

"Think, my Lady—who was it the last time you opened the door? This could be another droid sent to kill you," he warned.

For a moment my heart seemed to stop in my chest. *He could be right,* whispered a panicked little voice in the back of my head. *The whole world — hell, the whole universe — could be out to get you!*

But I couldn't live like that, couldn't give in to paranoia. I was still trying to deal with the idea that there was in fact extraterrestrial life out there, let alone the idea that I was supposed to go to some mystical planet and rule over it all from a golden throne. I couldn't let go of my humanity and my nice, normal world just because some tall, muscular stranger said so.

The knocking sounded again.

"Step back," I said sternly. "I'm going to get the damn door."

He frowned. "Then I am coming with you."

Chapter Eight

Charlotte

I went to the door with a glaring Kristoff right at my back. He was keeping to the shadows, such as they were, but I could tell his big body was coiled tight as a spring, ready to jump into action if he thought I was in danger in any way. God, he really took his job seriously! I had the uneasy feeling it was going to be next to impossible to get rid of him.

I have to admit, my heart was hammering in my chest as the door swung open. What if Kristoff was right? What if it *was* another assassin droid coming to attack me?

What met my eyes was the last person I had expected.

Dr. Drake Hunter stood there, his brown hair slicked back and a self-satisfied look in his baby-blue eyes. He was dressed in tight jeans and there was a motorcycle helmet under one arm. He was the "cool" doctor at North Florida Regional and he had every nurse, tech, and PA in the place swooning over him.

"Dr. Hunter?" I said blankly. "What are you doing here?"

He looked me up and down and gave a long, low whistle.

"Well, *hello* there, Charlotte. Aren't *you* looking lovely today."

I suddenly remembered that I was wearing nothing but the black lace teddy and the robe that went with it. Then again, it wasn't exactly like I'd had time to change, what with all the craziness that had happened to me in the last half hour.

"How can I help you?" I said, not bothering to keep the dislike out of my voice. I know lots of women who think that confidence is sexy—and it is, if you think the man being all confident and in your face can turn you on. But one shake of Dr. Drake Hunter's neatly manicured hand had been enough to let me know he couldn't do a damn thing for me sexually. Not that anyone could but still—his arrogance was annoying.

"Now, Charlotte…I think we got off on the wrong foot the other day." He gave me a blindingly white grin that all the other women at the hospital found completely charming and I just found irritating.

"You mean when you asked me out and I turned you down?" I said bluntly.

I'm not usually so rude but my heart was still pounding hard — here was *another* person from the hospital who shouldn't know where I lived showing up on my doorstep. Was he an assassin-droid? I didn't see a glint of silver in his blue eyes and he was a lot more articulate than the Carlos-thing had been but still, maybe whoever it was that wanted me dead was stepping up their game with an upgraded model.

Dr. Hunter's grin slipped a little but he clearly wasn't one to give up.

"Well yes — I was thinking I just caught you at a bad time," he remarked. "Your Attending said he sent you home so I thought maybe with a little privacy…"

"You thought if you cornered me at my home I'd agree to go out with you?" I demanded. "How did you even get my address?"

"I'm friends with Linda, in Records — she looked it up for me. She was actually pretty jealous when I told her why I wanted to see you. I, uh, think she has a little crush on me." He winked at me knowingly — damn, would *nothing* puncture his huge ego?

"I'm sorry," I said. "But I just don't think —"

"You don't have to think about it at all, baby." Before I knew it, he had captured one of my hands and was staring soulfully into my eyes. "Just come with me. I'll take you for a ride on the back of my Harley and then afterwards we can spread a blanket under the stars…"

"I don't think so," I began but suddenly Kristoff was standing beside me, glaring down at Hunter. His skin had taken on that strange gold sheen again that I had seen the night before in the ER and his eyes were whirling with rage.

"Hands *off*," he growled at the startled Dr. Hunter.

Hunter dropped my hand abruptly, but held his ground.

"Who *is* this?" he asked me, his eyes never leaving Kristoff's tall form. "Is he, uh, from another hospital?"

I blessed the fact that Kristoff was wearing the stolen scrubs and lab jacket from the hospital.

"Yes," I said quickly. "This is, uh, my brother, Kris."

"Your *brother?*" He raised his eyebrows skeptically. "Forgive me for saying so, but you two look nothing alike. What's the deal with his skin?"

"That's because I was adopted," I said, which was the one truth in the stew of lies I was telling. I ignored the skin question—there was no plausible explanation as to why my companion suddenly had a golden sheen to his dark tan skin. "Kris is visiting from Minnesota where he's a resident at St. Paul's."

"St. Paul's, huh?" Hunter frowned, clearly not buying it. "If he's here visiting on vacation, why is he dressed in scrubs?"

"He, uh, thought he might come with me to do afternoon rounds," I said weakly—I could feel my house of lies collapsing but I wasn't quite ready to give up on it yet.

"I thought your Attending sent you home to get some rest," Hunter said, still frowning.

"He did but I'm, uh, perfectly well rested now and I was about to go back," I said.

"Dressed like *that?*" He eyed me incredulously.

"I was about to put on my scrubs," I said. "You just...caught me at a bad time."

Hunter started to ask something else but Kristoff glared down at him.

"No more questions," he said in that deep, dark voice of his. "You will leave *now.* You are not wanted here."

"Well aren't you just fucking *rude?*" Hunter snapped at him. "Charlotte, I think you'd better reign your extremely tall brother in. If he even *is* your brother." He frowned. "Come to think of it, wasn't there an extremely tall patient who escaped from the psych ward today?"

"Was there?" I said, trying to sound unconcerned. "That's strange."

"Yes—a patient I heard *you* were treating in the ER last night." Hunter's face grew rigid. "What are you doing, Dr. Walker? You know this kind of thing is a serious breach of ethics."

Great, when he wanted to go out with me I was sweet little "Charlotte." But the minute he thought he'd caught me with another man—and a patient at that—I was suddenly the much more formal "Dr. Walker."

"What I do is none of your business," I said stiffly. "And speaking of a breach of ethics, I think getting a fellow employee's address so you can harass them at home is pretty unethical. In fact, I'm sure *my* friend, Marge, in Human Resources would *love* to hear about it."

At last he stepped back, his face dark with anger.

"Fine. I was trying to do you a *favor*," he snarled. "Just trying to brighten up your sad, pathetic little life."

"Thanks, but I don't need it brightened badly enough to go out with you," I snapped back.

I could tell from his face that I had gone too far. Dr. Hunter outranked me at the hospital—he was a Resident and I was just a lowly intern. I had just burned a bridge there was no rebuilding and it could have a serious impact on my future career.

"You'll pay for that," Hunter said tightly. "You just flushed your career down the toilet, little girl. Remember that the next time you want in on a surgery and you're stuck on endless rounds giving enemas and cleaning out stomas."

He turned and marched off, leaving me fuming with rage. Okay, so he hadn't been an assassin-droid after all. But I kind of wished he was—it would have been better than the conversation we'd just had and the inevitable outcome.

I went back in my apartment and slapped the door closed only to find Kristoff standing there, staring at me appraisingly.

"What?" I snapped. "I hope you're satisfied. Now he's going to go tell everyone at my work that I'm harboring a crazy escaped psych patient in my apartment."

"I wouldn't have been labeled 'crazy' or had to escape if you hadn't ordered me drugged and tied to that metal sleeping platform," he reminded me, frowning.

"Well, what was I supposed to do?" I demanded. "You nearly choked my friend Sebastian to death! And *he* was just joking around with me. I'm surprised you didn't try strangling Dr. Hunter just now when he got nasty with me."

"I didn't think you needed my help," he said mildly. "You acquitted yourself very well. I can tell already you'll make a formidable Empress."

"Not *that* again." I threw up my hands and went to sit back on the couch. "Look, do you know how *tired* I am? I've been up for well over twenty-four hours and the last hour of that has been running from an assassin-robot and arguing with a seven-foot tall alien who seems to think I'm the queen of the universe. Not to mention flushing my medical career down the toilet by insulting a Resident. It's *crazy*." I felt tears of self-pity pricking behind my eyelids and blinked them away angrily. "I just can't *deal* with this right now!" I said, my voice trembling much more than I wanted it to.

Unexpectedly, Kristoff's eyes softened and he came to sit beside me.

"My Lady," he murmured, looking at me earnestly. "I see how weary you are. Why don't you take your ease and sleep for a time? I will guard you that your sleep may be free of fear."

"You talk like an escapee from the Renaissance Festival, you know that?" I said, but there was no anger in my words, only a weariness so deep I felt it all the way down to my bones.

Suddenly I was so tired I could barely move and I wanted to sleep more than I'd ever wanted anything else in my whole life. When I woke up, I could fight with my new, unwanted houseguest some more but for now, I simply couldn't find any more energy to deal with him or any of the rest of the crap going on in my life.

"Sleep," Kristoff urged me.

I wanted to agree with him, get up, and go slide into bed. Even with the racket coming from Mr. Peterson's TV on the other side of the wall, I felt like I could sleep about a hundred million years. But I was so tired, I couldn't even nod my head, let alone get up and go to bed.

With a little moan of pure exhaustion, I scrunched down and

laid my head against the arm of the couch.

I'll just take a fifteen minute power nap, I told myself. *Then I'll get up and get everything worked out. But right now I just need some time…just a little time to recharge…*

So telling myself, I drifted off and knew no more.

Kristoff

I waited until she was deeply asleep and then I gathered her into my arms and carried her into her sleeping chamber. She sighed deeply and turned her face towards me, nuzzling against my chest in her sleep. The innocent gesture made my heart tighten strangely though I could not have said why.

I slid her between the sheets of her sleeping platform and debated taking off her outer garment, which was a type of robe. I didn't want to overstep the boundaries she might perceive between us but actually, there *are* no boundaries between the Goddess-Empress and her personal guard when it comes to such things.

As the Empress must be protected at all times, it is considered best to have her surrounded by attendants she can trust and so we of the Imperial Guard are trained in all aspects of personal care and comfort. We are able to give a soothing massage as well as fight off a would-be assassin. We are as capable of bathing and tending our Empress as we are of finding out and foiling a deadly plot against her life.

My old mistress, Sundalla the 999th never required such intimate services of me, though she confided in me a great deal. But I knew that past Empress's had used their Guards for much more than just protection. And why not? Our bodies are sworn to the service of she who sits upon the Golden Throne. We are there for the Empress to use in any way she sees fit.

There is no shame in such service—only honor and loyalty and the pleasure of a job well done.

I decided at last that Charlotte would sleep easier without her outer robe. Carefully, I untied the sash that held it closed and slipped it from her sleeping limbs.

Then I wished I hadn't done it.

She was too beautiful, lying there with her silky blonde hair spread over the pillows and her long limbs carelessly splayed. She was full figured, with ripe breasts and rounded hips—lush and gorgeous in a way I didn't think she was at all aware of. The tips of her pink nipples poked through the fragile black lace of her small sleeping outfit and the V between her thighs was capped with a mound of silky-looking blonde curls.

For a moment I thought of some of the other, more intimate duties I had heard past Guards had performed for their mistresses…and then I pushed the thought away.

I made myself pull the coverings over her, hiding her luscious body. It was wrong to think such things about the female I had sworn myself to. Wrong and strange. I had never had such problems in my service before. Of course, my old mistress was forty cycles my senior and had once confided to me that her desire for any male had died when her bonded mate and Consort had passed into the other realm.

It's only her blood calling to me, I told myself uneasily. *My chastity is dedicated to her along with my life. These feelings will pass…they must.*

Speaking of her exulted blood, I was cautiously relieved that, despite the large amount of it she had given me, Charlotte didn't seem to be showing any signs of the *Calet Sanguis,* also known as the Burning Blood. It is the sickness which most often occurs following the Culling of the Consorts ceremony, after the Goddess-Empress has given her blood to the ones the Council deems worthy of her attentions.

Of course she hasn't experienced the Calet Sanguis, I told myself sternly. *Your blood isn't rarified enough to call to hers, no matter how much of her own blood she pumped into you!*

It was a ridiculous thought and I pushed it from my mind. I was there to protect and serve—nothing else. Accordingly, I looked around for another way to serve her.

There was a pile of clothing which needed washing on the floor and I thought I remembered seeing a machine in the closet by her food-prep area that had pictures of clothing on it. Perhaps I could figure it out.

Gathering as much of the clothing as I could, I slipped out of her sleeping chamber and went to make myself useful.

Chapter Nine

Charlotte

I had the God-awfullest weird dreams while I slept—all about a snake made of flames that wrapped itself around and around me, crawling all over my body and making me itchy and restless and hot.

When I finally woke up, I thought I was still dreaming.

Stacks of neatly folded clothes were sitting at the foot of my bed and Kristoff was putting them away in my dresser, obviously trying to be quiet so as not to wake me. He had taken off the white lab coat—which was good because it looked like it was about to burst at the seams—and was just wearing the light green scrub. The thin material of the top was stretched tight over his broad, muscular shoulders.

"What...what are you doing?" I asked, sitting up and rubbing my eyes. It looked like he was cleaning but that couldn't be right—could it? The few guys I had been with before I gave up on dating wouldn't have been caught dead doing household chores. It was beneath them—unmanly. Yet I had never seen anything more masculine, somehow, than my huge, seven-foot tall, self-appointed bodyguard folding my undies.

Hey—he was touching my undies!

"Excuse me!" I jumped out of bed and went to rescue my best black lacy panties from his large hand. "What do you think you're doing?"

"Serving you, my Lady." He shrugged innocently. "Forgive me—did you want to wear those now?" His eyes drifted down to the area between my thighs and I remembered that the black lace teddy I was wearing didn't have any panties to go with it. Also, it had somehow hiked itself up so that my little mound of well-trimmed curls was showing.

"Oh my God!" I pulled the hem of the teddy down as quickly as I could. "How…why…don't look!"

"Forgive me." He turned his head away considerately while I pulled on the panties.

"Where's my robe?" I demanded, looking for it. "I don't remember taking it off—or getting in bed either!"

"I carried you to the sleeping platform and removed your outer garment so that you could sleep more easily." He spread his hands. "I ask your pardon if that makes you feel uncomfortable. I wanted only to serve you."

He looked so innocent that I felt bad accusing him of anything pervy. I still couldn't find my robe so I crossed my arms over my chest, frowning at him.

"I just…" I shook my head. "Did you actually do my *laundry*?"

"I protect and serve," he said simply.

"Okay, well…" I looked around and finally spotted my robe, folded neatly on the side of my bed.

"You don't need to fear to show your body to me, my Lady," he remarked as I put it on. "The Empress has no secrets from her personal Guard."

"Well *this* Empress does," I snapped. "I don't know you well enough to run around barely dressed. There." I felt better when I put my robe on, though I knew I would feel more in control if I was wearing scrubs and a lab coat instead.

Speaking of wearing scrubs, I noticed that Kristoff had reached beneath the stolen scrub shirt he was wearing and was rubbing his chest and abdomen, right where he had been wounded.

It reminded me that I was his doctor—or had been last night when I'd stitched him up and given him a blood transfusion. Since then he'd escaped from the hospital, run all the way here, and had fought off an attacker who wanted to kill me. Then he carried me to bed and let me tell you, I am *not* light. All that and I hadn't even thought to check his wound! What was wrong with me?

"Take off your shirt," I told him abruptly.

He raised his eyebrows at me.

"For what reason? Do you wish a different type of service, my

Lady? Because though my chastity is sworn to you—"

"No, no—nothing like that!" I said quickly, feeling my cheeks get hot. "I just want to examine your wound. The stitches I put in should dissolve when you're healed but that's going to be a while—I want to make sure you didn't pop any of them fighting that thing. Or doing laundry."

"As you wish." He tugged the shirt over his head, and spread his arms, displaying himself for me.

"Oh…" I whispered. His chest was absolutely mouthwatering—seriously, it looked like something out of a porno aimed at women or gay men. From the heavy musculature of his pecs right down to his eight-pack abs he was completely ripped. Of course, I had seen him the night before when I treated them but then I had been completely focused on saving his life. Now I could really appreciate what Sebastian had been going on and on about—shirtless, Kristoff looked like some kind of a Greek God.

The stitches—you're supposed to be looking at the stitches! an accusing little voice whispered to me.

Right…the stitches.

But there were no stitches to see. To my utter amazement, they were gone—and so was the wound they had been holding closed. The only thing left was a long, faint scar that started just under his collarbone and ran down his long, muscular abdomen into the waistband of his scrubs.

"What in the…how is this possible?" I asked out loud. Forgetting to be intimidated by his amazing physique, I stepped forward and examined him, tracing the long, nearly invisible scar with my fingertips. His skin was warm—almost hot—but not in a fevered kind of way. More like it was his normal body temperature. As before when I had touched him, I felt a strange tingle jump between us, like a low-level electrical current. I barely noticed it—I was too caught up in witnessing what appeared to be some kind of medical miracle.

Kristoff made no comment or complaint and it wasn't until I was starting to explore the end of the scar, under the waistband of his scrubs that he caught my hand in his own, much larger one.

"My Lady," he said, his deep voice hoarse. "I don't believe…I don't think it would be wise for you to go further."

I tore my eyes from the faded scar and saw that there was a different kind of "miracle" happening in his scrub bottoms. His thick, heavy shaft had come to full attention and was pressing hard against the thin green material. He was so long the broad, mushroom-shaped head was almost peeking out the top.

Blushing, I dropped my hand hastily.

"I'm so sorry. I've just never, uh, seen anyone heal that big…uh, I mean fast! I've never seen anyone heal that *fast* before," I stammered, feeling my cheeks get even hotter. Oh God, this was *so* embarrassing!

"Forgive me for the way my body reacts to you," Kristoff murmured. "It is…inexcusable."

"Well, I was kind of, uh, touching you." I cleared my throat. "Not that I meant to, you know, turn you on or anything. I just wanted to examine you. I can't believe you healed so rapidly!"

"Why are you surprised?" he asked, sounding surprised himself. "You healed me last night—you're a Healer, correct? Is that not your *La-ti-zal* power?"

"My *what* kind of power did you say?" I asked, frowning at him.

He sighed. "I keep forgetting that you're ignorant of the galaxy beyond you. Listen…"

He told me a lot of stuff about the Goddess of Mercy and the Ancient Ones, whom she had created and given the seeds of life to sew across the galaxy. And about *La-ti-zals,* who were females blessed with extra gifts from the Ancient Ones.

"Only I thought that the gifts were dormant until you left your planet's atmosphere," he remarked. "At least, that is how it worked for your other two friends, Lady Zoe and Lady Leah."

"What? You're saying that Zoe and Leah have, uh, special gifts too?" I frowned at him. "Seriously?"

He nodded. "From what I understand, Lady Zoe is an Opener and Lady Leah is a Healer. I thought you were one as well."

"No." I shook my head. "I don't have any special gifts. Except, well…" I trailed off, thinking of my touch-sense. But I had never told anyone about that before.

"What?" he asked. "Please, my Lady—I need to know."

"I…sometimes I know things about people when I touch them," I said reluctantly. I'd been keeping my secret for so long it made me feel naked and vulnerable to say it out loud.

"A Knower?" He frowned. "That is a rare talent indeed. Do you also have visions or dreams that portend the future?"

I thought of the strange dream I'd been having about a snake made of flames twining around my body and shook my head.

"No, my dreams are pretty much nonsense—like everybody else's. And the, uh, touch-sense—that's what I call it—usually just works the first time I touch someone. Like with you, I knew that you'd recently been fighting for your life and that I couldn't give you regular O neg blood because it might kill you. And—"

"And?" he prompted in a soft, low voice.

"And that's all," I said quickly. There was no way I was going to tell him the third thing I had picked up from him.

That of all the men I had ever touched, he was the only one I knew my body would react sexually to.

Just thinking about it made me feel hot and cold all over. I tried to push it out of my mind but it didn't want to go. The fact that he was standing there looking so damn sexy and mouthwatering didn't help any either.

"Um…you can put back on your scrub shirt now," I said, feeling like it would be safer not to have him half-naked right in front of me. "I don't know how it happened but you certainly seem to be healed."

"It was your blood," he said quietly, pulling the too-tight scrub top back over his broad chest. "It saved my life—but you should not have given it to me. I am not worthy to receive such a gift from the Goddess-Empress herself."

I sighed. So we were back to that again.

"About the Empress thing…" I began.

"I have been thinking," he said, before I could get going. "I have a small message cube that her majesty, Sundalla the 999th recorded for me to give to you before she Ascended to the Heavens.

It's tucked away in a secret compartment of my belt. If I could just get my armor I could show it to you. Perhaps it would change your mind."

I didn't think anything could change my mind about believing that I was supposed to be the ruler of the whole freaking galaxy but I was willing to watch the message out of sheer curiosity.

"Sure," I said, shrugging. "I'll watch it but I'll have to go get your armor first." I looked at the clock on the wall. "My shift starts in about an hour and a half and it's going to be at least twelve hours long so you'll just have to wait until..." I stopped because he was frowning and shaking his head.

"You cannot go to the House of Healing alone and unprotected," he growled. "It's been long enough since I incapacitated the first droid that another attack is imminent. Your enemies will be waiting for you to step outside your door to swoop in and kill you."

"What?" I put my hands on my hips. "I hope you don't expect to go with me—you're an escaped patient, remember? Security will be on you like a duck on a June bug the minute you step in the door."

"Neither of us is going," he said calmly.

"First of all, you don't tell me what to do," I said angrily. "And second, how are we supposed to get your armor if neither of us goes to the hospital?"

He frowned. "I think I know of a way. How enamored of you was that male I choked for disrespecting you last night?"

Chapter Ten

Charlotte

"Sebastian, you are the *best* friend, ever. I really mean that—thank you so much," I said.

"You're welcome. Is he with you *now?*" Sebastian looked up and down the empty hospital corridor, trying to catch a glimpse of Kristoff.

"I am." There was a shimmer in the air behind me and my huge, self-appointed bodyguard suddenly appeared. He was dressed as he had been when I first saw him, in the Roman-soldier looking armor with the molded golden breastplate, high black boots, and short leather kilt. He had the long golden sword in a sheath at his back and its hilt stuck up above his blue-black hair.

To be honest, he looked nothing short of amazing and the intense way he watched me made me feel strange inside—kind of shivery. It was like I had my own private gladiator, although it was hard to see how I merited such loyalty and devotion. I couldn't help thinking of the way he had looked at me and said, *"I am yours,"* as though it was an irrefutable fact that could never be changed.

Don't be silly, I told myself, looking away from that changing rainbow gaze. *He's just protecting you because you're the Empress or whatever. It's his job, that's all.*

"How does he *do* that? Just appear and disappear like that?" Sebastian asked, awed. He had reluctantly agreed to go to the hospital and bring the armor to my apartment, but only if I told him absolutely *everything.* Which I had tried to do, though Kristoff didn't like it. Still, I felt like I owed my friend an explanation and besides—telling it to someone else and having them believe it made me feel less crazy.

Not that there could be any doubt about Kristoff telling the truth now. Besides the heap of silver metal parts which was all that was left of the assassin-droid, his chameleon-like skin changing abilities, and the small crystal cube which projected a message from the previous Empress, who looked like a much older version of myself, I could now add the irrefutable fact that his technology was clearly not of this world. Case in point, he was somehow able to twist a knob on his thick leather belt and vanish into thin air, only to reappear when I least expected it.

"It is *Nicean* stealth tech," he explained to Sebastian who was looking at him with a kind of awe-struck lust. He clearly wasn't holding a grudge against Kristoff for strangling him the night before, even though I could see the marks of the big alien's long fingers still on his neck.

Yes, that's right—I said alien. There was no denying it anymore—Kristoff most definitely was an alien. An alien who had insisted on following me to the hospital when I refused to call in sick for my shift. But at least now that he had his armor he was able to make himself invisible while he watched over me.

"I wish I could get some of that tech," Sebastian murmured, looking over Kristoff's lean, muscular physique hungrily. "It would really come in handy when I go clubbing."

"It would not work for you," Kristoff told him shortly. "You need *Majoran* blood in your veins and the ability to change the color of your skin, hair, and eyes at will. We are chromatachromes—the tech simply enhances our talents."

"You can do all that?" Sebastian asked eagerly. "Show me!"

Kristoff looked at me and I nodded apologetically.

"Could you? He won't stop asking until you do."

"Very well." With a shrug, he turned his skin deep green, then violet, then back to the tan with a gold sheen which was what he most seemed to favor.

"Oh my *God*," Sebastian exclaimed. "He's like a sexy, muscular chameleon!"

"It's pretty amazing, all right," I acknowledged. Then I saw a nurse coming down the corridor. "Kristoff," I hissed, turning my head to him, but he had already disappeared. To anyone watching, it would look like Sebastian and I were alone in the hallway, perhaps discussing a patient. But I knew that Kristoff was just behind me, keeping an eye out for any potential threats, even though I couldn't see him.

"We'd better get to the Pit," Sebastian remarked. "Uh..." He cast a glance behind us. "How is he going to, you know, keep from bumping into people if he's shadowing you all night?"

"Don't concern yourself," rumbled a deep voice, pitched for our ears alone. "I will not give away my position."

It made the hairs on the back of my neck stand up to hear his voice coming out of what appeared to be empty air. I took a deep breath and tried to shrug off the feeling of being watched—not just by Kristoff but by some unseen enemy too.

"Why are you even *here* if everything he told you is true?" Sebastian demanded, as we walked towards the ER, which was still pretty quiet this time of night. "I mean, if you're really some kind of goddess or empress or whatever then what are you doing pulling a nine to nine in the Pit? You should be on your way to Glamour-planet, girl!"

"I can't just pick up and go like that," I exclaimed, telling Sebastian the same thing I had told Kristoff. "I have a life here! I worked hard to get into this program."

"Didn't we all," he murmured. "But if some massive, muscular, sexy alien showed up and told me I was supposed to be the king of his universe, I sure as hell wouldn't be hanging around here!"

"Well, I *am*," I said stubbornly.

"So then why is *he* still hanging around if you told him you're not interested in being the Queen of Everything?" Sebastian threw a look over his shoulder at my invisible bodyguard even though he couldn't see him.

"I can't, um, convince him to leave without me," I said. "He seems to think I'm still at risk."

"Then you shouldn't be in the ER," he pointed out. "You don't need to bring your stranger danger in here for all of us to share!"

"That's the thing—I don't think I *am* in danger. Not here in a crowded place, anyway," I said in a low voice, indicating all the people around us now that we were in the ER proper. "The assassin-droid came after me when I was all alone at home. As long as I stay busy and in a place with lots of activity, I should be fine."

"But why take the chance?" Sebastian demanded.

"Damn it, Sebastian—you're supposed to be on my side!" I exclaimed. "I can't just let this reshape my whole life! Even if I did decide to go, I have some loose ends to tie up here. Some patients I'm responsible for. Not to mention I'd want to give our Attending a damn good excuse before I suddenly disappeared off the face of the Earth."

Just saying that made a shiver go down my spine. That was the real reason I didn't want to go with Kristoff, even though I now believed him. I didn't want to leave my safe, normal existence and abandon the only planet I'd ever called home.

I know it sounds foolish, but I was more afraid of the unknown than I was of some possible killer lurking around the corner.

"So he's just going to shadow you and stay at your place until you change your mind?" Sebastian muttered.

"I don't know. I guess." I shrugged and reached for a chart. "Look, we'd better get to work."

"Okay…see you, I guess. Be careful." He gave me a cautious look and then threw a glance over his shoulder as well, as if Kristoff might be watching him.

I knew he wasn't though—he was too busy watching me.

Kristoff

I wished I could have convinced Charlotte to come with me at once. I had already signaled my ship, getting it ready to go. My best shuttle was cloaked in stealth tech, hovering in low Earth orbit, ready to descend the moment I called it to me. But I couldn't go until my new mistress was ready to come with me.

I considered taking her by force—simply picking her up and slinging her over my shoulder. She was light enough—it would be easy. It would also be for her own good. It was a fool's errand, shadowing her at the House of Healing, watching and waiting to circumvent any new attacks before they happened.

It was true, I told myself restively. Now that I had made contact with her and she believed me and understood I was telling the truth about the galaxy and her role in it, I should simply kidnap her and take her back to Femme One. There she could begin the Trials and prove she was the True Incarnation so she could take the Golden Throne.

Except I knew if I did that, she would never forgive me.

Though I hadn't known her long, I already knew my new mistress well enough to understand that she couldn't be bullied or coerced into doing something she didn't want to do. I remembered with admiration the way she had dealt with her male superior, who had come to her domicile seeking her sexual favors. Charlotte had sent him away and not gently either—which was good, such males deserved no gentleness when it came to the rejection of their advances.

Just thinking of the proprietary way he'd touched her made a low growl rise in my throat. *Mine,* came a thought, unbidden to my mind. *She is **mine** and the next time that bastard touches her I'll cut off his fucking hand!*

The vehemence of my feelings surprised me and made me uneasy. But of course, I was just protecting my mistress—or so I told myself as I threaded my way through the crowded halls of the House of Healing.

I watched as Charlotte assessed the hurt and injured and dealt out treatment. She worked with quiet efficiency and I saw as an observer what I had not been able to understand as a participant in this drama the night before—she truly loved her calling. Though her *La-ti-zal* power was not as a Healer, still she poured her whole heart into practicing her profession.

I saw that she knew when to be gentle and when to be brusque—saw how she worked with grim determination to save a child's life, who had come in after having some kind of allergic reaction. I saw how the little girl's parents hugged Charlotte and kissed her and cried with relief when it was clear their child was going to survive.

What an Empress she'll make! I couldn't help thinking in admiration. *She truly has a heart for her people.*

After Sundalla the 999th had Ascended to the Heavens, I had never believed that her successor could win the boundless admiration I'd had for the old Empress. And yet, almost against my will, I felt respect growing in my heart for my new mistress. I remembered the words of Sundalla the 999th when she had asked me to go search for her next Incarnation and keep her safe. She had begged me to show her new Incarnation the same love and devotion I had shown to her.

Though I had tried, I had been unable to give my promise, saying that I could never love and respect anyone as I did my old mistress. And yet the old Empress had known—she always knew somehow.

"When you find her...you will also find her worthy. Worthy of the same love and devotion you have shown to me all these years," she had told me. *"Now go, my dear Kristoff—the wisest and bravest of all my Guards. Go and seek her out."*

I had sought her out...and I was beginning to think the old Empress had been right. Now if only I could convince Charlotte that she belonged on Femme One instead of Earth... In the meantime, though, all I could do was watch over her and protect her.

But when the threat came, it was so cunningly hidden I almost didn't see it before it was too late.

Charlotte

I wished I could get rid of that "somebody's watching me" feeling. It wasn't just from having Kristoff somewhere behind me, shadowing me with silent stealth, either. I felt like someone else was watching—someone who wished me harm.

I told myself I was being foolish but I couldn't shake the feeling. It was creepy—like an itching sensation right between my shoulder blades.

Come to think of it—my whole body was beginning to feel itchy and strange. The skin of my arms and legs and torso felt tight. But when I ducked into the bathroom to check myself—after first letting Kristoff make sure no one else was inside—I saw nothing that could be the cause of my discomfort. No obvious rash—no reason my skin should feel inflamed.

I shrugged it off as paranoia—a psychosomatic outward manifestation of the inner turmoil I was feeling. But as the night went on, I began to feel more and more unwell—almost as though I was running a low-level fever.

Sebastian noticed it too. At around three in the morning, we had a lull in the action, which sometimes happens, even on the busiest night. Just a little quiet time when one set of patients had been taken care of and right before a fresh set comes in.

"Hey, what's wrong with you?" he asked, pulling me into an empty care area—the name we gave to the little, curtained off cubbies where we put patients as they came in to the ER.

"What…what do you mean?" I frowned and shook my head. "What are you talking about?"

"Your eyes are bright, your cheeks are flushed… I would say it was love but you look more like someone getting sick than someone falling head-over-heels. Uh…no offense." He looked all around us. "Is, uh, *he* still here?"

'He' meaning Kristoff, of course.

"I don't know," I said irritably. "I guess so."

As the hectic night in the ER had worn on and I had gone about my usual routine, the idea that a huge alien warrior was invisibly shadowing me had begun to seem unreal again. I had stopped being careful where I walked or how I moved and Kristoff, for his part, had never run into me once.

In fact, as I stood there feeling dazed and half drugged with the strange hot, tight sensation that had enveloped my whole body, it was almost easier to convince myself the whole thing was just a dream and I didn't actually have an invisible seven-foot tall body guard following me around at all.

"I mean it, Charlotte—you don't look so good. Here." Sebastian pulled a portable temperature gauge out of his lab coat pocket and poked it into one of the disposable plastic sleeves we use to keep from spreading germs.

"Sebastian—" I tried to protest but he shook his head.

"Uh-uh, sweetie—no complaints. Open up and say 'ah.' I need to know what's going on with you."

"Fine." I sighed and let him slip the temperature probe under my tongue.

I waited, not very patiently, until it finally beeped and Sebastian withdrew the probe and shucked the plastic sleeve into the nearby trash.

"Well?" I asked as he examined the unit.

"No." He frowned to himself in concentration. "No — that can't be right. Here — try again."

"What? Why?" I demanded, but he was already fitting a new plastic sleeve on the probe and sticking it in my mouth.

I put up with the process a second time and then a third — this time using my own temperature gauge because Sebastian thought something must be wrong with his — before I finally lost patience.

"No more!" I exclaimed, when he tried to take my temp a fourth time. "What does it say?"

"It can't be right." He frowned and finally showed it to me. "According to this, you're hypothermic."

I frowned at the reading on the gage — 92.6 — a full six points lower than the standard human body temperature of 98.6.

"What the Hell?" I muttered. "What does this mean? I don't *feel* cold — in fact, I feel like I'm burning up."

"You do?" Abandoning scientific methods, Sebastian put a hand to my forehead. "Your skin is like ice!" He looked really worried now. "I knew you weren't looking right. Charlotte, we need to run some tests and find out what's going on with you. This could be dangerous!"

"I'll be fine," I said, trying to wave him off. "I'm just still tired — that's all. I've had, uh, a lot happen today."

"I *know* that," he hissed. "And you've also possibly been exposed to some new pathogens today. Pathogens from a whole different *planet* when the Invisible Hunk came into your life! Remember that TV show we binge-watched together — *The Strain?*"

"Oh, please, Sebastian — don't be so dramatic," I said irritably. "I'll be fine — I just need a good night's rest."

"But Charlotte — "

"I know what may be the cause of this," a deep voice came out of the air behind me.

Sebastian and I both jumped and looked around guiltily, like kids with our hands caught in the cookie jar. So Kristoff *was* still there — he wasn't a figment of my imagination or a really vivid dream as I had sort of halfway been hoping.

"What is it?" Sebastian hissed out of the corner of his mouth, looking like somebody in a spy movie passing information while trying to look innocent. "If you gave my friend some kind of incurable alien disease—"

"It is not incurable but it's not easily solved either." Kristoff sounded unhappy. "I told you, my Lady, that you should not have given me your blood."

"What?" Sebastian demanded. "How is Charlotte giving *you* a transfusion of her super-rare blood going to make her sick? It's not like it was the other way around and she took *your* blood."

"It is the Royal Cycle beginning," Kristoff replied obliquely. I wished I could see him and try to read his face because his words weren't making any sense.

"What does *that* mean?" Sebastian hissed.

"That Charlotte must come with me to Femme One and soon— there is no medicine here on your primitive planet that can cure her," Kristoff said.

"Now, wait just a minute—" I began but that was when I heard another voice calling my name.

"Dr Walker!" a man's voice shouted across the ER. A familiar voice, I'm sorry to say. I looked up with dread and saw that Dr. Drake Hunter was glaring at me from the other side of the Pit.

"Oh *no*," I moaned, feeling my stomach turn over. God, could this night get any worse or weirder?

"What is it?" Sebastian asked. "What does *he* want?"

"I forgot to tell you but he came to my apartment earlier to ask me out again," I said under my breath. "Kristoff was already there with me and Hunter saw him. Then I told him to get lost. He, uh, wasn't very happy about it."

"And you talk about *me* being dramatic!" Sebastian's eyes were shining with excitement. "Girl, you are just *dripping* with hot, eligible men! I wish you'd tell me your secret."

"There's no secret involved," I muttered. "And I'd be happy to give you this particular 'hot, eligible' man. He's probably here to assign me to go mop vomit and change bandages in the burn unit."

"Hmm, he *does* look angry," Sebastian admitted.

"Dr. Walker, I'd like to talk to you *now!*" Hunter repeated, glaring at me. Great, so he was prepared to cause a scene.

"I'd better go," I muttered. "But I want you to stay here, Kristoff," I said to the empty air behind Sebastian.

"Under no circumstances." His deep voice was a protective growl. "I will not leave you alone with a male who wishes you harm."

"It's not like he's going to attack me," I said. "He's probably just going to say a whole lot of nasty things to me. Things that might make you want to snap and strangle him like you did poor Sebastian last night. I don't need that kind of a scene right now."

"I will not leave you," he insisted, his deep voice sounding tense.

"I'm the Empress, right?" I said, turning to glare at the empty space and wishing I could look him in the eyes. He was so tall I was probably eyeballing his chest—only I couldn't tell because he was invisible. "I'm the Empress so what I say goes! And I say *stay here.*"

There was a restive movement in the air, as if he was shifting from foot to foot angrily. But at last he said, in the coldest voice possible, "As my Lady wishes."

"Good." I took a deep breath and turned back to the glaring Dr. Hunter. "This hopefully shouldn't take long."

I crossed the ER floor, aware that the eyes of all the support staff were on me. Most of them knew by now that Hunter had asked me out and that I had refused him. None of them knew about our second, disastrous meeting, however. I could tell, though, by the angry look in Hunter's big blue eyes that *he* most certainly hadn't forgotten about it.

I was already feeling ill and a confrontation with a sexist asshole was the last thing I wanted right now. But it looked like there was no getting out of it so I squared my shoulders and walked up to him.

"Yes, Dr. Hunter?" I said quietly but clearly. "What can I do for you?"

"I need to talk to you. *Now,*" he snapped. "Come with me." He started to lead me away from the main ER but I tried to stop him.

"Dr. Hunter," I began. "If this is about this afternoon—"

"It's about a patient of mine whose orders you screwed up," he snarled. "You nearly Goddamn killed him!"

"What?" I couldn't help feeling shocked. Suddenly instead of having the upper hand and being the woman turning down a man, I was cast back in the role of the lowly Intern who had screwed up and was being dressed down by the enraged Resident. "There must be some mistake," I protested. "I don't have any of your patients on my schedule."

"That's what you think. Come with me and I'll show you." He turned away again but I was still reluctant to go.

"Dr. Hunter—"

"Dr. Walker," he said, rounding on me. "Do you want to do this here and now where everyone in the ER can hear about your *monumental incompetence?* Or do you want to discuss it in private?"

"In private," I said, feeling my cheeks heat with shame. I kept my chin up, though, as I followed him out of the ER, despite feeling every eye in the place on me. It was a good thing, I thought to myself, that I had ordered Kristoff to stay behind. There was no way he could have listened to the crap that was about to come down on my head without reacting.

Hunter led me down a dark hallway and into a dim, empty X-ray room. The X-ray tube was placed neatly on a pillow, resting on the fluro table and there were a pile of weights and sandbags in one corner and several lead aprons hanging from a rack.

I stood by the chest bucky as he closed the door and rounded on me, his eyes flashing.

"Dr. Hunter, I really think there's been some mistake—" I tried again but he didn't let me finish.

"I have a message for you," he said, taking a step towards me. I saw uneasily that his features had gone blank, though his voice still sounded angry.

"A message?" Without thinking about it, I took a step back. This situation was beginning to make me feel really uncomfortable, and not just because I was about to get chewed out.

"A message, yes. And it is this—*True Incarnation or not, you will never sit the Golden Throne.*"

"What?" I exclaimed, taking another step back. Suddenly the situation seemed horribly familiar—it was the exact same mess I'd been in when the Carlos-thing came after me. But that time I'd had Kristoff to save me. This time I had ordered him to stay away—how stupid could I be?

"You heard me, *Empress.*" Hunter's eyes flashed cold and silver as he reached for me. "You'll not live to be crowned. Tonight you *die.*"

"Get away from me!" I screamed but the lead shielding in the walls muffled my voice—I was pretty sure no one outside the door was going to hear me.

"Come to me. Do not delay the inevitable," the thing which had taken on Drake Hunter's appearance crooned. It came at me, hands stretched wide and I ducked wildly, trying to avoid it. I remembered well enough what had happened when the Carlos-thing had only brushed my skin with its hand. If this thing even *touched* me I could be dead.

It was between me and the door but there was a small control area in the back of the room where the tech would stand to take the X-ray. I dodged for the little cubby, trying to get through it so I could run through the Radiology suite and come out the other side.

Before I could get two steps, the thing caught me by the hair and yanked me back. "Don't fight your fate, *Goddess,*" it said and put its cold, cold hands around my throat, choking off the scream that was rising to my lips.

Suddenly the door of the X-ray room crashed open and Kristoff appeared, as from out of nowhere. The look of rage on his face was awful to behold—there was a fury like I'd never seen before in his whirling rainbow eyes which were switching colors too fast for my frantic brain to register.

"You shall not have her!" he snarled and then he drew the incredibly long sword which was strapped to a scabbard on his back. *A Great sword or a Bastard Sword.* My mind gabbled RPG gamer terms even as the thing's hands crushed my windpipe. I wished inanely that I was someplace safe, playing Diablo II with my friend Zoe instead of being choked to death by a killer robot thing.

Then Kristoff's sword arced through the air and Hunter's head parted company with his body. It spun through the air like a hairy bowling ball but as it whirled, I saw it change. Hunter's handsome features became smooth and blank and silver until there was nothing left when it hit the floor but a vaguely head-shaped shiny sphere.

The hands, however, continued to choke the life out of me.

"Goddess!" Kristoff growled, coming forward to yank the spasming hands away from my throat.

"You...came," I whispered and dissolved into a coughing fit. Thank God my windpipe wasn't crushed but I could tell I was going to have some serious bruising and I still felt light headed due to oxygen loss. "You came," I repeated when I could. "Even though...I told you...not to."

"I should have come sooner," he said grimly. "You can court-martial me for disobedience later, my Lady."

He was examining me anxiously as he spoke and just then Sebastian came rushing into the room.

"What did I miss? What happened?" he demanded. Then he saw the still-jerking pile of metal scrap that had been Dr. Hunter and his eyes got wide. "Oh my God! What *is* that?"

"Assassin-droid," Kristoff said grimly. "And I'm afraid it had nanites in its hands. See? Here—and here." He pointed to my throat, which now felt like it was on fire. "We have to get them out and then I need to get her up to my ship."

"No, no—" I started to protest but Kristoff took me by the shoulders and shook me.

"Listen to me, Charlotte," he said, using my name for the first time since I'd first seen him in the ER. "Your life is in danger here. Not only yours but the lives of all you hold dear! Do you know what these droids do? They attack someone you know—someone close to you—and suck out their life essence so they can make an exact replica. A replica that will lull you into a false sense of security so they can kill you!"

"You..." I choked. "You mean Dr. Hunter is really...really *dead?* And Carlos too?"

"Dead and sucked dry—unrecognizable husks, even to their loved ones," Kristoff said grimly. "The droid probably picked this male because it saw him leaving your residence. But it could just as easily picked *him*." He pointed to Sebastian who went pale. "Or someone else you love—a friend or family member."

"Oh my God," I whispered and coughed again. "I...I didn't realize."

"While you stay here on Earth everyone you know and love is *in danger*," Kristoff said harshly. "And you yourself are ill. I do not want to force your hand, my Lady—it is a crime punishable by death. But if I must take you to Femme One against your will in order for you to survive, then so be it. I will do what is in your best interests even if I am killed for it."

"No." I shook my head. "I don't...don't want you to be killed. I...I'll go."

"Good." He looked relieved. "But we have to do something about the nanites first."

"The MRI room," I said. "It's just down the hall." I took a step towards the door of the X-Ray room, stumbled, and nearly fell. My throat was on fire and my legs felt weak and wobbly.

"Where is it?" Kristoff stooped swiftly to swing me into his arms. He looked at Sebastian. "Lead me there."

The MRI machine at North Florida Regional was a closed bore, superconducting magnet which meant that the magnetic field was never off. For safety's sake, the door to the main magnet room is kept locked—so some idiot with a pacemaker or an aneurism clip won't ignore all the warning signs and wander into the magnetic field and kill themselves.

Luckily for me, there was a tech there, preparing to scan a STAT patient who was being sent down from the floor.

"What in the world?" she exclaimed when we appeared in her doorway with Kristoff holding me and Sebastian tagging along, wide-eyed.

"We need to get in the magnet room—*now!*" he exclaimed. "Get the key and unlock it—hurry!"

"I'm sorry, Doctor but I can't let you go in just like that!" the tech protested. "You haven't been screened! And you..." She eyed

Kristoff with his thick metal breastplate and greaves—not to mention the tall sword with its hilt poking over his shoulder. "You'll get sucked in and I'd have to quench the magnet to get you out!"

"She's right," I managed to croak. "Kristoff...can't come in."

"Then I'll go with her. Here, just bring her to the doorway," Sebastian snapped. Then he looked at the tech. "I'm Dr. Trent and I take full responsibility for this. Dr. Walker and I need to get in the magnet room and I promise you, neither of us has any implants or pacemakers or clips."

The tech looked like she wanted to protest but a growl from Kristoff got her moving. Grabbing the key, she unlocked the heavy, shielded door and swung it open so that we could hear the quiet pulsing of the superconducting magnet.

"Here." Sebastian stripped off his lab coat which held most of his electronics. Kristoff set me on my feet and Sebastian grabbed me by the waist, slinging my arm across his shoulder. He wasn't strong enough to carry me like Kristoff—then again, almost no one would be—as I said before, I'm not a lightweight—but he was able to help support me. Half walking, half dragging, we finally made it into the magnetic field.

I didn't even have to go into the MRI machine itself—the relief was immediate. The burning in my throat stopped and the feeling of doom which had been building inside me since the Hunter-thing wrapped its hands around my neck seemed to subside. I still felt dizzy and light headed, but I was able to stand on my own.

"Okay...I'm okay," I whispered to Sebastian and straightened up so I wasn't leaning on him quite so hard.

"Good—you're *heavy*." He took a deep breath and then looked anxiously at my throat. "The red marks are fading. How do you feel?"

"Better," I said. "But still not completely right."

"Come back out in the hall so I can take your temperature again."

He led me out to where Kristoff was watching anxiously and the tech was staring with wide eyes. Sebastian shooed her back to her room saying something about patient privacy. Picking up his lab coat, he found his temperature gauge and popped it under my tongue. When it beeped, he frowned anxiously.

"What?" I asked when he took the probe out of my mouth.

"See for yourself." He handed me the unit. "A fight and an adrenaline rush like you just had should have raised your temperature, not lowered it. But you're down to 89.8. That's not good, Charlotte. Really not good. How do you feel?"

"Hotter than ever." I tugged at the loose neck of my scrub top. "Like I'm burning up."

"It's the *Calet Sanguis* – the Burning Blood." Kristoff sounded as anxious as Sebastian looked. "It is part of the Royal Cycle, as I said before. Empress, you must leave this place now and come with me."

"He's right." Sebastian nodded. "You need to go, Charlotte."

It didn't seem I had any choice.

"All right," I said heavily to Kristoff. "How do we get out of here?"

"I need a large, open area to call my shuttle to," he said.

Kristoff snapped his fingers. "The helicopter pad. On the roof of the hospital."

"Let's go."

I would have walked but Kristoff swung me into his arms again as though I weighed no more than a feather.

"Lead the way," he told Sebastian.

Before I knew it, we were standing on the large, flat space watching as Kristoff did something to a control on his belt that presumably called his shuttle.

"He's like Batman with that thing," Sebastian, who had one supporting arm around me, murmured.

"Yeah – it's like an alien utility belt." I tried to laugh but it came out as more of a choked sob. "Sebastian," I said, "I'm scared."

"I know, hon but Kristoff seems to know what's going on with you and I sure as Hell don't," he said frankly. "Who ever heard of a sickness that makes your body hypothermic even though you feel like you're burning up? Also, we don't need any more killer robots tearing up the ER trying to get to you."

I knew he was right but it still made me want to cry. Where was this mysterious place I was going and would I ever come home again? Would I ever see the hospital or finish my internship? Something inside me doubted it—doubted it very much. And then there was my family. I wasn't very close to them—not because I was adopted but just because we had never quite clicked somehow. Still, I didn't want my mom to worry.

"All right," I said to Sebastian. "But promise you'll tell everyone—my family included—that I'm all right."

"I will." He was half crying now, too as he hugged me. "I promise I will."

And then a smooth black craft that looked like something out of a high-end car commercial, only with wings instead of wheels, landed silently on the helicopter pad.

"Come, my Lady," Kristoff said, taking my arm. "It's time to leave this place."

I gave Sebastian one final hug and then Kristoff was swinging me into his arms again and placing me gently in the strange, black craft.

The last thing I saw of Earth was Sebastian waving and the lights of the hospital receding into the night.

I didn't know when I would ever see either one again.

Chapter Eleven

Kristoff

Charlotte lost consciousness before the shuttle was halfway to my ship, still hidden on the dark side of the Earth's one lone moon. By the time I carried her inside my vessel, her pulse was weak and thready and her breathing was frighteningly shallow. Her skin was cool to the touch too, which I knew was a bad sign.

I had never heard of any Incarnation of the Empress having such an extreme case of *Calet Sanguis* before, but then, during the Culling Ceremony for the potential Consorts, the Empress usually only gave a few drops of her blood to each candidate to ingest.

Charlotte had given me a whole *bag* of her blood and I hadn't drunk it—she had pumped it directly into my veins. I supposed it wasn't surprising that she was in such a bad way. But I still had no idea what to do.

Even with my hyperdrive set on maximum capacity, there was no way I could get her to Femme One in time to save her. The seat of the Majoran empire, also known as Majora Prime, was located in the very center of the Goddess's Cloak, on the edge of the supermassive black hole that served as the central spire of the entire galaxy.

I was sent to save her and now instead, she's dying because of me. Because she saved me, I thought bitterly. *How amused her enemies would be if they knew that the new Empress's kindness accomplished what their fucking assassin-droids couldn't manage!*

I cradled her close in my arms, feeling a powerful emotion surge inside me. Charlotte wouldn't die—I couldn't allow it! And yet... how could I save her?

I couldn't think of a way.

Normally I have a very cool head under pressure—one cannot be trained in the arts of covert diplomacy without being able to stay calm even in the direst circumstances. But there was something about my new mistress that stirred me — stirred me so deeply I could barely think past my concern for her. My heart and mind were in turmoil and I couldn't determine a course of action.

I'm not a praying kind of male. As a rule, though I serve one who is supposed to be divinity made flesh, I do not believe in supernatural forces. And yet, as my desperation grew, I felt words rising to my lips — words I didn't even try to hold back.

"Goddess," I prayed aloud as I held Charlotte close. "Help me to save my new mistress! It's my fault she's sick — help me find a way to heal her before it's too late."

No one spoke to me from mid-air and the sky didn't open up to reveal the face of the Goddess of Mercy, but I felt a sudden calm come over me and the panic and guilt cleared from my brain.

Dr. Churika, I thought. *She would know what to do.*

Dr. Hanalan Churika had been the personal healer of my old mistress, Sundalla the 999th. She had stayed with the old Empress until the end and then, heartbroken, had judged it best to go back to her home planet of Denaris where she lived with her two mates. Denaris was much closer to Earth than Femme One — in fact, they were in the same quadrant of the galaxy.

Carrying Charlotte in my arms, I made my way quickly to the control and communication center of my ship. Cradling her head against one arm, I typed with my free hand, calling up the special code Churika had been given when she was in the service of the old Empress. This code activated a tiny chip in her arm which had been implanted when she had first been appointed the royal healer. The chip set off an alarm that would compel her to answer my call, no matter where in the universe she was or what she was doing.

Of course, that was when the old Empress was alive. Dr. Churika had no reason to answer the code now. But I prayed she would anyway.

"*Answer,*" I muttered impatiently. "Come on, Goddess-damnit! *Come on!*"

I hadn't drawn three breaths before my viewscreen flickered and Churika's wise face appeared.

"Hello? Who is this?" she demanded, her brows drawing low

in disapproval. "Who disturbs my retirement? And how dare you use the 'Empress in grave danger' code?"

"Because she is," I said grimly. "Dr. Churika, it's Captain Verrai. I have the True Incarnation with me—Sundalla the 1000th. But she is gravely ill. I need your help."

"You have? She is? Show her to me and tell me what's the matter!" the old female demanded imperiously.

I turned Charlotte's head gently and brushed aside some strands of long blonde hair to show her delicate features.

Churika leaned in close to her viewscreen and then sucked in a gasp.

"It's her—it's truly *her!*" I heard her mutter and she made a sign in the air, her wrinkled forefinger tracing a circle and pointing to the Heavens—the holy signal of the Goddess-Empress.

"I know," I said. "She has the rainbow aura just like Sundalla the 999th had. But she is deathly ill. I fear…" I forced myself to make my voice cold and dispassionate. "I fear she's going to die."

"Nonsense," Dr. Churika snapped, practical as ever. "Tell me her symptoms and how long she's been sick."

"I think she has the *Calet Sanguis* – the Burning Blood," I said. "But I've never heard of a case this extreme before."

"What?" The old female frowned. "How would she get the Burning Blood if you've just found her? There hasn't even been time for her to give her blood to any of the candidates for Consort yet. In fact, if you just found her, the Council hasn't even *picked* any candidates yet!"

"She didn't give her blood to a Consort candidate," I said, gritting my teeth against the shame of my admission. "She gave it to *me.*"

"*What?*" Dr. Churika looked scandalized, as though I had admitted to improper sexual contact with the Empress instead of just having some of her blood. "Why would she do that? And why would you take it? What happened?"

I told her about my fight with the first assassin-droid, my blood-loss and the subsequent blood transfusion.

"Goddess of Mercy!" the old healer exclaimed when I finished my explanation. "So she didn't just give you a few drops to drink—she *transfused* you with her own blood?"

I nodded. "I tried to stop her but by the time I realized what was happening, most of the damage was already done. I thought my blood wasn't exulted enough to call to hers at first because she had no symptoms. Then tonight, she started saying she was hot—burning up. Yet her temperature is well below normal and she's cold to the touch."

"Don't fool yourself, Verrai," Churika snapped. "Your blood is most certainly *not* exulted enough to call to hers. She needs a full-blooded Royal as her consort. But if she pumped that much of her own essence into a *rock* it would call to her. The problem here isn't the quality—it's the quantity."

I didn't resent her words in the least—I knew them to be true. I was a lesser noble—good enough to be the captain of the Goddess-Empress's Guard but not Consort material—not even in my wildest dreams.

"What must I do for her?" I asked. "Tell me how to save her."

She sighed. "How far are you from Denaris?"

"A solar day's journey—no more," I said. "The True Incarnation's home world, Earth, is a closed planet in the same sector as Denaris."

"Bring her to me at fast as you can," Churika ordered.

"What must I do in the meantime?" I asked, cradling Charlotte to me anxiously. "She's so cold and her pulse is too fast. Also, her breathing is shallow and rapid."

"She's going into the withdrawal stage of her Royal Cycle. When an Empress gives her blood to the Consort candidates, her body chooses which one it is drawn to and yearns for him. " The old female frowned. "Unfortunately, right now what her body is yearning for is *you*, Verrai."

"*Me?* But you just finished telling me I'm not Consort material!" I exclaimed.

"And you're not. But the new Incarnation's body doesn't know that. You've gotten so much of her blood in you it's created a false positive. Her body *thinks* you're meant to be her Consort, even though there's no way in the Frozen Hells you could be."

"What can I do?" I asked. "I cannot bond her to me."

"No-no!" Her faded eyes flashed. "You most certainly must *not* do that! It would be a sacrilege and treason of the highest order!"

"I'm aware of how unworthy I am to be with her," I said evenly. "So tell me how to keep her alive until I get to you without doing anything treasonous."

She frowned, considering. At last, she sighed.

"You'll have to warm her."

"That's fine," I said, relieved to have some concrete instructions at last. "I have some chemical warming blankets in my hold."

"No, no—you misunderstand." She scowled. "You'll have to warm her with your body. When an Empress Incarnate is in the withdrawal stage of her Royal Cycle, only the body heat of the one she's being drawn to will bring up her core temperature and ease the sickness she feels."

"But I'm holding her now," I pointed out, indicating the way Charlotte was curled in my lap, my arms securely around her. "And it's not helping."

Churika's scowl deepened. "She needs skin-to-skin contact, Verrai. Nothing else will do. Take off your uniform and those odd garments she's wearing—what *are* those anyway?"

"The uniform of the House of Healing she was working in," I explained. "As I told you before, she's been trained as a Healer, Dr. Churika—like yourself."

"Ah, that's right. An Empress Healer—imagine that!" For a moment she looked pleased—then she went back to scowling. "As I said—she'll need your bare skin against her own." She raised one crooked finger and shook it at me. "Only mind you don't do anything you shouldn't! Skin contact only—nothing more!"

"I've been chaste these past ten years in Sundalla the 999th's service," Churika," I said dryly. "I think I can manage a few more hours until we get to you."

"See that you do. And hurry—we don't need the Withdrawal stage to turn into the Needing stage. Though the Goddess of Mercy alone knows what may happen since she pumped so much of her blood into you."

"I'll set my hyperdrive to maximum," I promised.

"Do that. Hopefully I can do something for her. Then, when you get her to Femme One, she can have a proper Culling ceremony and choose a R oyal Consort."

The thought of Charlotte giving her blood to other males — of her body yearning for one of them until she felt the Need and had to go to him — made me feel tight all over for some reason. But I pushed the emotion away.

"We will be with you soon. I must go set a course and do what I can for my Lady," I told Churika.

The old healer nodded curtly and signed off. I did the same and went to plot our course, still holding Charlotte in my arms. I would heal her, I promised myself. Heal her of this affliction she had because of me — this false positive as Churika had called it. But I would be very careful when I did — I did not wish to push the boundaries between my new mistress and myself too far.

Chapter Twelve
Charlotte

I woke up in the dark, feeling horribly hot and tight all over my body. I had been dreaming of the snake again—the one made of flames that wrapped itself around my body and squeezed and squeezed until I couldn't get any air into my lungs. I didn't know if I was going to burn to death or asphyxiate or both.

All I knew was that I was burning up and I couldn't breathe.

"Help!" I tried to say, but my voice came out in a faint, panicked whisper. I simply couldn't get enough air to make much noise.

Still, someone heard me.

"It's all right," a deep voice said. "You're going to be all right, my Lady."

Whoever had spoken was taking off my clothes. I sighed in relief as the hot, itchy lab coat and scrubs came off, leaving me in just my bra and panties. The cool sheets beneath me felt so good on my fevered skin.

A big hand was touching my face—cupping my cheek. I sighed and leaned into the touch. It was warm, which shouldn't have appealed to me since I felt so hot myself. But somehow the sensation of it stroking my face felt amazing—like it was somehow exactly what I needed.

Only I needed more.

"Your skin is like ice, my Lady." The deep voice sounded worried this time.

I tried to say that I was burning up, not freezing to death, but I still couldn't make any words above a whisper.

"Hush," he murmured. "It's all right—I'm going to make everything better."

And then those big, warm hands began to touch me all over, stroking along my fevered skin, bring a soothing peace wherever they went.

I moaned breathlessly and arched my back up as he stroked over my shoulders and neck and upper chest—careful to avoid my breasts, though why, I didn't know.

The hands continued their journey, sliding down my torso and belly—carefully avoiding the panty region—and then caressing long and slow over my thighs and calves.

I can't describe how good it felt—how much I needed his touch— how much I *yearned* for it. And yet, the relief it brought was short-lived. As much as he stroked and caressed me, my body cried out for more. His hands stilled the fiery snake as it wound around my limbs and body, but only during the time he was touching me. The moment his long, gentle fingers moved on, it came back ten— no a *hundred* times worse than before.

My relief turned to distress and I began to moan and cry out, thrashing in the bed I was lying on. At least, I *assumed* it was a bed—I couldn't see anything in the dark but two faint colored dots dancing far above me.

"Please," I said, my voice a shaking whisper. "Please, it *hurts!* I...I'm *on fire!*"

The hands stopped and withdrew.

"I was afraid of this," the deep voice said. The speaker sounded as though he might be frowning.

"Afraid of what?" I demanded. "Please, can't you make it stop? I'm *burning!*"

"And yet your skin is like ice and your body temperature keeps dropping." He shifted in the dark beside me and the two colored spots high above me narrowed. "Very well, my Lady, it seems that propriety must wait upon survival."

"What?" I whispered, thinking—*He talks like someone from a Renaissance Festival!*

The minute the thought entered my brain, a rush of memories came with it and I realized who was the owner of the deep voice and warm hands.

"Kristoff?" I managed to whisper.

"Be still, my Lady," he warned. "You're ill because of all the blood you gave me—it caused your body to think I'm your Consort."

"What? What Consort—I don't understand," I said.

He sighed. "And I don't have much time to explain. I'll just say this—your body *thinks* it wants mine. You feel like you're burning up when actually, your core temperature is getting dangerously low. The only way for me to warm you up is to hold you skin-to-skin so that my heat can penetrate you."

"Yes, all right," I said, shamelessly eager. I knew I should have been reluctant—after all, I barely knew him. But at that point I didn't care—anything to make the burning stop! Anything to drive away the snake that was trying to strangle me!

"All right, my lady. I'm taking off my armor and uniform but leaving on my underclothes," he said.

There was a rustling and quiet clanking in the dark—probably his heavy breastplate being laid on the floor—and then he was sliding into bed with me, big and solid and amazingly warm.

"Oh!" I gasped as he put his arms around me. I burrowed into his embrace, trying to get my cheek against his hard, muscular chest. He felt so good against me but there was still too much cloth in the way. My bra and panties were barriers—impediments to the relief I desperately craved.

They had to go.

I reached behind me, tugging and yanking at my too-tight bra strap. Damn it, I had to get the freaking thing *off* me.

Kristoff seemed to understand what I was doing because he asked in a low voice, "My Lady, are you certain you wish to be bare-breasted with me?"

"Don't ask stupid questions," I panted angrily. "Just help me— *please.*"

He complied silently, reaching behind me to help unsnap the stubborn elastic. I shucked it off with a sigh of relief and threw it over the side of the bed. Then I started yanking on my panties.

These were easier to get off, but as before, Kristoff tried to stop me.

"My Lady…" His big hands were on mine, keeping me from making progress. "Do you really think this is wise?"

"Kristoff," I gasped—this isn't sexual, I *swear* it's not! I'm just in pain and I need…I don't know what I need. Just *more.*"

"As you wish." He hooked his fingers in the thin side straps of my panties then and pulled them down himself. I lifted my hips and helped him do it, eager to get them off—eager to get rid of anything standing between me and relief.

At last I was bare-ass-naked, as Zoe would have said. I reached for Kristoff, anticipating relief but there was still a barrier in the way. The undershirt and under-kilt he wore beneath his armor were keeping me from getting close enough.

I yanked at them, irrationally angry to have them in the way. They were keeping me from getting relief, damn it!

"Off!" I ordered imperiously, tugging at the soft, stretchy material. "Get it off *now.*"

Kristoff took off his undershirt but absolutely refused to take off the under-kilt.

"No, my Lady," he said firmly, pushing my hands away. "There must be *something* between us for propriety's sake."

"Fuck propriety!" I snapped. I was surprised to hear such language come out of my own mouth—I'm not usually much of a curser. But the feeling that I needed him—*all* of him—pressed against all of me just would not leave. I knew I ought to be embarrassed or ashamed to demand such a thing of a man I had only met a few days ago but I couldn't help it—my body wouldn't *let* me help it.

I needed him.

"My lady…" he began but then seemed to decide that there was no use arguing with me. "All right," he said, shucking down the rest of his undergarments so that he was completely bare with me. "I only hope you won't regret it later."

"Come here!" I said, ignoring the warning in his deep voice. "Please, Kristoff, I need you!"

He came, pulling me to him so that our bodies were flush

against each other, chest to chest. Well, he was so tall, it was more like my face to his chest but you get the idea—we were completely naked and pressed together as tightly as we could be.

So tightly I could feel his long, heavy shaft branding my inner thighs.

"Oh!" I whispered when I felt it throb against me.

Kristoff shifted restlessly.

"Forgive me," he muttered hoarsely. "It's inexcusable but I cannot seem to help myself, especially when you're so close, my Lady. I have been chaste for ten years but though I can control my actions, I cannot control the involuntary responses of my body."

"It's all right," I assured him and somehow, it was. Though it should have been a horribly embarrassing situation, I was finally beginning to feel some relief from the burning and breathlessness.

I'm a practical person—I always have been. Was it weird to be bare-ass-naked with a man I barely knew? Yes it was. But was it better than having the feeling that I was on fire and I couldn't breathe? Also yes—a thousand times yes. And besides, touching Kristoff wasn't like touching any other man I'd ever been with.

Not that I go around touching a lot of men. To be honest, after the attack by the drunk frat boy in college, I'd found the touch of most men slightly repulsive. Also, they couldn't do anything for me—my touch-sense told me at once the minute I made first contact. So what was the point?

Kristoff could definitely do something for me—my touch-sense had given me that message loud and clear. But as I had told him earlier, the current situation we found ourselves in wasn't sexual, despite our nudity. Well, not for me, anyway. I just wanted to be able to breathe and to get my body temperature normalized.

"Are you feeling better, Charlotte? I mean, my Lady?" he murmured in my ear.

"You can call me Charlotte," I assured him. "Any man who rubs his naked body against mine is close enough to be on a first name basis."

He made a soft rumbling sound and after a moment I realized he was laughing. Which was good—it broke some of the tension between us. It was the first time I had heard his laugh—he was a pretty serious guy, after all. It was a warm, pleasant sound that vibrated through my whole body, making me tingle.

I joined him and soon we were both laughing in the dark like lunatics with his arms wrapped around me and his big, warm body finally giving me the relief I craved so desperately.

At last our laugher tapered off and I found myself just cuddling in his arms. The worst of my desperate pain was over, which meant the situation should have gotten awkward fast.

Somehow it didn't.

"You saved me," I said, pressing my cheek to his slightly scratchy chest. "*Again.*"

He had the most amazing scent—warm and spicy and masculine. It reminded me of cedar and sandalwood and some kind of dark musk that made me want to get even closer and never stop breathing him in. His body was so much bigger than mine I felt completely surrounded by him—cocooned in his arms, utterly safe and protected. It was a sensation I'd never had before—not even as a child.

I never wanted it to end.

"It's my fault you're in this situation," he murmured, his voice a soft rumble in my ear. "If you hadn't given me so much of your blood... I shouldn't have let you."

"How could you have stopped me? You were out cold," I pointed out. "Also, you *needed* that transfusion. What kind of a doctor would I be if I stood by and did nothing when you needed help and I could give it?"

"So...you don't regret it? Despite the pain and discomfort it caused you?" He sounded faintly surprised.

"The patient comes first," I said firmly. "Although I've never, uh, quite been in a situation like this with a patient."

"As I have never been with my mistress," he admitted. "Is it helping you? You feel the burning ease? Your body seems much warmer than it was."

"It's helping," I said, wiggling a little. "Only..."

"What is it? Name what you need and you shall have it, my Lady," he murmured.

Damn—I was really kind of getting to like the way he talked. Even if it was kind of Renaissance-y.

"I feel like…" I took a deep breath. "I think it would help to have some pressure—*deep* pressure. Could you…I know this sounds weird, but could you, uh, lie on top of me for a minute? Kind of just…cover me completely with your…with your body?"

Okay, *now* I was finally getting kind of embarrassed. But this was what my body craved for some reason. And I didn't want to take a chance on the burning and breathlessness returning if I didn't give it what it wanted.

"As my Lady wishes," Kristoff murmured.

We had been lying on our sides, facing each other. With one swift move, he rolled me under him, covering my body completely with his own.

I should have felt smothered. He was so much taller than me that his chest was in my face. And his weight was considerable—at least three hundred pounds, I estimated, all of it pure muscle—pressing me down into the bed.

Strangely enough, despite his weight pressing me down, or maybe *because* of it, I was finally able to draw a deep breath and the last of the burning finally left my body.

"*Ahhh.*" I gave a little moan of pure satisfaction.

"My Lady?" Kristoff sounded a little worried. "Am I crushing you? I feel your pleasure in this new position but you're so small…so delicate."

I started laughing again—I couldn't help it.

"Why are you amused?" Kristoff demanded. He changed our positions, moving down so that we were face to face though he was still lying on top of me.

"Because." I giggled. "I am *not* delicate. In fact, I'm what you could call 'big boned' if you were being nice, that is."

"Your bones are like those of a bird," he protested. "So light I'm afraid I'll crush you."

"Believe me, I'm plenty solid enough—you're not going to crush me," I assured him.

"I just want to ease your pain—not add to it," he murmured.

"Don't worry," I told him. "I'm, uh, not feeling any pain right now. Not a bit. And...I like you on top of me. I don't know why though. I just seem to...crave it. Is that, uh, part of the Royal Cycle you were talking about earlier?"

"To tell the truth, I don't know," he admitted. "My old mistress — the Goddess-Empress before you — was well past her needing years when I entered her service. I have never been with an Empress who was young enough to choose a Consort before, so I don't know much about the process."

"Choose a Consort?" I asked, frowning. "What is that supposed to mean?"

"The Empress has...needs." He sounded like he was trying to be delicate. "Someone must slake them and so a group of Royal candidates are chosen by the Council of Wisdom for the Empress to pick from."

"So once I get to Femme One I'm going to have to choose some guy to, uh, service me?" I asked, unable to keep the incredulity out of my voice.

"Essentially." Kristoff's deep voice sounded flat in the darkness. "A male of Royal blood who will sit by your side as you rule and be sire to your children."

"God..." I sighed. "This just gets weirder and weirder. What if I don't *want* to, uh, choose a Consort?"

"You'll have to," he assured me. "The Empress must have someone to help assuage her hunger."

"Sexual hunger, you mean?" I asked flatly.

"Yes." He shifted restlessly and I was aware of his long, hard shaft pressing against my thigh. It stirred something inside me — something I'd never felt before. But I pushed the feeling away.

"What if I don't *have* any sexual hunger?" I asked bluntly. "I mean, I never have before."

Wow — I couldn't believe I'd just blurted that out. But it was true — it was like that part of my body was dormant.

"I mean, not that I've never had sex before," I hastened to explain. "Just that, well, it never actually, uh, *did* anything for me." Which was why I had given it up in college and hadn't bothered since.

"I have heard that a true *La-ti-zal* may not have sexual feelings until she finds the male who is meant to be her fated-mate." Kristoff sounded thoughtful. "So the fact that you have not had, ah, *desires* before does not surprise me, my Lady. But take my word for it, when you reach the *needing* phase of the Royal Cycle, you will have to have a male to help you quench your body's sexual thirst."

"I guess we'll see," I said neutrally. Secretly, though, I was thinking that if I didn't feel anything sexually now, in the position I was in, I would probably never feel anything.

I don't mean being naked and pinned to the bed under Kristoff's big, muscular form wasn't nice—it was *all kinds* of yummy. He smelled good and he felt incredible and he made me feel warm and safe and protected in a way I never had in my life. Also, I felt a kind of connection with him—something I had never felt with any male before. It was a deep-seated *rightness* I could neither explain nor deny, which was probably why I was so comfortable telling him things I hadn't told anyone else.

But still, though it felt good on all kinds of levels to be pressed naked against him, it didn't feel sexual—not to me. I could still feel how hard Kristoff was against my thigh and I knew he couldn't say the same. It didn't bother me. Though I felt his arousal, I had absolute faith in him that he wouldn't take advantage of me in any way.

I could probably spread my legs and let his naked shaft rub against my open pussy and he still wouldn't do anything I didn't want him to do, I thought. The mental image gave me a strange tingle which made me slightly uneasy. Why would I imagine such a sexual act? I had never been one to fantasize about sex—it simply did nothing for me. In fact, I had made up my mind years ago that I was probably asexual.

So why the tingle?

No reason, I told myself uneasily. *It was just a random thought. Don't dwell on it and it will go away.*

"My lady?" Kristoff's deep voice murmured in the darkness. "Are you well? You've been silent these many moments."

"Just thinking," I said.

"Would you care to share your thoughts? She who was Empress before you often confided in me."

I thought of telling him my idea about letting him rub himself between my legs and felt my face getting hot with a blush.

"Nothing important," I mumbled. "I was just thinking I feel like I've had enough deep pressure now." Which was true. My body felt like it had equalized and I felt like I ought to put a little distance between us. Somehow being so close, face-to-face and naked in the dark together felt dangerous in a way it hadn't before.

"Do you wish me to leave you?" he asked, rolling off me.

"No." I stopped him when he would have gone. "What if my symptoms come back? I couldn't stand that—they were *awful*."

"I understand," he murmured. "Do you want me to stay in the sleeping platform beside you and not touch you unless you feel them return?"

"Why would I want that?" I asked. Despite my feeling that it was somehow dangerous to be so intimately pressed against him, I still didn't want him to stop touching me completely.

"Well..." He cleared his throat. "Technically what we are doing is not at all proper. The Council of Wisdom on Femme One would be scandalized."

"I don't care about propriety," I said. "Or following some set of rules made up by people I didn't even know existed a few days ago."

"They will be *your* people, my Lady," he murmured, a faint reproach in his deep voice. "To rule over them properly, you need to care about their laws and regulations."

I sighed. "I didn't mean to offend you, Kristoff. Honestly, it's hard for me to wrap my head around the idea of ruling *anyone*. And so much has happened in the past two days. I guess I'm just *tired*."

"Then rest, my Lady." His voice was gentle. "And I will hold you or not, as you see fit."

"Just spoon me," I said, thinking that would keep us close without the danger of face-to-face intimacy.

"Spoon?" he asked hesitantly. "I'm not sure what that means."

"You know—like spoons in a drawer? Here, like this."

I demonstrated by turning my back to his chest and pressing against him so that his big, warm body cradled my own.

Kristoff accepted me into his arms but then I felt his big body stiffen and his pelvis draw away from my bottom. After a moment, I realized he was trying to keep his erection from pressing against my ass.

"Look," I said bluntly. "That doesn't bother me if it doesn't bother you. Like I told you before, this isn't sexual for me. It's about comfort. See?" To prove my point, I brought one of his big hands to my chest and nestled one of my breasts into his palm. It felt very pleasant—warm and safe. But not sexual, I told myself firmly. I felt that strange little tingle again and pushed it away.

Not. Sexual.

Kristoff stiffened again.

"My Lady, I should not—"

"Look," I said impatiently. "What was it you told me back at my apartment when you were folding my undies? You asked me if I wanted a 'different type of service.' What was that about if not something like this?"

He took a deep breath, and I felt his broad chest expanding behind me like a warm wall made of flexible steel.

"In days past," he said. "There are tales of Empress's whose Consorts were slain before they were done with their time of *needing*. In that case, it sometimes happened that the Goddess-Empress would choose one of her Imperial Guards to use."

"You mean...to use *sexually?*" I asked. "That sounds like sexual slavery."

"No—it is a great honor to be chosen so," Kristoff said earnestly. "But the rules of such servitude are very strict. First, the Empress must have no Consort at the time. And second, though she may use her Guard's body in whatever way she wishes, he is prohibited from using her in the same way."

"Uh...I'm confused. If they're, uh, having sex, aren't they using each other?" I asked.

"Not necessarily." He sighed. "I will be more explicit. When I said that the Empress uses her Guard, I mean that she may touch him—she may even, er, *rub* against him—in order to achieve a release. But he may not *touch* back or initiate any, ah, intimate behavior." He cleared his throat. "For instance, the way you put my hand you your breast—that would be permitted. But if I was to caress your breasts, to tease or suck your nipples into my mouth, to circle your stiff peaks with my tongue to make you moan, well, that would be wrong."

His words sent another one of those tingles through me and I felt my nipple, the one that was nestled in his palm, get tight and achy for some reason.

"Tell...tell me more," I said a little breathlessly. "What else isn't, uh, allowed? I mean, what couldn't you do to me if we were, uh, operating under those rules?"

"My Lady," he murmured, his breath hot in my ear. "It would also be forbidden for me to slide my hand down your belly to cup your sex."

"It...it would?" My voice was trembling but I didn't know why.

"It would," he assured me, his voice low and intimate in my ear. "And it would likewise be forbidden for me to spread your sweet pussy open and caress your slippery folds, seeking to find your Goddess-pearl and pleasure you by stroking it."

I could guess what a Goddess-pearl was and for some reason I found his words made me feel hot and tingly all over. What *was* this feeling? I couldn't understand it—I had certainly never felt anything like it before. It was strange and it made me feel uneasy, yet I didn't want him to stop talking.

"Tell me more," I murmured. "What else...couldn't you do to me?"

"I could not mount you, of course—could not breed you as you will need to be bred once the *needing* is past and your Royal Cycle comes to its apex."

"Oh?" I had my doubts about this whole needing and breeding stuff, but I was still plenty interested enough to want him to continue. "Go on."

"And I could not taste you." He shifted restively and I thought I heard a longing in his deep voice. "Could not part the lips of your pussy and pleasure you with my mouth and tongue, no matter how much I might desire it."

"So that's...something you, uh, like to do?" I couldn't believe I was asking him this. But we'd talked about just about everything else — why not?

"All Majoran males do," he assured me in a deep voice. "What greater pleasure is there than to be on your knees before your goddess, worshipping her pussy with your tongue?"

"Hmm..." I was the one who shifted this time, eliciting a soft groan from Kristoff as I inadvertently brushed against his shaft. "I, uh, that's interesting. And unusual."

"Do Earth males not feel the same way?" he asked, sounding surprised.

I thought of the two guys I'd tried having sex with before giving it up forever. One was my boyfriend in high school — a sweet, bumbling boy named Chad McGarth who couldn't have found my clit with both hands and a flashlight. He had attempted a few licks between my legs before taking my virginity in what was probably the most boring deflowering ever. His oral attentions reminded me of having a too-eager puppy trying to lick me and I had been glad when he stopped.

My second and last sexual experience was with a lab partner I'd had in my Freshman chemistry class in college. I'd felt intensely attracted to him — or thought I had. But when it came down to actually doing the deed, he couldn't turn me on any more than any other guy I'd ever met. I went through with the act anyway, mostly out of hopeful curiosity, to see if anything had changed since high school — it hadn't. He, too, had been willing to "go downtown" as he put it. But once again, it had done nothing for me and I had been relieved when we were finished and I could put on my clothes and go.

Shortly after that second attempt at sex was when I had been attacked. And that pretty much ended my sexual career, such as it was. Or wasn't, I guess.

"I guess some Earth males don't mind, uh, tasting a woman," I said thoughtfully. "But I don't think they crave it, either."

"Majoran males do," he assured me. "That is why so many of

the unmated males pay to be of use in the Temple of Goddess Pleasures."

I had no idea what the Temple of Goddess Pleasures was and I didn't intend to ask. I felt like we were getting off track a little.

"So, going back to the, uh, 'rules' we were discussing — about if I was an Empress without a Consort and I need, um, relief…"

"Yes?" he murmured.

"I guess what I'm asking is, you'd *never* be allowed to touch me?" I asked him. "Even if I ordered you to?"

"I could only touch you to serve you non-sexually," he explained. "For instance, to give you a massage or to bathe or dress you — all these things I am permitted."

"It sounds like the rules are pretty convoluted," I murmured.

"Some have said they are passing strange," Kristoff admitted. "As I said, it has been quite some time since they had to be invoked. Not since Sundalla the 887th, I believe, which was many generations ago. She lost her Consort when he fought and died in the Battle of Tr'zaq and chose one of her Guards to service her instead."

"But the point is, *I* can touch *you* if…if I feel like I need to? If it makes me feel more comfortable?" I asked.

"I am yours to command," he murmured and the soft, deep tone of his voice suggested he wouldn't mind being commanded. Wouldn't mind it at all.

Stop it, I told myself sternly. *It's not sexual, no matter what he thinks. You don't have those feelings — remember? Everything you've done tonight is just to alleviate your symptoms — the symptoms of the Burning Blood, as Kristoff called it.*

"So I can do *this,* if I want to?" To prove to myself that it wasn't sexual, I pressed my behind back against his warm pelvis, feeling his long, hard shaft thrusting against my ass.

Kristoff made a sound that was almost a groan in the back of his throat but didn't move away from me this time.

"Yes, my Lady. Do as you wish with me," he murmured, his deep voice hoarse.

"All right." I wiggled to try and get comfortable but though his body behind me was warm and solid and felt amazing, his shaft really *was* poking me. I changed position so that his thick length was nestled in the crevice between my buttocks. Not pressing inward or anything, just...cradled there. Ah...*finally* I was comfortable.

But was Kristoff?

He hadn't made any kind of protest or moved away from me, but I could feel the tension in his big body as he held me to him.

"Is this okay?" I asked him, feeling suddenly uncertain. "I mean, is it too, uh awkward for you?"

"It is...not a position I ever expected to be in with my mistress," he admitted at last. "But if it makes you feel comfortable and protected, I am pleased to be of service."

"But I don't want to do this if it makes *you* uncomfortable," I protested. "You have feelings too! Am I, uh, torturing you?"

"It's a sweet torture, my Lady." His deep voice was hoarse again. "I will willingly endure it if it serves your pleasure."

"Thank you," I said. "I can't explain it but, well, it makes me feel better to, uh, have contact with you. It makes me feel...safe. And I know my symptoms won't come back like this."

"Then it's good." He pulled me a little closer. "I want you to feel safe with me. I will protect you with my life, you know."

"I know," I whispered and I honestly understood that he would. "I'm sorry if it's, uh, hard—I mean *difficult* for you," I said. "But I guess you can probably find someone to help you take the edge off once we get to where we're going, right?"

I had to force the words out—the idea of him with another woman sent a bitter zing of jealousy through me, though I didn't know why. Still, it was only fair, right?

"Do you mean I might find another female and have her sexually?" He sounded shocked, as though I had suggested he go commit some kind of a blasphemy.

"Well, yeah—since you're not, uh, allowed to do anything with me. Not that I want you to," I added quickly. "I just mean with all your weird rules and everything..."

"I will not touch another female," he growled as though the very thought disgusted him. "*Never.*"

"I'm sorry," I said. "I didn't mean to offend you. Do you not, uh, have relationships with other women while you're serving the Empress?"

"I have not been intimate with a female for ten cycles—since right before I entered Sundalla the 999th's service," he growled, still sounding offended. "As I told you before, my chastity is dedicated to the Empress's service and I take my vows *very* seriously."

"Ten years? Wow—that's some dry spell," I murmured. "And I thought *I* held the record there."

"You have not…been intimate for some time?" he asked.

"No." I sighed. "Not since I was attacked by a drunk frat guy in college. After that I just didn't…want anything to do with it anymore. Not that it was great before that."

I felt Kristoff stiffen behind me, this time with rage.

"What was his name, this male who attacked you?" His voice was a low, fierce growl. "I will hunt him down and kill him."

"I don't know who he was," I said honestly. "It was dark and I couldn't see his face."

"The coward," Kristoff growled. "To attack a defenseless female in the darkness!"

"Not completely defenseless," I said sharply. "I *did* manage to fight him off. He…" I swallowed hard. I didn't like to remember the details of the attack. "He had me pinned and he was trying to spread my legs but I…I got a knee up and rammed him in the balls."

"Good." Kristoff's approval was sharp and immediate. "He deserved to have them cut off if he tried to take you—to take any female—against her will."

"I happen to agree," I said as lightly as I could. "But I left my butcher knife back at my dorm room so I had to content myself with kneeing him in the balls and running away."

"And you have feared to be intimate with a male since then?" he murmured.

"Not *feared* exactly." I sighed. "I told you, I've never had much in the way of sexual feelings. It just seemed like a lot of fuss and bother over nothing. And after the…the attack, I felt like doing it even less." I shrugged. "So I decided just to forget about it and concentrate on getting my degree."

It seemed incredibly strange to be lying naked in the dark with him and having such an intimate conversation when I hadn't even known him two days ago. Strange but somehow completely right. I hadn't even told Leah and Zoe everything that I had just told the big alien who was holding me so gently in his arms, and yet, telling Kristoff seemed natural somehow. I don't know how I knew it, but I understood instinctively that he would never betray my confidences or tell my secrets. And he wouldn't think less of me either, no matter how embarrassing they were.

"Well..." I sighed and settled down, my head pillowed on his muscular bicep. "I'm getting tired. It's been a long day...or night...or whatever it is."

"Then you should sleep," Kristoff murmured. "I will hold you and ward your dreams, my Lady."

"Told you..." I yawned, finding that I hadn't been lying—I really *was* tired. "You can call me Charlotte."

"That's not proper," he murmured, but I thought I heard amusement in his voice.

"I don't care." I yawned again and let my eyelids drift closed. "Don't care about propriety." Which was clearly evident by the way I was sleeping naked and spooned up against a strange man.

Only he's not so strange anymore is he? whispered a little voice in my head. *In fact, I think you're becoming quite **attached** to your new bodyguard.*

Doesn't matter if I feel attached to him or not—it's not sexual between us, I reminded myself, even as I nestled my breast into his big palm and pressed my bottom against his hard shaft. *Not even a little. The only reason we're so close is so my symptoms don't come back.*

It was true—I was sure of it. So then why did that strange little tingle follow me down into sleep?

Kristoff

It was, as I had told her, sweet torture to hold her lush body close and be unable to pleasure her. I couldn't help feeling the soft weight of her full breast in my hand, and the press of her ripe ass against my hard shaft was nearly maddening.

I wanted desperately to roll her sweet nipple between my thumb and fingers, drawing a low moan from her throat, and then to slide down between her legs and pleasure her with my mouth and tongue.

The oral pleasuring of a female — of his goddess — is what every Majoran male craves with all his being. In fact, bringing a female to orgasm in this way is the most effective way to make a Majoran warrior come as well. Show me a male who can kneel between his goddess's legs and make love to her with his mouth without coming and I'll show you a male made of stone.

I could picture myself between Charlotte's thighs right now — rubbing my cheeks against her soft mound of blonde curls, kissing every inch of her outer pussy first, then going deeper. Spreading the lips of her sweet sex to find her Goddess-pearl nestled in her inner folds like a treasure. I would bathe it with my tongue, tracing gently and firmly, savoring her secret flavor while she pulled my hair and moaned her delight, begging me never to stop, calling my name as I tasted her...

Stop! I ordered myself. *It can never be between you — don't torture yourself with such inane thoughts and fantasies.*

I tried to heed my own advice but it was hard...so hard. Especially with my new mistress curled lush and naked in my arms. I hoped that the healer waiting for us on Denaris would be able to give Charlotte something to help with her withdrawal symptoms.

I'm a strong male but I didn't know how much of this I could stand.

You'll stand as much as you have to — as much as the new Goddess-Empress deems necessary, Verrai, I told myself sternly. I thought again of the tale of Sundalla the 887th and her Imperial Guard. It was all written down in a hologramtic scroll in the Great Library of Femme One — it was one of the texts we of the Imperial Guard were made to study. It was meant to teach us that everything we did was only for our Empress's pleasure and our bodies were meant only to serve her.

Goddess — how I longed to serve her that way now! Especially after the long, intimate talk we had just had. It was much like the way I had used to talk to my old mistress, Sundalla the 999th, who confided in me almost from the start of my service to her. But the conversation I'd had with Charlotte held a special intimacy because she was curled naked in my arms as we spoke – I'd certainly never had *that* with my old mistress! Though the former Empress told me everything in her heart, she had always kept me at an arm's length physically – which was, of course, right and proper.

It was different with Charlotte. She pressed herself against me as she told me things – painful things – that I thought she might have kept secret in her own heart for many long years. It made me feel close to her, to feel that she trusted me enough to confide in me and know I would keep her confidences. We had talked the way lovers might talk – honestly and openly and the connection between us had been established as it hadn't been back on her home planet of Earth.

It felt almost like the beginning of a bond.

But I knew that could never be. Once we reached Femme One, the Council of Wisdom would appoint Consort candidates, Charlotte would give them each a few drops of her blood, and her true withdrawal would begin, leading her to the male who was supposed to be her mate.

Of course, all this would take place only *after* Charlotte had passed the trials to prove she was the True Incarnation. But I didn't anticipate much difficulty there – she had the rainbow aura. Though I was the only one who could see it, it proved beyond the shadow of a doubt that she was, indeed, Sundalla the 1000th. And the Council would see the truth of it during the trials.

Charlotte would be crowned, enthroned, and mated all within the space of days. And I...I would guard her the rest of my life and probably never hold her like this again.

It was the life I had chosen willingly and I had never regretted it. I didn't regret it now. I simply pulled her closer and buried my face in her hair, breathing in the warm, sweet scent of her.

Remember this, Verrai, I told myself. *Treasure this memory in your heart. It's the only time you'll hold the goddess you serve in such a way. It is an honor and a pleasure never to be forgotten.*

Chapter Thirteen

Charlotte

I woke to a feeling I'd never had before.

It started as that little tingle I'd been feeling before I fell asleep and grew into a warm glow that started somewhere in my pelvis and seemed to spread outward.

I lay there in Kristoff's arms, still half asleep, wondering what was happening to me. Was this another symptom of the Burning Blood disease I'd somehow contracted by giving him a transfusion of my blood? But it wasn't unpleasant—it didn't make me feel like I was burning up or that I couldn't breathe.

In fact it was kind of nice—a warm, tingling glow that seemed to encompass my whole body. It *did* seem to center on my breasts and the area between my legs, though.

I shifted a little and had to bite back a little cry as my nipple brushed against Kristoff's big hand. He was still cupping my breast as he had been when we fell asleep. Also, his shaft was still pressed against my ass. Which felt really interesting for some reason.

Experimentally, I shifted again, deliberately letting my sensitive peak rub against his palm, and nearly moaned. That felt good. *Really* good. Good in a way I had never felt before.

I thought back to the two other lovers I'd had back on Earth. Both had been especially eager to play with my breasts—I have big ones which a lot of guys like—although I'd always considered them a nuisance. But I'd never felt much of anything while they were pawing and fondling me—it just didn't turn me on.

Now, the lightest brush of my nipple against Kristoff's hand sent a hot spark of pleasure straight through me—from my breast all the way down to the area between my thighs. Why?

Speaking of the area between my legs, I was feeling a strange fullness and heat there. It made me press my thighs together, which caused an almost electrical jolt of pleasure to go through me. God, I was so *sensitive!* Why was that?

I had no idea why—I only knew the feelings were growing, filling me with a need that was as unfamiliar as it was frightening.

Back on Earth, I had never had these feelings. I had read about them, watched tons of TV shows and movies that included them, but never actually had them myself. I had tried masturbating but it didn't do a damn thing for me so I gave it up. Most days I lived entirely in my head. I felt like I had more in common with Vulcans—the race of beings who favored logic over emotion on the old Star Trek shows Zoe made me watch with her—than I did with my fellow humans.

Now I was feeling all-too human but I wasn't sure if it was a good thing or not.

Moaning softly, I spread my thighs, trying to ease some of the ache I was feeling. My pussy felt hot and swollen and throbbing. I wondered if it looked like it felt. The room had lightened some—a soft, overhead glow which seemed to come from the corners and cast a golden, indirect illumination almost like an artificial dawn. Being careful not to wake the still-sleeping Kristoff, I scooted a little away from him and opened wider, peering down at myself.

What I saw made me suck in my breath.

My pussy lips were puffy and pink, fuller than I had ever seen them. My clit, like a little pink pearl, was peeping out from between my glistening wet folds, as though begging for attention.

I had never seen myself look that way before. So...*ripe.* What was going on with my body? Why was I suddenly having feelings that had eluded me my entire life up until now?

"Gods...so *beautiful.*" Kristoff's low, hoarse voice behind me startled me. I looked up over my shoulder and realized he was surveying my body.

"Kristoff!" Feeling shy, I tried to shut my thighs. But the pressure and need were too much. With a little cry, I had to open them again, baring myself and my new, shameful desire to the man behind me.

"Forgive me, my Lady," he murmured in a deep voice. "But you need not be ashamed to show your body to me."

"I...I wasn't trying to, uh, show it," I said, my voice tight with embarrassment. "I was just...trying to figure out what's going on with me. I feel...strange today."

"Are you having pain?" he asked, sounding concerned.

"Not exactly..." I didn't know how to explain the throbbing, tingling warmth that seemed to radiate outward and center in my nipples and pussy.

"You may be entering the *needing* stage of your Royal Cycle," he murmured. "My Lady, would you permit me to perform a test?"

"What...what kind of test?" I asked uncertainly.

"A test for sensitivity. I believe it will help us learn what's happening to your body — such information could be vital when we get to Denaris."

"I...I thought we were going to Femme One," I whispered.

"We are. But given your extreme symptoms last night, I wanted to take you to a healer first. Don't worry — she was the official court physician to your predecessor, Sundalla the 999th. I trust her implicitly."

"Well, if you trust her then I trust her," I said. "But...why should you perform a, uh, sensitivity test now if we're going to a doctor?"

"To give her an idea of what stage of your cycle you're in," he said. "But if you'd rather not, we can wait until we get to Denaris and let Dr. Churika perform it. We should be in orbit soon."

I thought of letting a stranger I didn't know touch me...as opposed to letting Kristoff, who I was beginning to know and trust, do it.

It was no contest.

"Do it," I whispered. "Do the, uh, sensitivity test, Kristoff. I'd rather have you do it than anyone else."

"My Lady honors me with her trust," he murmured. "Very well, lie on your back and relax."

It was easier said than done — the relaxing part, I mean. My whole body felt tight as a wire but somehow I managed to make myself lay back and keep my arms and legs open, though I desperately wanted to close them.

Kristoff leaned over me, propped on one arm, and for a moment, he just looked at me, his eyes changing color rapidly as he took me in.

"Kristoff…" I murmured, shifting uneasily. "Is this, uh, part of the test?"

"Forgive me, my Lady—no it is not. I was just admiring your beauty. Your curves are so ripe and full."

"We call that being plus-sized on Earth," I remarked. "And it's not exactly considered a good thing."

"Truly?" He looked at me, frowning. "How can it not be? Your curves are formed in the likeness of the Goddess—they should be worshiped accordingly."

I didn't know how I felt about being "worshipped" but I did know that my body was aching for some reason. Aching and throbbing in a way that made me feel restless and anxious.

"Kristoff," I said, "when does this, uh, *test* begin?"

"Now," he murmured. Leaning over me, he began to blow a cool, ticklish stream of air over my heated skin.

You wouldn't think such a small thing would have much of an effect on me—well, you'd be wrong. Though he didn't touch me a bit—not with his hands, anyway—that cool stream of air seemed to light up my body like a Christmas tree.

"Kristoff," I whispered in a tight voice as he blew lightly across my nipples, which were now tight and aching. "What are you doing?"

"Gauging your sensitivity, as I said, my Lady," he murmured. "Do you feel yourself stirred when I do this?"

Stirred? Hell yes, I was stirred! But it was too embarrassing to admit.

"I…I guess so," I murmured, fighting the urge to press my breasts up to him and try to get those luscious lips of his wrapped around my nipples. Well, *that* was certainly something I had never craved before!

"Then I must continue lower, to gauge your reaction below," he murmured. "Can you allow it, my Lady?"

"I…sure. Okay," I said, my voice coming out slightly

breathless.

"Thank you," Kristoff said. Leaning over me, he blew that same, cool, ticklish stream of air over my body. Starting at my collar bones, he moved lower, past my breasts and over my trembling belly. Finally he reached the apex of my thighs.

I jumped and gasped when the cool air stirred the neatly trimmed curls on my mound. It was simply too much to bear—even though he was just blowing on the top of my pussy I felt like I was going to jump out of my skin.

Kristoff stopped at once.

"Ah—I fear you're too sensitive for me to test you here," he murmured.

Somehow I didn't want him to stop.

"No, I'm not," I protested breathlessly. "Please…please, don't stop."

He looked up at me, those amazing eyes half-lidded with an emotion I didn't dare to name.

"Very well, my Lady, but if I'm to continue, you'll need to spread your legs for me."

I did as he said without protest, spreading my thighs to bare myself completely. As I spread, I felt my pussy open as well—my outer lips so full and ripe they were spreading on their own to reveal my swollen clit. I had never felt so incredibly exposed with anyone—it was too much.

With a little cry of embarrassment, I reached down to cover myself. But Kristoff caught my wrist and brought my hand firmly back to my side.

"No, my Lady," he murmured, his voice slightly rough. "You must be open for me to finish the test. In fact, I will have to ask you to open yourself even more, since I am not allowed to touch you. Can you spread the outer lips of your sex for me?"

Blushing and trembling, I reached between my legs to do as he said. With the first and middle finger of my right hand, I spread my pussy open, revealing my inner sex completely, making myself more vulnerable than I had ever been with any man.

Kristoff groaned softly as he surveyed my open pussy.

"Gods," he muttered hoarsely. "So ripe...so beautiful..."

He was right between my thighs now, his face hovering over my pussy in a way that made me wonder if the sensitivity test was going to turn into something else completely. But though he was eyeing me like he was a man dying of thirst and my sex was exactly what he needed to slake his thirst, he held back.

"I will not blow on this area, my Lady," he murmured. "It is too sensitive, I am sure. Instead I will simply *breathe* on you and gauge your reaction to my breath."

"All...all right," I whispered. I bit my lip as he leaned forward, his mouth open almost as though he was going to kiss me.

Instead, he breathed out as he had promised. I felt the heat of his breath, bathing my open pussy and my clit throbbed in answer. I couldn't help myself—my hips bucked upwards in reaction and for just a moment, his mouth made contact with my inner folds.

"Oh!" I gasped, freezing in place. Unfortunately, the place I froze in was with Kristoff's hot, open mouth pressed to my pussy. Not only were his lips on me—I also felt his tongue, hot and wet, against my throbbing clit.

He seemed frozen too and for a long moment we stayed like that. Kristoff didn't move his tongue to taste or lick me...but he didn't pull away either. His eyes flickered up to meet mine and I saw an emotion that matched the one I was feeling in their shifting depths. I felt enveloped by his heat and wetness and desire.

Then I realized what I was doing.

"I'm sorry!" I gasped, pulling back and away from his mouth. "I...I didn't mean to."

Kristoff didn't say a word, though his lips were shiny with my juices. I saw him lick them slowly, as though savoring every bit of my essence. Then he rose and left the bed—which looked like a big shiny silver beanbag, incidentally—obviously putting some distance between us.

"Kristoff?" I said, feeling miserable. "I'm so sorry—I didn't mean to do that. I swear I didn't!"

"I am the one who has transgressed." He ran a hand through his hair in agitation and I saw that his cock was incredibly long and hard. "I should have moved my mouth at once—I should not have allowed myself to taste your honey, my Goddess."

"It was an accident," I said, sitting up. "We were just...*oh!*" My words ended in a little gasp because I had unthinkingly tried to close my legs. The motion sent a sharp bolt of painful desire through me and I shifted uncomfortably.

"What is it, my Lady?" Kristoff was looking at me anxiously.

"It's...it's nothing." I gritted my teeth. "I'm just, uh, really sensitive."

"That's not surprising," he said grimly. "From your reaction to the test I preformed, I'd say you were already well into the *needing* phase of your cycle."

"Needing *what* though?" I demanded, as he began to put on his uniform — or at least the under garments and the leather kilt. I was glad to see he was leaving the hard, metal breastplate and the other metal bits off for now.

"Needing a release — an orgasm." He frowned at me. "Perhaps I should leave you, my Lady. I don't believe you're so far into your *needing* that you can't help yourself with such matters."

"You mean...make myself come?" I asked bluntly.

"Yes. It should take the edge off your desire — at least for a little while." He spoke as though it was a simple thing — as though anyone could do it. Then he started to leave the room.

"Wait!"

He turned to me. "Yes, my Lady?" His deep voice sounded strained. "I need to see to the ship's orbit and you should, ah — *help yourself.*"

"I would if I could but I've never done that," I confessed, feeling my cheeks burn with the admission. "I mean, I've never, uh, been able to make myself come. I just...*can't.*"

Kristoff frowned and came to sit on the edge of the bed beside me.

"Of course, how stupid of me," he murmured. "You are a *La-ti-zal* as well as the True Incarnation. This desire you're experiencing is the first you've ever felt, isn't it?"

"It is." I nodded and swallowed hard. "And Kristoff, it's kind of — well, it's *scary.* I've never felt anything so intense. Can you…would you stay with me?"

His eyes, which had been hard with what I could only imagine was repressed desire, suddenly softened.

"Of course, Charlotte. Would you like me to hold you while you attempt to help yourself?"

My throat tightened at the way I felt when he used my name.

"Yes," I whispered. "Would you?"

"It is always my pleasure to serve you," he murmured. Sitting behind me, he drew me towards him until my back was flush against his hard, broad chest and his long legs were bracketing mine. "Lean back against me," he whispered in my ear. "And pleasure yourself."

I never would have believed I would allow myself to be vulnerable enough with any man to do what he was suggesting. But my body ached with need and I couldn't help myself. With a little moan I relaxed back against him, spread my legs, and let my hand drift down between my thighs.

Chapter Fourteen

Charlotte

It felt good as I spread my pussy and began to tentatively touch my inner folds—almost *too* good, in fact. Too intense. I was sure most women, by the time they got to be my age, knew exactly what to do to make themselves come. After many years of trial and error, they just knew what worked for them.

I didn't. Remember, masturbation had never done a thing for me back on Earth. And so, though it felt good to touch myself, I also felt clumsy and uncertain. I couldn't seem to find a good rhythm or establish the right connection. And the intense sensations were driving me crazy—making it impossible to get where I needed to go. I could feel my frustration growing along with my desire until I gave up with a little moan of aggravation.

"My Lady?" Kristoff made it a question.

"I know this sounds ridiculous but I *can't*," I told him. "It feels like I'm doing it all wrong somehow. I'm just not...getting anywhere."

"Would you like me to help you to help yourself?" he murmured in my ear.

I turned my head around to see him staring at me intently.

"Uh...how? Have you had special training in giving women orgasms or something?" I meant the words as a joke but he nodded with complete seriousness.

"Every Ma*jor*an male takes special classes in pleasuring a female as soon as he comes of age. It's mandatory."

"It *is?*" I couldn't imagine a society where learning to pleasure a female was mandatory.

"We take the pleasure of our females very seriously," Kristoff assured me. "We worship our females and what better way to worship than to give pleasure? Though I have not touched a female sexually in the last ten cycles, I do not believe my training has deserted me."

"Okay, I believe you," I said. "But if you're not allowed to touch me, how can you, uh, help me?"

"Like this. Viewer!" he said in a low, commanding voice.

At once, a rectangular metal rod rose from the end of the silver bed. The top third of the rod unfolded and then unfolded again and again and again until a flat screen made of hundreds of tiny squares was facing us. It was about two feet wide by two feet tall.

"This is mostly useful to communicate with the other rooms of the ship," Kristoff explained. "But it can also be used as a reflective surface. Reflect," he told the flat screen at our feet.

At once, the surface shimmered and a perfect picture of me leaning back against him, cradled in his arms appeared.

I blushed to see the way I was spread out with my hand between my legs. God, I looked so wanton! So *needy*. I started to close my legs but Kristoff put his big hands on my knees and gently opened them again.

"Never be ashamed of your beauty, Charlotte," he murmured in my ear. "Now watch…"

He took my hands in his and brought them to my breasts.

"Pinch your nipples," he ordered softly. "Just enough to feel the pleasure."

I did as he said, moaning softly as I squeezed my tight buds, sending sparks of sensation from my breasts straight down to my pussy.

"Good, that's good…enjoy your body," Kristoff murmured in a low, encouraging voice.

As I pinched and teased my nipples, he ran his big hands up and down my thighs very, very gently until my breath caught in my throat.

"A female needs to be brought to desire slowly," he lectured softly. "All parts of her body may be erogenous zones when touched correctly."

"That's wonderful, Kristoff," I whispered breathlessly.

"But...I've already been, uh, brought to desire. I just need to know how to help myself, um, reach the peak."

"Of course." He stopped stroking my thighs and reached for my hands instead. He brought my right hand down between my legs, beside my open pussy. "Spread yourself, my Lady," he murmured, his breath hot in my ear. "Open yourself and examine your treasures."

With trembling fingers, I did as he said, opening my pussy to put my throbbing clit on display.

"See how prominent your Goddess-pearl is," Kristoff said softly, pointing but not touching as we watched in the viewer. "You might think the right thing would be to rub it directly."

"That's...kind of what I was doing before," I admitted. "But the sensation was too intense—I couldn't stand it and I couldn't get anywhere with it."

"That is because the Goddess-pearl must be approached indirectly. She is shy and delicate and must be wooed before she gives up her pleasure. Here—give me your hand with just the forefinger extended, please, my Lady."

I curled back all the fingers but my pointer and allowed him to take my hand in his much larger one. He brought the finger to his lips and sucked it gently into the hot, wet depths of his mouth. I watched him and felt a long sigh fall out of me as he laved my finger with his tongue, his eyes never leaving mine.

"Kristoff..." I whispered.

He released my finger, letting it slip slowly from between his lips.

"You must touch the Goddess-pearl with gentleness."

He laid his first finger on top of mine, so that all I could see was his hand, not my own.

"Like this," he murmured. I watched, mesmerized, as he reached between my legs and began stroking, not directly against my clit, but along the side of it.

"Oh!" I whispered as I felt the pleasure again, but this time not so intense that I couldn't stand it.

"The Goddess-pearl may be caressed indirectly, sometimes for hours," Kristoff continued to lecture in my ear. "The female's pleasure can be built and then backed off many, many times in order to reach a more intense and satisfying peak."

"*Oh*," I moaned again, beginning to thrust my hips in time with his gentle stroking. I couldn't help it—the feeling of my own finger, guided by Kristoff's, and the image of him touching me in the reflective viewer was incredibly hot.

"If we were mated," Kristoff told me. "I would tease you for hours, my Goddess. And I would pleasure you in other ways as well before I let you come."

"How?" I whispered, hungry to hear more of his deep voice speaking forbidden things in my ear. "Tell me *how*."

"I would fill you with my fingers while you watched," he told me. "Fill you while I stroked your pearl with my other hand, penetrating you as I pleasured you."

The moment he said it, my pussy felt incredibly empty for some reason.

"Kristoff," I moaned. "Couldn't you do that now? Just...just this once?"

"Alas, I am forbidden, my Lady." He sounded almost as frustrated as I felt. "All I can do is tell you what I *would* do if I was allowed."

"Tell... tell me more then," I whispered. The slow, sensual slide against the side of my clit was driving me crazy—I felt like I was close but I wanted to hear more from him before I came.

"I would get on my knees, as I was a moment ago, and worship you with my mouth," he growled softly. "Gods, your honey is sweet! It would be my pleasure to spread your pussy wide and bathe your Goddess-pearl with my tongue until you came and released your honey for me."

"I...it would?" I gasped. "I...I thought...I wasn't sure if you...if you liked it when we accidentally, uh, touched."

"You mean when you brought your sweet pussy up to meet my mouth? Gods, yes, I *loved* it," he assured me in a low, hoarse voice. "It was all I could do to stop myself from spreading you with my tongue and taking you orally then and there."

The idea of him taking me—of Kristoff between my legs, going down on me and lapping my open pussy—was turning me on like nothing I'd ever thought or imagined before. Then again, the whole sensation of being "turned on" was still a completely new one for me.

New and amazing—suddenly I was right on the edge.

"Kristoff," I moaned, thrusting my hips up. "Oh, God—I...I think I'm close!"

"Of course you are, my Goddess," he growled softly. "You've been working your sweet little pussy against your finger—I can feel it. Can feel how your hips thrust as you caress your Goddess-pearl. It's time to let your pleasure reach the peak. Can you do that? Can you come in my arms while I hold you?"

"Yes!" I gasped and then something came over me—something as warm and overwhelming as a wave at the beach. It swamped me completely, taking away my breath, making my whole body go rigid with intense pleasure. "Oh!" I gasped. "Oh, *Kristoff!*"

"That's right, Charlotte," he murmured in my ear, his voice low and fierce with desire. "Come for me, my Lady—my Goddess. Let yourself go and *come*."

I did. I came so hard I swear I saw stars. My back arched, my toes curled, and I couldn't seem to stop moaning.

It was the first orgasm I'd ever had and it was *amazing*.

Kristoff

I held her as she reached the peak—held her and watched our hands, working together to give her pleasure. Gods, she was beautiful! Beautiful and perfect and not at all mine. I probably shouldn't be helping her like this. And yet, she had *needed* this release—how could I deny my mistress anything that she needed?

I couldn't.

And so I sat there holding her lush, naked body and watching as her berry-red nipples grew tight and her sweet pussy spasmed with pleasure. She looked so fucking beautiful when she came it hurt to watch her—and yet I couldn't look away. Couldn't do anything but pray that the moment would never end.

At last, it did, though. She collapsed in my arms, panting, her cheeks flushed and eyes bright with pleasure.

"Kristoff," she whispered. "That was...I don't know what that was. I've never felt anything like it."

"It was just your pleasure coming to a peak at last, my Lady," I told her, smoothing away a tendril of hair from her lovely face. "How do you feel now?"

"Tired." She yawned. "All wrung out somehow."

"The first pleasure for a *La-ti-zal* is very intense," I told her. "At least, that is what I was taught. Why don't you rest while I go make sure our course is good?"

"All right." She yawned again and let me lower her down to the sleeping platform and draw a coverlet over her still-naked body. But when I would have left her, she drew me down with one small hand on my shoulder. "Kristoff..." She said my name softly and drowsily—I wasn't sure if she wasn't already asleep.

"Yes, my Lady?" I said anyway.

"Thank you." She tugged at me and, to my surprise, kissed me gently on the lips. Before I could tell her how very improper her gesture was, she released me and curled into a ball under the coverlet.

"You are welcome, my Lady," I answered her but my only reply was her soft, even breathing.

I left her but before I went to the control area, I found my way into the fresher. A brief sonic shower left me feeling refreshed but in no way satisfied. My shaft felt like it had been hard for hours and at last I knew I could take it no more.

Leaning against one wall of the fresher, I fisted my shaft and began to stroke, thinking of my mistress, though I knew it was wrong.

Her soft hair and big green eyes...the way she opened herself and allowed me to help her touch herself—the way she shivered in my arms and called my name as she came...

And then my mind strayed to the most forbidden topic of all. That one brief instant when her pussy was pressed against my mouth.

I could still taste her honey on my lips—could still remember the feeling of her pussy opening under my mouth and her Goddess-pearl throbbing against my tongue. Gods, how I'd longed to taste her deeper — to thrust my tongue into her sweet well and lap up all her nectar while she moaned and cried and pressed against me!

Just the thought of it was too much for me. I came, my seed pumping out in jets that poured over my hand as I imagined giving my new mistress oral pleasure...as I imagined eating her sweet, creamy little pussy until she came all over my face.

Even in the midst of my pleasure, though, I knew I was doing wrong. I shouldn't want her like this—I shouldn't imagine doing these things with her. She was forbidden to me and she always would be.

But somehow I couldn't help myself. Though I knew it was certain ruin and damnation to want the Goddess-Empress for my own, I couldn't help wanting Charlotte.

Chapter Fifteen

Charlotte

"Dr. Churika will be with you shortly," an older male attendant with blue skin told us. "She has a...special case right now."

"Tell her Captain Verrai is here with his new mistress," Kristoff told him, frowning. "And she cannot wait long."

"Don't do that." I put a hand on his arm. "Really—I hate self-important patients who try to get in first because they think their time is more valuable than anyone else's."

"But my Lady, your symptoms—" he protested.

"Are under control for now," I told him firmly, although to be honest, I was already feeling that little tingle again, despite the intense orgasm he'd given me just a few hours ago. Or, I guess I had given it to myself, since he never really touched me. Although, it had certainly *felt* like he was touching me at the time, even though he was just guiding my hand.

Just thinking about it was enough to make me blush. I was starting to feel very confused about my relationship with the big alien. I knew he was supposed to be my bodyguard and we weren't supposed to have intimate contact. But I *wanted* intimate contact with him. Even now, standing right beside him without reaching over to touch him was hard.

It was like my body had somehow gotten addicted to his in the short period of time we had spent on his ship. Of course, that probably wasn't so surprising, considering that we had spent almost all of it naked and wrapped in each other's arms. But that had been necessary to keep back the symptoms of the Burning Blood syndrome, right?

Justify it any way you want, Charlotte, whispered a snarky little voice in my head. *The fact is you **liked** it and now you want more. But* *you can't have more — so deal with it.*

Shut up, I told it, even though I knew it was only telling the truth. *Just leave me alone.*

Kristoff was still looking at me with one eyebrow raised, as though he was trying to decipher what I was thinking. I knew he could already feel my emotions, through the strange bond we seemed to have formed, so my thoughts couldn't be far behind.

He looked absolutely mouthwatering in his full uniform with the molded breastplate, short leather kilt, and high, black boots. His skin was tan with just a tinge of gold today and I was glad he wasn't changing the color of it to reflect my mood. If he did, I bet it would be a cloudy gray-purple-blue because I was feeling so confused. Or whatever the colors of confusion are.

I decided *not* to think about the situation I was in. Instead, I sat in the small waiting room on a hard bench that seemed to be made out of purple and blue and pink seashells and looked out the open window at the gorgeous beach landscape outside. Being from Florida, I was used to beaches but we didn't have anything in the Sunshine State to top what Denaris offered.

The white sands glittered brilliantly in the pale blue sunlight and the azure waters were so clear they looked like glass. Tall, blue and purple trees swayed gently in a salt-scented breeze and overhead, strange creatures that looked a little like miniature, pink pterodactyls soared and swooped through the sky.

Denaris was a world that was mostly ocean at the poles but it was encircled by a chain of islands that wrapped all the way around it in an uneven, bumpy line with some more to the north and others more to the south. Kristoff had explained that the people here divided themselves into tribes — different tribes came from different islands but they often intermingled because of the strange practice they had of two men being mated to one woman.

"How does that even work?" I asked, when he explained it to me as we were docking the small shuttle in a parking area not far from the doctor's office. "They just have a three-way marriage and nobody ever gets jealous? That's hard to believe."

"It works because of the psychic bond between them," Kristoff had explained. "When they are very young, two compatible males find each other. They have some kind of medicine or plant which binds them together — I'm not sure exactly what it is. Anyway, they make a ceremony of it and from then on, the two of them are never parted."

"Aww, that's kind of sweet — like promising to stay with your best friend all your life," I remarked. It made me think of Leah and Zoe — I would have gladly promised to stay with them my whole life. It was too bad we'd had to go our separate ways — I missed both of them badly.

"There is a practical side to this 'sweet' partnership," Kristoff said dryly. "A female on Denaris will not mate a lone male because one male alone cannot form a bond with her or sire her children. Their DNA is such that two are required."

"Really? That's fascinating," I had remarked. "I wonder how the two guys in the relationship get along once they add the female in, though."

"Very well, actually," Kristoff said mildly. "One of them almost always has an alpha type personality while the other male is more beta. The alpha is the breadwinner, working outside the home to support the family while the beta stays at home to help with child-care and chores around the home. This leaves the female free to choose if she would rather have an outside career or simply stay home."

"Wow — what a great setup!" I had exclaimed. I knew many women who would give anything to have that flexibility, not to mention more help around the house.

"The Denarins think so," Kristoff had said mildly and that had been the end of the conversation because we were trying to find Dr. Churika's office.

I had been intrigued by the possibilities and now, as I looked out the window of the Dr.'s waiting room, I wondered about the Denarins I saw passing by. It was true that they most often seemed to be in groups of three — two males and one female. The male's skin tones varied widely, mostly seeming to fall in the spectrum of greens and blues. The females, on the other hand, mostly had pale, pearly gray skin.

It was fascinating to think that these people's biology had

developed in such a way as to make the two male/one female construct not only possible but vital to their survival. The bond between the males must be incredibly strong with no jealousy whatsoever…

"I tell you, I'm not sharing a female with *him!*" a deep, rough voice shouted, interrupting my thoughts. "He is from the Fang Clan and my sworn enemy."

"I have no wish to share with you either—or any of the Claw Clan," spat back an equally deep, though somewhat smoother voice.

Two large alien males, both over seven feet all, stormed out of the swinging silver metal door. They were followed by a tiny little female with pearly gray, wrinkled skin.

"Gentlemen, please," she said, frowning. "I am well aware that you were bonded accidentally, but as neither of you has any other prospects for finding a bond-partner, maybe you should try to make the best of the situation."

"You want us to make the best of this…this *fucking mess?*" demanded the one with the rougher voice. He had deep blue skin and light green eyes that snapped angrily.

"Mind your language you cretin—there are ladies present," hissed the other one, who had light green skin and deep blue eyes. "Off-worlder ladies, too—if I am not much mistaken." He eyed me with interest. "How do you do, *ma 'frela?*"

"She's fine," Kristoff said shortly, stepping in front of me. "And she's not in any way available."

"Forgive me." The green-skinned alien gave a short, polite bow. "It's just that my *companion* and I…" Here he threw a disgusted glance over his shoulder at the blue-skinned alien who glared back at him. "Were told that we could only be parted through the intervention of an off-worlder female. Specifically, one from a Closed Planet—a Pure One."

"I'm from a Closed Planet," I said, before I thought about it. Kristoff had told me as much when he explained about the Ancient Ones, the Twelve Peoples, and fact that I was a *La-ti-zal.*

"You are?" the blue-skinned alien asked eagerly.

"She's also *completely unavailable,*" Kristoff repeated, frowning at him.

"We have no interest in your female—or any female, for the purpose of mating her," the green-skinned alien said. "It's just that we were accidentally bonded at a clan-gathering." He glared at his companion. "And a wise-woman told us that the only way to break that bond would be to find a Pure One."

"And *I'm* telling you that's superstitious nonsense," the older woman with the gray skin who had followed them out, said, frowning. "Once you're bonded, you're bonded and there's nothing anyone can do about it. Look..." She put a hand on each of their arms. "I know you're from rival clans and you've both been loners all your lives, but a bond could not have formed between you if there wasn't some natural affinity there. Can't you just *try* to accept it?"

"Never," growled the blue-skinned alien. "I'm *not* gonna fucking accept being psy-bonded to a Fanger!"

"And I would sooner drown myself in the Green Hole as tie myself for life to a male of the Claw Clan," the green-skinned one said, frowning. He looked at Kristoff. "Could you give us the coordinates of the Closed Planet where you acquired your female?"

Kristoff glared at him. "I did not just *acquire* her—I am in her service. And I do not propose to tell you where you can 'get' one of her kind. Females should be protected—not exploited for your personal needs."

"Fine," the blue-skinned one growled. "We'll find it ourselves."

"Wait," I said, standing. The waiting room was so crowded with tall alien males I felt a little like a kid at a gathering of adults.

"Yes?" the blue-skinned one said roughly. "You have something to say?"

"I just...I wanted to know what you were going to do with...with the girl when you found her," I said.

"Nothing untoward, I swear to you, *ma 'frela*," the green-skinned alien said smoothly. "According to the wise-woman we visited, it would be enough to simply have her lay her hands on each of us at once. That alone would sever the tie between us and we could all go our separate ways."

"And...you wouldn't hurt her?" I persisted. "Or...abuse her?"

"What do you take us for?" the blue-skinned alien spat. "We might not be as into female-worship as the Majorans." He gave Kristoff a dismissive glare. "But we're still followers of the Goddess of Mercy. Females are to be cherished—not harmed."

"So…you just want to find a girl who can lay her hands on both of you at once and then you'll let her go?" I persisted, making sure that was all they wanted.

"That is all—we *swear*." The green-skinned alien looked at me earnestly. "And if we cannot find such a female to help us, we will be bound together in an unhappy and unwanted partnership forever." He threw another unfriendly glance at the blue-skinned male who glared back at him.

"All right." I took a deep breath, hoping I was doing the right thing. "Then…I'll touch you."

"My Lady—no!" Kristoff was already trying to get between me and the two of them.

"Kristoff, it's just a touch!" I said but to my surprise, the green-skinned alien was shaking his head.

"Forgive me, *ma 'frela*, but the touch must come from an unmated female who is not spoken for by another male in any way."

"He's right," the blue-skinned one said reluctantly, as though it pained him to agree with his companion about anything. "And I can smell from here how thoroughly your male has marked you."

I glanced at Kristoff, feeling a blush rising to my cheeks and saw him look back at me. I turned hastily back to the two alien males.

"Well, I still want to touch you," I told them stubbornly. When Kristoff started to protest again, I cut him off. "It's the only way, Kristoff," I told him. "The only way I can *know* for sure if they're telling the truth about not hurting the girl they want to find to help them."

"Yes, of course, my Lady…I see." He nodded reluctantly and stepped aside.

I stepped up to the two big males and held out my hands. The blue-skinned alien started to step up first but I shook my head.

"No — both of you. Both at once."

I don't know why it seemed important to touch both of them at once, but somehow I knew it was the only way I could get an accurate reading on them.

Silently, both of the big males held out their hands to me. I took them both at once, the green and the blue, and concentrated hard.

And then, just as I had when I touched Kristoff, I *knew*.

I got a rush of impressions — a huge grizzly bear-like creature roaring under the moon at night, a coiled snake-animal hissing in the dessert sand, and a deep feeling of reverence for females coming from both of them. These two would cut off their right hands before hurting a woman, I was sure of it. And I also felt their misery at being tied together in a partnership neither one had looked for or wanted. It seemed a shame they would be stuck together for life if they couldn't find someone to help them.

"All right," I said at last, releasing their hands and taking a step back. "Kristoff, you can tell them."

He sighed. "They probably would have found the Earth anyway — the Commercians are starting to advertise for their damn Alien Mate Index now to bring more customers in."

"The Commercians?" I frowned. "You mean the blue worms? The same ones that were trying to contact me?"

"The same." Kristoff nodded. "My Lady, why don't you keep your appointment with Dr. Churika while I speak to these two males." He nodded at the two large aliens who were waiting eagerly, now that I had okayed giving them the coordinates to Earth. I just hoped I had done the right thing — but my touch-sense had never given me false information and I trusted it now.

"Come." The older woman with the gray skin held out her hand to me. "If you would follow me?" she asked. She was wearing a long white robe that looked more like something a priestess would wear than a doctor's outfit.

"All right." I tried to smile, although I was feeling nervous at the idea of being examined. Don't they say that doctors make the worst patients? Well, they're right about that, at least in my case. Still, there was nothing else I could do.

I nodded once more at Kristoff and followed the doctor

through the door into her exam area.

Chapter Sixteen

Charlotte

"So how long have you been having these symptoms?" Dr. Churika eyed me suspiciously and frowned as she took my pulse.

So far she had looked at my eyes and ears, listened to my heart and lungs, and had wrapped some kind of full-length sleeve thing around my arm which I thought might be taking my blood pressure. It wasn't that different from having an exam back home except I wasn't sitting on an exam table. Instead, I was in a tank, up to my waist in some kind of pale green slime.

I wasn't very happy about the slime-tank, which I'd had to remove my clothing to get into, but Doctor Churika had assured me it was the only way she could get accurate readings on a *La-ti-zal*. Since Kristoff trusted her, I was willing to go along with the strange alien exam—but it still felt beyond weird to be standing there talking to her normally, as if I wasn't halfway immersed in warm green slime.

"I've been having symptoms about twelve to fifteen hours by now, I guess," I said. "I mean, it was last night when I was doing my shift in the ER that I started feeling hot. But my fellow intern took my temperature and found that it was below normal. In fact, I was verging on hypothermic. Later I started having shortness of breath—a feeling like something was strangling me until I couldn't breathe." I shivered at the awful memory. Thank goodness those symptoms hadn't come back!

"Mmm-hmm." Dr. Churika nodded thoughtfully and made some marks with a stylus on a thin, lighted pad which looked a little like a tablet except it was clear with a gold edge all the way around it. "And are you still experiencing any of these symptoms?"

"No—not since Kristoff, uh, held me." I cleared my throat, feeling awkward. It seemed like a strange treatment for any kind of sickness but it had certainly worked. "Um, he did a sensitivity test on me this morning," I volunteered, as she continued scratching on her tablet. "He seems to think I'm past the withdrawal stage of my cycle and into the, uh, *needing* stage."

"Is that so?" She looked at me sharply. "And what *exactly* did he do to you?"

"Nothing that's any of your business," I snapped, stung at both the nosiness of her question and the accusing tone she'd asked it in.

She frowned. "Your Majesty, as the personal healer to the Goddess-Empress I assure you *everything* about you is my business."

"But...but I can't *really* be the new Empress, can I? I mean, that's so bizarre!" The unreality of the whole situation hit me again. "I was born on Earth so how can I be a clone of the old Empress?" I demanded.

"Not clone—*Incarnation*," Dr. Churika corrected me sternly. "Between twenty and thirty cycles before the Goddess-Empress ascends to the Heavens, her next incarnation is born. For a time, they share a soul and both have the unique rainbow aura. When the present Goddess-Empress makes her Ascension to the Heavens, her incarnation is old enough and wise enough to rule in her place."

"And you're *sure* I'm the one?" I said.

"Kristoff is sure," she said firmly. "And he has the Vision—the ability to see the Goddess-Empress's rainbow aura. Besides, you look so much like the old Empress you could be her daughter. Not that she had any—there were only sons born of her union and I'm afraid none of them turned out very well. Such a shame." She shook her head.

"So...I'm genetically related to her in some way?" I asked. "I'm just trying to understand this. How can that be since I was born on Earth?"

"You share some DNA with the old Empress—most importantly a recessive gene—the royal or golden gene—which only one female in the galaxy may possess at one time. Except for the times during which your life overlaps with your predecessor and your successor," she added. "As to how you turned up on some backwater Closed Planet almost no one in the civilized galaxy has heard of, I have no idea. Some say the Goddess herself plants the seed of life that will grow into her next mortal avatar. But she chooses only the most worthy of vessels. Was your mother a female who was pure of heart?"

"I was adopted," I admitted reluctantly. "So I never knew my biological mother."

She grunted and made another mark on her pad.

"So...what does all this mean?" I said, feeling frustrated at the lack of information about the situation I found myself in. "What do I do now?"

"Now?" She looked up. "You'll go to Femme One, pass the Trials of Ascendancy, choose a Consort from among those royal males deemed worthy by the Council of Wisdom, and rule the galaxy."

"But...what if I don't want to?" I asked. "What if I just want to go back to Earth and finish my training to become a doctor?"

"If you want to be a healer, I'll train you myself," she said, nodding approvingly. "But my dear, there are many, *many* more lives you can touch and heal by being a good and wise Empress than by just being a healer."

I sighed. "Now you sound like Kristoff."

"Listen to him," she said firmly. "He was Sundalla the 999th's most trusted confidant and Guard. If she asked him to protect you, he'll do it even if it means giving his life. He won't play you false."

Her words confirmed my gut feelings about Kristoff but I had more questions—so many more.

"Tell me more about the whole Consort thing," I said, trying to pick my words carefully. "Is it...really necessary?"

Her faded eyes widened.

"Necessary? To have a Consort?"

"Right." I nodded. "I mean, if the Empress is the one who calls the shots—the one in power—then why does she have to have a man by her side at all?"

She snorted and shook her head, as if I'd just said something incredibly stupid.

"A Consort is necessary to slake the divine lust which will come upon you once your *needing* is ended and the *breeding* part of your Royal Cycle has begun," she said, frowning. "Only the seed of the proper male will be able to quench the fire you feel inside."

"But how can we be sure that's really going to happen?" I said. "I mean, I'm supposedly in the *needing* phase right now and I feel fine." Which was a bit of a white lie—the tingle I'd felt earlier was already growing. But I was so used to not having any sex drive at all, it seemed impossible that something which had always been inconsequential to me could somehow dictate my life.

"The needing you're feeling now isn't a true needing," Dr. said dismissively. "Nor was the withdrawal you had. That was just because you very foolishly gave Kristoff a transfusion of your own blood. The Goddess-Empress should only give her blood during the Culling ceremony in order to pick a true, royal Consort. Once you do that, you'll enter your true cycle and understand the need for a male to quench your lust."

"I gave Kristoff my blood because he was my patient and he needed a transfusion," I said stiffly. "I had no idea about any of this Goddess-Empress stuff but even if I had, I *still* would have given him the transfusion."

"Careful, my dear." The old doctor frowned at me. "What you're saying is only a hair's breath from blasphemy. The Goddess-Empress must *never* knowingly give her blood to a commoner."

"Kristoff isn't a commoner," I argued, beginning to get really pissed off. "Or even if he is, so what? He came to me and protected me before I even knew I was in danger. He followed me and refused to leave me alone even when I thought he was crazy for telling me I was supposed to be the Empress. He's saved my life multiple times—you can't tell me he's not qualified or worthy to have a transfusion of my blood!"

"Easy, child…" A small smile appeared at the corners of her mouth. "You sound like my Lady-Goddess Sundalla the 999th. She was always very adamant about her causes as well."

"Kristoff isn't a 'cause,'" I said, frowning. "As far as I can tell, he's my only friend in this whole mess. The only one who isn't trying to kill me or control me in some way."

"And that will be doubly true once you reach Femme One," she said, apparently unconcerned by my words. "But though he is a good and faithful guard, a guard is all he can ever be to you. I know the blood you gave him makes you feel drawn to him, but you'll get over that in a day or so once your blood has left his system."

"A day or so?" I raised my eyebrows at her. "Transfused blood should last a minimum of thirty to sixty days in a host body and it *can* last as long as one hundred and twenty days."

"Not the blood of the Goddess-Empress," she said dismissively. "Its special essence is absorbed into the host body in a day or so and then it becomes as normal as the host's blood. So don't worry, my dear—the drawing sensation you feel towards Kristoff will fade very soon."

"And then what? You think I'll treat him like dirt just because you say he's not good enough for me?"

I didn't know why I was getting so upset about this—it was pretty much what Kristoff himself had been saying to me from the moment we met—that he was just my guard and could never be anything else. But I've never liked elitist bullshit and I wasn't having it now.

"All I'm saying is you must have a *Royal* Consort, child," Dr. Churika said frowning. "Bear that in mind and don't do anything you shouldn't with your guard."

I thought guiltily of the way Kristoff had helped me pleasure myself and how good it had felt to come in his arms. Of how safe I had felt when he held me the night before and I talked to him about things I'd never told anyone else before. Would I really lose all the good feelings I had for him once the special essence in my blood was completely assimilated into his system? It didn't seem possible but the doctor seemed to take it as a matter of fact, not even open to discussion.

"You're silent," she said grimly, interrupting my troubled thoughts. "Which I take it means you've already done things you shouldn't."

"Anything I have or haven't done is none of your business," I said firmly, tired of listening to her crap. "I'm an adult and a doctor myself, you know. I don't have to put up with this kind of condescending treatment. In fact, I want to get out of this...this *slime* tank right now!"

To my surprise, she smiled again.

"Ah—so much like your predecessor! Come out and get dressed then." She nodded at my discarded scrubs. "Are those ugly, baggy garments *really* what healers wear on your home world?"

"They're called scrubs and they're very comfortable and practical," I said stiffly, clambering awkwardly over the high side of the tank and taking the towel she offered. To my surprise, I didn't have to use it much at all. The slime slid off my skin and went back to the tank, leaving hardly a trace behind when I got out of it.

Dr. Churika made a *tsking* sound with her tongue and shook her head. "You'll have to get used to court finery once you get to Femme One and I'm afraid it's not *nearly* as comfortable as those ugly Earth clothes of yours."

I didn't know what to say to that so I just kept quiet and pulled back on my underwear and scrubs.

"As I said before, you're not truly in your Royal Cycle yet, so I'm not going to prescribe any kind of suppressant for it as I might for an Empress who was having difficulty between the onset of her *needing* and her joining with her chosen Consort. If you have difficulties or renewed desires, just remember that they will pass."

"But...what if they don't?" I asked, remembering the overwhelming need I'd experienced before Kristoff had helped me to help myself earlier.

"They will," she said firmly. "They'll only last another day at most I should think, if not less. But if you *do* experience a problem, I'll recommend that you go to the Royal House of Goddess Pleasures."

"The what?" I asked but she was making a few final notes on her pad and turning to go.

"Kristoff can explain," she said. "For now, you need to get to Femme One."

"Thank you," I said stiffly. I wanted to add that I had about a million more questions but I got the distinct sense she was dismissing me.

I would never treat a patient that way! I thought resentfully as she nodded and left the room. *I wonder what the hell Sundalla the 999th saw in her?*

Whatever it was, Kristoff must have seen it too. I heard Dr. Churika explaining her diagnosis and everything she'd determined to him out in the hall, which further pissed me off—what about patient confidentiality, damn it? What about my right to privacy?

Dr. Churika acted like I had lost that right the moment she decided I really was the Incarnation of the Empress. But I was still a person with feelings—just because I shared DNA with some exulted dead person on another planet didn't change that fact!

Lifting my chin, I stalked past them and went out to the waiting room. Let them talk about me all they wanted to—this was still my life and I was going to live it the way I wanted to.

I hoped.

Kristoff

Charlotte was quiet on our trip to Femme One but I could feel her troubled emotions through the bond we had formed when I gave her my vow. She was unhappy and worried—my skin itched to reflect her feelings but I suppressed the urge sternly, knowing she would not like it.

There was another emotion, too, buried so deeply under the others I could barely feel it. It was there though, and it was strong— a deep current of desire was building inside her.

I told myself uneasily that it was of no consequence—that it would pass. In fact, Dr. Churika had been certain that this false *needing* Charlotte was going through would be over in a day— maybe even less. Considering that the transfusion had taken place two nights before, she was surprised it was still occurring at all. I was too, to be honest—I was certain that at any moment I would feel an easing of the lust inside my new mistress and then neither of us would have to worry about her false cycle any more.

And yet...part of me didn't *want* to feel her lust and desire for me disappear. I knew it was foolish and wrong, but I already desired her as I had never desired a female before. Knowing she returned my feelings, at least for a little while longer, made my own desire more bearable somehow.

I wished I could tell her I knew of her need and offer to help her with it again. But I knew I could not. Even wishing to do it was wrong—as her Guard, I should want only what was best for her. And wanting to be with me wasn't for the best at all. In fact, it would complicate matters immeasurably if she was still having desire for me when we reached Femme One.

Speaking of Femme One, I was pushing the hyperdrive to the limit and beyond and the center of the galaxy where my new mistress would rule was rapidly getting closer.

In only a solar day and a night we were there. I will add that Charlotte slept alone that night. And I let her, though I felt her longing for me through our bond. She wanted me to hold her again—I could see it in her eyes when I bid her goodnight as clearly as I felt it through our connection. But she was too proud and strong to ask and since her *needing* had not reached a fever pitch again, there was no reason to sleep in the same bed again.

Though I wanted to—the Goddess knows I did. I wanted so badly to hold her in my arms I ached with it.

But my needs were not important. What was important was transporting my new mistress safely to Femme One and allowing her feelings for me to fade and that was exactly what I intended to do.

When we finally reached orbit around the great, golden globe that is Majora Prime or Femme One, I told Charlotte to strap into the copilot's seat beside me.

"Wow," she breathed as we got nearer and nearer to the sprawling, gilded palace complex. "Is all that the palace? It looks more like a small city!"

"The palace doesn't only house the Goddess-Empress," I told her. "The Council of Wisdom who help her govern and make decisions all make their homes there. Also most of the Royals and some of the greater nobles. Not to mention all the support personnel—the maids and cooks and footmen and gardeners and many, many others who are on the palace staff."

"I thought you told me your mother was a noble," she said, casting a glance at me.

Though she was still in the baggy "scrubs" she'd been wearing on Earth, she'd had a sonic shower and had let down her hair. It hung down to her shoulders in a profusion of golden waves and her eyes looked very green. She was beautiful, though it was not my place to tell her so.

"My mother was a *lesser* noble and she wasn't even a native of Femme One," I told her, frowning. "Such distinctions are important—rank is everything at Court. I am considered a commoner by Royal standards."

"What—is there some kind of a caste system here? Are you untouchable just because you're only lesser nobility?" she demanded.

"Only untouchable to you, my Lady," I told her gently.

She blushed scarlet and looked away, making me regret my words. But I could feel her desire for me growing and I knew it was important to put some distance between us—even though it was the last thing I wanted to do.

As my mistress was being quiet, I concentrated on piloting the ship. I had decided to get as close as I could in stealth mode. Whoever had ordered and paid for the extremely expensive assassin-droids was doubtless waiting for news of our arrival. I needed to get Charlotte in to see the Council of Wisdom and have her declared the True Incarnation as soon as possible. After she was given official status at Court, it would be much harder to have her killed. Until then, our situation was going to be precarious at best, extremely dangerous at worst.

I got as close as low orbit before someone finally hailed me on the com-u.

"Unidentified craft," a vaguely familiar voice barked. "You are in violation of Femme One airspace. State your ID and intentions at once."

"This is Imperial One," I responded. "Y'lex is that you?"

"Captain Verrai?" the voice sounded startled. "We thought you were lost!"

"Lost?" I frowned. "Didn't T'zorin and the rest of my crew tell you I was on another mission?" *Someone* had known I was gone and what I was looking for—I was sure of it. Otherwise, why send the assassin-droids?

"T'zorin only returned a few solar days ago with the

Assimilation vessel you captured, Captain," Y'lex said. "They were attacked by pirates—he was the sole survivor. He's pretty shaken up."

"I see." I frowned, not liking what I was hearing. All the males I'd taken with me were hand-picked Imperial Guards with years of experience. Their loss would mean a hole in the ranks it would be difficult to fill. And with the new Empress to protect, it was a bad time to be short-handed.

"Do you want clearance to land?" Y'lex asked me.

"Yes, but not in the main docking bay," I said. "I'm going to the Empress's private hanger, near the Royal apartments."

"Yes, Sir, Captain." I could almost see Y'lex saluting. "Clearance granted."

"Good. And Y'lex—keep this quiet," I told him. "I don't want anyone knowing I'm here."

"Yes, Sir." He sounded puzzled but obedient.

"Good—Verrai out," I said.

"Y'lex out," he replied. "Oh but Captain—one more thing. You'll want to hurry if you're going to make it in time."

"Make what in time?" I asked, frowning.

"The Investiture, of course," he said, sounding surprised. "Isn't that why you came back? The True Incarnation of the Goddess-Empress is going before the Council in just a few minutes. If you don't hurry, you'll miss it."

Charlotte gave me a shocked look and mouthed, *"What?"*

I only shook my head sharply at her.

"Oh, I'll make it," I told Y'lex. "Don't worry—I'll make it in plenty of time."

Chapter Seventeen

Charlotte

"What is he talking about the Investiture of the new Empress?" I asked as Kristoff flew the ship into a small, private docking area in the side of the massive, golden building. "How can that be when you said *I* was the Empress?"

"You *are* the True Incarnation of the Goddess-Empress," he growled, frowning as he finished landing us in a large, dark space. "Whoever is going before the Council is an imposter. We just have to prove it."

"How?" I asked but he was already taking me by the hand and leading me out of the spaceship.

"Come with me and be quiet," he ordered. "We're going to take the back way—the old Empress's private entrance to the Council chambers. Almost no one knows about it so we should be safe."

"But...we're in the palace now. Doesn't that mean we're safe?" I protested as he pulled me along.

We left the large, echoing docking area and came to what looked like a solid stone wall. Kristoff knocked on it in a certain rhythm, which caused the door to appear like magic. He pressed his palm to the door and it opened just wide enough for him to whisk me through it.

"We're not safe until the Council has declared you the True Incarnation," he growled. "And even then you're still in danger—only of a subtler variety."

The hidden door led into a vast apartment with no windows. It was decorated richly with big, bulky, expensive looking furniture—most of it painted gold (or maybe *made* of gold, which seemed more likely)—and all of it extremely ornate. Wow—was this supposed to be my new living quarters? It was a far cry from the cramped, messy apartment I'd had back on Earth.

I didn't have much time to admire my new digs though—Kristoff was already reaching behind a huge, heavy tapestry that seemed to depict some kind of a battle scene to tap on the stone wall behind it.

Another passage opened and he pulled me through it, leading me into a claustrophobically tight corridor. It was pitch black but Kristoff seemed to know exactly where he was going. Keeping a firm grip on my hand, he pulled me along at a run through the tight, black space which was dusty with disuse.

"Kristoff," I gasped, as we finally came to the end of the corridor. "What are we going to say? How can we prove I'm who you say I am?"

"It would be easier if even one of the Councilors had the Vision as I do," he growled. He appeared to be knocking and patting the wall—maybe looking for another hidden doorway. "Unfortunately, that's not the case. I am the only male in the past fifty cycles to be born with the gift and the Council won't just take my word for it—especially not if they've already been poisoned by the lies of another. Which they must have—I can't think of any other reason they would Invest any female as the True Incarnation without making her go through the Trials."

"But—" I began but a low curse from Kristoff cut me off.

"It's blocked," he growled. "Someone has blocked the entrance to the Council Chamber."

"What does that mean? Do we have to go all the way back?" I hoped not. I'd never been claustrophobic before but here in this tight, narrow, lightless space, my heart was pounding and my palms were sweating.

"No. Just back to the exit beside the official Council Chamber entrance," he said. "I don't like this."

"You think it was blocked on purpose?" I asked anxiously as he turned us around and led me down a twisting side corridor I hadn't noticed before because I can't see in the freaking dark.

"Possibly. Or maybe someone on the housework staff who didn't know any better put something across the entrance. Impossible to know—we'll just have to be cautious."

He kept a tight grip on my hand and soon we were standing in front of another wall—or I assumed we were since Kristoff stopped and started tapping and knocking again.

This time, a doorway swung open, letting in some much needed light and fresh air. I wanted to get out of the corridor in the worst way—I felt grimy from being in the cramped, dusty space and my heart was pounding like crazy—but Kristoff made me wait until he looked.

"All right," he said at last in a low voice. "I don't see anyone coming in either direction. We just have to go down the hall and turn right—the entrance to the Council Chamber will be right there. The guards will know me and let us enter. Come on."

He pulled me out into a large, golden hallway with colorful jewel-toned frescos on the walls and ceilings. There were fancy statues carved from some pure white stone with silver and gold streaks running through it and the floors were made of something black and shiny that might or might not have been marble.

It was extremely intimidating, especially considering I was wearing scrubs that had been fresh two days ago and I was dusty and dirty from our trip through the secret passage. I doubted that anyone would think I looked like the new Empress. They were more likely to think I was a scullery maid escaped from the kitchen. Wait—did they have scullery maids here?

My random thoughts were interrupted as we ran down the corridor and turned the corner. Ahead of us I could see two vast, carved double doors made of some rich, dark wood and accented with golden handles.

But standing between us and the doors was something that made my blood run cold.

It was a Majoran male, probably an inch or two shorter than Kristoff and he was holding a knife in one hand—a *bloody* knife.

Behind him were two crumpled figures in armor a little like Kristoff's—they must have been the door guards but now they were obviously dead.

"Hello, Captain Verrai." The Majoran blocking us from the Council Chamber doors had a mad glint in his eyes, which were bright red. "What have you got there?" he asked, nodding at me. "Would that be the new Empress? She who is to carry on the male oppression in the Ma*jor*an system?"

"Get away from the doors." Kristoff pushed me behind him and reached for his sword, all in one swift movement.

"Ah-ah-ah. I don't think you should try anything, Captain."

I'd been so focused on the long, bloody knife in his right hand, I hadn't noticed his left. Now he drew it out from behind his back and I saw he was holding a small, black sphere with two lights blinking on it—both of them green. As I watched, he lifted it over his head and pressed something on it. There was a click and one of the green lights turned red.

Kristoff's eyes widened.

"No," he said hoarsely. "You can't!"

"Oppressor! Oppressor of the males!" the bloody-handed Ma*jor*an shrieked at me. He pressed the sphere again and the second light turned red. Then he wound up like a baseball pitcher about to throw a curve ball.

Everything seemed to happen in slow motion.

Kristoff dropped his sword and drew a dagger instead. With a flick of his wrist he cast it, almost casually, towards the would-be assassin. I saw it bury itself to the hilt in the other man's throat. A gout of bright red, arterial blood spurted out, leaving a trail than ended just a few inches from my feet.

Then I couldn't see any more because Kristoff dropped to the floor, dragging me with him, and pinned me beneath his big body.

Being pinned beneath him wasn't cozy or comforting this time, as it had been during my bout with the Burning Blood. This time his molded breastplate dug into my back and I could hardly breathe with his huge, muscular weight on top of me, pressing me down against the hard, cold marble floor.

I didn't have time to protest though—there was a deafening roar and a blinding flash that seemed to fill the whole world. I shrieked in fear but the explosion was so loud, I couldn't even hear myself. I felt Kristoff stiffen on top of me, trying to cover me more, to protect me completely.

Then my breath ran out and everything went fuzzy around the edges—I think I might have grayed out for a little while because I don't remember what happened next.

All I know is that I woke up to a very anxious Kristoff kneeling beside me and patting my cheeks.

"My lady? Charlotte?" he was asking in a hoarse, worried voice. "Are you all right?"

"Are *you*?" I asked, and coughed. "You were on top of me when...when it went off."

"Charlotte!" He pulled me to him, enveloping me in a hug so tight it was hard to breathe. "I thought I'd lost you," he muttered, his deep voice thick with relief. "Oh, Goddess..."

Then the double doors of the Council Chamber were thrown open with a bang and at the same time, the sound of booted feet running along the corridor came from the other direction.

"Captain Verrai?" An anxious voice asked.

Kristoff released me, making sure I could sit up on my own before he turned to the guard who was speaking.

"T'zorin? What are you doing here?" he demanded.

"The sentries at the Council Room door didn't answer voice checks. I started this way and then I heard what sounded like a shock grenade by the Council door. You all right?" the guard asked, wide-eyed.

"Fine." Kristoff picked himself up and held out a hand to me.

As he pulled me up, I saw that the backs of his arms were speckled with tiny drops of blood. "No, you're not fine—you're hurt!" I exclaimed, reaching for him.

"Just a few contact wounds. They'll heal," he said, pushing my hands away when I would have examined him.

"Kristoff—" I began.

"What is the meaning of all this?" a voice roared.

Looking up, I saw a very old man with a long blue beard streaked with white standing in the center of the opened Council Room doors. He was wearing a black robe and a heavy gold chain encircled his neck. He was completely bald but his incredibly bushy blue eyebrows almost made up for his lack of hair.

"What's happening out here? Who dares disturb the Investiture of the True Incarnation?" he demanded in that same, loud and angry voice.

"I do, Head Councilor Tannus ." Kristoff threw back his shoulders and took me by the hand. "Because you're Investing the wrong female. *This* is the True Incarnation of the Goddess-Empress. This is Sundalla the 1000th!"

Chapter Eighteen

Charlotte

Have you ever had that dream? You know the one—where you're at a job interview or a really important meeting at work where you want really badly to impress everyone. And then you look down and realize you're completely naked?

That was what I found myself going through when Kristoff dragged me into the extremely fancy Council Room to stand in front of a bunch of enormously important-looking people—only it wasn't a dream.

No, I wasn't completely naked, but I wasn't exactly dressed appropriately either. My scrubs were tattered and dirty—streaked with dust and grime from our run through the secret passage. My hands were bloody and when I walked, I felt a squishing in my right sneaker.

Looking down, I saw that the would-be assassin's blood had somehow found its way to my scrubs and shoe while I was pinned under Kristoff on the floor. From the knee down my right scrub-leg was a dripping mess of scarlet and so was my once-white tennis shoe. When I walked, I was leaving one bloody footprint everywhere I went on the pale gold, expensive looking rug.

Had I thought I looked like a scullery maid before? Now I looked like a cross between a dumpster-diver and a refugee from a terrorist attack.

My head was still ringing from the explosion and I felt fuzzy with shock. I was a complete mess and yet I had to stand there in front of the Council of Wisdom, which consisted of twelve old men, all dressed in long black robes and looking every bit as scary as the Head Councilor, and try to look royal while Kristoff told them who I was supposed to be.

"I'm sorry, Captain Verrai." The Head Councilor had resumed

his seat, which was at the head of a large, horse shoe-shaped table that encircled half the room. It reminded me of those long, raised podiums they use during Congressional Hearings. "I'm sorry," he continued. "But the True Incarnation has already been found and brought forward."

"She cannot have been," Kristoff said angrily. "*This* female has the rainbow aura of the Goddess-Empress." He nodded at me. "She and no other is Sundalla the 1000th."

"So you'd have us believe." The Head Councilor frowned. "But as I said, we already have the True Incarnation."

"Whoever claims this is lying." Kristoff's eyes flashed. "Who 'found' her and brought her forward?"

"Why, I did, my good Captain Verrai."

A tall, thin *Major*an with angular features and sharp, cat-like eyes came forward. He had a long, curling, blue-black mustache that made me think of a pirate in an old movie and his hair was neatly coiffed into an elaborate swirl on top of his head.

"Morbain," Kristoff growled, glaring at the other man. "I might have known it was you. Was it you behind the three failed assassination attempts on the True Incarnation? The last one right before the doors of the Council Room?"

"That's *Prince* Morbain to you, *commoner*," the man with the pirate mustache snarled. "And I don't know anything about any assassination attempts. Why would I bother trying to get rid of your little…well, whatever this is…" He looked me up and down and sniffed derisively. "When I have found the True Incarnation and brought her forward myself?"

"And who did you find?" Kristoff demanded. "Let me guess— a female from your own household who you've had complete sway over since birth."

"Well, as a matter of fact, yes," Morbain said mildly. "But you know how it is—sometimes the sweetest blossom grows right at your very feet. You have only to bend over to notice it. So it was with my lovely Eucilla. Come forward, my dear."

He beckoned to a figure standing in the shadows at the corner of the room. She stepped forward, into the light, and I what I saw made my heart drop straight down to my bloody sneakers.

She was absolutely *gorgeous.*

Long waterfalls of platinum blonde hair reached almost down to her knees and framed a pair of vivid green eyes. She was tall — six feet at least, which made me feel like a runt. And she had a perfect figure — all long and lean and willowy — seriously, she could have been a super-model back on Earth.

She was wearing a jewel-toned turquoise gown that wrapped around her size-two body tightly and flowed down her non-existent hips like ocean waves. A little gold and diamond tiara pinned on top of her perfect hair completed the look.

And I had thought I felt grubby before.

"*This* is the True Incarnation of the Goddess-Empress." Prince Morbain extended his hands as if to show off the girl's perfect beauty. "I think it's rather obvious when you look at them together that your female must be an imposter," Verrai."

"No, it is not *obvious.*" Kristoff seemed to be hanging onto his temper with both hands. "Because I have the Vision. This female..." He gestured at the tall, perfect girl who was looking down her nose at me disdainfully. "Cannot be Sundalla the 1000th because she has no rainbow aura. In fact, she has no aura at all — she is not even a *La-ti-zal.*"

"So you say." Morbain's eyes flashed an angry red. "But I say differently — I too have the Vision. And I have seen the truth. Eucilla here is the new Empress."

"You have no Vision except for your own greed for power!" Kristoff snapped.

"You dare not speak so to me! *I* am a Prince of the Blood!" thundered Morbain but Kristoff ignored him.

Turning, he addressed the Council of Wisdom instead.

"Are you really prepared to believe this male?" he demanded. "After all the assassination attempts he plotted against his mother? After all his treachery and lies? His mother forgave him his duplicity and the attempts on her life, but I cannot and neither should you!"

I sucked in a breath at that — I couldn't help it. Suddenly Dr. Churika's words came back to me — something about how the old Empress had never had daughters, only sons and none of them were any good? Was this Prince Morbain really the son of Sundalla the 999th? And had he actually tried to have his own mother killed? How awful! It was like something out of *The Tudors* or maybe *Game of Thrones.*

"How dare you?" Morbain was spluttering with rage. "How *dare* you make such accusations? My mother is not here to protect you any more, Verrai! I'll have you strung up by your own guts for such treasonous talk!"

"It's only treason if it's not true," Kristoff growled.

He turned back to the Council.

"So Morbain finds a weak female he can bend to his will, dresses her up and brings her to Court. And you're set to crown her Empress without so much as putting her through the Trials of Ascendancy?"

"But Captain Verrai," the Head Councilor said, frowning, his bushy brows pulled low. "She *has* passed the Trials."

"What?" Kristoff looked at him in disbelief. "All three?"

"Well...no." For the first time, the Head of the Council looked a little uncomfortable. "But she passed the most important one — the Orb and Scepter. They flew directly to her hands and as Prince Morbain pointed out, there is no clearer indication of the True Incarnation than the affinity of the Royal objects for the Goddess-Empress."

"Prince Morbain pointed it out and you decided to go along with it?" Kristoff growled. "Which of you are on his payroll, Councilor Tannus? Answer me that! How much did he pay to have you vote to skip the other two Trials and move on to the Investiture?"

"Why...you...how dare you accuse us of accepting bribes?" spluttered the Head of the Council and many of the other Councilors started shouting too. But one on the end — a younger Majoran with mahogany skin and thoughtful brown eyes — stood up and banged the podium table they were sitting at for silence.

"Councilors — *Councilors!*" he shouted. When they were quiet, he turned to face them. "Captain Verrai has made some accusations here today," he said. "Accusations which cannot go unanswered."

"They most certainly *can* go unanswered," exclaimed Head

Councilor Tannus. "We can send Verrai to the deepest cell in the dungeon and throw his grubby little imposter out on her ear!"

"Careful, Head Councilor," Kristoff growled, stepping in front of me. "Anyone who lays a finger on my Lady will have it cut off. And as for 'throwing her out on her ear,' well, she'll be in the right position to do that exact thing to *you* when she's proved to be the new Empress."

"You seem very sure of your choice, Captain," the younger Councilor with brown eyes said.

"I am." Kristoff lifted his chin. "I would stake my life on it. She has the rainbow aura—no other does." He cast a contemptuous glance at the tall, gorgeous blonde girl who was standing beside Prince Morbain.

"Very well," the young Councilor said. "I submit to this Council that the word of Captain Verrai cannot be taken lightly. He served our past Empress, Sundalla the 999th faithfully for ten cycles and she never had cause to doubt him. Can we do less than to listen to him now?"

"*Why* should you listen to him—because he served my mother?" Morbain demanded. "She was half mad by the time he came into her service. Old and blind and crazy as a—"

But he didn't get to finish because Kristoff was suddenly right in front of him, a dagger blade at the other male's throat.

"You will not speak so of my old mistress," he growled, his eyes blazing with fury. I had never seen him so angry. "She was wisdom and dignity and beauty personified and she deserved a hell of a lot better than a miscreant like you for a son!"

"Get your hands off me, commoner!" Morbain demanded, but I thought his voice sounded shaky.

"I'm not touching you—my blade is," Kristoff said, his deep voice cold. "And I'll ask you to remember that speaking ill of the Goddess-Empress—even one who has Ascended to the Heavens—is an offense punishable by public flogging or even *death*."

"Enough!" the Head Councilor snapped, motioning at Kristoff. "You've made your point, Captain Verrai. It is the judgment of this Council that both your, uh, candidate..." He motioned at me with distaste. "And Prince Morbain's candidate shall both undergo all *three* Trials of Ascendancy tomorrow."

"All three? *Tomorrow?*" Morbain looked aghast. "But we'll have no time to prepare!"

I sort of felt the same way myself. What were these Trials, anyway? Were they anything like the MCAT—the Medical College Admission Test? If so, I would need a hell of a lot more than one night to get ready.

But Kristoff was shaking his head and glaring at Morbain.

"If your female is all that you claim, she will need no preparation," he growled. "Charlotte needs none."

"*Charlotte*, is it?" Morbain's blue-black eyebrows rose nearly to his elaborately coifed hairline. "You call the female you claim is the True Incarnation by her first name? How very *familiar* of you. Seeing that you swear she is the new Empress, I trust you're keeping your hands to yourself? You do remember that for a commoner to touch a Royal in *that* way is blasphemy, do you not?"

For the first time, I saw Kristoff falter. At least, his cheeks went briefly red. Then he seemed to collect himself and his skin went back to tan with a tinge of gold.

"My Lady is the True Incarnation," he said, not answering Morbain's implied accusation. "And we will prove it tomorrow." He turned to the Council. "I ask that my Lady be granted the rights, privileges, and securities due to her station and that she be installed in the Royal Apartments both for her safety and as a sign of her status."

"Absolutely not!" Morbain roared. "My sweet Eucilla belongs in the Royal Apartments! Not that tattered little tramp Verrai dragged in here."

"Hey—" I began but the Head Councilor was already speaking.

"No one shall be installed in the Royal Apartments until we determine who is the True Incarnation!" he shouted. "For now, both candidates will spend the night in the Guest quarters."

"Head Councilor, the Guest quarters are difficult to defend," Kristoff protested. "There have already been three assassination attempts against my Lady's life in the past three solar days!"

"Then you must keep a good eye on her, Verrai," the Head

Councilor snapped. "And hopefully bring her to the Trials tomorrow in one piece."

Both Kristoff and Morbain started to say something else but the Head Councilor picked up a heavy looking pink crystal the size of my fist and pounded on the desk.

"Dismissed!" he shouted and that was that.

Chapter Nineteen

Kristoff

I took Charlotte by the hand and left the Council Room with a red haze of anger clouding my vision.

I wasn't surprised that Morbain had dared to bring forth an imposter — though it was an outrageous act of blasphemy, it was no more than I expected of the lying bastard. But that he dared to insult my old mistress, Sundalla the 999th and then threaten my new mistress... It was almost more than I could bear. Only knowing that I would be thrown in confinement where I would be unable to attend and protect Charlotte had kept me from slitting his filthy throat.

"Captain — what can I do?" It was T'zorin at my side looking anxious as we strode along the main hallway. Someone had already cleaned up the exploded remains of the would-be assassin — that was something, at least.

"Go ahead of us and do a complete sweep of the Guest quarters," I said. "Look for bombs, bugs, remote access devices — anything that could be harmful."

"At once!" T'zorin saluted but before he could leave, I put a hand on his arm.

"T'zorin," I said. "The trip back to Femme One with the Assimilation vessel — what happened?"

His eyes shifted uneasily. "Pirates, Captain! We barely got away with the ship intact and I...I was the only one who survived."

I could see his discomfort but there was something about his eyes that made me uncertain. I wanted to ask him more but just then Charlotte faltered and nearly fell.

"My Lady!" I turned and caught her before she could hit the floor.

"Sorry..." Her voice was a whisper. "Just...dizzy. I shouldn't have skipped breakfast, I guess."

"Skipped breakfast?" Then I remembered how I had offered her some nutrient paste for first meal, which is what most Imperial cruisers are stocked with, and she had refused it, saying she was too nervous to eat. But I didn't think that simple hunger was the only thing causing her faintness.

She'd been through a lot today—not the least of which was standing by my side as we faced down the Council of Wisdom— half of which I was willing to believe were in Morbain's pocket. Her face was smudged with dust and grime and her scrubs were splattered with blood—mine and the would-be assassin's.

She still looked beautiful.

"My Lady," I murmured, settling her more comfortably in my arms. "Let's get you to a safe place to dine and bathe and relax. You'll feel better soon, I promise."

"Hope you're right." Her eyes closed tiredly and she let herself relax against my shoulder. "Could hardly...feel worse."

"You care deeply for her, don't you?"

I looked over to see T'zorin looking at us with an unreadable expression on his face. I frowned.

"She is my mistress—and yours, T'zorin," I said sternly. "After her Investiture I'll have you and the rest of the Imperial Guard come to swear your vows. Spread the word among the other warriors— Sundalla the 1000th has arrived and she must be protected at all costs."

"Yes, Captain." He saluted again. "I'll go ahead to clear the Guest quarters now."

"Do that." I cradled Charlotte tenderly in my arms. "And have some refreshments sent for my Lady. She'll need her strength for tomorrow."

Charlotte

I faded in and out of consciousness as Kristoff carried me through the halls of the palace. I had a blurred impression of immense wealth—lots of marble columns, expensive looking art work, ornate carving, and servants dressed in black and gold livery scurrying everywhere.

Can't believe I'm supposed to live here, I thought blurrily as one opulent part of the palace faded into another and then another and yet *another.* It was as though someone had told me I was suddenly going to go live in Buckingham palace and not just live there—be the queen of the whole place.

How in the world could the Goddess-Empress deal with such a huge living arrangement? Then again, she wasn't just dealing with the immense city-sized palace and all the people who lived in it, she was also responsible for all the people on all the planets in the entire *galaxy.*

It was mind-blowing.

No, not she—you, whispered a little voice in my brain. **You're** *responsible, Charlotte so you better figure out how in the hell you're going to manage because this is getting awfully real awfully fast.*

God... I closed my eyes tightly, wishing I could faint again. But now that my brain was working—whizzing along with worry and uncertainty—unconsciousness refused to come back. I still felt weak from hunger and shock and I had the feeling that at some point in the future I was going to have some kind of freak-out due to nearly getting blown to bits by an assassin's bomb—but for now I was wide awake.

"Here we are, my Lady," Kristoff murmured as we entered a side corridor off the main hallway. There were several widely spaced doors and he took me to the farthest one at the end of the short passage.

The door, which was spotless white trimmed with gold, opened and a male servant wearing a black and gold uniform bowed us inside.

"This way, my Lord Captain," he said in a formal tone. "The quarters have been made ready as requested."

"And they're all clear." The other guard Kristoff had called T'zorin came out of one of the side rooms.

"Good." Kristoff looked down at me. "Are you well, my Lady? Can you stand?"

"I'm all right," I said, trying to make my voice sound normal. "I was just a little faint there for a minute—that's all."

He set me gently on my feet but kept an arm around my shoulders for support, which was nice. I leaned against him, feeling like he was my only friend in the whole, huge palace.

Friend...or something more?

I pushed the thought away and looked around. The Guest quarters weren't as opulent as the Royal Apartments which Kristoff had brought me through but they were still nicer than any hotel room I'd ever been in.

There was a round, brick fire-pit in the middle of a sunken living area, surround by low couches upholstered in some kind of lush, pale gray fur. Beside one of the couches someone had placed a little rolling, silver trolley bearing a selection of what looked like Majoran food.

I assumed it was food, anyway, but I couldn't be sure because all Kristoff had to eat on his ship were tubes of bland nutripaste. The paste was supposed to offer all the nutrition a full grown warrior needed for an entire day but it tasted like gummy, meat-flavored cardboard.

The elegant looking finger-foods arrayed on golden dishes were a far cry from the bland, meaty paste. I saw what looked like little round blue sandwiches with pink and purple filling, some flaky orange and yellow pastries as big as my fist that were completely square and some long, thin, straw like things with turquoise and fuchsia striping along their length. I didn't know what they were but I was so hungry I would gladly take a bite and find out. There was even an elegant looking mug with a golden rim and steam rising from the liquid inside.

My mouth started to water—despite all the craziness I'd been through recently, I realized I was really *hungry*. Also, that steaming cup was drawing me like a magnet. I knew the Majorans had probably never heard of coffee but any kind of hot, soothing liquid sounded good right now. Tea would be all right. So would soup.

"Is this for me?" I asked, as I stepped down into the sunken living area and went towards the snack trolley.

"Yes, my Lady. Of course. One of the undermaids just brought it from the kitchens." The servant in black and gold livery bowed elaborately to me, overlooking my crazy, dirty, disheveled appearance.

Kristoff was still talking to the other guard so I thanked the butler-guy and reached for the steaming liquid.

I could smell it even before I touched the elegant mug it was in. It had a sweet, slightly bitter aroma a little like hot chocolate. Mmm—I couldn't *wait* to taste it!

But just as I lifted the dainty mug, Kristoff looked up.

"My Lady, wait," he said urgently. "None of that has been tested for poison yet."

"Tested for *poison?*" I had been about to sip the delicious smelling liquid but now I pulled it away from my mouth abruptly.

It was a good thing I did. At that exact moment, the elegant mug shattered in my hand, spraying me with boiling hot liquid and incredibly sharp shards of glass.

I gasped and dropped what remained of the mug—mostly just the handle—on the polished hard-wood floor.

"Charlotte!" Kristoff was by my side in an instant. "Are you all right?"

"I don't know," I said and burst into tears.

Normally I'm not a girly-girl and I hate to cry in front of people but this was just too much. It was the freak-out I'd felt coming on and I have to say I didn't think I could be blamed for it. I'd nearly been killed so many times in the past few days it was ridiculous. From the two assassin-droids, to my close call with the Burning Blood disease, to the crazy activist guy with the bomb whose blood was still soaking my shoe, I'd been through a lot.

Having my mug explode like a grenade in my hand on top of everything else was just too much.

Through my tears I could hear Kristoff ordering everyone out of the guest suite. The prim and proper butler servant was apologizing again and again, sounding aghast at what had happened and the other guard, T'zorin, was saying that he was sorry he hadn't thought to check the food.

At last, though, they all left and Kristoff locked the door behind them.

Then he came back to me and peeled off my scrub shirt, pulling it carefully over my hair and trying not to let any of the sharp little shards cut me any more than they already had. He moved me away from the mess on the floor and took off my scrub bottoms too, and my blood soaked shoes and socks.

Through it all I stood there sobbing, tears pouring down my bloody, dirty cheeks as he stripped me to my underwear. Now that the tears had started, I didn't seem to be able to stop them—I didn't even try.

Kristoff sat me on one of the couches and kneeled in front of me to examine me.

"It's all right now, Charlotte," he murmured, softly but firmly, taking my face in both his big hands and looking me over for injuries. "You're all right, my Lady."

"I...I don't *feel* all right," I managed to gasp, through my tears.

"But you are." He looked at me seriously. "Thank the Goddess you only have a few scratches. If you'd actually brought that cup to your lips the explosion could have blinded you."

This made me cry even harder. To think that I was now living in a place where people came at me with bombs and my freaking coffee mug could explode like a grenade at any minute—it was *awful!*

"I...I don't want to be here," I managed to say at last. "I don't want to have to deal with this! I want to go home—go back to my old life on Earth!"

"I know, my Lady," Kristoff murmured. "And I am so very sorry but you can't."

He sat beside me and tried to put his arm around me but I pushed it off and buried my scratched and cut face in my hands.

"This place is horrible! We haven't even been here an hour and someone has already tried to kill me twice!"

"I suspect the mug wasn't so much an assassination attempt as a warning." Kristoff sounded grim. "Morbain wants us to know he's willing to do anything he has to in order to eliminate the competition."

"Who *is* he anyway?" I swiped at my eyes and looked up at him, finally regaining some control. "Is he really the, uh, son of your old boss? Of the other Empress?"

"He is," Kristoff said heavily. He sighed and ran a hand through his blue-black hair. "He has always desired the throne for himself though it is against a thousand generations of custom and religion to allow a male to sit upon the Golden Throne."

"Was he behind the crazy activist guy with the bomb too?" I asked. "What was he yelling about? The oppression of the Majoran males or something?"

Kristoff sighed. "There are a few malcontents—males who do not like the way our society works—the fact that most males worship their females as goddesses. They want a patriarchal society—or say they do, anyway. Most of them are just males who have been unable to bond with a female and they're bitter about it. But Morbain makes use of them, pretending he's sympathetic to their cause. I'm sure he thinks he could use their hatred as a stepping stone to gaining the throne."

"He seems like a horrible person," I said, wiping at my eyes again. "I mean, who tries to have their own *mother* killed?"

"It grieved my old mistress terribly." Kristoff looked sad. "She blamed herself—said that she had spent too much time ruling and not enough mothering her children. It was one of her deepest regrets."

"Well just because she didn't make it to all of his little league games is no reason to order a hit on her," I said sharply. "Or to try and blow up her successor. If I *am* her successor."

"You are, my Lady." Kristoff took my hands in his and looked earnestly into my eyes. "You alone have the rainbow aura. I wish you could see it as I do." He cupped my cheek in his big, warm hand and murmured, "It's so lovely. So perfect."

For a long moment I stared up into his shifting eyes, their colors changing so rapidly I could hardly track them. My heart seemed to stop in my chest and I felt myself wanting him—felt the desire I'd been trying to push down and ignore come bubbling up to the surface in an undeniable flood that threatened to swamp me. It had been days since the transfusion—why hadn't this longing I felt for him faded? If anything, it had grown stronger…

"Kristoff," I whispered hesitantly, leaning towards him. He leaned towards me too. He was going to kiss me—I knew he was. I could feel him wanting to and I *wanted* him to—so badly I could hardly breathe.

But then he looked away and dropped his hands.

"My Lady," he said, his voice becoming more formal and businesslike. "Perhaps you will feel better after you're bathed and fed."

I felt a surge of disappointment but I tried to cover it and sound unconcerned.

"Uh, a bath would be nice. But I think I've lost my appetite." I looked around him to the once-inviting snack trolley which was now littered with shards of glass.

"Nevertheless, I'll have something sent up along with a poison tester," he said. "You have to eat something—you must be strong for tomorrow."

"For the Trials of, uh…"

"Of Ascendancy," he said, getting up. "I know you must have many questions and I will do my best to answer them. But let me draw your bath first."

I sighed. "All right. I'm sorry I got so emotional there for a minute."

"My Lady…" His deep voice softened and he took my hand again. "You have every right to be upset. But I promise you, it will not always be like this. Once you're upon the Golden Throne, your status will keep you safe for the most part. And for rest, I will always be by your side. I swear I won't let you be harmed."

"Well…" I sighed. "I guess I'll have to take your word for it. I'm just scared right now, you know?"

"Of course you are. Frightened and hungry and tired. Let me draw your bath and we'll see if I can make you feel better."

"You don't have to wait on me," I protested as he rose and went towards one of the side rooms where the bathroom presumably was. "I can manage myself."

"Absolutely not." Kristoff looked scandalized. "The Goddess-

Empress does not bathe or wait upon herself."

"Wait...what? You're going to, uh, *bathe* me?"

The thought made me feel suddenly shy, even though I'd spent almost all of the night before last pressed naked against him. *And don't forget the way he held you in his arms and helped you come,* whispered a little voice in my head.

Yes, but that had been when the desire inside me was at a fever pitch—I had needed to come so badly I hadn't minded being on display, just as I had needed to breathe too badly during my bout with the Burning Blood to mind being pressed naked against his big, hard body.

But I was cured of the Burning Blood—or at least past that stage in my "cycle"—and though the sexual need was still growing inside me, it hadn't yet reached the fever pitch that would allow me to just toss all my clothes to the wind and not mind being intimately washed by my huge, muscular bodyguard. In fact, just the thought of it sent a hot shiver down my spine that was equal parts embarrassment and desire.

"Really," I said to Kristoff. "You don't have to do that. I've been bathing myself since I was five. I can manage."

"No you can't. Normally you'd have a female attendant for such matters but I trust no one at the moment." He looked grim. "And I am trained to such service, as well as to guard and protect you."

"You are?" I said and then remembered how he'd washed and folded my laundry back home. "Oh, I guess you are. But I mean, you really don't *have* to."

He frowned. "My Lady, there were two attempts on your life today. I want to check you over thoroughly and make certain I haven't missed any injuries you might have incurred."

"Well..." I bit my lip and shrugged. "Okay, I guess if you feel like you have to."

His eyes softened for just a moment.

"I *want* to, Charlotte," he said softly. "I want to serve you—to make you feel better. This has been a difficult day for you. Please, let me tend to you."

When he put it that way, I could hardly refuse.

"All right," I said, biting my lip. "If you really want to."

"I do." He turned and went into the other room, leaving me alone on the plush gray couch in my bra and undies trying to ignore the tingling of need that was turning into a throbbing between my thighs.

Chapter Twenty

Charlotte

I hadn't been sitting on the couch long, listening to the rushing of water in the other room, before I decided to try and get more comfortable. I started to stretch out and reached for one of the puffy cushions that littered the plush gray surface of the couch. When I moved it, something long and slender rolled into view.

It was a long, golden cylinder about the length of my forearm and the width of one of my fingers. It looked a little like a baton because it had two golden spheres on either end of it.

I started to reach for it, then I remembered the innocent-looking coffee mug. Heart pounding, I opened my mouth to call for Kristoff and that was when the strange golden rod came to life.

There was a buzzing hum and a screen that appeared to be made entirely of light suddenly projected out of it. The screen was about a foot long and two feet high and for a moment it was completely blank.

I didn't know what to make of it. Was this yet another assassination attempt? Should I be screaming my head off for Kristoff and diving under the couch?

Then it flickered and a small figure, about the size of a Barbie doll appeared on it, rendered in perfect 3-D. She was clearly someone important because she was wearing an expensive looking jewel encrusted gown and a crown on her head. She had blonde hair about the color of mine and deep green eyes.

"The Annals of Historical Preservation and Re-enactment present the history of Sundalla the 887th and her Chosen Guard," a small, tinny voice announced. "Now it came to pass that Sundalla the 887th of the line of the Goddess-Empress lost her chosen Consort and she was sorely grieved," it continued.

On the screen, the richly dressed woman buried her face in her hands as though she was crying.

"But Sundalla the 887th was still in her *needing* years," the voice said. "She did not wish to take another Consort but after a time, she cast her eye upon one of her Guards and he was fair in her eyes."

A new figure appeared on the screen—a tall, muscular male with the familiar gold-tinged skin. He had blue-black hair like Kristoff and the same changeable eyes too. The woman looked up at him and then reached to touch his cheek. The man took her hand and, very gently, kissed her palm. The looks they were giving each other were practically burning up the little screen they were projected on. Clearly she had the hots for him and just as clearly, he returned her feelings.

"And so the Council of Wisdom decreed that the Empress might take her Guard to use for her *needing* and thus the Empress made use of him, though he was not allowed to do more than serve her," the voice concluded.

On the lighted screen, the scene suddenly became X-rated. The Empress and her Guard were in bed and he had his hands over his head, gripping the headboard. He was gazing up with adoring lust at the Empress who was naked and sitting astride him. She was rocking her hips in a deep, grinding rhythm and it was clear that she was "using" him very thoroughly indeed. Her full breasts swayed, her nipples tight and pink and her mouth was shaped in to an "O" of pure pleasure.

"Oh my God!" I breathed, unable to pull my gaze away from the hot scene. How had this scroll gotten here and was it for real? I remembered Kristoff saying something about Sundalla the 887th and her Guard and how she was allowed to touch him sexually even though he couldn't touch her but somehow I hadn't pictured it quite so *graphically.*

"My Lady? Your bath is ready."

Kristoff's deep voice startled me and I gasped and tried to cover the incriminating scroll with a pillow. Panic made me clumsy and I only succeeded in knocking the damn thing off the couch and across the room. Not only that, the blow somehow turned up the sound effects. I could hear deep, masculine groans and feminine moans and panting along with the slapping sounds of really hot sex coming from the scroll now.

To my horror, it rolled *right up* to Kristoff's feet and stopped there, showing sex that would have done any porn site on the Internet proud.

"My Lady?" He looked up at me, his eyebrows raised. He had cleaned up some himself and he looked a lot fresher and more relaxed than he had before he disappeared into the bathroom. He had also taken off his breastplate and the metal parts of his uniform, leaving his broad chest bare, though he was still wearing his boots and the short, leather kilt.

He looks gorgeous, I thought.

And he looks like the guy on the porn scroll too, whispered a snarky little voice in my head. *And you look like the Empress on the scroll. Look at the way she's riding him!*

"I don't know where it came from," I said, nodding at the scroll, feeling my cheeks get hot with a blush. "It was just here on the couch and it popped on and then the voice said it was a historical document and it seemed okay until it suddenly went all porno and—"

"It's all right." He picked up the scroll and stared at it thoughtfully as the hot scene continued. "This is the holo-scroll we Imperial Guards are made to study before we take our vow to the Goddess-Empress."

"You...you are?" It was my turn to raise my eyebrows at him. "Do you, uh, expect to have to, um, *service* your Empress like that?"

Kristoff shook his head.

"No, but we are made aware that it is a possibility. We are dedicated to our Royal mistress heart, mind, and body—to use as she sees fit."

"Well I want you to know I wouldn't, uh, *use* you like that. I mean, unless you *wanted* me to, I mean," I said quickly. "I mean—"

"It's all right, Charlotte." He gave him a little half-smile. "Soon you'll have a Royal Consort and you won't even think of things like this." He nodded at the scroll in his hand where the Empress was now performing a position I was pretty sure was called "reverse cowgirl" on her guard, who was loving every minute of it.

"What if I do, though?" I dared to ask. "What if...what if it *was* somehow like that...between us, I mean?"

His eyes went suddenly half-lidded and he looked at me directly.

"Then it would be my pleasure to be at my Lady's service," he murmured.

I felt my breath catch in my throat and my heart started to pound. The desire inside me, which had been simmering just under the surface, suddenly spiked, making my nipples feel tight and achy. The place between my thighs was hot and swollen and I felt the *need* move through me like a wave.

"Kristoff..." I began but he did something to the scroll that shut it off.

"My Lady, your bath will grow cold," he said softly. "Will you come with me now and allow me to bathe you?"

"All right," I said, my voice coming out shaky. I started to stand but before I got two steps, Kristoff was there, sweeping me into his arms. "You don't have to carry me," I protested.

"But I want to. Besides, there are still shards of glass on the floor—I don't want you cutting your feet."

I couldn't argue with that. I allowed him to carry me into bathing room which turned out to be made of deep blue marble shot through with veins of pure gold. There was a big round tub on a pedestal in the center of the room made of the same stone. Over it hung a gorgeous chandelier that seemed to be made of a million tiny golden lights hovering in mid-air. How they stayed together and kept their shape, I didn't know but they made a soft, musical hum that was incredibly soothing somehow.

Kristoff carried me over to the steaming tub. There were three steps leading up to it and he placed me on the top one. Then he helped me remove my bra. I blushed and tried to cover my breasts as it came off but he shook his head.

"No, Charlotte," he murmured. "Don't hide yourself from me. Let me examine you and make sure you're all right."

I let my arms fall to my sides and bit my lip as he palmed my breasts, careful not to touch the sensitive nipples, as he examined me for cuts and abrasions.

There were a few places where the exploding mug had marked me but for the most part, I was okay. Kristoff frowned when he saw one long, shallow cut running from the inner slope of my breast, almost to my nipple.

"I'll put some healing salve on that after I've bathed you, my Lady," he murmured, tracing it gently. "There will be no scar—I promise."

"O...okay," I whispered, my tongue feeling clumsy and thick in my mouth. God, having his big hands on my bare breasts like this was driving me *crazy*. And even though he was being careful to avoid my nipples, I still felt his warmth and wanted more.

"You have such lovely breasts," Kristoff murmured as he finally finished his examination. "It would be a shame to let anything scar them."

"Th-thank you," I stuttered, feeling naked all over again.

And then he was kneeling before me and reaching up to hook his fingers in the sides of my panties. I blushed and held on to his broad shoulders as he brought them slowly down and helped me step out of them.

"So lovely, my Goddess," he murmured, still kneeling before me.

"I'm all dirty and scratched up," I protested. Not to mention I wasn't exactly a size two like my supermodel competitor for the throne. But Kristoff didn't seem to care.

"You're beautiful," he murmured. "And you'll feel better after I bathe you. Here—let me help you into the tub."

Rising, he took my hand and helped me step into the warm, steaming water. I hadn't noticed before but there were some kind of deep red pedals floating just on the surface. They perfumed the bath, giving it a sweet, slightly spicy scent that was instantly addictive.

"Mmm..." I moaned softly, letting myself sink into the tub. God, it felt *wonderful*. Much better than the weird sonic-shower Kristoff had in his spaceship. I could feel all the tension in my tired muscles leaking away, making me feel limp and peaceful.

"Feeling better?" Kristoff sounded slightly amused, as though he took pleasure in watching me relax and enjoy myself.

"Much," I admitted. "This is wonderful—thank you, Kristoff."

"You're welcome, my Lady. Now let's see to your hair."

Before I could protest, he had picked up a cup and was pouring the scented water over my hair. He was very careful not to get any in my eyes and after a moment I just relaxed and let him do it.

Next he scooped thick cream from a pink glass jar and rubbed it between his palms.

"Is that some kind of shampoo?" I asked, as he began to massage it into my hair.

"It will cleanse your hair and make it shiny and soft," he murmured, still working it into my wet hair.

I moaned softly at the delicious feeling of his strong fingertips massaging my scalp and washing my hair. God, he hadn't been kidding when he'd said he was trained for service as well as for combat—the way he was working the sweet cream into my hair with such firm yet gentle strokes felt *amazing*.

Kristoff seemed to realize I was enjoying his ministrations because he took a long, long time to finish washing my hair. At last, though, he rinsed my long, wavy strands until they were squeaky clean. Then he put something that looked like a pair of furry black gloves on his hands.

"What are *those?*" I asked, watching as he scooped a different kind of cream out of another jar and started rubbing his black-clad hands together to make a sweet-smelling lather.

"Bathing implements," he said blandly. "Would my Lady be so kind as to stand so that I may bathe her?"

"What? Why do I have to stand up?" I protested, feeling shy all over again.

"That I may bathe you properly," he murmured. "Please, my Lady."

"Well...all right."

Reluctantly, I stood up, dripping and covered all over with the scarlet petals. When I rose out of the water, Kristoff sucked in his breath, making me think something was wrong.

"What? What is it?" I looked down at myself anxiously.

"Nothing, my Goddess. You're just so *beautiful*." Kristoff's deep voice was slightly hoarse and the way he was looking at me, so intensely, made me blush.

"Thank you," I whispered, fighting the urge to try to cover myself. But though I still felt nervous to be naked in front of him, I also liked the feeling of his gaze on me—of those hungry eyes roaming over my body. It made me feel hot and desirable and beautiful, just as Kristoff had said.

"My Lady," he murmured. "May I wash you?"

"I'm all yours," I said, my breath coming out in a little gasp.

"If only you were," Kristoff murmured under his breath, so softly I almost didn't hear it.

"What?" I asked but he was already washing me.

He started at my shoulders and the nape of my neck and worked his way down my arms in long, clean strokes. He did the same for my front, palming my full breasts as he had before to wash them with gentle, circular strokes. This time, I noticed, he didn't avoid my nipples. Was it because he was wearing gloves? Or because the act of bathing me counted as "service" instead of sexual?

"Why are you allowed to touch me there now? To touch my, uh, nipples when you didn't before?" I heard myself asking. "Is it because you're serving me? By bathing me, I mean?"

"Naturally." Kristoff looked up at me. "Would you prefer I didn't touch you there?"

"No," I whispered. "I'd prefer if you did it *more*."

I didn't know where I got the boldness to say such a thing but I couldn't help it—the desire was growing in me and I wanted his hands on my body too badly to lie about it.

"My Lady," he murmured, plucking gently at my tight nipples with his long fingers. "I would not take advantage of you under the guise of service but since you asked for a deeper cleansing…"

"Ah—Kristoff! Yes, please!" I gasped, thrusting out my breasts for him to give him easier access. His gentle torture was sending sparks of pleasure straight down to my pussy, which felt swollen and hot.

He looked at me, his eyes hot and half-lidded.

"Does my Lady wish me to wash her lower?" he asked in that soft, deep voice of his.

"I...yes, I do." I whispered, biting my lip. *"Please, Kristoff."*

Without a word he began stroking his big warm hands down my sides and hips to reach my thighs.

I thought he would reach between my legs right away but he didn't. Instead he took his time, washing my back and legs and pelvis and belly gently, firmly, and *extremely* thoroughly until I thought I was going to explode.

"Kristoff..." I said, hearing the need in my voice.

"Yes, my Lady?" he murmured innocently.

"Please, I need..." I didn't know how to say it but he understood.

"I know what you need, Charlotte," he said, looking me in the eyes. And then finally —*finally* – he got to my pussy.

I moaned softly as one gloved hand reached between my legs to cup my sex. I was still standing up in the tub, the water up to my thighs and Kristoff was kneeling on the steps in front of me.

"Spread your legs for me," he murmured, looking up at me. "Let me bathe you."

"All...all right." I opened my thighs, feeling shaky and weak with desire. In fact, I was so shaky I had to lean forward and brace myself on one of Kristoff's broad shoulders.

"That's right, my Lady." He looked at me, his eyes filled with the same desire I felt myself. "Hold on to me if you need to."

His big hand in its soft, silky glove rubbed gently across my outer pussy lips. A moan caught in my throat as he washed me there and yet, after a moment a new moan rose—this one of frustration. Because though he was rubbing gently against my swollen outer mound, his long fingers still hadn't entered me to caress my heated inner folds, where I needed him most.

"Kristoff..." I begged. "Please, I need...I want..."

"As I said, my Lady, I would not presume to take advantage under the guise of service."

"But...but I need *more*." I heard the desperate, needy note in my own voice but I couldn't stop it somehow.

"I can only wash what is presented to me," he murmured, giving me a meaningful look. "Now if I was to be presented with *more...*"

I understood what he meant. Feeling shy and on fire with need at the same time, I straightened up and shook back my damp hair. Then I reached down and spread myself open for him, baring my throbbing clit as I had when he'd been teaching me to touch myself. Only this time I didn't want to do that—it was Kristoff's touch I yearned for—his touch alone I was burning up for.

"Ah, my Lady," he murmured hoarsely, his eyes on my aching clit, now proudly on display. "Your Goddess-pearl is so hungry—so swollen with need."

"It needs to be washed," I whispered, looking him in the eyes. "Please, Kristoff, wash me—serve me as I need you to."

"With pleasure, my Lady," he murmured.

And then his big hand found my sex once more, his long fingers in the silky black glove just cupping me at first but then dipping delicately into my wet folds to caress around and around my throbbing clit—though he still didn't touch it directly.

"*Please,*" I moaned, feeling half crazy with desire. "Please, Kristoff—I can't stand much more!"

It was true—I felt like my legs were made of spaghetti and I was going to fall over at any moment. I had to grip one of his broad shoulders again to stay upright.

"As my Lady wishes," he murmured and then, at last, the tip of one long finger found the swollen bud in the center of my folds and began to slide gently over it. From side to side he slid, back and forth over my aching clit—the gentlest motion imaginable and yet it filled me with pleasure so intense my knees almost buckled.

I gave a low cry and the hand I had braced on his broad shoulder fisted tight. Sparks of sensation leapt through me, igniting my body like a single spark from a campfire can ignite a whole forest. As Kristoff's fingertip continued its slow, teasing slide across my throbbing clit, I threw back my head, my hair hanging long and damp down my back and moaned without shame.

"Oh, *Kristoff!*"

"Gods, Charlotte..." Kristoff's deep voice was ragged and I

looked down to see that he was watching me, a hungry expression in his eyes. "You're so fucking *beautiful*," he growled softly. "And so close to coming... are you not?"

"Yes," I whispered. God, *yes."*

"Then come for me, my Goddess," he rumbled, his eyes filled with lust I felt echoed in my own body. "Come as I serve you."

"Ahh!" I gasped, my body obeying his command without question. "Oh, Kristoff —*yes!"*

After so much build up the orgasm was intense. I felt my body responding helplessly to his deep, commanding voice and the gentle but firm way he was caressing my clit. Not just responding, but going super-nova. My toes curled, my belly trembled, and my back arched. I had to grip his shoulders with both hands this time, to keep from falling.

Inside I could feel my inner muscles clenching and even in the midst of my pleasure I felt incredibly empty inside. I wanted something more — I needed to be filled. That emptiness and need hadn't become a burning, out of control force inside me — not yet. But I sensed that it would, some time in the future.

For Kristoff's part, he stayed with me, watching me hungrily as I came on his gloved hand, giving it up for him and calling his name as I pumped my hips shamelessly, trying to make the incredible sensation last. If my first orgasm at my own hands had been good, this one was infinitely better. Maybe because it was Kristoff touching me — Kristoff giving me the pleasure so intense I thought it would never end.

At last it did though, and I felt myself collapsing, panting and gasping, into the still-warm water.

Kristoff caught me and lowered me gently, letting my head rest on the edge as the soothing liquid lapped all around me. He stripped off the gloves without a word and rinsed me, his bare hands on my flesh this time, deliberate and possessive.

I purred with sleepy pleasure and arched under his touch as he cupped and stroked my breasts and caressed gently but firmly between my thighs. *This* was what I had been needing — the release I had been aching for almost from the first time he'd touched me and held me.

Why couldn't it be him? I thought drowsily as I felt his big, warm hands sliding deliberately up and down my naked body. *Why couldn't Kristoff be my Consort? Who cares about status or rank or cast or whatever it is they make such a big deal about here?*

It was Kristoff who had come for me back on Earth. Kristoff who had protected me. Kristoff who had saved me again and again, risking his own life to do so. I knew the desire I felt for him was supposed to fade when the effects of the blood I had given him wore off but it wasn't—my feelings for him were only getting stronger.

"Kristoff," I murmured as he lifted me out of the tub and began toweling me off with a big, warm, fluffy piece of blue fabric. "Why does it have to be this way?"

"What way, my Lady?" He sat me on the edge of the tub with the towel around my shoulders and began combing out the tangles in my hair gently and expertly.

"Why do I have to pick some other guy—some other *male*—as my Consort?" I asked, frowning. "I don't want to be with some stranger—I want to be with *you*. Why can't we be together like Sundalla the 887ᵗʰ and her Guard were?"

His face grew grave.

"Never say that, Charlotte," he said, shaking his head. "You're a Goddess and I'm nothing but a commoner. The idea of the Goddess-Empress mated to any but a Royal is sacrilege—blasphemy of the highest order."

"But why? Who says?" I demanded. "Why should they get to decide who I marry, er, mate with? You said you thought half of them are in Morbain's pocket anyway." I had a sudden thought. "You know, if I could shake hands with them or touch them in some way, I might be able to find that out. My *touch*-sense usually tells me if someone is friend or foe."

He frowned. "It is forbidden for the Empress to have physical contact with the Council of Wisdom. The law states there must remain between them a divide, in order to preserve the balance of male and female powers."

It was my turn to frown. "There sure are a lot of rules about who I can and can't touch around here. Not to mention who I get to spend my life with." I looked at him again. "Kristoff…"

"Don't speak of taking me as your Consort again." His eyes were hard and his face was stern. "For your own safety, I beg you my Lady—put the thought far from your mind."

How can I? I wanted to say. *When your hands on me feel so right…so good?* But at the look on his face, the words stuck in my throat.

"I still don't think it's right," I said as he finished with my hair and started rubbing some kind of cool, green gel over the scratches I'd gotten from the exploding mug. "And…I don't feel those, uh, *cravings* Dr. Churika said would fade getting any less. If anything they're stronger than ever."

He frowned. "She will be here tomorrow to attend you after the Trials of Ascendancy. We can ask for a prescription to cool your lust then."

"It's not just lust," I protested. "I want to be with you—want to *touch* you. To feel you hold me like you did that first night." I looked at him pleadingly. "Could we do that again tonight? I mean, sleep in the same bed together?"

He looked indecisive as he capped the jar of gel and put it away. "I shouldn't…if word got out it would be devastating to your reputation."

"But you're here to protect me," I pointed out. "And I'd feel so much safer if you were right there with me. Also, you had the other guard sweep the place for bugs, right? So who's going to know?"

"I'll know," he said in a low voice and sighed.

"What does that mean?" I asked, frowning.

"Never mind." He shook his head. "If it would ease your mind for me to share your bed tonight, my Lady, then I will serve you in that capacity gladly."

"It would." I thought longingly of how good it felt to be wrapped in his muscular arms—of how safe and warm I felt. No one could hurt me when Kristoff was holding me like that—I was sure of it. "It *really* would," I repeated, though I doubted he would actually hold me. Still, just having him near would be comforting.

"Very well." He picked me up, towel and all, and carried me

into another room like a sleepy child. By now I was getting used to being carried all around by him and I didn't even protest. I just rested my head on his broad, bare chest and breathed him in—that warm, masculine, spicy scent that was uniquely Kristoff.

I thought of how much I loved feeling safe in his arms. It had seemed so alien and strange to me the first time I was close to him but now it represented safety and security. I knew to my bones that when I was in Kristoff's arms, I was being held by a male who would kill or die to protect me—who would spend his last breath keeping me from harm.

I was almost asleep, worn out with the intense pleasure he'd given me and the crazy events of the day. I woke up a little though, when he set me down on a vast bed covered in a shimmering, coverlet of rich scarlet.

"Hey, don't leave me," I protested sleepily as he left the bed and went to rummage in a large ornate armoire-looking piece of furniture on the other side of the room.

"I'm just getting you something to sleep in, my Lady," he said. "It wouldn't be proper for us to sleep in the nude together, as we did when you had the Burning Blood."

I sighed unhappily. Being naked with him was *exactly* what I wanted—what my body craved. But I wasn't surprised that it wasn't allowed. Now that we were on Femme One, the rules seemed to be different—different and much stricter.

"Okay," I said. "But I don't want to wear a pair of granny panties and a flannel gown just to be proper. I can't stand being hot while I sleep."

"I will bear it in mind. Although I have no idea what 'granny panties' are," he rumbled.

"Just find something light, please," I said. "I'm a Florida girl—I don't do heavy PJs. In fact, I usually just sleep in an old t-shirt."

"Very well."

Kristoff pressed a hidden button on the side of the tall, carved armoire—which looked surprisingly like a piece antique of furniture you might find on Earth. Suddenly a glowing holo-pad made of red light appeared on its side. It had lots of squiggly looking characters I supposed must be an alien alphabet.

Kristoff had explained to me how the Commercians had been sending translation and immunization viruses down to Earth through the hole in our ozone layer. The viruses enabled me to understand just about any spoken language in the galaxy but apparently that was only good for speaking—reading was another story.

Great, was I really going to have to learn to read all over again in a different language? I supposed so. After all, I could hardly be expected to rule over these people if I was illiterate in their written language. Just another thing to add to my growing list...

Prove I'm the real Empress—check. Rule the known galaxy—check. Try not to fall in love with my hot Guard—check. Learn a whole new language— *Wait a minute...* Was I really falling in love with Kristoff?

If I was, I'd better stop it now, at least according to Kristoff and everyone else I'd talked to.

It's nothing, I told myself uneasily. *It's just a side-effect from giving him that blood transfusion.*

But if so, why wasn't it fading? Why did I want to be with him more, not less? Why—

A soft beeping sound from the armoire cut off my troubled musings and I saw Kristoff open one wooden door and pull a white, silky garment he had apparently ordered by tapping into the holographic keyboard.

Okay, so maybe the armoire *wasn't* so Earth-like and antique-y after all.

"Here, my lady." He came over to the bed, holding the garment. "Take off your towel and lift your arms," he said.

Obediently, I did as he said, waiting like a child to be dressed. I would really have to be careful, I was getting used to being pampered and taken care of by my muscular alien bodyguard. If I didn't watch it, I'd forget how to get dressed and brush my hair and take a bath on my own.

Not that I'd mind forgetting if Kristoff is taking care of me, I thought as he slid the light, white garment over my head. It continued to amaze me how he could fight off would-be assassins and stand up to the Council of Wisdom one minute and then be gentle enough to bathe me and comb out the tangles in my hair the next. He'd said he was trained to protect and to serve but it still seemed strange that such a huge, alien warrior could be so gentle and tender.

"Is this garment to your liking, my Lady?" he murmured, breaking my train of thought.

"Oh..." I looked down at what I was wearing. It was a kind of nightdress with spaghetti straps and it came down to my mid thighs. The fabric it was made of had the delicacy and richness of silk and the lightness of thin cotton. I ran my hand over it delightedly, feeling the ultra-soft material whisper under my fingertips. It was lovely.

"My Lady?" He raised an eyebrow.

"Yes, thank you, Kristoff. It's perfect." I smiled at him and then had to smother a yawn. "Oh, I'm sorry. Suddenly I feel like I can hardly keep my eyes open."

"It's been a long day. A *very* long day." He sighed wearily. "Well, let's tuck you in."

"And you too," I said, frowning as he started to peel back the rich crimson spread, revealing silky silver sheets beneath.

He frowned. "Actually, I thought it might be best if I slept on top of the covers while you sleep underneath."

"What? No!" I protested before I could stop myself. "No, you'll...you'll be cold," I said, trying to explain my sudden outburst. "I don't want that. It's better if we sleep under the covers together. Unless..." I bit my lip, looking up at him. "I mean, unless you don't, uh, want to."

He sighed and raked a hand through his hair.

"No, I *do* want to, Charlotte," he said in a low voice. "But I shouldn't."

"Who's going to know?" I asked again. "Just you and me and we won't tell anyone—all right? What happens on Femme One, stays on Femme One—right?"

He threw me an uncomprehending look which made me feel dumb—of course my cultural reference had gone right over his head. But then he shrugged and nodded.

"As you wish, my Lady. I will sleep beneath the covers with

you but I still think it would be better to limit our contact."

"All right." I sighed. It seemed to be the best I was going to get. Not that I was surprised—though I *was* a little hurt.

"Let me ready myself for sleep," Kristoff said.

He went back to the armoire. This time it produced a pair of long, black sleeping trousers that seemed to be made of a slightly heavier, silkier material than my light nightdress—almost like satin.

Kristoff turned his back to me and pulled off the rest of his uniform before pulling them on. Then he got in the vast, comfortable bed beside me and murmured, "Light's out."

At once the room was plunged into darkness.

I bit back a little cry, feeling suddenly all alone in the strange, alien room and the vast bed. Though Kristoff was beside me, he was an arm's length away. Now that I couldn't see him again, I felt suddenly cold and alone.

I huddled beneath the rich blanket thinking how everything here felt *wrong*. The sheets were too heavy and silky compared to my cheap cotton ones back home and the pillow was much too puffy, compared to the flat one back on my Earth bed. It even *smelled* wrong—kind of like an expensive hotel room I knew I couldn't afford, if that makes any sense.

I thought longingly of my bedroom back on Earth—who knew how many hundreds of light years away. Of my internship, which I would never finish. Of Sebastian, who was snarky but still a good friend and of Zoe and Leah who were far, far away. Kristoff had told me, during our journey, that my two good friends had both been taken off Earth as well, by other alien males. Supposedly they were both happy now, on another planet at the far opposite end of the galaxy. I hoped to be able to see them at some point but for now, they were light years from me, just like Earth was.

I've never been so far from home in my life, I thought and felt a hot tear trickle down the side of my nose. *And it's not even my home anymore. For all I know, I'll never see it again...*

The thought made me cry more as a debilitating wave of homesickness hit me. I put my fist to my mouth and tried to muffle my sobs but I couldn't hold back and soon my shoulders were shaking with them. Great—so much for being cold and logical like a

Vulcan. This was my second time crying in less than two hours—I was in real danger of turning into a girly-girl here. The kind of girl who cried at sad movies and those awful animal abuse prevention commercials.

It made me feel so weak—I *hated* to be weak. And yet I still couldn't stop crying.

Suddenly I heard Kristoff shift in the bed beside me.

"Charlotte," he said, soft and low. "Are you unwell?"

"I…I'm fine," I said, trying to make my voice sound strong and certain. Instead, my words wavered all over the place and ended in a sob.

"No, you're not. Come here."

He reached for me but I held back, evading his seeking arms.

"No," I said, trying to stop crying. "No, you said…said it wasn't allowed. That we should keep a proper distance between us."

"Fuck propriety," he said, sounding angry. "Hearing your grief hurts my heart. Come to me now and let me hold you."

He swore so rarely that the profanity shocked me a little. I allowed him to gather me close and wrap his arms around me. I molded myself to the side of his big, muscular body and only then did I start to feel better.

My tears tapered off to sniffles and the horrible, intense longing I'd had for home gradually faded.

Because this is home now. **Kristoff** *is home,* whispered a little voice in my head.

I was too tired to argue with it. Sighing I snuggled closer and breathed in his delicious scent.

"Thank you," I whispered.

"Oh, Charlotte…you may not thank me later." He sighed and carded one big hand gently through my hair. "But for now, sleep and take your ease. Tomorrow's Trials will come soon enough and you need to be well rested."

That's right—the Trials! I had wanted to ask him more about the Trials I was going to go through the next day to prove I was really the Empress.

But now that I was safe and secure in his arms, a weariness so deep and profound I couldn't fight it seemed to overcome me. I opened my mouth to ask a question and a yawn came out instead.

Tomorrow – I'll ask tomorrow, I thought, snuggling closer to the broad chest and wrapping one leg over his thigh.

And then I fell asleep to the gentle rhythm of his breathing and the soothing feeling on his hand in my hair.

Chapter Twenty-one

Kristoff

We slept so deeply I didn't waken until a pounding on the door shattered my sleep.

"Captain? Captain are you up?" It was T'zorin's voice.

I sat up, my heart pounding. I was completely entangled with Charlotte — her silky limbs entwined with mine in a way that would be considered *most* improper — if not outright blasphemy — by the members of the Council of Wisdom. The Goddess-Empress was not to have such intimate physical contact with any but her Consort and that only *after* she was mated.

Speaking of things the Empress wasn't supposed to do with anyone but her Consort, I had been skirting dangerously close to the line last night the way I had pleasured her. I had told myself it was an act of service — just part of the bathing process. But if I was honest, I had to admit that it was much, *much* more than that.

I could still remember the moment when she reached the peak — the way she called my name and clung to my shoulders as the pleasure overtook her. Gods, she was so beautiful — so wild and wanton and free. It almost hurt to remember it and yet I couldn't forget — the look on her lovely face as she came on my fingers was burned into my memory forever.

After that, I had wanted to be strong — to put some distance between us. But when she begged me to share her bed, what could I do? I knew it was weak to give in to my desire to be near her, but I couldn't help myself. More and more I was having feelings for my new mistress I had never had for the old one. Though I had loved Sundalla the 999th with all my heart, our relationship had never been physical. With Charlotte, it was completely different — we had been drawn together when I was trying to save her from the Burning Blood and now it seemed impossible to extricate ourselves.

Case in point, the way we'd slept entangled last night. I had been trying so hard to keep her at arm's length for her own good. And yet, when I heard her soft sobs in the darkness, a part of me had melted. I had felt her pain, her wish for her home world as clearly through our bond as though she had spoken it aloud. I couldn't resist holding her then, even though I knew it was improper and that it would probably only throw fuel on the fire that was our attraction for each other.

As I held her close and stroked her silky hair, soothing her until her pain and misery changed to contentment and peace and she fell asleep in my arms, I had reflected that it was a good thing she couldn't feel my emotions as I could feel hers. A good thing the bond between and Empress and her Guards was strictly one way.

Because make no mistake about it—I wanted Charlotte as much or more than she wanted me and I was damn glad she didn't know it. I no longer thought it was just a byproduct of receiving so much of her blood, either. I was deeply afraid that I was in danger of falling in love with my new mistress—which would be a disaster.

I can't love her, I thought as I disentangled myself from her gently and went to open the door where T'zorin was still banging and calling my name. At worst, if someone guessed my feelings, Charlotte could be brought before the Council of Wisdom to answer for her infidelity. At best, it would just be my own secret pain—a thorn lodged in my heart which pricked me every time I saw her with whatever Consort she ended up with. Even now, the thought of her sharing another male's bed made a low growl of rage rise in my throat—a growl I had to swallow back down as I went to the door.

"What is it?" I asked, opening it to find T'zorin standing there with a worried look on his face.

"Captain, the Council has voted to move the time of the Trials of Ascendancy up by two hours," he said. "Has no one told you?"

"Not until now. This is Morbain's doing," I growled. "When are the Trials starting?"

"In half an hour. I thought I'd better come tell you since you weren't in the Grand Hall yet."

I swore loudly. If I didn't have Charlotte in the Grand Hall in time, she would forfeit the challenge and Morbain's candidate would be crowned by default.

"Will she be ready?" T'zorin inquired.

"We'll be there," I said grimly. "Don't worry—and thank you for coming to tell me."

"I'm here for you, Captain. We'll stand strong together." He saluted. "And I want you to know I'm sorry about the exploding mug—I checked every other part of the guest suite but the undermaid had just brought the tray in before you came."

"And have you found out who the undermaid was that delivered the tray?" I asked sharply.

He nodded. "But I don't think she had anything to do with what happened. Some other agent was behind it."

"And I can guess who," I said sourly. "T'zorin, there was something else—a scroll left behind one of the cushions. It was, ah…" I cleared my throat. "One of the historical documents—the one dealing with Sundalla the 887th and her chosen Guard. I think someone left it here on purpose for Charlotte to find."

He shook his head, frowning. "If so then whoever left it did so after I had already checked the room. I swear I was thorough in my sweep—something like that would not have escaped my notice."

"All right then." I sighed. "We'll just have to double security. I want a double guard posted on the True Incarnation's door at all times. Make sure they're males we can trust."

"Yes, Captain." He saluted.

"Good. Dismissed. I'll see you at the Grand Hall."

He nodded and left with the look of a male who has much to accomplish and not much time to accomplish it in.

I knew how he felt.

Charlotte

"Get up! We have to hurry."

"Wha…what's going on?" I blinked blearily, trying to focus on what Kristoff was saying.

"Morbain has gotten the Council to move the Trials up in hopes that you'll forfeit by missing them," he explained, all but pulling me out of bed. "Come, we can't be late."

"Oh!" His words woke me up and got me moving. "But I don't have anything to wear or — "

"I'm taking care of that." He was already typing rapidly on the holographic keyboard by the clothing-producing armoire. "Here — eat this." He turned around for a moment to toss me a familiar looking tube.

I groaned. "Not more nutrient paste!"

"It's all we have time for and you're going to need your strength," Kristoff told me. He threw a stern look over his shoulder. "Eat it, Charlotte."

I didn't want to — I'd had plenty of the bland, meaty, cardboard-tasting stuff on the trip from Earth to Femme One but there didn't seem to be much of a choice.

Popping off the top, I squirted a cold, slimy mouthful onto my tongue and shuddered as I made myself swallow it. Despite its disgusting taste, my stomach growled and I realized how hungry I was. I'd hardly had anything to eat the entire previous day. I finished off the tube just as Kristoff finished typing.

"This should work." He drew a long, sheathe-like gown made of a shimmering silvery-gold material out of the magic armoire and held it out to me. "Quickly — we need to get this on you."

"I don't know." I eyed the gown doubtfully. "That looks like it's going to be awfully tight. I'm not exactly as skinny as my competitor, you know."

"She's an imposter," Kristoff growled, pulling my nightdress over my head and starting to put the golden gown on me, despite my muffled protests. "And she's *too* thin — this dress will show off your curves."

"Well, she's not too thin for *my* planet," I said, as my head popped out of the top of the shimmering gold dress and my arms followed. "In fact, she's pretty much perfection."

"That doesn't change the fact that she's an imposter. Or that she isn't one tenth as lovely as you are, my Lady."

He adjusted the gown and frowned thoughtfully.

"Come look in the viewer."

He led me to another room where there was a 3-D mirror thing which showed how the gown fit. And let me tell you—how it fit was *tight*. It clung to my curves in a way that made me look like a too-full hourglass overflowing at both ends. The sheathe-like dress started right at mid-boob and then continued down, cinching in at the waist, clinging to my thighs and ending in a mermaid-bottom that started at my knees and belled out into a rustling mass of fabric in a kind of short train behind me.

"Kristoff," I protested, tugging at the top, which showed a lot more cleavage than I liked. "I really don't think—I mean, this isn't me at all!"

"You need to look regal," he said, frowning.

"Well, I'm not going to look anything but crazy if I can't move," I said. "This thing is killing me!"

"Here." he made some kind of adjustment to the gown and abruptly I could breathe a little easier. It still *looked* much more revealing than I liked but at least I didn't think I'd faint from oxygen deprivation while wearing it. "Well?" Kristoff asked, raising an eyebrow. "Better?"

"I guess," I grumbled. "But I'm afraid I'm still going to look crazy—look at my *hair*."

I have naturally wavy—almost curly hair that I normally keep confined in a tight ponytail at the back of my head. It's just easier that way and I don't want it getting in my face when I'm dealing with an emergency situation at the ER. Now, however, it wasn't just in my face—it was all *over* the place. Belatedly, I realized that I shouldn't have gone to bed with it damp—now I was paying the price.

"I don't have any makeup with me either," I pointed out to Kristoff. "Not that I wear a lot but as my mom used to say, everybody needs a little help. Right now I look like a crazy woman in a pretty dress."

"Come here—we can take care of all that if we hurry." He was already leading me into another room.

"What? Are you a hairdresser and make-up artist too?" I asked, frowning. "That seems like a lot of training on top of being a bodyguard and a warrior."

"Naturally not—we'll use the auto-coif. My old mistress had all the Guest quarters fitted with them a few cycles ago."

As he spoke, he gestured to a round, black, circular platform in the center of the room. There was a control panel on the wall, again in those strange alien letters I would soon have to learn.

"What am I supposed to do?" I asked, as he positioned me on the circle and went back to the control panel.

"Just hold still," Kristoff was already punching in commands. Suddenly, the circle I was standing on lit up and began to glow iridescent blue. Then a shimmering cylinder that seemed to be made of pure light descended all around me.

"Uh...Kristoff?" I asked uncertainly. I wasn't *exactly* feeling claustrophobic because I could see through the cylinder to where he was punching more commands into the control panel but, I still didn't like being confined to a small area.

"Hold still," he ordered again. "I'm setting it for the lightest application. Your beauty doesn't need much augmentation."

"Application of *what?*" I demanded and then the light cylinder moved inward and I had a feeling of warmth that seemed to envelope me from the top of my head all the way to the bottoms of my feet. Speaking of which, I didn't have any shoes on. Why were we worrying about hair and make-up when I was still barefoot?

Before I could point that fact out to Kristoff, I felt the strangest sensation all over my face. It was like a thousand butterfly wings caressing my cheeks and chin and lips and brows all at once—a light but continuous fluttering all over. It wasn't unpleasant but it *was* unexpected and I had to steel myself to hold still as Kristoff had ordered.

At the same time, I became aware that something was tugging at my hair Not just one something though—about a thousand somethings were pulling gently, doing something to my unruly waves that I couldn't begin to guess. Again, it didn't hurt, but it did feel weird. Like someone was lifting every stand of hair on my head at once. What the hell was going on?

I didn't have long to wonder because the whole process took less than a minute. Almost before I knew it, the shimmering light was withdrawing and the iridescent blue circle I was standing on faded back to black.

"What just happened to me?" I asked, when it seemed safe to talk. "I meant that was *weird*. Did that machine comb my hair or something?"

"More than that. Come back to the viewer."

Kristoff was looking extremely pleased with himself as he led me back to the 3-D viewing room. What I saw made me suck in my breath in surprise.

"Oh," I whispered, putting a hand to my cheek. "Is that really *me?*"

From the neck up I had been completely transformed.

My face was lightly but expertly made up. My eyes had been turned into smoky, sultry green jewels and my lips and cheeks had been touched with purest carmine red. My hair was swirled into an elegant up-do with little curling tendrils artfully arranged to frame my face.

I felt like I was looking at a stranger—a really *pretty* one but a stranger nonetheless. I hadn't looked this good even when I dressed up to go to prom in high school or when I was in a friend's fancy, formal wedding.

"This is...amazing," I whispered, reaching up to touch my other cheek. "I can't believe that's really me."

"It's really you, my Lady," Kristoff murmured. "The dress and all the work of the auto-coif are simply like the setting to a beautiful jewel. They haven't changed a thing—only enhanced it. And now we have to go or we will be too late."

"Okay—oh, wait!" I said. "I forgot—I don't have any shoes on."

Kristoff cursed and looked at the chronometer on his wrist.

"I knew I was forgetting something! But there's no time now— your dress hides your feet, at least."

"But—" I started to protest but he was already taking me by the hand and leading me out of the guest suite.

As we left, a group of guards dressed much like he was—(and when had he had time to get into his uniform? I didn't know)—fell into position around us, completely surrounding us on all sides.

"Who are *they?*" I murmured to Kristoff as we rushed down the broad hallway — the black marble floor cold under my bare feet.

"An honor guard. They will accompany you everywhere you go until I'm certain you're no longer in danger," he said. "Come — the Grand Hall is just ahead. We'll be just in time."

"But the Trials!" I exclaimed. "You never told me anything about them! What are they? What am I supposed to do? I mean, I'm assuming it's nothing too physical or you wouldn't have dressed me up like this but I just don't know —"

"You will see," he said, giving me a swift glance. "Truly, my Lady, it's better if you know nothing about them until you encounter them. Just remember, whatever happens and whatever you are asked to do, do it without fear. You are the True Incarnation and no harm will befall you. Do you understand?"

That sounded kind of ominous but we were already at the large, gilded double doors that led to a hall crowded with people. Very *tall* people, as it turned out. Anyway, there was no more time to ask questions — I decided I would just have to trust him.

"Yes," I said. "I understand."

"Good," he said and pulled me into the room.

Chapter Twenty-two

Charlotte

"Kristoff Verrai, Captain of the Imperial Guard and his candidate for Goddess-Empress," announced the tall footman in black and gold livery standing just inside the large double doors.

There was a murmuring in the crowd of people—all of whom were extremely richly dressed and most of which had the same deep blue-black hair as Kristoff. A few of the women had changed their skin and hair and eyes to match my competitor's, I saw. There was a lot of platinum blonde hair and sharp emerald eyes. Their men had skin that varied with the mood of their females—a lot of them seemed to be a bright, swirling, orange-pink at the moment. I wondered if that was the color of curiosity.

Since Kristoff had explained about Majorans being chromatacromes and so able to change their skin and hair and eye color at will, none of this surprised me. But I'd be flat out lying if I said it didn't *unnerve* me, because it sure as hell did. It was weird to be in a crowd of super tall alien people who were constantly changing color like living lava lamps—though I supposed I would have to get used to it since they were my people now.

As the crowd parted, we saw another podium-like table where the Council of Wisdom were already seated. Prince Morbain and the lovely girl he'd called Eucilla were standing in front of them and Morbain was very clearly consulting a watch—or what Kristoff had called a chronometer—as though he was marking off the time.

"You can stop counting the minutes—I am here with the True Incarnation in plenty of time, despite your attempt to move the Trials without letting me know," Kristoff said flatly, as we came to join them in front of the Council.

"Are you really? What a pity." Morbain looked up, giving him a bland stare. "But as for moving the Trials, I only did it for the sake of the respect I feel for our esteemed Council of Wisdom. Our wise

Elders have much to attend to, it isn't right to make them wait on such inconsequential matters."

"The Investiture of a new Empress is no small matter, Prince Morbain," said the youngest council member—the one with brown eyes and brown skin that I remembered from the day before. He looked at Kristoff. "Captain Verrai, is it really true that no one came to notify you of the change of time?"

"No one but one faithful guard—without whom we would have been late and forfeited the Trials. Which I am certain is Morbain's true reason for the time change," Kristoff growled.

"But this is highly irregular!" protested the Councilor. "I gave orders myself to a footman to alert you."

"You'd better find out what happened to him then," Kristoff said blandly. "Because he never found his way to the door of the Guest quarters."

"But—" the Councilor began. Just then, a footman in black and gold livery stepped forward and whispered in his ear. The Councilor's light brown skin went suddenly pale and he looked up. "His body was found just now, stuffed in the kitchen pantry" he said in a stunned voice. "His throat had been cut. This…this is an outrage!"

"Are you surprised?" Kristoff asked him. "After I told you about the three attempts already made on my Lady's life—one of them right outside your Council Room yesterday? And to that I must add a fourth as her drinking vessel exploded in her hands yesterday just as she was about to take a sip of *langra* tea."

"All this is most shocking and dreadful," Head Councilor Tannus interrupted, frowning. "But it is *not* the reason we are gathered here in the Great Hall today. We are here that the Trials of Ascendancy may be completed by both candidates for Goddess-Empress. Are the candidates ready to begin?"

I could see Kristoff scowling at the way the Head Councilor was ignoring the issue of the many assassination attempts that had been made against me. The youngest Councilor still looked outraged and I thought a few of the others looked distinctly uncomfortable. But no one moved to contradict the Head Councilor when he changed the subject to get down to business.

Eucilla stepped forward, brushing a lock of platinum blonde hair gracefully out of her lovely face.

"I am ready to prove I am the True Incarnation, oh honorable Councilor," she said in a clear, well-modulated voice. She held her chin high and today she was wearing a pure emerald dress that set off her eyes perfectly. Her feet were strapped into extremely high heels that made her six inches taller — she towered over me in my bare feet, making me feel like a shrimp.

"Remember," Kristoff murmured in my ear. "*You* are the True Incarnation, Charlotte. Step forward and claim your place without fear."

"I'm, uh, ready too," I said, taking a step forward as he'd said and trying not to sound as nervous and unsure of myself as I felt.

"Very well." The Head Councilor banged on the podium-table with the fist-sized pink crystal which seemed to be a kind of gavel. "Then let us adjourn to the Testing Suite, which has been made ready for you."

My honor guard surrounded me once more and with Kristoff by my side, we all marched out of the Grand Hall and then down the broad main hallway for what seemed like forever.

At last we came to a smaller offshoot — a dim side passage that looked like it didn't get much use. Here the Head Councilor stopped the whole procession and raised a hand over his head for silence. The crowd of Majoran nobility slowly stopped talking and waited expectantly.

"This is the corridor of the Trials," he said, his voice carrying surprisingly well in the packed hallway. "It is forbidden for any save the candidates, their companions, and the Council of Wisdom to enter and see the Trials."

There were grumbles of disappointment but I got the feeling the Majoran nobles and Royals weren't that surprised. Myself, I was relieved. I didn't want all these strangers watching me do…whatever it was I was going to have to do. Plus, there was no Earthly way they could all fit into the much smaller passageway we were about to enter.

"Come," Kristoff said, taking my arm firmly as the Head Councilor led the way into the dim corridor.

We were behind Morbain and Eucilla and they were so tall I couldn't see around them but soon we stopped and the Head Councilor turned to face us.

"Back, please—away from the Trial doors," he said, motioning peremptorily at us.

Once everyone took a step back, against the right wall of the corridor, I saw that the left wall had three doors in it at widely spaced intervals.

"Three Trials of Ascendancy have been ordained for the finding and delineation of the True Incarnation," Head Councilor Tannus said, his bushy blue-black eyebrows drawing low on his forehead. "They should be sufficient but if for some reason there is no clear choice…we do have the *fourth.*"

Some of the other Councilors sucked in their breath at this and looked at him uncertainly. I looked at Kristoff to see if this meant anything to him but he merely stared straight ahead, his handsome face impossible to read.

God, I *really* wished he would have briefed me on what was about to happen!

"And now for the first Trial," the Head Councilor said. "That of the Orb and Scepter."

"I believe Eucilla should be allowed to go first," Morbain said, stepping forward.

I looked at Kristoff to see if he was going to object but he simply nodded serenely. "Let her."

"Very well." Casting a somewhat uncertain look at Kristoff, Prince Morbain stepped forward, holding Eucilla by the elbow. "Go, my dear—claim what is rightfully yours. What you have already claimed *once before,*" he said, raising his voice grandly so that it carried out to the waiting nobility beyond the small corridor.

"As it is agreed, the Lady Eucilla shall have the first Trial," the Head Councilor said. Stepping forward, he opened the wide, black door outlined in gold. "And Lady, ahem—I am sorry, *what* was your name again?" He stared down his nose at me.

"Charlotte," I said, beginning to get sick of his arrogant bullshit. "Charlotte Walker."

"Yes, well—Lady *Charlotte* then—you may stand in the doorway and watch. After Lady Eucilla has had her turn, it will be your time to enter."

"But what are we supposed to *do* in there?" I asked as Eucilla walked through the door, as stately as a queen. "I don't know anything about any of this."

"You require an explanation?" His bushy eyebrows went up in disbelief.

"I'd like one, yes," I said, trying to keep the irritation I felt out of my voice. "Along with a little courtesy. I don't think that's too much to ask."

"Oh, very well." He rolled his eyes as though I was being childish by asking. "Within the first Trial room is the royal Orb and Scepter—those implements which the Goddess-Empress holds as she sits upon the Golden Throne. The Orb and Scepter are imbued with sentience and they long for the touch of the true Goddess-Empress's hand. In fact, it is said that they will fly from their pedestal to the hand of their true mistress the moment she steps into their immediate vicinity. Watch," he added, motioning at my competitor.

Eucilla had taken a step into the long room which was bare except for the rich gold and crimson pattern that completely covered the walls and made it look like the inside of a Faberge egg. At the end of the small, jewel-like area was a pedestal with two black silk cushions on it.

On one cushion was lying a large gold implement about the size of a baseball bat. It had a ruby as big as my fist on one end. On the other cushion was what looked like an immense crimson-red pearl about the size of a soccer ball. It was encrusted all over with diamonds and trimmed with gold, making it glitter and gleam like an exotic, expensive fruit in the dim, warm light.

"Wow," I breathed, looking up at Kristoff. "And those are supposed to fly to my hands the minute I walk in the room?"

"They will fly to the *True Incarnation's* hands," the Head Councilor sneered, correcting me rudely.

"Charlotte *is* the True Incarnation, Councilor," Kristoff said, his voice filled with quiet menace. "I'd have a care how I spoke to the future Empress if I were you."

The Head Councilor opened his mouth to retort but just then Eucilla took another step towards the pedestal and both the Orb and Scepter jerked up from their black silk cushions and flew to her waiting hands.

"You see?" Morbain exclaimed triumphantly. "And that is *exactly* what happened yesterday! Which is why we should stop this travesty right now and invest Eucilla as the True Incarnation."

I looked at Kristoff whose rainbow eyes were narrowed. What was going on here? He'd told me that *I* was the True Incarnation of the Goddess-Empress. So then, why had the Orb and Scepter flown to Eucilla?

"Let the Trial continue," he said, frowning at the Head Councilor. "It is now time for my Lady Charlotte to enter the chamber."

"But..." I looked at him uncertainly. "But they already..." I gestured at Eucilla, who was standing there holding the Scepter in one hand and the Orb in the other, looking unbearably smug.

"Go on, Charlotte," he said in a low voice. "All will be made clear. You will see."

Hesitantly, I stepped into the small room. The floor and ceiling were the same gold and red pattern as the walls, which only contributed to the feeling of being inside a Faberge egg or else a very large jewelry box.

I wasn't sure what I was supposed to do, since the Royal implements had already flown over to Eucilla. So I just took a few steps inside the door and stopped there, staring at her.

"Put out your hands," Kristoff instructed me. "Call them to you."

"Um...okay." Feeling like a fool, I turned towards Eucilla, who was giving me a distinctly unfriendly look, and held out my hands to her—or rather, to the objects she held.

"Here guys," I said, looking at the golden baseball bat and the diamond encrusted soccer ball. "Come here now."

I sounded like I was calling dogs at the park and for a minute I felt ridiculous. Then something strange started to happen.

I saw Eucilla stiffen and quiver. The knuckles of the hand holding the Scepter tightened and went white and she clutched the Orb to her chest, her long fingernails digging in between the diamonds. Her whole body seemed to shake all over, as though from effort.

And then, suddenly, the Orb broke free and came whizzing at my head like a bad pitch gone wild.

I gasped and ducked but it didn't hit me. Instead it waited until I straightened up and then nudged my arm gently, like an animal wanting attention.

"Oh...okay." I held out my open hand and it settled in my palm like a tame bird. I ran my hands over it wonderingly — I had never seen so many diamonds all in one place in my entire life — except in movies about the mob, of course.

Aside from the diamonds, there was something strange on the Orb. I frowned as I brought my hand away and a thin string of nearly invisible, gluey substance extended from the Orb's jeweled surface to my fingertips.

"What the —" I began to mutter but just then I heard a muffled shriek and looked up.

Eucilla was still trying to hold the scepter — hanging onto it with both hands now as it whirled around like a possessed baseball bat.

"Don't let go!" I heard Prince Morbain hiss at her in a low voice. *"Don't let go!"*

But the Scepter apparently decided that it had had enough. Rising up high, it came straight down, giving Eucilla three sharp raps on the top of her head with the sharp ruby-knob on its end. Since she was still holding it by the handle, it looked bizarrely like she had decided to hit herself in the head with it, but I didn't think that was the case.

At the last blow, she gasped and let the Scepter go free. It came whizzing at me too, just like the Orb had. I almost ducked again, but then I decided to hold my ground.

Sure enough, the Scepter came to a stop before me, hovering in midair, and nudged me very gently on the arm. I held out a hand and the long golden handle of it fitted neatly into my palm.

The Scepter was very heavy and I noticed that it, too, had the same gluey strings that had been on the Orb. But even as I opened my palm to examine them, the sticky strings melted away, leaving no evidence that they had ever been there in the first place.

"Nothing. This means nothing!" Prince Morbain was declaring as Eucilla rubbed the top of her head and glared at me as if *I* had knocked her over the head with the Scepter myself. "Let the Trials continue! It is our right to have all three Trials!"

"Of course he says that *now*," Kristoff said, coming up beside me to murmur in my ear. "Though I'm certain it was a different story yesterday when he somehow made it appear that the Scepter and Orb had an affinity for the imposter."

"There was some kind of transparent, gluey *strings* on both of them," I said, nodding down at the implements in my hands.

They hummed with life and I felt as though I was holding two very excited dogs who were just barely keeping themselves under control. You know how it is when a dog is really, *really* happy to see you but you tell it to stay, so it does, but its tail is still wagging like crazy? It was like that.

"That would certainly explain how Morbain made it appear that the implements had an affinity for Eucilla when they didn't." Kristoff sounded thoughtful.

"My Lady Charlotte," the Head Councilor interrupted, giving me an irritated look. "If you would be so kind as to place the implements back in their respective resting places so that the Trials can continue?"

"Oh, sure. Sorry," I said. Going back to the pedestal with its golden lighting and two black silk pillows, I placed the Orb and the Scepter gently back in their places.

Both of them popped up again and began to hover after me, for all the world like dogs that can't stand it when their master is about to leave.

"No, no, you guys," I said sternly. "I need you to stay. *Stay.*" It should have felt weird to be talking to inanimate objects except these objects *weren't* inanimate. I got the distinct impression that they had thoughts and personalities. Not very complex thoughts, to be sure, but still, they weren't your ordinary, run-of-the-mill Royal implements either.

The Orb and Scepter stopped in mid-hover and then slunk back to their cushions, like dogs with their tales between their legs.

"Good boys," I told them, hoping to take the sting out of my scolding. "I'll see you later, I'm sure."

"You mean you *hope* you will," Eucilla hissed at me. She had stopped rubbing the top of her head but her lovely mouth was twisted up as though she'd been sucking lemons. "The only way you'll see the Orb and Scepter again is when *I* am holding them as I sit on the Golden Throne," she added.

"I don't know," I said blandly. "I could be wrong but it didn't seem to me that they *wanted* to be held by you. I mean, if that whole knocking you in the head thing was any indication."

"You...you little off-worlder *beggar*," she spat, as though it was the worst insult she could think of. "You'll see—*I'm* the True Incarnation! I've known it since I was a child. I was *raised* to be the next Goddess-Empress."

"Indeed you were, my sweet. Now come, the second Trial is about to begin." Prince Morbain took her by the arm and led her from the room.

Kristoff took my arm as well.

"What's next?" I asked, under my breath.

"You'll see," he said obliquely. "Just remember that you are in no danger. Do whatever is asked of you and do not fear."

It was the second time he had told me not to be afraid, which made me really nervous. The Orb and Scepter Trial had been easy but we still had two more to go—three, if the Councilors decided to include the dreaded fourth Trial, whatever that was. What was coming up next?

I didn't have long to wonder.

"This is the Trial of Flame and Scale," the Head Councilor intoned, when we were all standing before the second door. "Within this chamber lives the Royal fire drake—a living symbol of the unbroken line of succession dating from the very first Goddess-Empress, Sundalla the First. The drake will tolerate only the touch of the True Incarnation. Your Trial is to go into the chamber and touch the scales of the Drake, then return."

"Once again, I feel Eucilla should go first," Morbain said importantly.

"Actually, both candidates may complete this Trial at the same time," the Head Councilor said. "But it is absolutely forbidden for anyone else to enter the chamber."

"A fire drake?" I said, turning to Kristoff. "Is that what I think it is? I mean, it's been a good long time since I went to the Renaissance Fair but that sounds an awful lot like a dragon."

"I don't know what a dragon is," he murmured back. "But I do know that nothing in that chamber will hurt you, my Lady."

"But—"

"Are you ready, candidates?" the Head Councilor asked, his hand on the golden doorknob.

"Yes, of course we are, Head Councilor," Morbain said smoothly. He turned to Eucilla and I heard him murmuring, "Remember, it's most likely sleeping. Just go in quickly and quietly, touch the tip of its tail, and come straight back."

"But why must I be quiet?" I heard her ask petulantly. "*I* am the True Incarnation—you said so yourself, Morbain! Surely the drake will not hurt me."

"Just do as I say," he hissed. "And be quick about it."

The Head Councilor opened the door and Morbain all but pushed her inside.

Of course Kristoff didn't push me—I stepped across the threshold myself, with no idea of what I could expect to find.

Inside it was much larger than the first, small jewel-box room. In fact, I estimated it was about the size of a football field. There was nothing in it but a high, green hill that gleamed in the dull light, with two large trees on either side of it.

I looked around for the fire drake but I didn't see anything even remotely resembling a dragon. Could it be in the branches of the trees? Or maybe on top of the big green hill?

Eucilla was walking purposefully towards the far end of the large room, heading for the hill and trees, so I did too. I was pretty sure she knew more about this Trial than I did since she had someone to brief her. I wished again that Kristoff would have at least given me a *clue* as to what I was supposed to face during these Trials instead just deciding, for whatever reason, that it was better to let me figure them out on my own.

The floor of the large room was carpeted in some kind of dark blue-green moss which felt soft and cushy to my bare feet. It was a pleasure to walk on—for me, anyway. Apparently not so much for Eucilla, though. She was tottering in the high, stilt-like shoes strapped to her feet. Their sharp heels kept getting entangled in the moss and causing her to almost trip. If I had been her, I would have kicked the damn things off, but that wouldn't have looked very dignified. And I had a feeling that looking dignified was very, *very* important to Eucilla.

Despite her shoe troubles, she got to the huge green hill and the trees on either side of it before me, though not by much. I was about to say something to her when a flash of motion in the branches of the tree beside me caught my eye.

The trees were as tall as oaks with brownish-black trunks and leaves a teal so dark they were almost black. So when a flash of gold flickered in those dark leaves, it made me look.

There, sticking its head out from between two teal leaves, was a perfect little miniature dragon. Not a lizard or a snake—an actual *dragon* about as long as my hand from the tip of my middle finger to my wrist. It had an elongated snout and large, jewel-like eyes that whirled as it considered me. When it sat up on the branch I saw it had tiny wings too—gold with red and black webbing. It looked like an exquisite golden statue come to life.

"Hi there, little guy," I said to it. Could this be the fire drake? It didn't seem nearly as frightening as I'd thought it might be. "How about coming here for a minute?" I said to the little dragon, holding out a hand, palm up to it. "I'm supposed to touch you but I'm pretty sure it's okay if you touch me instead."

It hesitated for a moment, then stepped out onto my hand. Its little claws were sharp and its skin was dry and very hot—in fact, I could feel the heat of its tiny body radiating against my palm as though I was holding a live coal instead of a living creature.

"Hey, buddy..." Carefully, using just one fingertip, I stroked the top of my new friend's head. The whirling jeweled eyes half closed with pleasure and it made a soft humming sound I took to mean it was enjoying itself. I stroked it again and was so caught up in the enchanting experience I forgot to look and see what Eucilla was doing until I heard her voice.

"Well, *hello* there," I heard her coo. I looked up to see that she was staring at another miniature dragon that was peering at her from a higher branch of the tree. "Aren't you just *adorable,*" she gushed, as it cocked its tiny golden head from side to side, studying her. "Morbain said you'd be big but just look—you're *tiny.*" She cast me a defiant glance. "I see *you've* already got one."

I shrugged. "He just came to me. They're cute, right?"

"Hmmph." Apparently she was done talking to me. Instead, she held out her hand to the little golden dragon, which was slightly larger than the one I had. "Come here," she said in a coaxing tone. "Come to the True Incarnation as you're supposed to, now."

The dragon sniffed her hand, cocked its head to one side...and bit her middle finger.

"Ouch!" Eucilla cried, snatching her hand away and glaring at the dragon, who almost seemed to be laughing at her. "Why you little—oh no, you're not getting away that easily. Come here—*come here!*"

She made a snatch at the dragon but it darted away. Eucilla, however, was clearly not one to give up easily. She grabbed the branch the little creature had jumped to and began to shake it vigorously.

With a sharp sound of distress, the miniature golden dragon fell out of the tree, onto the soft moss below.

"Got you!" Eucilla snatched it off the ground before it could skitter back up the tree. "Let's see you try and bite me *now,*" she exclaimed, holding it in front of her face, but not so close that it could reach her with its spiky little teeth.

"Be careful," I said sharply, putting my own little dragon carefully back on the tree branch he'd come from. "You're hurting him!"

"Well, he hurt *me.*" Petulantly, she squeezed the little creature until it squeaked in distress.

"He was probably frightened," I said angrily. "Stop it, Eucilla! Put him back!"

"I'll do no such thing. I—"

She was interrupted by the high, keening wail coming from the little dragon in her hand. At once, about a hundred little golden heads stuck out from the trees on either side of us and other miniature dragons took up the cry. It got so loud I had to put my hands to my ears.

"Stop it! Stop that dreadful racket!" Eucilla exclaimed. "If you don't, I'll make you sorry! I am the True Incarnation—I'll have the lot of you destroyed if you don't *shut up.*"

And then the hill moved.

It was just a motion in the corner of my eye at first—something I barely saw because I was so focused on the little dragon clutched tight in Eucilla's hand. But then it moved again and I turned to face it.

What I saw made me feel cold all over. The little dragons abruptly fell silent and in the sudden stillness I swore I could hear my own heart pounding in my ears.

"Eucilla," I whispered breathlessly, my mouth so dry I could hardly talk. "Eucilla, put it down *now.*"

"It bit me," she said, her eyes still trained on the little dragon. "I'm not done with it yet! Besides, I'm *supposed* to touch it."

"Well you'd better get done in a hurry," I told her, still facing the hill which was no longer hill-shaped. "Because I don't think that's the fire drake we're supposed to be touching." I pointed with one shaky finger. "Look."

"What are you *talking* about?" Reluctantly, she turned her head to look at what I was pointing at. Her eyes grew wide and she gasped.

The hill was a hill no longer. It had uncurled itself, revealing that what I had taken for a moss-covered mound of dirt was actually an enormous back. A long, snaky neck had uncoiled to point a huge head directly at us.

Once when I was a kid, my adopted parents had taken me up to Washington DC to visit the Smithsonian museum. My favorite part of that trip was the Natural History museum with all the animals. Specifically, I loved the dinosaur exhibit. I still have a picture of me standing beside a Tyrannosaurus Rex skull, completely dwarfed by the huge fossil.

That was kind of the way I felt now except the creature facing us was no fossil. Also, it was at least *twice* as big as a T-Rex and it looked mad as hell.

"Oh my Goddess," Eucilla whispered, staring at it. "Oh my *Goddess.*"

"*Drop... the little... dragon,*" I hissed at her from the corner of my mouth. Dimly I was aware of Morbain shouting the same thing at her from the doorway. But the door was so far away, on the other end of the football field-sized room, it was hard to hear him. "Drop it," I repeated. "I think that's a baby and this is the mother. If she thinks you're hurting her baby..."

"*Oh.*" Understanding flooded Eucilla's face, which had been nearly drained of prettiness by the fear that was stamped on her perfect features. "All right—it's all right," she said in a shaking voice to the huge dragon which was watching us with whirling jeweled eyes as big as basketballs. "I'm letting your baby go, see? I'm putting it down."

Up until now, both of us had been frozen in place. Now, as Eucilla reached up to place the little golden dragon back on the tree branch with his brothers and sisters, I saw the dragon's huge eyes tracking us. Suddenly, it opened its mouth and let out a roaring, hissing screech that made my eardrums bulge.

"Ahh!" I clapped my hands over my ears in pain and Eucilla fell to her knees, crying.

The huge head lifted and the jaws stretched wide, showing razor sharp, serrated teeth as long as my arm. The fire drake blew a huge plume of flame into the air, white-hot and as bright as a jet from a blow-torch. The temperature in the room went up by what felt like twenty degrees and the cold sweat that had popped out on my skin suddenly turned hot and desperate.

Eucilla shrieked and started trying to scramble to her feet in the ridiculous heels.

"Run! We have to *run!*" she babbled.

"No!" I caught her arm, dragging her under the shelter of the tree with me.

"Let me go!" She batted at my hands frantically. "I have to get away from here! This *creature* is *mad*. It doesn't understand I'm the True Incarnation!"

"Stay right here." I shook her, making my voice stern, as I did when I spoke to unruly patients. "Don't you see—she's protecting her babies! She won't burn us as long as we're close to them because she might burn them, too. If you run, you'll make yourself a target because you'll be far enough from them for her to breathe fire at you."

At last I saw my words were sinking in. Eucilla's eyes grew wide and she stopped struggling against my hands on her arms.

"You...do you really think so?" she whispered. "I mean, are you *sure?*"

"Of course I'm not sure," I snapped. "I didn't know anything about this stupid Trial, unlike you. But it seems logical. Look at the way she's looking at us."

The mother fire drake—because I was pretty sure that was what she was—had stopped screaming and shooting fire for the moment, and now she had lowered her massive head again and was looking at us, the huge eyes whirling with some unknown emotion. She almost seemed to be...*waiting* for something.

Could it be that she was waiting for either Eucilla or me to complete the Trial?

You need not fear. Nothing will hurt you. Kristoff's words came back to me. He'd been right about the first Trial...could he be right about this one too?

And was I really going to have to go touch that enormous head I saw pointed in my direction?

I can do this, I told myself. *I'm not afraid of animals—even big animals. I loved riding horses as a kid.*

Of course, horses aren't twice as big as a Tyrannosaurus Rex and able to breathe fire. But if I really was the True Incarnation of the Goddess-Empress, as Kristoff claimed, I should be able to walk up to the massive fire drake and touch it without harm.

Of course if he was wrong, I would probably get burned to a crisp or bitten in half or both. I had a sudden vivid mental image of the bottom half of me still standing on the moss while the top half of me disappeared in flaming chunks down the hot, red gullet.

Don't think that way — in fact, don't think about it at all, I told myself. *Just do it.*

Taking a deep, shaky breath, I took a step away from the shelter of the tree and towards the massive dragon. Its hide was thick and pebbled, a deep green with an iridescent gold sheen that reminded me a little of Kristoff's tan and gold.

Kristoff. Kristoff said I couldn't be hurt. That nothing in these trials could hurt me. I held on to that thought like a lifeline as I took another step forward and then another.

"What...what are you *doing?*" Eucilla breathed, looking at me as though I was crazy. "Are you *mad?*"

"I'm going to touch it," I said, keeping my voice low and soothing. "I'm supposed to."

"No, you're not — *I* am!" She jumped up suddenly and started to totter towards the huge head on her stilt-like heels.

The fire drake, which had been quiescent, suddenly came to life and let out a mighty snort from the vast nostrils on the end of its snout. The snort sent out a hot black cloud of smoke and ash, directed right at Eucilla, who shrieked as it enveloped her.

"Go back," I hissed at her from the corner of my mouth. "Go back under the tree where you're safe, you idiot!"

The smoke cleared and Eucilla was left standing there, her lovely gown blackened and her pale skin and hair completely gray from the ash and smoke. She looked like she'd decided to take some time out of her busy schedule of being a rich bitch and moonlight as a chimney sweep.

"That's *it!*" she stormed, tears of rage cutting tracks down the grime on her cheeks. "I'm leaving! It doesn't matter if I touch that...that *thing* anyway — I already touched a little fire drake. So I don't have to touch the big one!"

She turned and started flouncing away, stumbling and tripping in her angry haste as her heels caught in the moss.

It was the heels that saved her life.

The huge green head swiveled to face her retreating back and the jaws opened, just as they had before. I saw that the dragon was about to breathe fire again but it happened so quickly, there was nothing I could do to stop it. The best I could do was shout a warning.

"Eucilla!" I yelled. *"Duck!"*

"What?" She turned her head to see me and her shoes got tangled in the moss. With a little cry, she fell over just as the fire drake belched a burning gout of flame directly at her.

Eucilla hit the moss covered ground and the stream of white-hot flame went directly over her head—setting the back of her long hair on fire.

"Crap!" Visions of patients in the burn unit back home flashed through my mind and I acted without thinking. Rushing out of the safety of the tree, I ran to Eucilla, who was shrieking and rolling around ineffectually on the ground as her long hair flamed.

"My hair! My *hair!*" she shrieked, sitting up and batting at her head which only spread the fire. Honestly, didn't they teach stop, drop, and roll on this freaking planet?

"Get down," I ordered her. Grabbing her shoulders, I tried to force her to the ground. But panic had made her strong and she fought me back, shrieking and crying.

"No...*no! Leave me alone!*" she sobbed.

"You have to smother the fire!" I shouted at her. Then, realizing that I wasn't getting through to her, I looked for something to smother it myself. There was nothing in the flat, mossy landscape I could use. Then I looked down. Well, nothing but my dress.

Hurriedly, I grabbed at the flowing material of the bottom of my dress and began ripping at the seams. Luckily it was sewed right at my knees and I was able to yank it off all in one glittery, flouncy piece.

As soon as I did, I rushed at Eucilla, who was still screaming and waving her arms, and tackled her to the ground, wrapping her head in the yards and yards of silvery-gold material as I did so.

She shrieked even louder but the sound was muffled by the

train of my dress. I pushed her down and squeezed her head tight, heedless of her flailing. Only when I was sure the fire was out did I lift the material and take a look at her.

"You...you...how *dare* you?" she spluttered when her face, still gray from the dragon's ash, came into view again. "I'll have you hanged by your thumbs from the palace walls for assaulting me, so everyone can see what happens to one who hurts the Goddess-Empress when I ascend the throne!"

"You're welcome," I said dryly. "I was just trying to put out the fire before you went up like a human torch."

"You..." Her voice trailed off and her eyes got wide. "Oh my Goddess," she whispered faintly.

In the craziness with the fire, we had both forgotten about the source of it. Now I felt a presence looming over my right shoulder. When I turned to look, I saw that the dragon was *right there.* Literally, not even a foot from my face.

As my friend Zoe would have said — holy shit.

"It's going to *burn* us," Eucilla whimpered, beginning to cry again. "It's going to burn us to a *crisp.*"

"No," I said. My voice was shaky and my knees felt even shakier but somehow I managed to make myself stand. "No, she's not."

Nothing will hurt you...have no fear...have no fear...

I risked a glance at the doorway, so far away across the massive room. I could see the figure of Morbain gesturing at the figure of the Head Councilor who was gesturing back angrily. Kristoff, however, was simply leaning against the doorway with his arms crossed over his broad chest and watching me quietly. He was too far away for me to see his eyes but I knew they would be a rainbow of shifting colors as jewel-bright as the dragon's.

Only I have the Vision, he'd told me. *Only I can see the rainbow aura that surrounds you, my Lady.*

His eyes, so much like the fire drake's. Could it be...could it be that *she* could see the aura *too?* The rainbow aura which was supposed to surround me — which was invisible to everyone else?

I looked at her and saw she was watching me intently.

"I'm sorry," I said to her, using a low, soothing tone. "I'm sorry we invaded your...your nest and bothered your babies." I took a step towards her, though I could hardly believe I was doing it. "Forgive me," I said, holding out a hand to her.

To my mingled relief and disbelief, the dragon snorted softly and nudged my outstretched hand with her scaly snout. Her skin was hot—much, much hotter than that of her baby's—but she only touched me for a moment.

After that one, brief caress, she shook her head and turned, ambling back towards the trees where dozens of little golden heads were watching from between the branches and squeaking for their mom.

The moment she got settled between the two trees, a hundred little golden dragons came rushing out of the leaves and swarmed all over her, looking like bright, jeweled ants next to her massive bulk.

The mother fire drake snorted again, this time a sound of contentment, and settled her head between her huge front paws. But her eyes continued to watch Eucilla and me, as though she wouldn't be completely at rest until we left her chamber.

"Come on," I said and tried to help Eucilla to her feet.

"Get *off* me." She pushed me away and got up on her own, still tottering on the ridiculous heels.

"We have to go," I said but she was already on her way towards the distant door, tottering along with as much dignity as she could muster.

Walking behind her, I saw that most of her hair had been burned off in the back and she was probably going to have some pretty nasty second degree burns on her exposed scalp. The ER doctor in me wanted to rush after her and talk about treatment options but I could tell my help wasn't wanted. Instead, I plodded after her, heading for the doorway where Kristoff waited for me.

Speaking of burns, my own hand should be blistered all to hell from the touch of the dragon—it had been like pressing my fingers to a red-hot stove. But when I lifted my palm to look, I saw I was unharmed. *Nothing will hurt you,* Kristoff had said, and he had been right.

I was just sorry that Eucilla had been burned so badly. I had a feeling that she really *did* think she was the True Incarnation. It was an idea that someone—probably Morbain—had been feeding to her since childhood. And as pretty and tall and perfect as she was, I could see how it would be an easy lie for her to swallow. After all, she certainly *looked* like an Empress. Or she had before she tangled with the dragon, anyway.

Well, at least one good thing will come of all this, I thought to myself as I walked over the soft moss with the dragon's glittering gaze still weighing on my back like a golden stone. *It will put an end to the Trials. There's no way Morbain can claim Eucilla is the True Incarnation after all what just happened.*

Chapter Twenty-three

Kristoff

"This proves nothing—*nothing!*" Morbain declared, his voice ringing in the small corridor. "Eucilla is the True Incarnation and you cannot prove otherwise!"

I stared at him in weary disbelief and Charlotte shook her head.

"Did you see what happened in there?" she whispered, looking up at me.

I bent down, the better to hear her words.

"Yes, I saw," I murmured. "You were beyond brave, my Lady. You have the courage of a warrior."

"Only because I trusted you," she said softly, looking into my eyes. "You told me nothing would hurt me and I believed you." She frowned. "Although I wish you would have given me a *little* warning about what was waiting for me. I was pee-your-pants-scared in there!"

I had to stifle a laugh. Her way of talking tickled what some would have said was my nonexistent sense of humor at times.

But there was nothing humorous about what was taking place now.

"*She* caused the Fire Drake to burn Eucilla," Morbain was shouting, pointing at Charlotte. "She confused the beast with her off-worlder scent and caused it to behave wrongly."

"That's so like you, always twisting the truth, Morbain," I said, glaring at him. "Charlotte *saved* Eucilla from certain death not once but *twice* when she put out the fire on her head and stopped the fire drake from killing her!"

"She did no such thing! She is an imposter and should be disqualified at once!" Morbain bugled, his eyes bulging with rage. "Head Councilor Tannus, I *demand* satisfaction!"

The Head Councilor frowned and I wondered again if he was in Morbain's pocket. I wished I could have Charlotte touch him—even for an instant—to use her *La-ti-zal* powers of Knowing. It would be good to know if the male had been paid off or if he was just being stubborn because he didn't want another strong Empress to ascend the Golden Throne. He had never liked my old mistress, Sundalla the 999th because he had been unable to control her. Though the Goddess knew, he certainly *tried.*

"Head Councilor Tannus," I said to him. "I think it's very clear what happened in the chamber of the Second Trial. Two candidates walked in and only one walked out unscathed. Look at my Lady Charlotte—there isn't a scratch or a burn on her. While Morbain's candidate...well..." I gestured at the still-smoking Eucilla who was pouting, with her ash-covered arms crossed over her chest. No words were needed to convey the obvious—or so I thought.

At last the Head Councilor made a decision.

"It is the ruling of this Council that the first two Trials are inconclusive," he said, glaring at Charlotte and myself. "And so we will continue with the Third Trial, if both candidates agree."

Words of outrage rose to my lips but Charlotte tugged at my arm and shook her head.

"Don't," she whispered when I bent my head to hear her. "Don't bother. I'm not afraid to go through another Trial."

"I do not fear for your safety, my Lady," I told her softly. "But for your honor. Morbain seeks to discredit you."

"Let him try." She lifted her chin and looked at the Head Councilor. "Councilor Tannus, I don't mind doing the Third Trial but I want Eucilla to have some medical attention first," she said calmly. "She has second degree burns on the back of her neck and her scalp. They need to be treated or they're only going to get worse. Also, she got a bite on her finger from one of the baby dragons. That needs to be disinfected and bandaged too."

For the first time, the Head Councilor looked surprised and I saw some of the other Councilors murmuring among themselves in apparent shock. I wasn't surprised, though—Charlotte was first and foremost a healer. I had seen back on her home planet of Earth how seriously she took her profession. That she demanded medical attention, even for the imposter who sought to take her rightful place on the Golden Throne, was just part of her nature.

"Well," the Head Councilor began. "I suppose we could wait while the other candidate goes to the medical wing of the palace…"

"No!" It was Eucilla, her red eyes narrowed, her lovely mouth twisted down into a pouting frown. "She's just trying to get rid of me! I'm not going *anywhere.*"

"I'm trying to get you treatment before those burns start suppurating," Charlotte said sharply. "You must be in pain, Eucilla. Let the doctors or healers or whatever they call them here treat you!"

"I'm not leaving!" The other female's eyes flashed. "*I* am the True Incarnation. And I'm staying here to *prove it!*"

Head Councilor Tannus shrugged.

"Very well. Then let us proceed with the Third Trial—the Trial of Fruit and Stone."

He led us down the corridor to the third and final door on the left-hand wall. Without ceremony, he threw it open, revealing a room only a sixth the size of the last chamber. In the center of the room grew a single tree with long, flowing branches, crowded with glittering fruit.

"Behold, the Tree of Wisdom," he said, motioning to its spreading branches, some of which hung so low their fruit was only inches from the mossy ground. "On it grows the Royal fruit—the *oppols* of gold." He indicated the bright, glossy golden-skinned fruit. "Only the True Incarnation of the Goddess-Empress can pluck and eat this delicacy. All others—"

He didn't get to finish because Eucilla had already rushed into the room and was grabbing for the fruit.

"I am the True Incarnation," I heard her muttering to herself. "I am—I can do this! This is easy!"

It didn't look easy, however. Though the fruit had looked so accessible when the Councilor first opened the door, now it seemed to hop away from her seeking hands, going from branch to branch just as she was about to pluck it.

With a cry of pure rage, Eucilla grabbed one low-hanging

branch and shook it, wrestling it as though it was a living opponent. After a moment, she stood up, shaking herself free of the curling leaves and holding out one of the large, gleaming *oppols*.

"I got one!" she shrieked. *"I got one!* I'm the True Incarnation! I am — *me!* Not her — *me!*"

Then she opened her mouth and took a massive bite out of the fist-sized fruit in her hand.

Or tried to, anyway.

There was an audible crunching sound, but not of fruit being bitten into. It was the sound of bones breaking — of *teeth* breaking, I thought.

Eucilla gave a muffled shriek and pulled the *oppol* away from her mouth. There was a bloody stump where one of her front teeth had been. As for the fruit, it was completely unmarked except for a smear of blood on its glittering golden side.

"As I was about to say," the Head Councilor said waspishly. "Only the True Incarnation of the Goddess-Empress can pluck and eat the fruit because to all others it has the consistency of stone."

"It's not stone!" Morbain exclaimed. Grabbing the Royal fruit from Eucilla's hand, he wiped the blood off and held it out. "This fruit is clearly unripe. That's why it hurt Eucilla's mouth. No other reason!"

"Charlotte, you know what you must do" I murmured to her and she looked up at me with understanding.

"All right," she whispered back. "But it seems kind of mean — like rubbing salt in her wounds."

"You have to," I told her. "There must be no doubt that you are the one and only True Incarnation."

She sighed and nodded, then stepped quietly into the room. She walked over to the Tree of Wisdom but before she could even reach for an *oppol,* one fell neatly into her palm. The commotion at the door had stopped and even Morbain had fallen silent as the onlookers realized what was happening.

"Come, my Lady," I said to Charlotte, raising my voice so that it carried. "Take a bite of the Royal fruit."

Charlotte brought it to her mouth and took a large bite. There was another crunching sound—this one the sound of teeth sinking through the crisp flesh of a ripe fruit—and she held the *oppol* up so that everyone could see the bite she'd taken from it.

It was easy enough to see—the inside of the fruit was a gleaming sapphire blue which showed up against the golden skin perfectly. As was the small dribble of blue juice that ran down her chin before she wiped it away.

"You see?" Morbain bugled. "Now *that* fruit is ripe. Eucilla, my love, take a bite of *that* one."

"Give me that!" Eucilla snatched the fruit from Charlotte's hand and sank her teeth into it.

There was a third crunching sound and I could tell by her howl of pain that it was her teeth that had given way, not the fruit.

Eucilla flung the *oppol* away from her but not before I saw that her *other* front tooth was now just a jagged, bloody stump as well. She ran to Morbain, tears streaming down her dirty cheeks.

I looked at Morbain wearily as the girl wailed in his arms.

"*Now* will you admit that Eucilla is not the True Incarnation?"

"Never." He glared at me and then looked at the Head Councilor. "I invoke my right as one of Royal blood to demand the Fourth Trial!"

Charlotte

There was an audible gasp in the room and all the members of the Council of Wisdom looked shocked.

What in the hell was the Fourth Trial, I wondered. Was I going to have to walk over live coals or scale the side of an active volcano or swim through a lake of man-eating sharks or what?

Whatever it was, I trusted that it wouldn't hurt me. I knew that because only Kristoff's face remained serene even as everyone around us had gone pale with terror.

"Very well." The Head Councilor had a grim look on his face but he nodded anyway. "Follow me," he told us.

I had thought he would lead us out of the narrow corridor where the doors to the first three Trials were located. Instead, he turned and led us deeper into it. Soon, I saw why.

In a shadowy alcove at the very end of the dim passage, was a fourth door. This one, though, wasn't made of gold or even trimmed in gold in any way. This one was dead black and there was an elaborate-looking locking mechanism on the golden knob, which was twice as big as the knobs on the other doors.

The Head Councilor stopped in front of the black door with the oversized knob and then began doing something weird with the thick gold chain he wore around his neck. Pretty soon he had detached part of it which looked like a kind of medallion. He twisted and turned it at strange angles and soon he was holding something vaguely key-shaped.

"Within this room is something so deadly that only I, as Head of the Council of Wisdom, or the Empress herself may open it," he announced, holding the medallion-key up.

"Why?" I asked. "Does the Empress get a key too?"

"No, of course not." He gave me a disdainful look. "When the True Incarnation is at last brought to light and Invested as the Goddess-Empress, her touch on the knob will be enough to open it."

Stooping down, the Head Councilor fitted the medallion-key into the locking mechanism of the huge knob. Then he twisted it and threw it open with a flourish, revealing what was beyond a doubt, the prettiest room I'd yet seen in the palace.

It was like an indoor arboretum with a high, vaulted glass ceiling through which pinkish light filtered down onto an idyllic tropical garden. A lush carpet of blue-green grass led from the doorway all the way to a pretty little golden bench with curving legs and a curlicue-back. There was a narrow path of golden gravel leading to the bench, winding its way between flowering shrubs and spreading bushes with their broad, turquoise leaves.

Tall trees shaded the path and in their branches, I could see bright, jewel-like creatures that looked a little like chipmunks or squirrels only their fur was brilliant blue and emerald green and ruby red instead of dull brown or gray. There was even a little blue brook, babbling its way across the landscape.

All-in-all, it looked like the perfect place to sit and read a book.

"Oh," I whispered to Kristoff. "It's gorgeous! What's so bad about it?"

"Behold," the Head Councilor intoned dramatically, before Kristoff could answer me. "I give you...The Garden of *Death.*"

Well, I guess that answered *that* question.

"The Garden of Death?" I asked, looking at it doubtfully. "Um, how exactly is it deadly?"

"It's not—to the True Incarnation," the Head Councilor said, staring at me significantly. "To the Empress, this place can be a refuge—a place of much needed solitude in which no one can bother her."

"Why?" I asked blandly. "Is there some kind of electrical field over the entrance that fries anyone who tries to go in except her?"

"A shrewd guess, my Lady." This time it was the youngest Councilor—the one with the brown skin and eyes—who answered. "There is, indeed a barrier between this room and the next, but only to contain that which lies within."

"And what 'lies within'?" I asked, feeling like the phrase—and indeed, this whole scene—was entirely too dramatic. "I mean, what's inside that's so dangerous?"

"Poison." Morbain's eyes gleamed in the dim light. "Every surface within that garden is infused with the deadliest poison in the known galaxy. The very air within is a poisonous fume that would sear the lungs of anyone but the Empress—or one that she is touching skin-to-skin."

"If the air leaked out into the rest of the palace, it could kill everyone in the whole place," Kristoff explained quietly. "That's why there is an invisible barrier held in place here...and here." He nodded at the top corners of the door and I saw two little black boxes with blinking red lights on them—presumably generating some kind of field to contain the deadly air of the garden.

"Of course," he continued. "It doesn't stop anyone from going into the room—it just keeps the poisonous air inside from getting out and spreading. And it also stops any projectile weapons—any shot from a blaster or any other kind of firearm cannot get through. That way the Empress can sit with the door open without fear of any kind of assassination, should she so choose."

"Go back a minute," I said, looking at Morbain who was still giving me a challenging look, as though he was waiting for me to run screaming at the idea of an entire garden filled with poison. "What did you mean it would poison anyone except the Empress and someone *touching* her? How does that work?"

"The Empress may convey her immunity to the Garden of Death through skin-to-skin contact," the Head Councilor said. "In this way the Garden may serve as a safe room for her and her loved ones in case of an attack. As long as she continues to touch them, they will not come to harm. However if she lets them go—even for an instant..."

"Oh, okay. I get it," I said.

It had seemed strange at first to have a room full of deadly poisons in the middle of a busy, crowded palace—like a terrorist attack waiting to happen. But I could see how it would be helpful for the Empress to have a safe place for herself and her loved ones to retreat in case the palace was attacked. Then I had another thought.

"What about the chipmunk-looking things though? How are they still alive in there?"

"The *terlings,* you mean?" the younger Councilor asked, motioning to the jewel-colored animals scampering in the branches of the trees.

"Sure, I guess. Are they immune to all the poison in the, uh, Garden of Death?"

"Naturally so." He nodded. "The *terlings,* my Lady, are the most vicious, bad-tempered rodents in this or any other world. They will leave the Empress alone but if they feel that their territory is being invaded they will spring to action and attack anyone else."

Wow—attack chipmunks. This place just kept getting better and better.

"Thank you for your explanation," I said politely, keeping my thoughts to myself.

"And these are not even the most dangerous creatures that live in the Garden of Death," one of the other Councilors said eagerly. "There are also the *Heart-bursts*—snake-like creatures who have the most poisonous bite in the known galaxy. Their venom kills almost instantly — causing the heart to swell and explode within the chest."

"And again, I'm guessing they don't attack the Empress — just everybody else?" I asked. I was sensing a theme here.

"He nodded. Mostly they stay hidden in the trees and bushes."

"Is there an antivenin?" I asked, the doctor part of my brain getting interested. I had never heard of a snake whose venom made someone's heart swell up and burst in their chest cavity.

"There is, but it's hardly ever effective. If the patient — "

"So only the True Incarnation can go in without getting killed?" Eucilla interrupted. She spoke with some difficulty, her words mushy due to her two missing front teeth.

I wished she would just give up and go seek some medical attention. It was painful to watch her standing there with her skin and dress all gray from ash and soot, her teeth broken, and her hair half burned off. She had been so lovely and now she looked like a broken toy a child had been careless with — a Barbie doll thrown in the fireplace to melt. But despite everything we had been through, she still had the gleam of determination in her eyes.

I thought I had never seen anyone before who was so willfully self-deluded.

"Yes, exactly my dear," Morbain said, still giving me a challenging look. "Which is why no one but the True Incarnation would *dare* to enter. A regular person — an imposter — would scarcely last five seconds within those walls. The plants would cut them like knives, the touch of the water in the stream would be as acid, eating away at their flesh, and the very air would sear their lungs until they fell down and died in *agony*."

This last description was clearly aimed right at me. He was letting me know why I didn't dare to go into the forbidden garden. Trying to scare me out of trying so that I would concede the victory to Eucilla.

But after dealing with living inanimate objects that whizzed at my head, fruit that turned to stone in the wrong hands, and facing down a freaking fire-breathing *dragon*, I just couldn't find it in me to be very frightened of the pretty little garden.

Apparently, neither could Eucilla.

"So only the True Incarnation can go in and live and going in will prove once and for all that I am the one!" she exclaimed.

Morbain frowned. "Well, yes my pet but I don't think—"

"I'm the one!" Eucilla shouted, running for the doorway.

I saw at once that the idiot was going to get herself killed, trying to prove a point that wasn't true. Jumping after her, I barely caught her wrist in one hand as she teetered in the doorway in her ridiculous heels.

"Eucilla wait—this is suicide," I protested, trying to keep her from crossing the threshold.

"For you, maybe." She flashed me a look and then surged forward, through the doorway and into the lovely, idyllic garden.

I hung onto her wrist grimly as we went, knowing she could be killed if I let go. Sure enough, since I was touching her, neither one of us were harmed. I could breathe easily and the plants and bushes that brushed us didn't hurt a bit.

I wished I could go sit on the golden bench and watch the blue water in the little brook ripple and babble and just rest for a minute. It felt like these stupid Trials had been going on for ages and I was tired and hungry, despite the tube of nutripaste Kristoff had made me eat that morning.

But there was no rest while Eucilla was with me. The minute we got into the garden, she began fighting me.

"Let go! Let me *go!*" she demanded, trying to twist loose of my grip on her wrist.

"No." I hung on tight. "If I do, you'll die."

"*You'll* die, you mean," she hissed. "Since *I* am the True Incarnation. You're only holding on to me to save your own miserable life."

"Eucilla, my dear, you've made your point." Morbain's voice sounded high and strained. "We can all see that you've entered the Garden of Death and no harm has befallen you, so you must be the True Incarnation. You can come back now."

"She's only come to no harm because my Lady Charlotte is keeping her from it by staying in contact with her," Kristoff said sternly. "Without her touch, your candidate would die."

"Not true! Head Councilor Tannus, I demand that my Lady Eucilla be declared the True Incarnation at once so that this travesty can end!" Morbain exclaimed.

Still fighting with Eucilla, I turned my head to see that the Head Councilor was nodding, as though this actually seemed like a reasonable proposition to him.

What was going on with this guy? Either he was deep in Morbain's pocket or he was working some agenda of his own.

Kristoff was staring at him and Morbain angrily and the other Councilors were murmuring amongst themselves.

"My Lady Charlotte," Kristoff said to me, raising his voice to be heard over the babble. "You must release your grip on Eucilla's arm."

"No," I said grimly, thinking of the Hippocratic Oath I'd taken. "First, do no harm." Well, I would be doing a hell of a lot of harm by letting go of Eucilla. She was a real piece of work but she didn't deserve to die just for being a delusional idiot.

Kristoff frowned. "My Lady, it is the only way to prove the truth of the matter."

"I don't care," I said, still gripping her arm. "I'm not going to let her die. You don't understand, Kristoff—she really *believes* she's the one."

It was true—now that I was in firm contact with Eucilla, my touch-sense told me so. She really, honestly believed that she was meant to be the next Goddess-Empress and she refused to let anything change her mind. Also, she was spoiled, entitled, and came from an immensely rich family. But I could have guessed all that without my *La-ti-zal* powers.

"Let me go!" Eucilla stormed, still trying to twist away from me. "You off-worlder, imposter, piece of commoner trash! Let...Me...GO!"

As she screamed the last word, she stomped down on my bare foot and shoved me with her free hand as hard as she could.

I fell in the grass on the side of the golden gravel path, my toes throbbing and the wind knocked out of me from the fall. Eucilla, meanwhile, stood tall in the garden laughing and doing a little happy-dance of triumph.

"You see?" she shrieked, jumping up and down, which caused the *terlings* to stand up on their little hind legs and begin chattering angrily. Eucilla paid them no attention. "Do you see?" she yelled, waving her arms wildly. "This proves it! This proves that *I* and I alone am the..."

Her words ended in a horrible, wracking cough. A panicked expression crossed her once-lovely face and her hands went to her throat. A hoarse gasping sound came from her mouth and she stumbled to her knees and then toppled over into one of the flowering bushes beside the path. Immediately the *terlings* came rushing over, scampering over her fallen form, scratching her with their sharp little claws.

"Eucilla!" I said, or tried to say, anyway. I had fallen really hard when she hit me and I was still struggling to get some air back in my lungs.

"Ah...gah!" she gasped, her long body fishtailing in the bushes, trying to throw off the jewel-colored chipmunk-creatures. I was horrified to see that the lush, turquoise leaves were cutting her flesh like knives and the flowers were leaving angry red welts over her skin and face. Her dress protected most of her torso and legs but her feet, strapped into their high heels, had landed in the little babbling brook. As I watched, the innocent-looking water began to *melt* her footwear, which was smoking and letting off an acrid stench like something dissolving in acid.

Grimly, I got to my feet, even though it felt like the foot Eucilla has stomped on might be broken. I tried to walk mainly on my heel, to keep the pressure off my throbbing toes and arch, as I hobbled around to where she lay, stretched on the deadly grass.

"Shoo! Shoo!" I brushed at the *terlings* and they scampered away, still chattering angrily.

Grabbing Eucilla's arms, I began to haul her towards the doorway. But though she looked so willowy and thin, she was heavy—*really* heavy. Also, I was trying to drag her through the thick grass and out of the bushes that seemed to want to hold on to her. It was almost as if the plants were *hungry* and Eucilla was the only food they'd seen in a long time.

"*Uhhh*," I gasped, taking a firmer grip and yanking harder.

"Come...on!" But no matter how hard I pulled, she wasn't budging.

Suddenly, someone was beside me.

I looked up and saw Kristoff, reaching for Eucilla's limp form. Already welts had formed on his gold-tan skin where some of the branches of the bushes had brushed it and there were cuts on his arms where the leaves had sliced him.

"Kristoff, no!" I gasped. "You'll *die!*"

"Not if you let go of her and hold on to me," he said grimly.

I saw at once what he meant and reached for his muscular bicep. The moment my skin touched his, he drew a deep breath and the tight, strained look left his face.

"Ahh—that's better. Don't lose your hold on me, my Lady," he said, taking a firm grip on Eucilla's arms.

"I won't," I promised.

I think Kristoff wanted to pick Eucilla up and carry her, as he had done for me so many times. But as I had noticed earlier, the hungry branches of the bushes she had fallen into did *not* want to give up their prey. In the end, he had to drag her out by her arms, as I had been trying to do. Luckily, being so much stronger than me, he was actually able to do it. After what felt like forever, we were able to pull Eucilla out of the deadly garden.

As soon as she was out, I had Kristoff lay her out on the floor and felt for a pulse.

Nothing. No breathing either. I wished desperately that I was back home in the Pit where I could call for a crash cart. But I had to do the best I could.

"You," I said pointing to the Head Councilor, "Go get a healer *now*. Well, don't just stand there!" I yelled when he just stared at me like I had grown a second head. "This woman needs medical attention. Get me a healer who has the antidote to this poison!"

After another look at me that was half angry, half frightened, he finally scurried off to do as I said.

"What can I do, my Lady?" Kristoff was kneeling beside me on the cold, black marble floor.

"Chest compressions," I told him. "Straddle her and position your hands one on top of the other. But first find the xiphoid process and go up two fingers…shit—do you people even *have* a xiphoid process? Never mind—I'll find out myself."

As it turned out, Majorans do have a xiphoid process, which is that little nubbin of bone that sticks off the end of your sternum. Under my direction, Kristoff started doing chest compressions while I did rescue breathing, tilting Eucilla's head back to open her airway and checking every few cycles to see if we were getting back breathing or a pulse.

We weren't.

Finally, a female Majoran in a long, white robe appeared. She had a business-like air of efficiency and her long, dark blue hair was tied back in an approximation of my own pony-tail back home. She was carrying what looked like a sleek, silver suitcase which I hoped had a defibrillator and plenty of meds inside.

"Move please." She brushed me and Kristoff aside and I let her because I could tell she knew what she was doing. Still, I couldn't help filling her in.

"Patient is an adult female who breathed in known poisonous fumes in the, uh, Garden of Death." I still felt ridiculous saying it. "She also fell into the grass and shrubbery which resulted in cuts and abrasions, as well as chemical burns along her face and arms."

"How long was she inside?" The Majoran doctor looked up at me briefly.

"I don't know," I said miserably. "Maybe five minutes? But for some of that time I still had hold of her, so she wasn't hurt. It was only after she got away from me that the poison began to take effect."

"So you went in too? And *survived?*" Her eyes widened and went yellow briefly—the color of surprise? I didn't know.

"This is Lady Charlotte of Earth, the True Incarnation of the Goddess-Empress, Sundalla the 1000th," Kristoff told her. "The Garden of Death could not harm her."

"Your Majesty!" The healer was already kneeling but she bowed as low as she was able.

"Never mind about me," I said irritably. "What about her? Can you save her? Do you have the antidote to the poison she breathed and touched?"

"I do." She popped open her silver suitcase and got out a vial of blue liquid which she proceeded to load into some kind of hand-held device with a lot of tiny, short needles attached, which I assumed was some kind of hypodermic. But before she could administer it, Kristoff touched my arm.

"My Lady—look."

"What is it?" I looked down at the spot he was pointing to—or rather, *spots*. There were two bright blue fang marks on the inside of Eucilla's arm, just beside her right elbow. I'd missed them before because I was too busy trying to do CPR and get her heart started again to check her over like I should have.

"*Heartburst* bite," the Majoran doctor said quietly. She felt again for Eucilla's pulse, shook her head, and began to dismantle her elaborate looking hypodermic.

"*Heartburst?* What the hell is—" I began, and then I remembered what one of the Councilors had been telling me, about the deadly snake creature that lived in the garden whose venom was the most toxic of the known galaxy.

"I'm sorry, your Majesty," the doctor said somberly. "If I had gotten here at once, I might have been able to help. But as long as it's been, I'm afraid her heart has already burst within her."

I sat back on my heels wearily and swiped a hand over my forehead.

"No wonder CPR didn't help," I said, half to myself. "We were trying to restart her heart but there was no heart to start again."

"I'm sorry," the doctor said again. "It is, of course, your Majesty's right to punish me for not getting here quicker."

"*Punish* you?" I looked up at her in disbelief. "Of course I'm not going to punish you for losing a patient—I lost her too. If anything, this is on me. I should never have lost my grip on her. I should have tried harder to drag her out."

"Charlotte," Kristoff said in a low voice. "You can't blame yourself for this. You did everything you could."

"No." I straightened up, lifting my chin. "No, you're right, Kristoff, I'm *not* entirely to blame." I rose to my full height—which wasn't easy since the foot Eucilla had stomped on was throbbing—and rounded on Morbain. "This is *your* fault," I said, pointing one trembling finger at him. "*You* filled this poor girl's head with nonsense about how she was the next Empress. You told her from the time she was a child that she would grow up and rule the whole galaxy when what you really wanted was to rule *through* her!"

A shocked gasp went up from everyone assembled and from the corner of my eye, I could see Kristoff shaking his head as though trying to get me to stop. But I was so angry I couldn't stop—didn't *want* to stop. I didn't care what anyone thought of me—I just wanted to let Morbain know exactly what I thought of *him*.

"*You're* the reason she's dead," I said, my voice shaking with rage. "You killed her as surely as if you'd put a gun to her head and pulled the trigger yourself! You are a *murderer!*"

There was another shocked gasp and I saw that Morbain's face was red and twisted but not with sorrow—with rage.

"Why you..." His mustache quivered and little white dents appeared on either side of his generous nose. "You...you little..."

"I believe the word you're looking for is your *Majesty*," Kristoff said in a low, menacing voice. He had risen smoothly to his feet to stand beside me. His sword was out and naked in his hand. "For Lady Charlotte *is* the True Incarnation of the Goddess-Empress," he went on, glaring at everyone assembled, including Head Councilor Tannus who was back and looking very angry. "And as such, I demand that we hold the Ceremony of Investiture *here* and *now*."

"What?" the Head Councilor exclaimed. "But that is most irregular! We cannot hold the ceremony anywhere but in the Council Room proper."

"I don't think so," Kristoff growled. "Too much could happen between this part of the palace and the Council Room. You know as well as I, Head Councilor Tannus, that the ceremony mostly consists of you conferring the title upon the worthy candidate and declaring to the Goddess and everyone present that she is indeed the True Incarnation."

"But...but I..." Clearly the Head Councilor felt backed into a corner and just as clearly, Kristoff didn't care.

"Can you deny that Charlotte is the True Incarnation?" he demanded. "She has passed through all four of the Trials of Ascendancy and lived, while her competitor has not."

He nodded down at Eucilla's body, which was being quickly and quietly removed by several of the Imperial Guards to my mingled relief and regret. I hate losing a patient—even a bitchy, bratty, entitled one with delusions of grandeur like Eucilla had been.

Morbain's mouth worked under his pointed pirate mustache, as though he wanted to say something and the Head Councilor had a sour look on his face but apparently neither one of them could refute Kristoff's claim.

"All right," Councilor Tannus finally said. "Let me confer with the Council of Wisdom."

"Do not confer too long," Kristoff said, frowning. "My Lady is weary and in need of rest and aid—see that you do not keep your Empress waiting."

Chapter Twenty-four

Charlotte

I don't know if it was Kristoff's words or the way he was glaring at them, but the Council of Wisdom didn't take long to confer. Almost before I knew it, I was standing surrounded by a circle of men—the High Council at my front, and my honor guard and Kristoff at my back.

"Charlotte of Earth," High Councilor Tannus said, giving me the nastiest look possible. "By the power invested in me by the Goddess of Mercy, she who gave the seeds of life to the Ancient Ones and bid them fill the galaxy with all living things, I do now pronounce that you are, in fact, the Goddess-Empress, Sundalla the 1000th and Invest you with all the titles, rights, and privileges attached to that designation. Long may your Majesty live."

At the moment he spoke the words, something very strange happened. I felt a rush of power go through me—like a warm, electrical wind that made every part of me tingle. It was the same kind of rush I'd felt when Kristoff made his vow to me, what seemed like a hundred years ago back on Earth. Only this was even more intense—as though something bigger than myself was filling me up, like water in a cup.

"Oh!" I gasped and put my hand to my head, wondering if my hair was all standing on end—it certainly felt like it.

"My Lady, are you well?" Kristoff murmured in my ear.

"Is she all right?" I heard one of the other guards ask—it was T'zorin, I thought dimly, the one who had warned us that the Trials had been moved up. The one Kristoff trusted. "I was at the other end of the hall—couldn't see what was going on. What happened? Is the Empress all right?"

"I...I'm fine," I whispered, taking the arm Kristoff reached out to steady me with. The moment we touched, I felt the same, electrical sizzle I'd experienced the first time I touched his skin. Only this was a hundred—a *thousand* times more intense.

I shivered as a deep wave of *needing* washed over me. Need that was bigger than me overwhelmed me—*filled* me. My nipples were suddenly tight, tender points at the tips of my breasts and between my thighs I was wet and swollen and ready.

"*Kristoff,*" I moaned, turning to look at him. "I…I need…"

His eyes grew wide and he shook his head, a desperate signal to be silent. Somehow I managed to keep the words inside me but I couldn't control the *need* the pulsed through me like a heartbeat—throbbing and pounding and *growing* with every breath.

The Goddess's need, whispered a voice in my head. *You are filled with the Goddess and her needs are not small.*

"The True Incarnation has been Invested," someone shouted—it might have been the Majoran doctor, who was still there in the crowded small hallway of the Trials. "Long live the new Goddess-Empress! Long live Sundalla the 1000th!"

Other people took up the chant and soon it had spread to the crowd of waiting nobles and royalty in the broad main hallway outside.

"Long live the Empress! Long live the Empress!"

"Come," Kristoff said, bending down so I could hear him over the noise. "We need to get you to the Royal Chambers." He looked at T'zorin. "You go ahead of us and make certain they're all clear. And make damn sure no one and nothing goes in or out until we get there!"

"Yes, Captain!" T'zorin saluted and began weaving his way through the crowd.

Kristoff had me by the arm and was leading me out too. I tried to follow him but the moment I forgot and put weight on my hurt foot, a bolt of pain went through me, making me gasp and sink to the ground.

"Charlotte?" He looked back at me, his eyes filled with fear for me. It was that look on his face, more than anything else, that made me realize we were in a vulnerable and dangerous position. No wonder Kristoff wanted to get us out of here and back to the safety and privacy of the Royal Chambers. "Are you well? What happened?" he asked.

"I...my foot. She...Eucilla stomped on it when she was trying to get away. I don't know but I think she might have broken it," I said in a rush. The one good thing about the intense pain was that it drove the desire out—at least a little. So when he bent and scooped me up into his arms, I could feel his body against mine without moaning in need.

It was a good thing because everyone was watching us, including Morbain and Head Councilor Tannus, both of whom were staring daggers in my general direction. If I had started writhing in Kristoff's arms or trying to kiss him—the way I badly wanted to do—we could have been in real trouble.

Poor Eucilla—who would have thought by breaking my foot she was doing me a favor?

And then we were in the middle of the mob, the honor guard surrounding us and barely clearing a path. It seemed that now I was officially the Goddess-Empress, everyone wanted a better look at me.

"Bow!" Kristoff roared, holding me tightly as he surged forward like a man fighting against a strong current. "Show the proper respect and bow before your new Empress, people of Femme One!"

Reluctantly, I thought, they began to do as he said. They probably would have bowed more readily to Eucilla—she had certainly looked the part more than me and everyone had expected her to win the deadly contest we'd just played together.

God, I couldn't think of that now. Nor did I want to think of the pulsing desire that was growing inside me like a ball of energy threatening to explode and turn me into a shivering mass of mindless lust.

The feel of Kristoff's hard body against my own, the spicy, warm scent of his skin, the way he carried me, so strong and sure...everything about him made me want him. Want him so badly I thought I would die if I couldn't have him. And yet, somehow I held back, mindful of the many, many eyes that watched us as we went.

But God, what was happening to me? And how long could I

stand this before I snapped?

Kristoff

"No, no—you're fine. Just fine." Dr. Churika snapped her medical case closed and stood up.

"What? How can you say that?" Charlotte's voice was terse and angry. She'd objected to having Dr. Churika attend her—asking instead for the under-healer who had tried to help us with Eucilla at the Garden of Death.

I had explained, as patiently as I could, that the other healer had not been vetted yet or taken the Oath of Loyalty. Until I could look into her background and be sure of her completely, she wouldn't be allowed to attend the Empress.

"I don't care about any of that," Charlotte had muttered. "She knew what she was doing—I could tell. And she wouldn't be dismissive of me and...and what I'm going through right now."

"And what *are* you going through?" I'd asked her, frowning. I had felt the surge of energy that went through her during the pronouncement of Investiture—everyone in the hall had. It had rippled outwards in waves—a great flow of divine power that proved beyond the shadow of a doubt that Charlotte was indeed the True Incarnation.

But there was something else too—the need I had seen in her eyes when I touched her—the desire I felt thrumming through her lovely body was both intense and immense. I knew it was there but I wanted to hear her say it—to know exactly what we were dealing with before we called the healer in.

"You know what it is," Charlotte had said, looking up at me. "And you know what I need."

To that, I had no answer—not one she wanted to hear, anyway. I could feel her yearning for me—it was matched by mine for hers. But we could never be together and there was no use in belaboring the point.

Just then, Dr. Churika had been announced and our conversation had been cut short. The healer had examined Charlotte with her usual brisk efficiency, given her an injection in the hurt foot—which was only badly bruised and not broken—and pronounced everything to be fine.

"I'm *not* fine," Charlotte told her again, glaring up from the rich, golden brocade settee in the sitting room where I had deposited her when I finally got her back to the Royal Apartments.

"I assure you, your Majesty, that foot will feel as good as new in just a few minutes. The injection I gave you is a fast healing agent which will—"

"It's not my *foot* I'm concerned about," Charlotte said through gritted teeth.

Churika raised her brows. "And what is it that concerns your Majesty?" she asked dryly.

"It's these feelings—this *need*—which you said would fade as the effects of my blood left Kristoff's system." She glanced at me and I looked calmly back, willing my face to remain neutral. I had felt her trembling in my arms as I carried her through the crowd back to the safety of the Royal Chambers. Her lust had licked at me like a flame, teasing me with what I could never have.

"Hmm...this is still an issue?" Dr. Churika frowned. "That's most irregular."

"Not only is it still an issue, it just got exponentially worse when I was confirmed, uh, I mean *Invested* as the True Incarnation," Charlotte told her. "It hit me in this massive wave—I feel like I'm going to *crawl* out of my *skin* if I don't get some..." Her eyes lingered on me, hungry and full of desire. "If I don't get some relief."

The healer saw where Charlotte's eyes had wandered and her face took on a stony, disapproving expression.

"Well, it's common knowledge that the Empress needs a Consort—you're probably just longing for yours. I'll recommend to the Council of Wisdom that the Ceremony of Culling be scheduled for tomorrow and you can choose a Royal Consort very soon."

"No." Charlotte's voice was tense and angry. "I don't *want* some stranger I've never met before! I don't want anyone but—"

"You cannot always have what you want, child, even if you are the Empress," Churika said sharply before Charlotte could speak my name. "As for the need you feel now, I'll schedule a trip for you

to the Royal House of Goddess Pleasures this very evening. Bathe
and dress yourself and be ready to go."

"But—" Charlotte began.

"Not another word," the older female said sternly. "I will not
hear blasphemy spoken in my presence, not even from the mouth of
she who rules us all."

"So it's blasphemy to be with the one man in the whole
universe I want?" Charlotte demanded. "If that's the case, I don't
think much of your religion. And I don't remember converting to it,
either."

"You converted when you were Invested as the True
Incarnation," Churika snapped. "Kindly remember that you are the
Goddess-Empress and act like it, instead of a spoiled brat throwing
a tantrum because she cannot get her way."

Charlotte's eyes got very wide and for a moment I thought she
would shout or possibly even throw something at the older female's
head. She certainly looked angry enough to do either or both. But
she simply took a deep breath and closed her eyes for a moment.
When she opened them, her gaze was every bit as steely as Dr.
Churika's.

"Thank you for your medical opinion, Dr. Churika," she said in
a calm, level voice. "I will certainly take it into consideration."

Churika blinked, looking surprised.

"Very well, your Majesty," she said shortly. "I'll see to the
details of your visit to the House of Goddess Pleasures."

"Do that." Charlotte nodded. "Now I'd like some time to
myself. It's been quite a day and I need to recuperate."

"Of course." The other female was still looking at her warily, as
though she wasn't sure what Charlotte might do next. I wasn't sure
myself. I could still feel the need surging inside her, as well as the
simmering anger she felt against Dr. Churika—who really had
overstepped her boundaries just now. But there was something else
in her—a seed of doubt had been planted. I wished I knew why.

For a moment we all just stood there and then Charlotte
nodded at the healer.

"You're dismissed."

Churika looked like she wanted to say something else but she didn't quite dare. At last she simply gave Charlotte an abbreviated bow and left.

"My Lady?" I said, going to sit beside her on the gold brocade settee. She looked weary and worried and so lovely it made my heart ache.

"Kristoff," she said in a low voice. "Do you think I'm acting like a spoiled brat? Like Eucilla was?"

"No, my Lady," I murmured. I took her bare feet onto my lap and began to rub the injured one very, very gently. Her bones were so delicate that her foot was barely as long as my hand, from fingers to palm.

"I hope not," she said in a low voice. "And I know that I'm responsible for an awful lot of people now." She put her face in her hands. "I made a pretty bad start of it, didn't I? I already lost one."

"Eucilla died because of her own foolishness — not through any fault or failing of yours," I told her, my heart aching for her grief and sorrow.

"I should have been able to save her," she said in a muffled voice. "I *hate* losing a patient."

"She wasn't your patient. She was your rival and an imposter to the throne," I reminded her.

"She didn't know that." She pulled her hands away from her face. "That bastard Morbain — I saw it when I touched her, you know. The way he filled her head with lies and dreams and swore she would be the Empress when she grew up and came of age. Eucilla was just a spoiled little girl and he poisoned her mind, Kristoff! He made her so sure of being something she wasn't that she died for it." She shook her head. "I can't forgive that or forget that."

"Then remember it," I said gently. "But don't take her death on yourself, my Lady. You don't deserve that guilt."

"Thank you." She sighed and lifted her chin. "I try to remind myself of that but it's always hard when you lose a patient — and she *was* my patient, even if it was only for five minutes. So don't say she wasn't."

I nodded gravely, acknowledging her statement, though I

didn't really agree with it. Still, it was like Charlotte to think in such a manner. I had never met anyone with so much personal integrity, such fierce courage and loyalty…and such loveliness.

My heart swelled and I had to look away and concentrate on rubbing her hurt foot again. My old mistress had spoken truly when she said that when I found her successor I would find her worthy of the love and devotion I had shown to her. Sundalla the 999th would have liked Charlotte. She was so like my old mistress and yet she was also her own person, strong and stubborn and wholly worthy of admiration and service.

I only wished I could serve her in the way she wanted me to. In the way that she *needed* so desperately. Even now, when I was only touching her feet, I could feel the electric tension between us. It made me want to take her in my arms and worship her with my body, not just my heart.

"So," Charlotte said, her tone deliberately light. "Tell me about this, uh, House of Goddess Pleasures. What is it and how in the world is it supposed to help me with my, um, my *problem?*"

"It is a place where unmated females can go to get their needs met and unmated males can worship them."

Her eyes narrowed. "Worship *how* exactly?"

I explained the process and her eyes went wide.

"What? Kristoff, I can't do *that."*

I frowned. "I am afraid you have no choice. Dr. Churika is still the Royal Healer. If she has prescribed a course of treatment for you, you'll have to go through with it."

"Well, I…I want a second opinion," she sputtered, clearly upset. "I want…I need…"

"What you need, Charlotte, is someone to take care of you," I interrupted in a low voice. "You won't get through the Culling Ceremony otherwise. You need to be calm and collected tomorrow—not 'ready to crawl out of your skin' as you put it."

She reached out tentatively to cup my cheek in her hand.

"I like when you call me by my first name," she said softly. "I mean, 'my Lady' is nice too, even if it does sound kind of Renaissance-y. But when you call me by name it's more…intimate somehow." She blushed as she spoke the words but she didn't drop her eyes or take her hand from my cheek.

"My Lady," I said again, deliberately using the honorific. "Please don't change the subject. I happen to agree with Dr. Churika on this particular point—you need a deep release and the House of Goddess Pleasures is the best place to get you one."

She bit her lip. "But...I don't want to let some *stranger* do that to me!"

I turned my face into her hand and placed a gentle kiss on her palm, my heart drumming beneath my ribs. Gods, how I wanted her!

"I don't want anyone else touching you either," I admitted in a low voice. In fact, the thought made me sick inside. "But I swear to you, my Lady, I will make certain of your safety. I will not let you be hurt," I told her fiercely.

"You will?" She looked at me pleadingly. "I mean I'm sure you will. But do I *really* have to go through with this"

"Charlotte," I said softly. "You need this release."

"All right." She dropped her eyes. "I...I guess I'll try. I just don't know if I can go through with it."

"When your *need* grows great enough, you will be willing," I assured her, thinking of some of the stories I had heard of Empresses past.

When their *needing* was on them, their lust could be truly legendary which was one reason it was so important that the Consort be a fit male who had a drive to match the Empress's own. It was one of the criteria the Council of Wisdom considered when choosing candidates from the Royal males available.

Charlotte sighed. "I guess I'll just have to take your word for that."

"Come," I told her. "Let us get you fed and bathed and prepared for tonight."

Chapter Twenty-five

Charlotte

"I can't believe I'm actually going to do this," I muttered to myself as the golden carriage made its way through the crowded halls of the palace, which was so large there were actually roads inside to get from one area to another. It really was like a self contained city with a market district, several theaters, numerous restaurants, beauty salons, and everything else you could think of.

So far we had been staying in the section which was reserved for the Royals — the Royal Sector it was called — and it was where the Empress and the Council of Wisdom made their homes and ruled from. But now we were going to an area outside that sector — to the House of Goddess Pleasures.

I had been piecing together more information about the place we were going and what I found out surprised me. It was, as Kristoff had told me, an establishment where unwed Majoran females could seek sexual pleasure without any shame, blame, or social repercussions.

But it wasn't some kind of a whore house staffed by gigolos. Rather, the Majorans considered it a kind of temple — a place that was sacred to the Goddess and to the goddess-hood of all females everywhere. Because of that, it was staffed by unmarried Majoran males who had to pay dues in order to serve there. They were specially trained by the priests who ran and oversaw the place in the arts of pleasuring a female in various ways and they were *always*, Kristoff stressed, extremely respectful.

I tried to imagine something like that working on Earth and just couldn't see it. There were still too many places on my home world where women were objectified or treated like chattel to be bought and sold. There was still too much sexual shaming going on. But in the Majoran society it was believed that every woman had a little spark of the Goddess within her and they were worshipped by their males because of it.

Not to say there weren't some males who disapproved of the situation or disliked it—I was pretty sure Prince Morbain and the Head Councilor of the Council of Wisdom were living proof of that. But most Majoran males seemed to dote on their females and treated them as if they were more precious than gold.

The way Kristoff treated me.

I tried not to think about that. Tried not to think about the fact that tomorrow, during the Culling Ceremony, I would give my blood to at least three candidates—none of whom I had ever seen before—and all picked for me by the Council of Wisdom. Out of those candidates, supposedly I would feel drawn to only one and he would become my Royal Consort.

Right now I couldn't imagine being drawn to anyone but the man sitting beside me, scanning the crowds outside the carriage's opaque glass windows, ever protective and always on the alert for anything or anyone who might pose a threat to me. I realized what I was doing was the equivalent of falling in love with your bodyguard but why was that so bad? Especially when he was so strong, and brave, and handsome, and muscular...

Stop it, Charlotte, I lectured myself. *You can't have him and you know it. For some reason it's supposed to be some kind of a sin or sacrilege and no matter how stupid that seems, you're supposed to be ruling these people now. You can't start your reign by disrespecting their religion and throwing their customs in their faces.*

But no matter how much I lectured myself, I couldn't overcome the burning need that was still growing inside me every minute. Under the special gown I was wearing, my nipples were tight and achy and the place between my thighs felt swollen and tender with desire—a desire I could do nothing to satiate myself.

I knew because I'd tried.

I had insisted on bathing myself for that express purpose. At first Kristoff had adamantly refused, but I insisted and I think he finally got the hint. I took a long leisurely soak in the huge, blue marble tub and tried taking care of business.

It didn't work.

Or rather, it *did* work but it wasn't enough. It seemed like no matter how much I touched myself, the need was never satiated. And believe me, I tried until the water went cold around me and I was beyond frustrated. My clit felt hot and swollen, ready to come at the lightest touch but every orgasm I gave myself seemed to barely ease the *need* inside me. At last I had to admit I needed something deeper—another way to satisfy my desire.

Finally, Kristoff had knocked on the door and demanded admittance. I sat up quickly, letting the tepid water cover me and told him to come in.

He took one look at my flushed and guilty face and shook his head.

"My Lady," he said in a low voice as he sat on the edge of the tub. "It won't help."

"What won't help? What do you mean?" I stuttered, feeling like my face must be as hot as the bathwater was cold by that time.

Kristoff simply gave me a look. "Don't forget that I can feel your emotions through the link I share to you," he said matter-of-factly. "I know what you've been doing in here and exactly how unsatisfied you still are, my Lady."

"I...you..." I'd felt suddenly ashamed, and even more naked than I already was, somehow.

Kristoff must have felt my mortification because his deep voice got a little softer.

"I know you're trying to please yourself, to take care of your need on your own, but you *can't*, Charlotte. You've reached the point where you need someone else to help you."

I bit my lip, unsure of what to say. "This whole thing where you can feel my emotions," I said at last. "It seems really unfair. Why can't I feel yours too?"

He shook his head. "The bond between the Empress and her Imperial Guards goes in one direction only. The only way you could feel my emotions is if we were mated and I bonded you to me."

"And how...how would you do that?" I asked, my heart suddenly pounding much harder.

"Through sex...making love." Kristoff's voice had been a soft, deep growl. "True mating and bonding sex requires deep penetration and the male must fill his goddess with his seed."

"So...that's all it takes?" I whispered, squeezing my thighs together under the water as I imagined him inside me, filling me, fucking me... "Just penetration and, uh ejaculation?"

"No." He shook his head. "If that was all, half the population would be wrongly bonded to a mate who wasn't suitable for them. We believe there is, for each person in the galaxy, a 'fated mate' – one whom you are destined to be bonded to for life. This is determined by the Goddess of Mercy, who is always seeking to propagate love among her people. When you make love with that one person the Goddess has meant for you, then and *only* then can a bond be formed."

"What if it's a person everyone else thinks is wrong for you?" I asked softly. "What then?"

Kristoff had stroked a strand of hair out of my face and looked at me. There was sorrow and regret in his rapidly shifting eyes.

"The will of the Goddess usually prevails. But not in all cases. Sometimes there are higher callings, my Lady. Now, will you allow me to help you from the bath and get you dressed? I have a light meal prepared for you and then we'll make our way to the House of Goddess Pleasures."

That had been the end of our conversation—and the end of me trying to "take care of" my problem myself. If Kristoff was right— and he had been right about everything else so I had no reason to doubt him—then what I needed was an outside touch. That was because the Goddess needed physical worship and as her scion here in the physical realm, I shared her needs and channeled them.

I didn't know how much or how little of that I believed but I had felt the immense surge of power when I had been Invested as the True Incarnation of the Empress, not to mention the hot wave of lust and need that had followed it. I thought it was probably better to err on the safe side and do what Kristoff said was necessary.

But I couldn't help wishing it was Kristoff who was going to take care of me. *Please, Kristoff, can't you promise me you'll be the one to help me in the House of Pleasures? I wouldn't mind going there and doing this if it was you.* A dozen times the words rose on my lips and a dozen times I swallowed them back down.

You can't ask that of him. He's not allowed to or he would have said so—you know he would have. You'll just have to deal with it, I lectured myself. *And besides, maybe it won't be so bad. It's all going to be completely anonymous. Just try to relax and enjoy it…*

Right. There was no way I was enjoying this, no matter how much my body declared that it needed a release. But there was no way out of it now—I would just have to suck it up and deal with it.

Sooner than I liked, the golden carriage pulled up before a tall, temple-like structure made of smooth, white marble. Four graceful columns flanked an arched entryway and there were people of both sexes ascending and descending the marble stairs that led up to it.

Kristoff got out first and motioned for me to pull my hood over my face to hide my identity. Many of the other women I saw were also wearing hoods or cloaks, though some wore masks instead. The males wore black leather masks that concealed their features, and I understood that other steps were taken inside to further preserve anonymity.

"Come, my Lady," Kristoff murmured, handing me down from the carriage, which was drawn by a lovely white horse-type creature with six legs instead of four. It snorted and tossed its head, its silky mane flying as I stepped down, holding tight to Kristoff's hand.

He led me up the marble steps and I kept my head down, glad that no one seemed to have recognized me.

Beneath the long, hooded cloak I wore, I felt my special Goddess Pleasure gown shift against my bare skin. It was made of the same thin, silky material as the sleeping garment Kristoff had gotten the magic bureau to make for me and it felt strange to be out in public in what felt like a nightdress.

Only this nightdress had several *special* features.

I preferred not to think about them now, however. I was just glad that the hooded cloak covered everything and dreaded taking it off.

At the top of the steps, we were met by a priest with brownish-tan skin in a long gray robe. He had serene gray eyes that matched his robe and an air of calm about him.

"Good morrow, my Lady. Good morrow, Sir," he greeted us.

"Have you come to be served and to be of service both in turn?"

"Are you Brother Selbert?" Kristoff asked in a low voice.

"As a matter of fact, I am." The priest nodded. "How can I be of assistance?"

Kristoff leaned closer and spoke in a low voice I couldn't catch. The priest's gray eyes widened and flickered over to me for a moment. Then he nodded.

"Of course. Come with me, if you please."

I wasn't sure what Kristoff had said—something about discretion probably, because instead of leading us through the broad, main entrance, the priest led us around to a smaller, more private door. He rapped on it and after a moment it opened and he ushered us inside.

"This is the private area where goddesses of Royal blood may receive pleasure and release," he told us in a low voice. "My Lady, if you would come with me, I will show you to a private pleasure chamber."

"I...don't know." A sudden attack of nerves made my hands shake and my palms sweat. Was I *actually* going to do this? Was I really going to go into a "pleasure room" and let some stranger touch me?

I can't do this, I thought. *I just **can't.***

"My Lady, you need this," Kristoff murmured to me. "Please go and do not be afraid. I swear that I will personally make certain he who attends you has only your safety and best interest at heart."

"All...all right," I whispered. "I'll try, I guess."

"Is my Lady unused to being pleasured?" the priest asked, frowning a little.

"She comes from a place where there are no Goddess Pleasure Houses," Kristoff explained. "She is as a maiden who has never visited the Pleasure House before."

"I see." The priest inclined his head. "Well, my Lady, I vow to you that all who serve here have had extensive training and can be extremely gentle if you so desire."

"As to that..." Kristoff cleared his throat. "I have a specific request regarding who shall be allowed to touch and service my

Lady."

He leaned in to speak to the priest again and I saw the other man's gray eyes grow wide and then narrow.

"I don't know," he said, frowning. "Such a request is...*most* irregular."

"It is necessary," Kristoff said firmly and I wondered what his request had been. He probably wanted a background check on the guy who was going to be "servicing" me—ugh, just *thinking* that word made me cringe. I really didn't see how I could go through with this.

"Well..." The priest still looked doubtful, but at last he nodded. "Very well."

"Thank you." Kristoff looked at me. "It is arranged, my Lady. You can go to the pleasure room with confidence and find your release."

"Um, sure. Thanks, I guess," I mumbled. I still wished it could be Kristoff that touched me—Kristoff that pleasured me. Once more the words trembled on my lips and once more I swallowed them down.

"Come," the priest said and this time, I went with him.

What else could I do?

Chapter Twenty-six

Charlotte

"This is the pleasure room," the priest with quiet gray eyes announced, opening a small ivory door, elaborately carved and outlined in gold.

Inside, I saw a small, round room as plush and luxurious as the inside of the genie bottle in the old *I Dream of Jeannie* re-runs I used to watch as a kid. The rounded, curved walls were decorated in patterns of gold, peacock blue, and teal and there were cushions in the same array of colors everywhere. Bisecting the room was a long, royal blue curtain that went from the curved ceiling all the way down to the floor, cutting the room exactly in half. The floor, which was gold and green, was made of a firm pillow-type material that gave when I stepped on it. Hanging overhead was an elaborately curved lamp which gave off a dim, golden glow and the faintest, spicy hint of incense.

"Please remove your shoes, goddess," the priest murmured. "And here is Aliza who will help you prepare and answer any of your questions before your pleasure attendant comes in."

"Welcome, my Lady." Aliza bowed low as I stepped out of the soft golden slippers Kristoff had given me to wear with my gown. She was a girl not much younger than me with the dark blue hair of most Majorans and a serious look on her lovely face.

"Um, hi," I said uncertainly as the priest bowed and left, shutting the door behind us. "How are you?"

"I am of no consequence," she said, bowing again. "It is you who have come here seeking service and release."

"Um, not really." I could hear the nervousness in my voice but I couldn't seem to stop it. "See, I really didn't want to come here. It was my doctor's idea—I mean, my *healer's* idea. But I really don't think I need this. I mean, I feel fine so maybe I should just go."

"No, my Lady—you must *stay.*" Somehow Aliza had insinuated herself between me and the exit door, blocking it with her body. "You don't need to be nervous," she said gently. "I understand it's your first trip to a pleasure house but I swear to you that you will find only pleasure here—never shame or pain. Unless pain is what you wish?"

"Pain? Oh, no—no, I'm not, uh, into all that 50 Shades stuff," I babbled. "I mean, I guess I could see the bondage part of it being fun but whips and chains just don't...don't do it for me. I mean..."

I trailed off, seeing that she had her head cocked to one side and was looking at me curiously.

"Never mind," I said miserably. "I guess the best thing to do is just get it over with."

"Get it over with?" Her eyes widened. "My Lady, it is our hope that you will never wish the pleasure to end."

"Uh, you can keep hoping that then," I said. "Anyway, please just tell me what I'm supposed to do and what's going to happen?"

"First we must remove your cloak." She suited actions to words, unfastening the cloak from around my neck and taking it away to drape it over part of the long, cushioned blue couch against the wall.

I shivered and wrapped my arms around myself at once, trying not to let the gown I was wearing gape open.

Remember I said that the gown had "special features"? Well, it did, in the form of two long slits on either side of the front of it, right over my breasts. That wasn't a problem as long as my nipples weren't hard, but once they got tight and achy with need, as they were now, they poked out the slits in the front of the gown. Actually, Kristoff had explained as he was putting the gown on me, the slits were meant to allow the entire breast to poke out of the dress for easier access.

The bottom of the long, silky gown, was cut in a wide, inverted V with the point right below my navel. Which meant it left my sex completely bare. I had begged to wear even a tiny pair of panties but Kristoff had told me sternly that undergarments were not allowed in the House of Goddess Pleasures because they interfered with the access of the pleasures attendants servicing the females who had come for a release.

So now I stood there, barefoot and exposed, crossing my arms over my chest where my nipples kept wanting to jut out of my gown and squeezing my thighs together to hide my sex. I had trimmed the golden curls between my thighs considerably during my bath but they still felt horribly visible in the dim light of the pleasure room.

"My Lady, you have no need to hide yourself or be nervous," Aliza said, coming back to me. "Let me instruct you in what is to happen during your pleasuring."

"Okay, thanks," I said numbly. I felt a little like I had the one and only time I'd gone to get a massage when the attendant told me to take everything off but my underwear and lay on the massage table face down and practically naked. The massage had been a birthday gift from Zoe, who thought it might help me "loosen up."

She was wrong.

Getting a massage had been a horribly uncomfortable experience because I just couldn't relax. I don't mind touching other people when I examine them as a physician because that's part of the job. But I *don't* like strangers touching me. Not even well-meaning strangers who only want to help me.

Something told me the "pleasuring" I was about to undergo was going to be about ten times worse than the massage. After all, during a massage, they only touch the non-sexual parts of your body. Unless you go to one of those skeevy places that offers 'happy endings' I guess, but they're really more for men. At least, I had never heard of a woman going to one.

Which is because women don't usually feel comfortable letting strange men touch their erogenous zones—at least not in the culture I was from. Majoran culture appeared to be completely different but just because I was supposed to be their Empress didn't mean I could suddenly adopt their attitude about letting strangers grope my lady bits. In fact, just the *thought* of some strange man pawing my breasts and feeling between my legs was enough to make my entire body clench with dread.

Ugh, I really, *really* didn't want to do this!

"Come with me," Aliza said, taking my arm and leading me to

the curtain. Now that I was closer to it, I saw that it wasn't all one whole piece of cloth. Instead, it was made of long strips, each about as wide as my hand, which were strung together.

"What am I supposed to do?" I asked. There was a knot of tension building in my stomach that made me feel slightly ill.

"Simply kneel upon the floor and press your breasts through the slits in the curtain," Aliza said, as though it was the easiest thing in the world. She took my hand and helped me get settled in the position, nudging me forward until my breasts were thrusting out through the curtain. "Make sure to keep your legs spread wide as well, my Lady," she said, nudging me again until I opened my knees. "The one who is to service you will come in through the door at the other side of the curtain and kneel before you to pleasure you with his hands and mouth."

"Will he be wearing a mask?" I asked, my mouth so dry I could hardly speak. I couldn't believe I was in this vulnerable, sexual position with my bare breasts out in the open and my thighs spread wide to show my naked sex.

"He will, my lady," she assured me. "And in addition, I can dim the lights if you so choose."

"Yes, *please*," I said fervently. In my opinion, the less I could see of the guy who was "servicing" me and the less he could see of me, the less awkward this whole thing would be.

"As you wish." She looked up. "Lights, dimmest setting. And soothing music, too, I think."

At once the already low lighting sank to the level of a single candle, making it difficult to see anything in the small, plush room. From somewhere the soft, hypnotic sounds of a flute began to play. It didn't do a thing to soothe me, though—my nipples were tight with fear and I felt cold all over.

"And now I will leave you to get your release."

Aliza bowed and I realized that once she left, I would be committed to going through with this crazy thing.

"Wait!" I said quickly, looking up at her from my vulnerable kneeling position. "How long exactly is this, uh, going to last?"

"Why, until you have a release of course, my Lady," she said, as though it was self explanatory. "Though if you have need of more than one release, simply tell your pleasure attendant and he will continue until you are completely satiated."

"Yeah, right," I mumbled under my breath. As if I would put myself in for more of this than I had to.

"Well, if there is nothing else, then I will take my leave," she said again.

"Wait!" I exclaimed. "Wait, there *is* something else!"

"Yes?"

My eyes were adjusting to the dim lighting and I could see that Aliza was looking at me with a patient expression in her eyes.

"Um..." I tried to think of something—anything at all—to stall, to keep her from leaving. But my mind was suddenly a complete blank.

"I shall leave you, then," Aliza said, a mysterious smile playing around the corners of her mouth. "And do not worry, my Lady. I think you will find your pleasure attendant very much to your liking."

As if I could like a stranger—any stranger—who came in the dark room and groped me. But before I could think of anything to say to stop her, she left and the pleasure room door *snicked* shut behind her.

Can't believe I'm doing this. Can't believe I'm actually going to let some stranger—

The soft sound of the door behind the curtain opening cut off my train of thought as cleanly as a surgeon's scalpel.

Oh my God, I thought to myself. *Oh my God, he's here! He's right across from me behind the curtain! Here we go!*

There was a soft sound of heavy footsteps muffled by the cushioned floor. Though I couldn't see him, it immediately gave me the idea that my "pleasure attendant" was a very large guy. Well, most of the Majoran males seemed to be pretty big. I was sure I hadn't seen a single one under six foot six and most of them seemed to be closer to Kristoff's height of over seven feet.

Kristoff! I thought longingly as I heard the man on the other side of the curtain approach. *I wish it was you! I don't want anyone else!*

But what I wanted didn't seem to matter. There was a soft rustling behind the curtain and I got the impression that whoever it was had knelt in front of me.

I got tense, waiting for big, unfamiliar hands to grab my breasts and start groping between my legs.

Instead, he touched my knees.

I know, right? It was weird. And at first I was sure he was going to run his hands up my legs and right between my thighs. But he just sat there, silent and motionless, with his big, warm hands on my knees, which of course, were sticking out between the slits in the curtain.

Okay, so maybe he was a knee man? Which was weird, especially considering that my breasts were also sticking out of the slits in the curtain. Maybe it was too dim in the room for him to see properly. But he should still know that my boobs wouldn't be down where my knees were. What was going on?

"Um..." After a long moment, I cleared my throat, not sure what to say. "You, uh, *do* know you're touching my knees, right?"

There was a soft sound of ascent and a deep voice murmured, "Yes, my Lady."

"Okay. And you further know that my boobs, I mean my breasts, are up here, right?" It felt funny to call attention to my breasts when I'm usually wishing a guy would look me in the eyes instead. But since we were here to do this, we might as well get it over with.

"Do *want* me to touch your breasts?" the deep voice asked softly.

"I...um...well, you're *supposed* to, I think," I said, trying to keep the tremble out of my voice.

"That isn't what I asked you." The big hands finally moved, sliding slowly up my thighs. But he was touching the tops of my thighs—*not* angling inward to go for my sex. My nerves tingled at the light touch and I felt the flame of *need* within me, which had been almost extinguished by my fear and uncertainty, suddenly blaze to life again.

"I...I'm not sure what I want," I said, my voice soft and breathless. "I...I'm afraid."

"I know," he murmured. "I can feel you tremble."

I felt those big, warm hands begin to move again, sliding slowly upwards from my thighs to my hips.

They were on my side of the curtain now and I looked down, wishing for the first time that the light wasn't quite so dim. I wanted to see him a little better—well, what I *could* see of him, anyway which was mostly just his hands and his muscular forearms. His long, strong fingers were splayed, resting lightly on the swells of my hips.

"Hey," I said, slightly breathless. "I, uh, thought you were supposed to stay on your side of the curtain."

His hands moved up, dipping inward to caress the curve of my waist.

"You have a lovely shape, my Lady," he murmured, ignoring my halfhearted protest.

"I...um...thank you," I whispered uncertainly.

The hands continued their journey, sliding up my sides and over my shoulders to lightly caress the hollow of my throat and the sensitive sides of my neck. Against my will, I felt a tingle of pleasure at his gentle touch and I had to bite back a moan. God, and he hadn't even touched the parts he was supposed to touch yet! What was going on with me?

The hands moved again, sliding down the sides of my breasts and then cupping their undercurves in his big, warm palms. I shivered, though he still hadn't come anywhere near my nipples, which were tight with need and fear.

"You're going very slowly," I blurted out. "I mean, not that that's a bad thing. I'm not complaining or anything I just..." I trailed off, realizing I was babbling.

Shut up, Charlotte, I told myself fiercely. *Just shut up and let him get this over with.* But for the first time, I wasn't as certain that I *wanted* it over with.

"I was told to be gentle, as this is your first time at a pleasure house, my Lady," he murmured. "Do you wish me to be rougher?"

"What? No!" I exclaimed, feeling half panicked. "No, please don't!"

There was a soft laugh from the other side of the curtain.

"Never fear, my Lady. Your body is beautiful. I will worship it gently and with reverence."

Finally I felt his hands move up and then he was sliding his thumbs gently over my tight, aching nipples.

I gave a little gasp and jumped. The spike of pleasure I got from such a small gesture scared me. Scared me because I realized I felt *drawn* to this strange man behind the curtain. And how could that be when I didn't feel drawn to anyone but Kristoff?

Kristoff! The thought of him filled me with a longing so deep and wide I felt like I might drown in it. I couldn't do this — couldn't let another man touch me — pleasure me. Not when I wanted only Kristoff.

"I'm sorry. I thought I could do this but I can't...I just *can't.*"

I started to pull away but then his fingers closed over my sensitive nipples, squeezing gently and dragging a moan from my lips.

"Why, my Lady?" he murmured. "Why can't you allow yourself to be pleasured? Is it because you long for another?"

"Yes," I whispered breathlessly. "Yes, that's it exactly."

"And what, may I ask, is his name?" the deep, soft voice inquired as he rolled my nipples gently between his thumbs and fingers.

"*Ah...*" I gasped. "His...his name is Kristoff."

"And he is the one you burn for? The one you desire?" A gentle tug at my ripe buds accompanied the question, making me moan again.

"Yes," I whispered. "I want him so...so much. But I can't have him. It...it's not allowed."

"The love of a Royal female for a low born male she cannot have," he murmured. "We hear this tale often here at the Royal House of Goddess Pleasures."

"You...you do?" He was still pinching and twisting my nipples and the gentle torture was driving me half insane.

"We do. Did you know that such couples often meet in just such a place as this?" he asked softly. "For here they can come together anonymously as pleasure attendant and pleasure seeker and do things that would otherwise be forbidden."

"I...I didn't know that," I whispered.

"It's true, my Lady. I have even heard tell of a Lady who fell in love with her guard. Though he was sworn never to touch her intimately, he had no choice but to follow her when she went to the House of Goddess Pleasures. He had sworn, you see, to see to her safety in all matters. And since he felt he could not trust any other male to safely give her a release, he took the matter upon himself."

"You mean he...he switched places with the pleasure attendant?" I asked breathlessly. God, every time he pinched my nipples I could feel sparks of pleasure going straight to the spot between my thighs! Already I felt swollen and wet there. I spread my legs a little wider, trying to get comfortable.

"Even so," the low voice murmured. "And so he came to her and pleasured her and brought her many sweet releases while she called his name, none the wiser that it was actually he who was touching her."

Somehow, through the haze of pleasure, his story started to make sense.

"What are you telling me?" I asked, wondering if what I was thinking could possibly be true.

"I am only telling you of things that have happened here in the past," he said. "But, my Lady, if you so desire this 'Kristoff' then why do you not pretend that I am he?"

"You...you certainly talk like him," I said and then moaned as he stopped pinching my nipples a moment to knead my breasts with his big hands. "Very...Renaissance Fair."

"And what does he call you?" he inquired in that low, hypnotic voice.

"He calls me 'my Lady' a lot," I whispered. "And also...Charlotte."

"Charlotte," he murmured and I could feel his hot breath through the curtain. "Do you like the way I've been touching your sweet breasts? Or was I too rough with your tender nipples? Maybe I should suck them and make them better?"

"Yes," I whispered. "Yes, *please.*"

"Ask me to do it, then," he murmured. "Say, 'I want you to suck my nipples.' And call me by *his* name when you do."

"Kristoff?" I said uncertainly. "You want me to call you Kristoff?"

"Yes, my Lady. It would be my pleasure and, I believe, yours as well."

"Kristoff," I whispered. "Please...suck my nipples."

"As you wish, *Charlotte,*" he murmured. And then I felt one tight peak being pulled into his hot, wet mouth and he sucked me hard, making me moan and sway against the curtain helplessly.

"Gods, I love your breasts," he groaned softly, when he finally released my first nipple. "So full and ripe. So perfect, my Goddess."

I moaned as he sucked my other nipple into his mouth and reached through the slits in the curtain to bury my fingers in his hair. It was thick and I threaded my fingers through it as I pressed my chest up to meet his mouth. He was torturing my nipple with his tongue, circling the aching bud slowly and stopping every once in a while to nip very gently with his teeth until I thought I was going to go crazy.

"Oh," I whispered, needing no prompting this time. "Oh, *Kristoff.*"

"That's right, Charlotte," he growled softly, releasing the second nipple. "Call me by name. And tell me what else you need."

"I...Kristoff, I need a release," I whispered, telling the truth. "I need to *come.*"

"Of course you do my Lady." One big hand stole down to slide between my legs. I felt him cup my vulnerable, open pussy in one big hand.

"*Oh...*" I whispered, the sound falling off my lips like a moan.

"I can feel how hungry your sweet little pussy is, Charlotte," he murmured through the curtain that still separated us. "I can feel how wet and swollen you are."

As he spoke, one long finger slipped between my slippery folds and began to slide gently around and around my aching clit, never quite touching it.

"Ah!" I gasped. I couldn't help thinking that this was exactly the way Kristoff had touched me when he bathed me. Again the thought entered my mind...what was the true identity of the man on the other side of the curtain? And then the idea was driven out of my head as the pad of his thumb began to slide back and forth over my tender bud, back and forth...back and forth until my knees trembled and I had to reach through the curtain to grab his broad shoulders for support.

"Tell me you want this, Charlotte," he said, his low voice fierce with desire. "I want to hear you say you like it."

"I *do* like it," I whispered, moving my hips in time with his slow, intense rhythm. "I *love* it!"

"Call me by name," he insisted. "And tell me what you like."

"I...I like it when you...when you pet my pussy, Kristoff," I whispered, the words catching in my throat as he continued the slow, maddening caress.

"Good, that's good, my Lady," he murmured. "Are you getting close to a release, do you think?"

"Yes!" I gasped. I could feel my orgasm hovering on the horizon, just out of reach. But if he kept stroking and petting my swollen, sensitive clit I knew it would soon overwhelm me, just as it had the night before when Kristoff was bathing me so thoroughly.

Just as I was beginning to feel the beginning swells of it, however, the big hand was withdrawn.

"What...why did you stop?" The words were almost a sob in my throat. "I was really *close.*"

"I know, my Lady. But it occurs to me that this Kristoff of yours wouldn't want you to come on his fingers."

"He...he wouldn't?" I was trying to follow what he was saying but my disappointment in not being allowed to reach the peak was so sharp it was hard to feel anything but *need.*

"No, he wouldn't," the man behind the curtain murmured. "Not when you could come on his tongue instead."

"Come on his...what do you mean?" I felt my need turn to uncertainty. As I've said before, this particular activity was never high on my wish list.

"I mean I want to taste your pussy, Charlotte," he growled softly. "I want to spread your thighs and lick your clit until you come, riding my tongue."

"I...you...you do?" The hot, dirty words left me almost breathless. I felt a renewed surge of desire rush through me.

"More than anything," he assured me. "But I don't want to do it with this curtain in the way."

Abruptly the curtain parted and I saw him looming over me for the first time.

He was tall—tall and very muscular, just as I had suspected—and bare from the waist up. There was a mask obscuring the top part of his face but there was no mistaking those broad shoulders, or the rapidly shifting rainbow eyes I saw behind the black leather mask.

"Kristoff?" I whispered, reaching up to touch his cheek. "It...it's really you?"

"Yes, my Lady," he murmured. "Who else would I entrust with your safety? I couldn't take the chance that a strange male might hurt you when he touched your most sensitive areas. I had to undertake your pleasuring myself."

"So you...you've been the one touching me?" I whispered.

Slowly, he nodded. "And now I'm going to taste you."

"I..." I felt suddenly shy at the idea. "I don't know, Kristoff."

A smile touched the corners of his sensual mouth.

"Who is this 'Kristoff' you speak of my Lady? I am but a humble pleasure attendant, sent to satisfy your needs and give you a release."

"I see," I said, feeling a shiver of need run through my body. "And how exactly are you going to do that?"

His eyes behind the black leather mask grew hot and heavy-lidded.

"I'm going to carry you to the couch, my Lady, and lay you down so that you can open for me completely. Then I'm going to spread your thighs wide and pleasure you with my tongue. I want to fuck you with it—fuck you deep and long and hard until you come all over my face."

"Oh..." I felt almost faint with desire at his hot words. He almost never swore, so when he did, it sent a little tingling shock through me. But that wasn't the only thing making me tingle—the naked desire in his eyes was making me crazy. This was the first time he'd openly acknowledged how much he wanted me—that he needed me as much as I needed him.

"My Lady..." He stood and swooped me up into his arms. "Will you let me bring you to the couch?" he murmured. "Will you spread yourself for me and let me taste you?"

"Yes," I whispered, unable to help myself. "Yes, Kristoff. If...if you really want to."

"It's all I've wanted from the first moment I saw you," he admitted, his deep voice hoarse with desire. "Gods, Charlotte, if you only knew how I desire to worship your pussy with my tongue."

"I...I didn't know you felt that way," I whispered as he carried me over to the cushioned couch and lay me down on it.

"All Majoran males desire to worship their goddesses so," he assured me, kneeling between my legs. "My Goddess, I want you so badly...want to bury my face between your thighs and taste your sweet honey straight from the source."

Before I could answer, he ducked his head and rubbed his rough cheek against the tender mound of my sex. He inhaled deeply, his eyes flickering with lust and then rubbed the other cheek against my cleft as well, almost as though he was bathing in my scent.

"Gods, you smell so good," he groaned softly. "From that first accidental kiss aboard the ship, I've dreamed of nothing but this. Spreading you open and licking your pussy deep and long and hard."

I remembered the kiss he was talking about, when his lips had accidentally made contact with my sex during the sensitivity test he'd performed on me. Had he really been thinking about tasting me since then?

Apparently so, because his eyes were still heavy-lidded with desire as he leaned down to press a warm kiss to the top of my mound.

"Charlotte," he said, looking up at me. "I will try to be gentle but I want you very badly."

"Maybe...maybe we should just start with a kiss. Like we did before," I suggested breathlessly.

He made a low sound of ascent in his throat.

"Perhaps we should at that. Can you spread your outer lips for me, as you did before? Can you open your pussy for me, Charlotte, and let me kiss you?"

Blushing and trembling, I did as he asked. Reaching between my thighs, I used two fingers to spread open my outer pussy lips, revealing my slippery inner folds and my aching clit.

"Your Goddess-pearl is so beautiful," Kristoff murmured. "So swollen with need, my Lady."

"It *is* really achy," I admitted softly. "It...it almost hurts, Kristoff."

"In that case, I must kiss my Lady to ease her pain," he murmured. Leaning down, he placed a hot, open-mouthed kiss on my spread pussy.

For a moment it was exactly like the accidental kiss he'd given me while we were aboard his ship. Then I had felt his tongue against me, but he hadn't moved it at all. This time he held still for a long moment...and then licked me, pressing his tongue deep into my pussy and dragging upward to slide over the tender bump of my clit.

Sparks of pleasure shot through me and I moaned and bucked my hips. It felt so good it was almost too much. I gasped and bit my lip as he did it again...and then again, lapping my open pussy as though I was his favorite flavor in the whole world.

"Gods," he muttered hoarsely, looking up at me. "You taste so good, Charlotte. And I can feel your Goddess-pearl swelling under my tongue."

"Having you taste me...lick me...it feels *amazing*," I whispered breathlessly. "I...I never thought it could feel this way."

He leaned down and swirled the tip of his tongue around my swollen clit. I moaned and bucked against him again, shamelessly offering myself to his hot mouth and seeking tongue.

"That's good." He looked up, his eyes filled with lust and need behind the black mask he still wore. "Open yourself completely, Charlotte."

"I...I thought I *was* open," I said, my heart pounding. "What...what else do you want?"

"This." Reaching under me, he twined his long, muscular arms around my legs, splitting my thighs wide open, baring my pussy for him completely.

I gasped at the sudden feeling of vulnerability. Not only was I open—he was *holding* me open—holding me down. And since he was exponentially stronger than me, there was nothing I could do to stop him. Nothing but give him what he wanted.

"I'm going to lick you deeply now, Charlotte," he told me, his eyes heated behind the mask. "Going to penetrate your pussy as deeply as I can with my tongue and taste your sweet honey right from your cleft."

"All...all right," I said softly. "I...I won't try to stop you."

"I want you to do more than just submit to my tongue inside you." The look in his eyes was incredibly intense—almost scary. I felt my breath catch in my throat as a need that matched my own blazed from them.

"What...what else can I do?"

"Give yourself to me, my Goddess," he murmured. "Press back against me. Feed me that sweet little pussy and fuck yourself on my tongue—*hard*."

"Oh God, Kristoff..." When he talked to me that way and looked me in the eyes so directly as he told me exactly what he was going to do to me and what he wanted me to do in return, I felt like I might melt into a puddle right there on the couch. Or else catch fire from the intense heat between us.

"Promise me," he said, bending to rub his cheek against my pussy mound once more. "Tell me you'll give me what I want and you won't stop until you come on my mouth."

"Yes," I whispered, loving this new, aggressive side of him. He was always so deferential to me, so protective and careful. But here and now in the pleasure chamber he was different— possessive...hungry...*dominant*. "Yes, Kristoff—I'll give you what you want."

"Good," he murmured. "That's very good, Charlotte."

Then he pulled me closer and bent his head to press his tongue long and hot and wet, deep inside my open pussy.

I moaned and bucked against him, as well as I could. He had such a tight grip on my thighs I couldn't do much more than roll my pelvis. Which I did, moving to meet him as he stroked deep inside me, tasting me as deeply as he could.

At the same time, he shifted his grip on me so he could reach between my legs. The pad of one broad thumb came up and began to slide over my swollen clit once more in that hot, back and forth motion that drove me completely crazy.

Gasping, I reached for something to hold on to and found my hands buried in his thick, dark hair.

"Kristoff!" I moaned helplessly. "Oh, God, *Kristoff!*"

Hearing his name on my lips seemed to drive him wild. He tongue-fucked me even deeper, pressing long and hard inside my channel as his thumb continued to caress my aching bud until I felt like I was either going to come or pass out from the pleasure. I writhed against him, crying out—his name a prayer on my lips.

I don't know how long it lasted, only that it seemed to go on forever as the pleasure built and built until I could barely remember my own name.

All the need, all the desire that had been building inside me from the moment I had been Invested as the True Incarnation seemed to hit me at once. The orgasm felt like an explosion—something so strong it might rip me apart. I cried and gasped and begged, unable to help myself, unable to stop the moans that came from between my lips.

Through it all, Kristoff just kept tasting me, driving his tongue deep in my pussy as he stroked my clit in that same, slow, deliberate rhythm which refused to be hurried no matter how much I begged and cried and rolled my hips.

God, I thought. *Good…so good!*

And it was—incredibly good. I rode Kristoff's tongue and mouth, just as he had told me to, and I had never felt anything so intense in my entire life.

I never wanted it to end.

Kristoff

I never wanted it to end.

Having Charlotte under to me, spread as wide as possible, her soft, pink pussy open for my seeking tongue was a fantasy I had only dreamed of and had never expected to fulfill.

Shouldn't be fulfilling it now, whispered a harsh voice in the back of my head. *You should have let the pleasure attendant take care of her, as was the original plan.*

I had tried to follow the plan—the Goddess knows I had. But when we'd gotten to the House of Goddess Pleasures and I had seen the fright—the outright panic in Charlotte's big, green eyes—I hadn't been able to go through with it. Not to mention the fact that the idea of another male touching her in any way—especially sexually—sent a surge of possessive rage through me I could hardly control.

You'd better learn to control it, whispered that same, acerbic inner voice. *The Culling ceremony for the Consort candidates is tomorrow. The day after that she'll belong to another male—a Royal who deserves her touch. One who will bond her to him and bring her pleasure as often as he wants.*

The thought made a possessive growl rise in my throat and the urge to bond Charlotte to me—to claim her for my own—came over me so strongly I could barely hold myself back.

Instead of plunging my shaft into her, I concentrated on fucking her with my tongue. One release wasn't enough. I wanted to make her come again and again—to feel her honey flowing and taste her sweet nectar on my lips, knowing I was the reason for it.

Determined to make our encounter last, I brought Charlotte to the edge over and over, making her writhe on the pleasure room couch as she called for me—called my name and mine alone—at the moment of release. I told myself that no matter what else happened or who her Consort turned out to be, we would always have the memory of this night together. The one night when I had allowed myself to give her what we both so desperately needed, though I knew it wasn't right.

At last she lay panting and spent, shying away from my tongue as though the sensation was too intense when I bent to lick her again.

"Kristoff," she whispered, her sweet voice husky from crying and moaning for so long. "I...I don't think I can take any more."

"Very well, my Lady." I placed a soft, chaste kiss to her mound and unwound my arms from around her thighs. She tried to sit up but the pleasure had made her weak. I had to help her get upright on the couch and then I sat beside her.

"That was...*amazing,*" she whispered weakly, looking up at me. "How did you do that? How did you make me come again and again like that?"

I allowed myself a small smile. "Didn't I tell you Majoran males take special classes in pleasuring females?"

"Well, you must have been at the head of the class," she said, answering my smile with her own. "Because that was an A plus performance with some serious extra credit thrown in."

"I was happy to serve you," I murmured, taking her hand in mine. "No, *more* than happy—it was the fulfillment of my deepest and most forbidden fantasy."

"Well, I can't say I ever fantasized about it before, since I didn't really have much of a sex life back on Earth," she said, sounding thoughtful. "But you can bet I'll be fantasizing about it now." She looked up at me shyly. "You really liked it that much?"

"Tasting your sweet pussy...hearing you call my name...pull my hair...buck against my tongue?" I licked my lips, savoring the taste of her nectar. "Oh, yes my Lady. I *loved* it."

"But what about you? Did you, uh, get any relief?" She reached for my still-hard shaft but I moved her hand away gently.

"Forgive me, my Lady but that is forbidden. I am the one attending you, not the other way around."

"That hardly seems fair," Charlotte protested.

"Nevertheless, that is the way it is." Not that I didn't want her sweet, soft little hands on my shaft—it would be an intense pleasure. How I had kept myself from coming while I tasted her, I would never know but I wasn't about to let her make me come now.

I had already broken enough rules for one night.

"All right. I'll let it go—for now. But next time—"

"There can be no next time," I interrupted her. "I'm sorry, my Lady but this night is all we can have together."

"But...but I thought..." She shook her head. "I mean, you said this happens all the time. A Royal and a non-Royal who want to be together meet at the Pleasure House—right? So why can't we meet here again?"

"Only unmated people may meet at the Pleasure House," I told her gently. "In another day or two you'll be bonded to your Royal Consort and then I can be nothing more to you but the Captain of your Guard, as I was to my old mistress."

"But I don't *want* another Consort!" she insisted fiercely. "Who made the stupid law that the Empress has to marry a Royal anyway?"

"I believe it was the Council of Wisdom—to preserve the divinity of the Royal bloodlines," I told her. "No male without the blood of a past Goddess-Empress running in his veins can be allowed to bond with the present Goddess-Empress."

"But that's ridiculous," she protested. "Who cares about the bloodlines?"

"The Council of Wisdom," I said. "As well as the priests and priestesses in the temples of the Goddess of Mercy, of whom you are meant to be a corporeal scion. And because they care, all of the Majoran system cares."

She sighed and looked down at her hands.

"All right, I get it. I don't want to throw my new people's religion in their faces or flout their customs or break their rules." She looked up at me. "But isn't there *some* way of getting the law changed?"

I shook my head regretfully.

"My Lady, you are the thousandth ruler in an unbroken chain of Goddess-Empresses. The tradition against Royalty interbreeding with the other, lesser nobility or commoners has been in place since Sundalla the first and by Sundalla the 100th it was made a law. Now it is part of our religious beliefs. It would take a miracle by the

Goddess herself to change it."

She frowned. "Do you really believe in her? In the Goddess?"

I thought of the panicked prayer I had offered to a deity I didn't really believe in back when it had seemed Charlotte might die of the Burning Blood. A prayer which had been answered...but by the Goddess, or a simple whim of fate?

"I don't know," I said honestly. "I never used to. Now...I'm not sure."

"I'm not either," she said and sighed. "But it does seem like if I'm supposed to be the Goddess's scion, feeling her emotions and feeding her needs and desires here in the mortal realm, I should get to pick *who* I fulfill those desires with."

"But you don't get to," I said gently. "The Council of Wisdom, which is meant to balance the Empress's power, are the ones who will bring forth suitable candidates."

"Who did the old Empress marry—er, bond to?" she asked. "The one before me, I mean."

"I never met him," I said. "He died before I came to serve at Court. But I do know he was not one of the Council of Wisdom's choices for my old mistress. He was, in fact, the General of her entire armed forces." I frowned. "The Head of the Council—Councilor Tannus in fact—was most displeased that Sundalla the 999th went against his wishes, but there wasn't much he could do about it. The General had the entire might of the armed forces at his back."

"Really?" Her eyes widened. "So then there *is* hope! We *can* go against the Councils' wishes!"

I shook my head. "The General was still a Royal. He just wasn't one of the candidates the Council had deemed worthy for the Empress."

She frowned mutinously. "I don't like the idea of a panel of old men getting to pick who I spend the rest of my life with! Especially not that Councilor Tannus—I'm almost sure he and Morbain are in bed together."

"What?" I asked, slightly shocked. "You think they—"

"It's just an Earth saying that means they're in cahoots. You know—that they're working together," she explained, seeing my blank look at her strange Earth vernacular. "I don't trust them is what I'm trying to say—either of them! Did you see how Tannus kept on letting poor Eucilla go through Trial after Trial, even after it was obvious she couldn't have been the True Incarnation? He could have stopped it but he just kept agreeing to everything Morbain said."

"I agree that *did* seem to be the case," I said. "And I wouldn't hesitate to urge you to look outside the candidates the Council offers you if you don't find one that's pleasing to you. But you must look to a Royal—not a commoner or a minor noble like myself."

Charlotte sighed and looked down at her hands again. "We have a saying on my world—the heart wants what the heart wants." She looked up at me, the *need* clear in her lovely green eyes. "I can't help it, Kristoff—my heart wants *you.*"

I felt as though someone was ripping me up inside—shredding my heart with the sharpest dagger imaginable. It was nearly unbearable and yet, for my Lady's sake, I knew I must bear it—bear it for the rest of my life.

"As mine wants you, Charlotte," I told her gently, taking her hand in mine. "But this *must* be the last time we speak of it. Come..." I rose and tugged her to her feet. "Our time in the pleasure room is over. We must go back to reality and try to forget this ever happened."

"I can't forget," she whispered, her eyes bright with unshed tears. "I don't *want* to forget."

I drew her to me and leaned down to taste her mouth—a sweet, forbidden kiss I could never repeat. The dagger in my heart had turned dull now—a throbbing pain I knew I would never get over. Knowing that she must go to another male was like knowing I must die...and yet continue to serve, staying at my post and protecting the woman I loved while she loved another.

It was agony.

It was the way things had to be and there was nothing I could do to change it.

"We must forget," I whispered to her. "And now we must go."

I found her cloak and put it on her, pulling it low to cover her face and hide the tears that slipped silently down her cheeks, each salty drop like another stab to my already wounded heart. I would have given anything to dry those tears but it was beyond my power. I could do nothing to help—nothing to ease her pain which I felt through my bond to her as clearly as I felt my own.

Chapter Twenty-seven

He who had been Count Doloroso chafed within the bonds of his new Majoran host body. Since assuming the identity and life of the Imperial Guard, T'zorin, he had been waiting for a chance to get the Earth girl—the *La-ti-zal* called Charlotte—alone for his own purposes. But it was impossible—that damn guard, Kristoff, was constantly with her, never leaving her side even for an instant. In the guise of T'zorin he had gotten as close as he could, making himself indispensable—trustable. Yet still Kristoff would never leave her.

I need to get her alone, he thought, pacing the corridor outside the Council Chambers. *I need to take her someplace no one will dare to come after her, someplace safe from where I can make my demands. But where?*

Actually, he had an idea of where he could take the new Empress once he had her. The problem was getting her alone in the first place. How could he separate her from Kristoff? How could he get her away and breed a whole new race of Organic Assimilated unless—

"So everything is set for the Culling Ceremony tomorrow evening?" a soft, familiar voice murmured, coming from the narrow corridor just around the corner from him.

Doloroso froze, listening intently, barely daring to breathe.

"Indeed it is. She'll not suspect a thing until its too late." The other voice was also familiar—familiar and gloating, Doloroso thought. "All you have to do is be certain she gives her blood. Once I ingest it, she'll be drawn to me like a *twila* moth to an open flame. You *did* make certain that the other candidates are not as, ah, *suitable* as myself, correct?"

"It was the first order of business," the other voice said. "And I pushed a new declaration through as well to make certain she cannot pick another Royal besides the ones we offer as candidates."

The voice turned hard. "I'll not have another Empress run rough-shod over me in the way Sundalla the 999th did."

"Yes, my mother *was* quite willful," the other male replied. "It was good thinking on your part to close that loophole. Something tells me this new Empress is every bit as willful as her predecessor."

"Willful and unfortunately, gaining in popularity," the first voice said. "Someone took a vid of her trying to save Eucilla after the Trials and it's been spreading like wildfire among the commoners and nobles alike. The people already love her for her courage and if they get behind her en mass…"

"Don't worry about that," the other male said. "I've planted a few, shall we say, *failsafes* in case things don't go according to plan."

"I won't ask what they are," the first voice said.

"Good. I'll only tell you if you need to know. Now I must get back."

"I will see you at the Culling banquet tomorrow evening. Be ready."

"I will. And never fear, my friend—the two of us will rule the galaxy together. Whether the new Goddess-Empress likes it or not."

The voices ceased and after a moment, Doloroso was certain they were gone. So there were other players in this game—well and good, he didn't care. What he had heard only confirmed what he had already known—whoever held the Empress held the key to the entire galaxy.

Doloroso just had to be certain that *he* was the male who held that key.

Chapter Twenty-eight

Charlotte

"My Lady, you have a long distance vid-call."

Kristoff's deep voice was cool and aloof. After our hot encounter in the House of Goddess Pleasures the night before, he had become withdrawn and distant in a way that hurt me more than I could say. I knew he was just trying to put some much-needed space between us, especially considering the illicit nature of our feelings for each other, but it felt like a personal rejection. He had refused to sleep in the bed with me last night and I had cried myself to sleep, so miserable I could hardly bear it.

Deal with it, I told myself dully for what seemed like the thousandth time. *You can't have him and after the way you've been moping around, he probably doesn't even want you anymore, anyway.*

Only I didn't think that was true. I saw the desire in his eyes, when I turned and caught him watching me. He still wanted me as badly as I wanted him—maybe even more. But we could never be together and all because of a stupid tradition which had turned into a law which had become part of the Majoran religion somehow.

You rule these people now—or you will once you're crowned, I reminded myself. *You can't start out by crapping all over their religion.* I knew it was true but it still felt like someone was digging my heart out with a dull spoon every time I thought of spending my life with someone other than the man I had fallen in love with.

Well, maybe it wouldn't be so bad. Everyone kept telling me that once I gave my blood to the prospective candidates at the Culling ceremony I would feel incredibly drawn to one of them and desire no one else. Of course, I had also been told that the effects of giving my blood to Kristoff would fade and *that* hadn't happened, so how could I believe—

"My Lady, did you hear me?" Kristoff asked, breaking into my morbid line of thought.

My Lady. All day long he had been calling me that—not once had he called me by name as he had last night when he was tasting me and bringing me to the peak again and again. His way of addressing me had seemed charming at first but now I was getting sick of it. I just wanted to hear him call me "Charlotte" but I had a feeling he never would again.

I looked up at him dully. "I'm sorry, what did you say?" I was bone-weary from staying up late crying the night before, and from all the religious rituals and purifications I'd been going through all day to get me ready to be crowned and enthroned, after I chose my Consort.

"I said you have a call," Kristoff repeated. "I had it routed to the private conference area in the back of the Royal Apartments. If you'd like to follow me?" He indicated the narrow hallway which ran the length of the Royal Residence and raised his eyebrows at me.

"Fine," I said. "But can you at least tell me who it is? I don't really feel ready to start making rulings or doing trade negotiations or whatever it is I'm supposed to be doing as the Empress. I need to consult with some experts first—someone who can bring me up to speed on what the last Empress was doing."

Kristoff's icy gaze softened a little.

"You won't have to worry about trade negotiations or royal duties to take this call, my Lady," he said. "In fact, I think you'll be most happy when you see who's calling."

The only thing that would have made me happy at that moment was being in his arms and knowing I could stay there. But I couldn't say that aloud—it would only make things harder. Instead I lifted my chin and tried to look as cool and collected as he was.

"All right, thank you. I suppose I have time to take a call before the banquet tonight."

The Culling Banquet—which I was *not* looking forward to—was supposed to be a lengthy and important affair which took place right before the Culling Ceremony itself. I was going to be dressed in a ridiculously heavy getup which consisted of a rich brocade dress of forest green worked all over with golden embroidery which

Kristoff had ordered specially made for me. I was sure it would look spectacular—he had impeccable taste, after all—but I didn't feel like getting dressed up and presiding over a table-full of snobby Royals who would be scrutinizing my every move and word. In fact, I really didn't—

My thoughts cut off abruptly when Kristoff led me into a small room with a wide viewscreen covering one entire wall and I saw the two familiar faces glowing on its lighted surface.

"Zoe?" I asked, my eyes widening in disbelief. "Leah? What...how... I don't even know how to start! Why are you calling me and why didn't you call me before?"

"Charlotte!" they both squealed and I thought Zoe looked so excited she might just crawl through the viewscreen.

"We're so sorry we couldn't call earlier," she said, her red curls practically crackling with excitement. "But the distance between Femme One and Eloim is crazy long—it messes with communications."

"So how are you calling me now?" I asked, blankly. "Did you boost the signal or something somehow?"

"No, we're actually on our way to see your coronation," Leah said, looking as excited as Zoe. "We weren't sure if we could all go first because of Sadie's crown..."

"The Star of Compassion isn't supposed to be parted from me or Eloim—my new home planet—for at least a year," Zoe put in, touching a glowing pink jewel which she wore at her forehead. "But I talked to her and she agreed to make an exception and come off planet with me."

"Wait—you *talk* to your jewelry now?" I said, frowning.

"Only because it has a sentient creature that lives inside it," Zoe said a touch defensively. "Anyway, even *after* my Star agreed to come with me to see you, we still weren't sure we could go because of Grav."

"That's my new guy." Leah was beaming. "He's had some, uh, problems in the past but your friend, Kristoff, issued a pardon for him. So the four of us—me and Grav and Zoe and her guy, Sarden—are all on the way to see your coronation ceremony."

"Uh...a pardon?" I looked at Kristoff who nodded and gave me a small smile. "I thought you would agree with the ruling, my Lady. Gravex N'gol was instrumental in saving and protecting your friend's life, as well as in apprehending Count Doloroso, the Assimilated criminal who was trying to abduct her for nefarious purposes."

"Oh, well in that case…"

"Here, you have to meet him," Zoe exclaimed. "Him and Sarden both. Wait just a second!"

There was a brief pause and then the viewscreen was suddenly filled with four faces instead of two—only two of the faces were male and extremely alien.

"This is my sweetie, Sarden." Zoe was snuggling up with a seven-foot tall alien who had dark red skin, golden eyes, and horns like the devil. "He's the one who dragged me through the bathroom mirror at my old work in the first place. Well, with a little help from the Commercians, of course."

"The Commercians?" I said frowning. "Those blue worm guys, right? You know they kept trying to contact me for the longest time? In every shiny surface in the house—they even popped up on a scalpel when I was assisting in a splenectomy! I thought I was going *crazy*."

"Oh dear…" Leah put a hand to her mouth. "Um, I'm afraid that was my fault. See, when I decided to go with Grav, here…" She nodded at the blue alien male who was built like a Mac truck and had curling black ram's horns at the sides of his head, "I didn't want you to worry, like we worried about Zoe. So I paid them to give you a message that I was all right." She frowned. "Didn't you ever get it?"

"I never let them finish," I confessed. "I was so convinced I was seeing things that I ran away every time the worm guy started talking."

"Well, even if you didn't get the message, you know what's going on now," Zoe said brightly. "Humans are not the only intelligent species in the universe. Not even close—there are trillions and quadrillions and quintillions more in our galaxy alone!"

"Yes, I know," I said dryly. "And now I'm apparently

supposed to be ruling over all of them."

"We know." Leah looked at me, wide-eyed. "How are you dealing with that?"

I gave a glance back at Kristoff, who was still standing silently at my back.

"I'm...dealing with it," I said. "As well as I can." I didn't want to go into the personal problems I was having—not with both their mates and Kristoff in on the conversation.

"You're taking good care of Charlotte, aren't you?" Leah asked, looking at Kristoff rather than me. "You promised you would if I gave you her location."

"I am doing my utmost to protect the Goddess-Empress from harm," Kristoff said shortly.

"And what about Doloroso?" the blue alien with black horns— he had black eyes too, I saw with white irises—asked in a deep, gravelly voice. He was talking to Kristoff, not me. "We heard he got away again."

"Actually, no," Kristoff said. "The Assimilation ship was attacked by pirates and only one of my men survived but he did manage to bring it in to Femme One."

"Only one?" Sarden, the alien with the red skin and golden eyes frowned.

"The rest were killed." Kristoff shook his head. "It's made me regrettably short handed during a time when I could use more Imperial Guards, not less. But I am seeing to the Goddess-Empress's safety myself."

"Who is Doloroso?" I asked, frowning.

Zoe filled me in briefly on the weird body-jumping villain who was apparently a sentient computer program that could download himself into different hosts and take them over.

"Only what he really wants is to start a whole new race of computer babies with *La-ti-zal* mothers so they'll have special powers or something," Zoe said. "So watch out for him!"

"He's not a threat anymore," Kristoff assured her. "His ship was brought back to Femme One and he has not made a reappearance. I think it's safe to assume that he is finally dead."

"It's not safe to assume *anything* about Doloroso," Zoe objected. "We thought he was dead the first time and he came after Leah. You have to protect Charlotte from him!"

"Kristoff *is* protecting me! He's saved my life more times than I can count," I told her. "He's really..." I glanced back at him, the words dying in my throat. How could I describe him, my Guard who had risked his life to save mine so many times? *Amazing, incredible, strong...the man I'm in love with and can never have.*

"I think..." Kristoff looked at me shrewdly. "That my Lady Charlotte would enjoy speaking to her friends without male interference."

"Think you're right," Grav growled in his deep voice. He made a stiff bow to me. "Your Majesty."

"Your Majesty," Sarden echoed, also making a deep bow before straightening up. He looked at Kristoff. "Keep us informed, Captain Verrai, and let us know if there's anything we can do to help during the coronation. We're in communications range now and we'll be coming into orbit around Femme One very soon."

"I'll keep that in mind, thank you." Kristoff nodded at both of them. "And now I'll take my leave."

Everybody bowed again and then Kristoff left the room and the other two alien males left the viewscreen, leaving just Zoe and Leah and myself to talk.

"Whew..." Zoe fanned herself with one hand and grinned at me. "Okay, that Captain of the Guards guy is *hot!* Are you getting some of that, Charlotte?"

"Zoe!" Leah protested. "You know Charlotte doesn't like to talk about her love life! And besides, she's the Empress of the whole entire galaxy now. She's got more important things to think about."

"Actually, I don't." I sighed. "I mean, I should, I know...but I just can't."

"What?" Zoe leaned forward, her blue eyes turning shrewd. "All right, Charlotte—we can see something is bothering you. Spill it."

Always in the past when I'd felt like my friends were prying into things that didn't concern them, I had clammed up fast. But this time, I was so miserable and upset I couldn't help myself. When

Zoe told me to spill everything that was going on, I did.

"...so we can never be together," I finished, after talking for almost a solid half hour in which my two best friends had listened quietly, their eyes getting wider and wider.

"Whew!" Zoe whistled and shook her head. "That's some story, Charlotte!"

"I can't believe everything you've been through," Leah said sympathetically. "All those assassination attempts! And it's *awful* that you can't be with the man you love."

"It's the law, apparently," I said miserably. "And Kristoff is too honor-bound to break it."

"*You* break it then," Zoe said. "You're the Empress—can't you do what you want?"

"It doesn't work like that, Zoe," I said, patiently. "Just because I'm the Empress doesn't mean I can tell everybody to go to Hell and marry whoever I want to."

"I would think that's *exactly* what it means," Zoe said. "I know *I* would."

"I'm sure you would," I told her, grinning a little. Zoe always had been the most adventurous of the three of us.

"Well every law has a loophole—isn't that what you always used to tell us when you were a paralegal?" Leah asked practically, looking at Zoe.

"Not this one," I said glumly. "It's been in place for a thousand generations. Kristoff says it would take an act of the Goddess of Mercy herself to change it now."

"Pray about it then," Zoe advised. "The Goddess is real—she'll hear you."

"You really think so?" I looked at her doubtfully.

"Absolutely." Leah nodded. "Something is going to work out—you'll see."

"I hope you're right." I sighed. "But I'm afraid you're not. I just..." I trailed off, shaking my head.

"You just want to bond with the man you love," Zoe finished for me sympathetically. "We know how it is, Charlotte—really we do. Leah and I didn't think we'd get to stay with our guys either, but it all worked out in the end."

"Well," I began but just then there was a rapping at the door and Kristoff stuck his head in.

"Forgive me for interrupting, my Lady but the Culling Banquet is in half an hour. We really need to get you ready."

"All right, thank you," I told him. "Just let me say goodbye and I'll be out in a minute."

He nodded shortly and withdrew.

"Culling Banquet? What's that?" Zoe asked.

"It's this huge elaborate feast before the Culling Ceremony which is where I give three drops of my blood to three different candidates who the Council of Wisdom—a bunch of old men I don't even know—has chosen for me as possible Consorts. Then, supposedly, I'll be irresistibly drawn to one of them. The candidates, I mean—not the Council of Wisdom guys."

"So *the Council* gets to pick who you'll spend your whole life with?" Leah asked, frowning. "That hardly seems fair."

"To me either," I said. "But apparently that's how it's done and it would be *sacrilege* to suggest I get to pick my own husband." I couldn't keep the bitterness out of my voice.

"Hang in there, Charlotte," Zoe said, getting a stubborn look on her pretty, freckled face. "And don't give up—you have to advocate for yourself!"

"I'm trying, *believe* me," I said. "But this is kind of a difficult situation to advocate in, you know? I'm trying to be respectful of my new people's religion and customs."

"Well they need to be respectful of you too," Leah exclaimed. "I can see why they would want a Council to balance the power of the Empress but this isn't a trade negotiation or a whatever it is you're going to be doing once you get on the throne—this is your *life*. And believe me, Charlotte, if your alien guy is anything like ours is, once you bond to him, it'll be for life."

"Leah's right," Zoe said seriously. "This is a lasting arrangement. Most of the Twelve Peoples don't even know what divorce is. Once they're bonded, they stay together until one of them dies. It's no joke."

I felt myself go cold all over. Bonded for life to a man I didn't even know? A man who was picked for me by the Council of Wisdom, who I was pretty sure didn't even *like* me? *A man who isn't Kristoff,* added a little voice in my head. This was going to be horrible. What was I going to do?

"My Lady…" It was Kristoff again at the door. "We really *must* get you ready," he said sternly.

"Hey!" Zoe was frowning at him from the viewscreen. "You—Kristoff."

"Yes?" He frowned at her politely. "Is there something I can do for you? My Lady is about to be late for a very important state banquet."

"Let her be late then," Zoe said recklessly. "*She's* the Goddess-Empress of the universe—let the guests wait on her a little. It won't hurt to let them know she's in charge of her own life. And speaking of that…" She pointed at him. "What are you doing about this thing between the two of you?"

"Zoe!" I hissed at her, mortified.

"No, I'm sorry, Charlotte—you two are obviously crazy for each other but you're pussy-footing around the issue and nothing's getting done!" She scowled at Kristoff. "If you love Charlotte, you have to *fight* for her!"

"If you knew the situation here on Femme One, you'd know I've been doing nothing *but* fighting for my Lady," Kristoff said, frowning. "But what you're asking me to do would compromise her reputation and ruin her standing with the Council of Wisdom and the peerage of the entire Majoran system."

"Who cares about them?" Zoe said, frowning. "And who says Charlotte has to be the Goddess-Empress anyway? It's not like she applied for this job—she basically got forced into it. Why doesn't she get a say? What about her happiness?"

"Zoe," I said, rubbing my temples where I could feel a tension headache forming. "It's just not that simple."

"This is love, Charlotte," she said. "It's never simple. But that doesn't mean you should give up all sense of self and just blindly sacrifice yourself for a bunch of people you never met before a few days ago."

"My Lady," Kristoff said. "We really *must* go."

"I have to go," I told my friends. "Thanks for calling me."

"We'll see you soon." Leah shot me a sympathetic look. "Stay strong, Charlotte. We'll be there for your coronation."

Zoe just shook her finger at me. "Remember what I said. *Think* about it."

Then the viewscreen went black and their beloved faces faded from view. Kristoff rushed me into the next room to get dressed and made-up but I couldn't help thinking of Zoe's words. If only I could follow her advice and do what I wanted to do—love who I wanted to love.

I knew it was impossible, but I couldn't help wishing, just the same...

Chapter Twenty-nine

Charlotte

"Well, well, my dear—aren't you looking especially fetching tonight?"

I gritted my teeth and looked at the golden plate, as wide as a hubcap, which was sitting in front of me. Though I tried to ignore it, I could see the reflection of Prince Morbain, sitting right beside me at the banquet table. Not only that, but Head Councilor Tannus was directly across the table from me, though at least *he* didn't seem inclined to talk.

It really was a huge table with literally hundreds of other seating options. Whoever had made the seating arrangement and put the odious Morbain directly beside me and the surly Tannus across from me would be in big trouble if I found out their identity. I needed to talk to the chamberlain of seating charts or whoever it was and make sure it never happened again.

Still, here we were and since everyone else was already seated, it didn't seem likely that I would be able to change seats, especially since I was smack-dab in the middle of the enormous table in a special throne-looking chair. Morbain was seated on my left and the seat on my right was empty. I had tried to get Kristoff to sit there beside me but he had declined.

"I am sorry, my Lady," he'd murmured in a low voice. "But that seat is kept empty on purpose. It is the seat your future Consort will occupy once you choose him."

Of course then I wanted him to sit to my right more than ever but he was standing behind my throne-chair instead, keeping a watchful eye on everyone at the table. He'd told me that my status as the True Incarnation would do much to keep me safe but it was clear he was still being vigilant and protective, which I very much appreciated.

"I *said* you're looking radiant tonight, my dear," Morbain repeated, stroking his curling pirate's mustache and leering at my cleavage, which the forest green feasting gown emphasized with its low-cut bodice.

I gave him the most withering stare I could.

"That's Goddess-Empress or Sundalla the 1000th to you," I said, biting the words out slowly and clearly. "*Not* 'my dear' or any other endearment or nick-name you might think up, Morbain."

Several of the Royals around us sucked in their breath and I saw glances and whispers being exchanged all up and down the long table. Head Councilor Tannus scowled, as though I'd said something shocking.

I didn't give a damn. I wanted nothing to do with a murderous, conniving asshole like Morbain and I didn't care who knew how I felt.

Morbain's smile became a bit forced.

"Technically you're not the Goddess-Empress until you've been crowned and ascended the Golden Throne," he pointed out. "Until then you're simply the True Incarnation."

"Fine," I snapped. "Call me that, then. Or better yet, don't call me anything at all. Let's just eat and each pretend the other doesn't exist."

Morbain opened his mouth, no doubt to give an angry retort, but just then the middle of my hubcap-sized golden plate slid to one side and a steaming pot of bubbling, dark blue broth rose out of the table.

"Oh!" I jumped a little in the huge, padded chair. "What in the world?"

"This is *quantro,* my Lady," Kristoff murmured in my ear. "It's considered a great delicacy. You dip the *palas* in the *quantro* pot and they will turn into whatever delicacy the chef has prepared for you."

"Dip the *what* into the pot?" I asked, frowning. But just then, a servant in the gold and black palace livery set a plate of small green and blue balls beside the boiling blue broth.

"Those are the *palas,*" Kristoff said. He nodded to a long, skinny pair of golden tongs next to my plate. "You pick up the *pala* of your choice and dip it into the pot..." He gestured to the blue, bubbling broth. "In order to reveal the secret tidbit the chef has prepared just for you. But first..."

He reached into a fold of his uniform and withdrew a silver wand with a blinking red light on the end of it. This he proceeded to wave over both the bubbling broth and the green and blue balls—which ranged in size from a walnut to a lemon—until the light turned from red to green and began to glow.

"All right, my Lady," he murmured in my ear. "You may dine in safety. There is no poison on or in your food."

"Thanks," I muttered and he nodded and resumed his place, standing behind my chair.

"Well, well—your Guard is certainly very *protective* of you, my dear. Excuse me—I mean, *True Incarnation*," Morbain remarked as I picked up the golden tongs and looked at them doubtfully.

"Can you blame him?" I snapped. "I've nearly been killed three or four times in the space of the last week. Apparently *someone* doesn't want me on the throne. Can't imagine who *that* might be." I glared at him as I spoke but he didn't even have the grace to blush or drop his eyes.

"A most regrettable state of affairs, I'm sure," he remarked, picking up his own tongs. By now, a pot of the bubbling blue stuff had appeared in front of everyone at the table and the servants had finished placing the plates of blue and green balls in front of all the other diners as well.

After a moment, I became aware that everyone at the table was looking at me expectantly.

"True Incarnation," Head Councilor Tannus said, looking down his long, boney nose at me across the table. "It is customary for the Goddess-Empress to take the first bite at a banquet of state."

"Oh. Oh, of course," I said, feeling foolish and put on the spot. Quickly I grabbed one of the little blue balls at random and dunked it into the bubbling blue broth.

Of course, I had no idea how long it was supposed to cook but after a moment I checked my tongs and saw that the blue casing around the tidbit of food had melted, revealing...

A long, green, writhing *slug*.

"Ugh!" I exclaimed involuntarily and nearly dropped my golden tongs.

"Oh, a *perech* grub—and still alive too!" Morbain exclaimed. "Such a delicacy!"

"It…it's *supposed* to be alive?" I asked in a low voice.

"Most assuredly! They're quite a rarity this time of the year— normally they only spawn in the rainy season. Why?" He raised one pointed black eyebrow at me. "Is it not to your taste?"

"We…on my planet, we don't usually eat slugs. Especially not live ones," I said, still revolted by the wriggling green slug dangling from my golden tongs. It was as long as my hand and dripping with clear, viscous slime.

"A great pity—you're missing out on a delicacy," Morbain remarked. "Still, until you eat it, no one else can eat their food. The Goddess-Empress must take the first bite—or gift it to someone at the table."

I looked up and saw that it was true—no one else at the table had taken a single bite. Most of them were holding other bits and pieces of food in their tongs —although none of them seemed to be slugs—and staring at me expectantly.

Oh my God—was I actually going to have to *eat* this thing? Was I going to have to eat a *live slug*?

I knew what Zoe would have done—she would have thrown down the tongs and demanded to speak to the chef. She was never shy about sending things back at a restaurant—even a swanky one. But this wasn't a restaurant—this was my first official banquet with the people I was supposed to be ruling over. I couldn't let it appear that I thought their food was disgusting—even though it really, *totally* was.

I brought the slug closer to my mouth, thinking about the blonde girl who gets sold to the barbarians on *Game of Thrones*. There's a scene where she's pregnant and has to eat a whole, raw horse's heart in order to make her baby strong or something crazy like that. It cements her place as the barbarian queen and later on she gets to ride dragons or something—I don't know, I only remember the parts Zoe made me watch. *Anyway*, I told myself, *at least a live slug isn't as disgusting as a raw horse's heart.* But somehow I couldn't make myself believe it.

"What is the matter, True Incarnation?" Head Councilor Tannus pitched his voice to carry to everyone seated at the table. "Do you not find our food to your liking?"

"Of...of course not," I managed to say. "I mean, of course I do. I'm just...considering which end to eat first."

"One usually starts with the head," Morbain recommended helpfully. "That way you can save the tasty intestinal tract for last."

That was it—I was going to puke. I could feel my gorge rising and I had to swallow hard in order to keep the light lunch I'd had earlier down. Kristoff had told the kitchen staff to make me several light meals by now and none of them had involved anything alive. Why did I have to deal with this now, in public, in front of every single Royal in the palace?

"You *can*, of course, gift the first morsel of food to a fellow diner at the banquet," Morbain hissed in my ear. "Would you like *me* to eat the grub for you, my dear?"

I didn't want to have anything to do with him but it seemed like the only way out. Because I just couldn't put that green, slimy, wriggling slug in my mouth—I just *couldn't.*

"Fine." I dropped the slug onto his side plate carefully. "Have it."

"Why, thank you." Morbain stabbed the squirming creature with a sharp, two-pronged fork. There was a high-pitched shrieking sound, which seemed to come from the hapless slug, and then he shoved it into his mouth and bit down hard, cutting off the cry of pain abruptly. A brown string-like thing squirted out from between his lips and landed on his chin. Without missing a beat, he scooped it up with one finger and examined it.

"What..." I felt more nauseous than ever. "What is *that?*"

"The intestinal tract, as I told you." He offered it to me on the end of one stubby finger. "Are you quite certain you don't want it?"

"Positive," I said, wondering if it would cause a horrible scandal if I puked under the table. "You...you go ahead."

"Suit yourself." He shrugged and slurped it up like a long

brown spaghetti noodle, making me cringe.

"My Lady," I heard Kristoff murmur, leaning down to speak in my ear. "Are you well?"

"Fine...I think." I swallowed hard, feeling some of the nausea start to recede. "I just...couldn't eat that."

"You should have given it to someone else, then." He sounded unhappy. "The gift of the first morsel of food on the Empress's plate is reserved for her Consort or a treasured favorite."

"What?" I glared at Morbain, who was dunking a lime-sized green ball into his bubbling broth and carefully not looking at me. I felt like I had been tricked, especially when I saw a slight smile hovering around Councilor Tannus's thin-lipped mouth as he ate a morsel from his own pot.

"Just don't do it again," Kristoff advised and straightened up, standing guard behind my chair.

"Fine," I muttered, more to myself than him. "I won't."

Deciding to try again, I picked an egg-sized green ball this time. I dunked it in the boiling blue liquid—which was really too gummy to be broth—and waited until the outer covering melted.

A writhing, green and purple beetle with three inch-long antenna was revealed, caught in my tongs.

I gasped and dropped the golden utensil. It clattered against my plate and the bug—which was as big as one of those giant roaches we have down in Florida—skittered off down the table.

People began to murmur and all eyes were on me until Morbain reached out and stabbed the beetle with his two-pronged fork. He popped it into his mouth and ate it with a disgusting crunching sound, grinning at me as he did so. Everyone relaxed and started eating again—everyone but me, that was.

"My Lady, are you all right?" It was Kristoff, leaning down to whisper in my ear once more.

"No," I whispered back. "Kristoff, what is going *on* here? This is nothing like the food you've had served to me in the Royal Apartments! Why do I keep getting live slugs and roaches?"

He looked unhappy. "Someone must have told the Royal chef that you enjoyed exotic cuisine. I will disabuse him of the notion in the future but for now there is nothing I can do."

I could guess who that "someone" had been. I had been set up to make it look like Morbain was a friend or favorite of mine somehow—but why? Would it really gain him that much status to eat food that was meant for me? Possibly, I supposed, but it was too late to worry now. I would just have to go on with the feast and try to pretend I was eating my own food from now on.

Picking up the golden tongs, I grabbed another little round ball and dunked it in the boiling blue goo. After a while, I lifted the tongs just about an inch out of the broth and peeked at what was in them.

Something hissed at me and a forked tongue flickered in my direction.

Grimly, I plunged the tongs back into the bubbling pot and waited until I thought the weird food item must have drowned. Taking another peek I saw that I was right. It hung limply from the tongs, looking like a drowned snake with three heads and two tails. Great—I was supposed to eat this thing?

Instead, I discretely let it slip back into the pot and grabbed another ball to dunk in the goo.

For the rest of the banquet, that was what I did—dunking the balls in the goo to kill whatever emerged and then just leaving them in the broth. Soon my pot looked like a witch's stew filled with dead insects, slugs, worms, and even something that appeared to be a tiny bat, all boiling in a slimy dark blue broth. It was disgusting but at least it appeared that I was participating in the feast.

I was extremely glad when a servant rang what sounded like an immense gong and announced, "Royals of Femme One, the moment you have been waiting for has finally arrived! If you will all adjourn to the Culling Chamber, we can begin the Ceremony."

Kristoff

Everyone rose and I took Charlotte by the elbow and led her away from the table. Surrounded by her honor guard, we traversed a long hallway and then went down a long flight of steps that led to a vast, arching double door made of silver.

This chamber was used only once a generation when the

Empress chose a new Consort. The staff, I saw, had done a good job of cleaning it and making it ready to receive the crowd of Royals who were to attend the Culling Ceremony. It was a large auditorium with a stage at the end of it which had been set up specifically for that purpose.

I didn't like putting Charlotte up on the stage until I had to — it made her too much of a target, in my opinion. Instead, I stood at the foot of the steps, waiting until the entire crowd was seated and the Council of Wisdom had taken their places on the stage.

Then, and only then, did I lead Charlotte up the steps and seat her on the golden, throne-like chair in the center of the stage which had been prepared for her.

She moved carefully but gracefully in the heavy green gown I'd had made for her. I reminded myself to order her lighter outfits in the future. She wasn't as big or as strong as a Majoran born Empress would have been although, to my eyes at least, she was twice as lovely as any other female in the room.

Stop thinking of how lovely she is and just concentrate on protecting her, I told myself as I got her seated. *This is the last time she'll want you, anyway. After she gives her blood to the candidates, she'll begin to long for one of them.*

I wondered who the three the Council had chosen were. Usually it was an array of young Royals, all picked from the foremost families. Young males around the Empress's age with impeccable bloodlines and the blood of past Goddess-Empresses flowing in their veins.

I couldn't see for sure who it was, though, because of the black cloth barrier stretched in front of the candidates. As was the tradition, the barrier hid them from both the prying eyes of the audience, and the gaze of the Goddess-Empress herself. In this way, she was supposed to be able to make a completely impartial decision. After the three the Council had picked had ingested her blood, she should begin to be drawn to one of them. Often the result was instant, though sometimes it took hours or even days to determine the true Consort.

I thought of how Charlotte had seemed fine at first, after giving me her blood, and then how the Burning Blood disease had set in later. Would she have the same delayed symptoms when one of the

Royal lineage consumed her blood or would she be immediately drawn to the right male for her?

I pushed the thought away. I didn't want to know. Didn't want to stay here and watch as the female I loved was drawn to another. But this was my fate—my destiny. I had sworn my vow to my mistress—had promised to be faithful unto death. I was willing to be killed or maimed in her service and this should be no different.

Except the idea of seeing her with another male *was* different somehow. I felt that I would rather have my sword hand chopped off than see her in the arms of another. Anything would be better than the stabbing pain of losing her forever.

I thought of how I'd heard her weeping in the night and had been unable to go to her. I had told myself that it would only make it harder for both of us if I gave in again and held her while she slept. Now I wished that I had done it, wished that I had the memory of holding her one last time to carry me through.

Then Head Councilor Tannus rose and began to speak and I stepped to my place, behind my Lady's chair.

The Ceremony of Culling had begun.

Chapter Thirty

Charlotte

"The Ceremony of Culling is a time honored tradition. It is the best way, determined by the Council of Wisdom, to help the new Empress find her true Consort," Head Councilor Tannus intoned. His voice boomed out over the audience and I thought he must have some kind of microphone on, though I couldn't see any wires or any kind of headpiece on him.

He was standing beside me on the stage, holding a long, engraved golden dagger with a wickedly sharp looking point. Standing beside him was another Councilor, holding a small silver tray with three tiny crystal cups that looked like miniature shot glasses.

"Behind the barrier," Tannus continued, "Are three candidates, deemed worthy by myself and other members of the Council of Wisdom. As you all know, the Empress-to-be will give three drops of her blood to each. As she does not know their identities, this will provide a completely impartial way for her to choose which Consort is most suitable for her. She may be drawn to the correct male at once or it may take some time. Eventually, however, she will seek him out and he will be invested as her Royal Consort during her coronation ceremony."

There was a polite smattering of applause and I got the idea that everyone here already knew the rules of the Culling Ceremony and Tannus was just repeating them to be official.

To me, the whole thing seemed a lot like the old Dating Game show and I was the "lucky bachelorette." Behind the black curtain to my left, I could hear coughing and shuffling, as if the three candidates were getting restless. I would have to pick one of them but instead of asking cute and kooky questions to determine my true match, I would be giving them my blood to drink. Also, we wouldn't be going on an all-expenses-paid cruise to the Bahamas at the end of it—we would be stuck together for life.

Okay, so maybe *not* so much like the Dating Game.

"And now for the sacrifice of Royal blood," Tannus said. "If your Majesty would please extend your right hand?"

I held out my hand, eyeing the ceremonial dagger in his grip, but before he could stick me with it, Kristoff intervened.

"Your pardon, my Lord Councilor," he said in a low voice. "But my Lady's life has been threatened more than once in the time since she has gotten to Femme One. If anyone is to pierce her flesh, it will be me, with my own dagger."

"What?" Tannus blustered. "Why, this is most unusual! You can't just—"

"I can and I will," Kristoff said firmly. "Unless you'd like to hold up these proceedings to have the ceremonial knife tested for possible traces of poison?"

"You...you accuse me of—" Tannus began, his face turning red.

"Assuredly not," Kristoff said smoothly. "But has the knife been in your keeping the entire time before the ceremony? If you turned your back on it, even for a moment, a would-be assassin could have dipped the tip in deadly poison. It is a risk I do not intend to take." He looked at me. "My Lady, if you would extend your hand?"

With Tannus still blustering and protesting in the background, I held out my hand to Kristoff and he unsheathed one of his own daggers and wiped it carefully on a clean, white cloth.

"My Lady, I would not pierce your flesh or bring you pain for any lesser reason than this," he murmured, cupping my hand in his.

"I know," I whispered, feeling numb. He looked amazing in his gladiator-type uniform with his broad shoulders and the golden chest-plate gleaming. My hand tingled where he touched me and I felt a deep longing to be in those strong, muscular arms. To be held by him, just one more time. But now wasn't the time—not with every single Royal and noble in the palace watching.

"I'll be quick," Kristoff promised. He pressed the tip of his razor-sharp dagger into the pad of my middle finger and I felt the tiniest pinch. When he withdrew, there was a ruby drop of blood welling at the end of my finger.

Quickly, the Councilor with the tray stepped forward and held out the tiny crystal shot glasses. I squeezed exactly three drops of blood into each one and then Kristoff knelt beside me and bandaged my finger in another clean, white cloth.

"And now," Head Councilor Tannus said, taking the tray from the other councilor and glaring at Kristoff. "I will give the Royal blood to the three candidates which have been chosen as worthy."

He stalked around behind the black curtain and I heard the soft clink of crystal on silver as he started handing out my blood samples.

"Take these and drink," he commanded grandly, his voice carrying out into the auditorium through the invisible PA system. "That it may be known if you are the chosen of the Goddess-Empress or if you are to be Culled."

Then I heard something I was pretty sure *wouldn't* carry over the hidden microphone.

"Eh…what's this then?" a thin, reedy voice asked. "You woke me up from m' nap to give me one tiny glass of ale? That's not enough to quench m' thirst!"

I frowned. Who in the world could *that* be? Whoever it was, they certainly didn't sound like a *young* man.

Then another voice spoke up—this one high and querulous.

"I don't *want* to drink that! Nasty!"

"Now, Egmon," murmured a softer, feminine voice. "You promised Muhmuh you would drink it like a good boy. Remember once you're done you get a sim-sim candy to take the taste away."

"But it's *nasty!*" whined the voice. "Don't *wanna!*"

I frowned and looked at Kristoff to see if he was hearing this as well. From the puzzled look on his face, he was. He had told me the candidates would be chosen from men around my age—no more than five to ten years younger or older than me on average. So why did the voices I was hearing sound like a grandpa and a little boy?

For a moment I was frozen to my seat. If I got up, every eye in the auditorium would be upon me. All the most important people in the palace would be staring at me and wondering why I was profaning their ritual.

Then again, if I *didn't* get up and go investigate, I would be letting someone else decide my fate for the rest of my life. What were a few moments of public embarrassment to that?

Stand up for yourself! I could almost hear Zoe shouting in my head. *Don't let them steamroll over you, Charlotte! Find out what's happening back there.*

Taking a deep breath, I rose from the throne-like chair.

"Your Majesty…" One of the other Councilors was immediately by my side, a worried look on his face. "Your Majesty, where are you going?"

"I'm going to find out what's going on." I gave him the coldest look imaginable. "Now would you please step aside, Councilor."

He held his ground, blocking the way between me and the curtain.

"I really don't think that's advisable, Majesty," he said, frowning and rubbing his hands together nervously. "You see, it's still too early for the blood the candidates have ingested to be having any effect on you and it's really not customary for the Empress to see her potential consorts before she feels drawn to one."

"I don't care about what's customary," I snapped. "I want to know what's going on back there. Now, *move*."

"You heard the Empress." Kristoff was suddenly at my side, his skin glowing a burnished gold. It was a mute reminder to everyone assembled of my status, since only the Imperial Guards were allowed to maintain a golden skin color and then only in the presence of the true Goddess-Empress. He had a hand on the hilt of his dagger and a dangerous look in his eyes. "Will you move or not?" he asked in a low voice.

The audience of Royals and nobles had begun muttering among themselves but I ignored them. I just wanted to find out what was happening behind that black curtain that was going to affect the rest of my life.

"This is *not* proper!" The Councilor looked scandalized but at last he moved aside and let Kristoff and me past.

Well, in for a penny—in for a pound. Since everyone was staring at me, I decided I might as well make a dramatic gesture.

I walked to the black curtain and tugged it as hard as I could. I had only meant to pull it back but the fabric it was made of must have been weak—maybe with age since this room only got used once a generation. Anyway, I heard a low ripping noise and suddenly the entire curtain fell to the ground at my feet.

Everyone in the crowd gasped at what was revealed—including *me*.

Sitting on three chairs were my candidates, who were supposed to be within five to ten years of age difference from me. Only it looked like whoever had picked them didn't know how to count.

An old man who looked to be about ninety was blinking owlishly at me and clutching an empty shot glass in one gnarled hand.

Opposite the old man, was a little boy who looked to be around five or six. He was accompanied by his mother who was staring fearfully at me and trying to get him to drink the three drops of blood, which he was adamantly refusing.

And sitting between them, looking like the cat who had gotten the cream, was Prince Morbain himself.

He was holding an empty shot glass and as I watched, he reached over and snatched the little boy's glass from his mother's hand.

"Give me that!" he exclaimed and then, watching my reaction, he downed the three drops of blood in one gulp and smacked his lips. "Mm-mm! Delicious!"

"Why you...you..." Words failed me but they didn't fail Kristoff.

"What is the meaning of this?" he demanded of Tannus, who was still standing there with the silver tray looking smug and self-satisfied.

"This is the Culling Ceremony, as you well know, *Guard*," Tannus snapped, glaring at him. "Kindly restore the curtain and take the Empress away—she doesn't need to see these males until she feels drawn to one of them."

"She will never feel drawn to either a little child or an old man as you well know," Kristoff growled. "The age difference is too great—her blood will not call her to either of them."

"A pity, isn't it?" Morbain smiled widely, his teeth streaked red with my blood. The sight made my stomach roll. "But that is the way of it. Grandfather Yulip and young Master Egmon here were the two males in the palace with the most Royal blood in their veins and so the Council had no choice but to choose them as candidates. Well, except for myself of course—I have more Royal blood than anyone else, being the son of the late Sundalla the 999th."

"Which makes any kind of joining with you some kind of weird, horrible *incest*," I exclaimed, feeling sick. "I share DNA with your late mother! And even if that wasn't the case, I could never be attracted to *you!*"

"You share a few genes only," Morbain replied, smiling evilly. "It's not enough to hinder our joining, my dear. And I *shall* call you 'my dear' or 'my darling' or maybe even 'my little slave' if I so choose. Because very soon now you will be enslaved to the desire you feel for me." He preened as he spoke, throwing out his chest and stroking his long mustache, which I was beginning to think made him look less like a pirate and more like the eccentric artist, Salvador Dali.

"You shall call my Lady by her title or I'll cut out your tongue," Kristoff growled, stepping forward and unsheathing his sword. "And never speak of enslaving her again—Charlotte is the Goddess-Empress and she will rule herself and her people as the Goddess guides her—not on any whim of yours, Morbain!"

"Here now!" Tannus stepped forward, bristling self-importantly. "These are sacred proceedings! You cannot profane the ritual by drawing a blade!"

"You mean the way you've already profaned it by rigging the results?" Kristoff demanded. "Tell me something, Tannus—did you and Morbain act alone or was the entire Council privy to this blasphemy?"

"I can answer that question," I said grimly. Striding forward, I grabbed Tannus's free hand in one of my own and let my touch-sense take over.

At once I knew three things—that he and Morbain were plotting to rule together, using me as a puppet figurehead... that he had hated the old Empress... and that he intended to have me killed if things didn't go according to his plan.

The last made me gasp and step back so fast I almost stumbled. Kristoff had to catch me.

"What is it?" he murmured. "What did you see, my Goddess?"

Before I could answer, Tannus was shaking the hand I had grabbed above his head and shouting,

"Blasphemy! Corruption! The True Incarnation has *touched* a member of the Council of Wisdom! This cannot be!"

"Oh, do be quiet, Tannus." To my surprise, it was Morbain talking. He had risen from his chair and come to stand a cautious distance from Kristoff's blade. "Stop making such a fuss," he told the Head Councilor. "It doesn't matter if she *touched* you or not—we still have the upper hand. I've had her blood! Any moment now she'll be after me, panting like a bitch in heat."

"Watch your language." Kristoff put the tip of his blade to Morbain's throat, his eyes whirling with rage. "If you speak so of my Lady again I swear I'll kill you," he snarled at Morbain.

Morbain gave him a sharp look.

"You love her, don't you *Guard?* So much that the thought of her with another is nearly driving you mad. Is that not right?"

Kristoff growled and surged forward. I think he really would have cut off Morbain's head but I put a hand on his arm.

"Kristoff, don't! They'll put you away and I won't have anyone to protect me," I pleaded.

He growled again, a possessive, inhuman sound that sent shivers down my spine. I could feel the tension in his muscles, could see his strong jaw clenching with rage. He really did want to kill Morbain and after years of treachery on the prince's part, I couldn't blame him. But I didn't want to lose him either.

"Kristoff," I pleaded.

At last he backed away and re-sheathed his sword.

"Stay away from my Lady," he said, pointing at Morbain. He turned to me. "My Lady Charlotte, I believe it is time for you to invoke your right to give your blood to another Royal male, just as your predecessor, Sundalla the 999th did in her time."

For a moment my heart leapt, but then I realized he wasn't talking about himself. He was nodding at the crowded auditorium where the Royals in attendance were watching with wide, uncomprehending eyes. There were literally dozens of hot alien males in the right age range and with the right bloodlines to choose from. But I didn't want any of them.

"I don't—" I began but Tannus interrupted in his self-important voice.

"I am afraid it will be quite impossible for the Empress-to-be to choose another Royal to give her blood to," he said, looking down his nose at me. "Only yesterday the Council of Wisdom voted on a motion to keep her from seeking outside our recommendations—for her own safety, of course," he added.

"What?" I demanded. "You can't just do that! You can't just run my life and dictate exactly who I'm supposed to marry—er, pick as a Consort! This was supposed to be a scientific process—it's the only reason I agreed to it in the first place!" Well, that and the fact that I hadn't wanted to offend my new people. But seeing as how I was up on the stage in front of all of them making a scene, I was pretty sure that particular ship had sailed.

"Actually, we *can*." Tannus gave me a nasty smirk. "One of the reasons the Council of Wisdom exists is to impart wisdom to the Goddess-Empress herself. To that end, we must determine who is the best male to be your Consort."

"So you considered and came up with *Morbain?*" I demanded. "What's *wrong* with you people?"

Tannus sniffed. "I had thought your Majesty would be *pleased* with our decision. After seeing the way you favored the Prince at the banquet—giving him the first *and* the second bites from your plate I thought—"

"That was fixed and you know it," I snapped. "Someone told the cook all I wanted for supper was bugs and slugs and creepy crawlies! Of *course* I wasn't going to eat that!"

"You will never carry out this plan," Kristoff told Morbain and Tannus who were both smiling in a most unpleasant way.

"My dear Guard," Morbain said. "We already *have.*" He looked at me and winked, making my stomach roll. "When your *needing* begins, you know where to find me, my dear. I'll be seeing you soon. *Very* soon I should think."

Then he strolled off the stage laughing, leaving me standing there in front of the crowd with a knot of uncertainty and dread in my stomach.

What was I going to do?

Chapter Thirty-one

Kristoff

I was so enraged it was difficult to see past the red haze that covered my vision as I ushered Charlotte back to the Royal Apartments. The urge to seek out Morbain and kill him at once was almost overpowering. Only knowing that Charlotte would be left alone without a protector if I did so kept me from hunting him down and chopping his lying, duplicitous head from his body.

Speaking of Charlotte, I could feel her fear and worry strongly through the bond I had with her. And who could blame her for being afraid? Tannus and Morbain had basically conspired against her to hand the power of the throne over to the last person who should have it.

I couldn't count the number of plots I'd foiled against my old mistress and Morbain had been behind all of them. A male like that deserved to be killed, not crowned Consort.

Consort. Just the thought of Morbain's greasy hands on Charlotte's cool, white flesh made my stomach churn. If I had to see that...if I had to stand by and watch while he touched and took my Lady in the way that I was forbidden to ...

I shook my head fiercely. The idea was too much. I honestly thought it might drive me mad to watch the female I loved to distraction given to the male I hated most in the galaxy. My mind simply wouldn't be able to stand the strain without snapping. I would wind up killing Morbain or myself or both of us if that happened.

And yet, how could it be stopped? Morbain had Royal bloodlines and he had ingested twice as much of Charlotte's blood as was needed to form a connection between them. Even now she might be feeling a pull in his direction.

I looked at Charlotte. She was pacing up and down the living area of the Royal Apartments, a large room decorated in gold finery with a long, low couch and a fireplace at one end. One of the maids had lit a fire and it glowed red and warm, filling the large chamber with a ruby-gold light that made Charlotte look even more beautiful in her green banqueting gown. It swished and swirled around her, reflected in the three-paneled viewer which was opposite the couch—a place where the Empress could check her appearance one more time before appearing in public.

Her beauty overwhelmed me but I tried to ignore it and concentrate on the bond I had with her instead. To my dismay, I could feel the lust already growing in her. The need and desire boiling to the surface like an overfull pot. She was very close to the breeding part of her cycle—if she had not already reached it.

"My Lady," I could not stop myself from saying. "I...feel the need in you. Are you...do you...?" I knew I ought to ask if she wanted me to escort her to Morbain, but somehow I couldn't get the words out.

She looked up at me sharply.

"Do I need someone to scratch my itch? Yes, I do—very badly, in fact. But is it going to be Morbain?" She made a face. "Hell no, it's not."

"But if you are drawn to him..." My throat wanted to lock on the words, to never let them out. "If you *want* him..." I finally choked out.

"I don't want anything to do with him!" she snapped. "And I don't care how much of my blood he drank—he could drink it by the gallon like two percent milk—I still would never want him." She crossed the distance between us and looked up at me. "I want *you*, Kristoff."

"My Lady," I whispered. "You cannot mean..."

"Kristoff..." She lifted her chin, the light of determination flaring in her lovely green eyes. "I don't care about the rules anymore. I'm not going to abide by the Council's regulations if they feel free to break or manipulate them any way they want."

"I understand why you would feel that way," I said carefully. "But my Lady, no matter what wrongdoing has gone on, I am still not of Royal blood. I cannot be your Consort."

"Fine. Then I won't have a Consort."

"But you must!" I protested. "Someone must help slake the *need*. Your Royal cravings…"

"Can be just as easily satisfied by *you*." Reaching up on her tiptoes, she took my face in her hands and looked intently into my eyes. "Kristoff," she whispered. "I want you to help me—the way Sundalla the 887th had her Guard help her."

"My Lady…" I felt her *need* so strongly it was all I could do to stop myself from taking her then and there, as she was asking me to do. But I couldn't let myself, no matter how much I might want to. "Charlotte," I said, my voice hoarse with desire. "I want you as you want me. But the union between Sundalla the 887th and her Guard was sanctioned by the Council of Wisdom."

"Screw the Council of Wisdom," she said, frowning. "They're corrupt. Or at least Tannus is. Do you know what I saw when I touched him?"

I shook my head, almost afraid to know.

Charlotte took a deep breath. "Taunus would kill me if he could—he'll try to if things don't go according to his plan."

"What?" I glared at her. "You Saw that when you touched him?"

She nodded. "That and the fact that he and Morbain have been conspiring together for a long time now. Oh, and he hated your old mistress—my predecessor."

"He didn't like that she defied him in her choice of Consort," I said bitterly.

"Well, I'm defying him too," Charlotte said firmly. "If I can't have you as my Consort, then I won't have any Consort at all."

"The Council of Wisdom won't stand for it," I said.

"They'll have to," she said grimly. "I was willing to go along with their rules and bow to their religious authority when I thought everything was impartial. But tonight, after what we saw at the Culling Ceremony…" She shook her head. "I'm not playing by their rules anymore, Kristoff."

I knew I should advise her to play along with the Council, to give Tannus what he wanted. He was, after all, the most powerful person in the galaxy, after the Empress herself. If he truly wanted her dead, it would become a full time job keeping her alive and safe. In short, he was a dangerous male.

But I couldn't bring myself to do it. It was partly the unfairness of the situation but even more than that, I couldn't bear the thought of the female I loved being given to another.

"Very well," I said in a low voice. "Then I will help you defy the Council. Just tell me what you want of me, my Lady."

"I want *you* Kristoff." She pulled me down and I let her, sealing my mouth to hers for a kiss. Her mouth tasted as sweet as the *lizten* berry wine that had been served at the banquet and her sweet, feminine scent intoxicated me. I felt my shaft throbbing beneath my uniform and knew I wanted her as I had never wanted another female.

But we must at least *try* to work within the confines of the law.

"My Lady," I said, my voice husky with need, when we finally broke the kiss. "You know how much I want you but in order to keep to the letter of the law where an Empress and her Guard are concerned, *you* must take and use *me*. Not the other way around."

"All right." She was already shedding her gown, her skin creamy and glowing as she stepped out of the rustling green fabric and stood naked before me in the firelight. Her nipples stood out pink and tight from full breasts and I could see the way her outer pussy lips were swollen with need, allowing her Goddess-pearl to show itself.

It was all I could do not to drop to my knees and bury my face between her thighs right then and there—Gods, how I longed for the taste of her! The feel of her pulling my hair and crying my name as she had at the Pleasure House was fresh in my mind. Just the memory of it made my shaft so hard it hurt.

But now that we were back in the palace, the rules were different. I must only let her touch me and I must not touch back. I must give my body to be used and not use hers in return. And above all, I must not spurt my seed inside her and seek to bond her to me. Penetration was allowed, only if she impaled herself upon me. Allowing myself to come inside her, however, most certainly was not.

It was hard, so hard but if we were questioned by the Council I needed to say that we had been guided by the laws Sundalla the 887th and her Guard had used.

Promising myself that I would not violate the precepts of those that had come before us, I undressed as well—or started to, until Charlotte stopped me.

"No, let me," she murmured, after I finished removing my chest plate and greaves.

I stood silent, watching her beautiful body and full curves in the firelight as she stood on tiptoe to remove my undershirt. When she bared my chest, she rubbed her cheek against it, making a soft sound of desire in the back of her throat. When she took off my kilt and underclothing, I had to clench my hands into fists to keep from reaching for her.

And when we were both finally completely nude in the firelight, it was all I could do not to wrap my arms around her and take her there on the floor on the rich fur rug before the fireplace. Somehow I made myself hold still while she continued to explore me.

I must be strong, I told myself. *I must allow myself to be taken without taking.*

But Gods, I didn't know how long I could hold out against the desire that threatened to consume us both.

Charlotte

I couldn't believe how bold I was being. Part of it was due to the *need* inside me, urging me on—the same need I'd been feeling since Kristoff had taken me aboard his ship and I'd had the Burning Blood. Only now it had intensified by a factor of about a thousand. I had the feeling that I was entering the breeding stage of my cycle and I would need to have sex very soon or suffer some serious consequences.

What I was feeling had nothing to do with the fact that Morbain had drunk some of my blood—I was sure of that now. I felt absolutely no inclination to go to him. In fact, the idea of letting him touch me in any way made my stomach turn. It was Kristoff I wanted—Kristoff who was right for me and always had been. I was absolutely certain of that.

And that was the other reason I allowed myself to be so bold with him. He was the one I wanted and he had admitted to wanting me too. Even knowing he couldn't react and could only accept my touch without touching me back made me feel bold and hot. I *liked* the idea of being in charge—of touching and teasing him and making him every bit as hot and needy as I felt.

So I let myself do what I wanted—what I had *always* wanted to do, if I was honest—from the first moment I started to feel for him. I explored his big, hard body, running my hands up and down his muscular chest and back, stroking down to circle around the aching length of his shaft without actually touching him there.

A low groan rumbled deep in his chest and I saw his big hands clench into fists at his sides. It gave me a thrill, knowing how I was affecting him.

Growing bolder, I gripped his thick length, loving the way it throbbed in my hand. It was like holding a hot bar of lead, one that pulsed in my fist, eager for my touch. Kristoff threw back his head and groaned again, this time louder as he pumped helplessly into my hand.

Suddenly I wanted to taste him as he had tasted me the night in the Pleasure House. Sinking to my knees before him, I rubbed my cheek against his shaft, breathing in his dark, masculine musk. It sent a shiver of desire through me so strong I couldn't help myself. Leaning forward, I swiped my tongue over the broad, plum-shaped head of his cock. A taste as salty as the sea flooded my mouth, making me want more. Getting even more daring, I opened my mouth and took him between my lips, struggling to take as much as I could—which wasn't much more than the head—he was simply too big.

Kristoff's eyes fluttered open and he looked down at me, an expression of shock on his face. I know because I was looking up at him while I sucked him and swirled my tongue around his throbbing shaft.

"My Lady, no!" he exclaimed hoarsely, trying to draw away from me. "You must not abase yourself so before me!"

"It's not abasement—it's pleasure," I said, releasing him at last. And it was. Though I had never cared for this act before, I found it intensely enjoyable now. Just knowing that I was affecting Kristoff so deeply was enough to make my nipples hard and my sex wet with desire.

But Kristoff was shaking his head.

"My Lady," he murmured, raising me to my feet. "If you truly wish there to be intimate kisses between us..." He sank slowly to his knees before me, looking up to hold my eyes with his. "If that is what you wish, then I beg you will allow *me* to do the kissing."

"But...how?" I asked, looking down at him. He was so close I could feel his hot breath against my breasts and I knew what he meant, though not exactly how he thought he could accomplish it without breaking our self-imposed rules. "I thought I was the only one allowed to touch or, uh, taste. That you just had to let me, um...*use* you."

"And so you shall—use me to the fullest." Kristoff's eyes blazed and his voice was deep with lust. "Let me show you."

He rose and went to the long, gold brocade couch to one side of the fireplace. Sitting down in front of it, he leaned back until the tops of his shoulders were pressed against its cushions. Then he laid his head back until he was resting against the couch looking up at the frescoed ceiling, filled with dancing shadows from the firelight.

I saw what he wanted at once but it made me feel nervous and extremely exposed.

"You want..." I couldn't make the words come out of my mouth.

"I want you to ride my face." Kristoff lifted his head and looked at me, desire filling his beautiful, alien eyes. "Come, my Lady...spread your thighs and use me...rub your sweet, open pussy against my tongue...feed me your honey as you find your pleasure against my mouth."

"I...don't know." I bit my lip. "You know I love it when you...when you taste me, Kristoff. But can't we do it the way we did the other night in the Pleasure House. You know, with you on top?"

He shook his head regretfully. "Forgive me, my Lady but in

order to remain within the precepts set by the Council for Sundalla the 887th you must find your pleasure with me and I am not allowed to help you or touch or take you in any way."

"Why?" I asked. "Why is it so wrong for you to touch me back?"

"Because..." Something heated flickered in the depths of his eyes. "Though we are deferential to our females and treat them as goddesses, Majoran males have a deeply primal mating urge. If I allowed myself to touch you and taste you the way I so desperately long to, it might push me too far—to the point beyond which I cannot control myself anymore. And if I go past that point..."

"What?" I asked, when he trailed off, shaking his head. "What would happen?"

"I wouldn't be able to stop myself from taking you," he said in a low voice—almost a growl. His eyes went half-lidded with need. "Wouldn't be able to stop myself from claiming you—*fucking* you, Charlotte. Fucking you and coming deep in your pussy—bonding you to me."

As always when he talked dirty to me the hot, deeply sexual words spoken in his low voice sent a shiver of desire straight through me. God, *that* was what I wanted—what I needed so badly I could almost taste it! The feeling of him pumping into me, thrusting deep and hard, filling me with himself and claiming me in no uncertain terms.

But Kristoff had said it couldn't be. I would just have to take what I could get.

"Come, my Lady," he murmured, his eyes still lazy with lust. "Come ride my face and feed me your sweet pussy. I'm longing to taste you again."

Feeling a shiver of desire run down my spine, I did as he said. Going over to the couch, I knelt on the rich gold cushions and positioned myself with my thighs on either side of his upturned face. His mouth was right under my pussy but I still felt reluctant to rest my weight on him.

"Come down," Kristoff murmured, looking up at me. "Let me taste you."

"I feel like I'm going to hurt you," I protested.

He gave a deep, rumbling laugh. "How? You're tiny. And so sweet and succulent—I only want to taste you again. Please trust me, Charlotte."

Oh. I kept forgetting that though I was plus-sized back on Earth, our size difference here did actually make me small, if still pleasingly plump. I knew how strong Kristoff was—I had seen and felt his strength in action. I could trust him to support me and I didn't have to fear that I'd hurt him.

"All right," I said at last. "But let me know if it's too much."

"Never too much...never too much of your honey, your sweet taste, my Goddess," he murmured and I heard the lust in his voice and knew he meant it. It was strange to contemplate but Majoran men seemed to enjoy giving their females oral pleasure more than they liked getting it themselves. At least, Kristoff certainly did.

Gripping the back of the couch in both hands, I spread my thighs wider and lowered my open pussy to his hot mouth.

Kristoff

Being surrounded by my Charlotte that way, feeling her all around me, her sweet, open sex pressed to my eager mouth was almost more than I could bear. Her warm, feminine scent filled my senses and her pussy, already slippery with honey, was the most delicious thing I had ever tasted.

I felt a surge of desire like nothing I had ever felt before—an urge so deep and primal I could scarcely fight it. The urge to take her, to fuck her and bond her to me, ensuring that no other male would ever lay a finger on her as long as we both lived.

Mine, growled a possessive voice within me as I penetrated her sweet entrance with my tongue and slipped deep inside her. *Mine and no one else's!*

I fought the urge with all my might. Fought it and won— barely. Somehow I was able to lie quiescent against the couch and simply allow my sweet lady to ride my face, rubbing her open pussy against my seeking, hungry mouth.

For she was doing that now—she was trusting me, trusting in

my strength to support and pleasure her. My cock throbbed as one small hand came down to grip my hair and she worked herself against me fiercely, pressing her inner folds against my lips and mouth, soft sounds of need coming from her slender throat.

That's right, my Lady, I thought, wishing we had a true two-way bond so that she could feel what I felt and hear what I thought. *Rub yourself against me – ride my face…take your pleasure with me.*

I repositioned slightly and put out my tongue, cupping her sweet sex as best I could without touching her with my hands. I could feel her Goddess-pearl swelling against my tongue and taste her honey flowing as she rubbed against me, soft, helpless little sounds falling from her lips as she curled her fingers tighter in my hair, her pleasure overcoming any fear she'd had about trying this new position.

Come for me, I thought, my cock throbbing, nearly delirious with need and pleasure. *Come against my face – feed me your honey, my Goddess. Let me pleasure you until you cannot stand it any more and the pleasure overwhelms you.*

With a soft cry, that was exactly what Charlotte did.

"Kristoff," she moaned, grinding against me. "Kristoff, please…*please!*"

Her grip tightened in my hair until it was a painful pleasure and I felt her clench around me, her Goddess-pearl throbbing against my tongue. Her thighs quivered and I tasted fresh nectar and swallowed it eagerly, hungry for her delicious flavor, so salty/sweet and perfectly Charlotte.

She finished at last, quivering against me, soft little moans still coming from her throat. I waited until she at last dismounted and cuddled beside me, pressing her small, soft body to mine.

"Mmmm… Kristoff, that was so good. But…" She looked up at me, her green eyes luminous in the firelight and still filled with the *need.*

"My Lady?" I asked softly. "What is it you desire?"

I knew what I desired – what my body was urging me to do. I wanted to take her here and now, to spread her legs and thrust long and hard into her sweet center, to fill her with my seed and claim her. But I couldn't…I mustn't. Instead I held still, my cock throbbing rigidly between my thighs, waiting on my lady's pleasure.

Charlotte

"You know what I desire—what I *need*," I said, feeling the throbbing, unfulfilled ache between my thighs. "That was wonderful, Kristoff—*amazing*. But I need more. I feel...so empty inside."

"You need to be filled." His voice was a low, lustful growl and I suddenly remembered what he'd told me—that he had to be careful not to reach the edge of his control so he wouldn't take me and bond me to him.

But I *wanted* to be bonded to Kristoff. Wanted it so badly I could barely stand it. I didn't give a damn for what the Council of Wisdom said anymore—those cheating, lying bastards. If they weren't going to play by their own rules, well, neither was I. I wanted Kristoff and I was going to have him, I decided. Not just as a sex toy to get off against—I wanted him to bond me to him—to form a permanent connection that couldn't be broken or denied.

How, though? My Imperial Guard was so honor bound he was determined to follow the rules. Determined not to go too far.

Well, maybe I can push him too far, I thought, a plan forming in my mind. And from the look in his shifting eyes, it wouldn't take much of a push.

I knew what I was going to do.

"Yes," I whispered, climbing into his lap and leaning over to kiss him. "I need to be *filled*. But not just filled—Kristoff, I think I've reached the breeding part of my cycle. I need to be bred—I need *you* to breed me."

"My Lady, no!" His voice was a low groan. "To breed you I would have to not just penetrate you but also spurt my seed inside you. And that I cannot do."

"Why not?"

As I spoke, I gripped his rigid shaft in my hand, feeling him throb against my palm, and leaned forward to kiss him. My nipples brushed against his broad, bare chest as I pressed forward, taking his mouth possessively. Kristoff didn't kiss me back but he groaned again when I lapped at his lips and chin, which were still shiny with my juices. Looking down, I saw that once more, his big hands were clenched into fists as though he was holding himself back by sheer force of will from claiming me the way I so desperately needed to be claimed.

Tasting my own secret flavor on his mouth was almost more than I could stand. I nearly impaled myself on him right then and there but I knew if I did, I wouldn't be able to get the reaction I wanted out of him. Instead, I contented myself with rubbing against him, letting the broad head of his cock part my pussy lips and stroke against my wet, open folds without quite penetrating me.

Kristoff groaned low in his throat, looking down to see the erotic sight of his shaft parting me and slipping into my open pussy.

"Gods, my Lady...you're driving me *insane*." His voice was a lustful growl. "Come down on me—fill yourself with me and use me until you come on my shaft."

"And if I do?" I said, rubbing the broad head of his cock directly over my aching clit. "What happens then? I get to come but you don't?"

He closed his eyes briefly, a look of almost pain coming over his face.

"That is how it must be. I cannot breed you—cannot fill you with my seed. It might form a bond between us."

Which was why he had to be so still while I rubbed myself against him, I suddenly understood. If he allowed himself to move, even a little bit, his animalistic instinct to claim and bond me to him would take over.

That was exactly what I wanted.

"Kristoff," I murmured in his ear, still rubbing against him. "Don't you *want* to come inside me? Don't you *want* to make me yours?"

"You know I do." His eyes blazed. "But it's blasphemy. Even what we're doing now is walking close to the line of sacrilege."

"Who says it's blasphemy or sacrilege for us to be together just because I supposedly have Royal blood and you don't?" I argued softly. "The Council? Who cares what they think anymore? I didn't grow up thinking I was anything special, Kristoff. And I don't think I am now. I'm just a woman who wants her man. Who wants her man to take her. To *breed* her." I pressed against him hard, making him groan as I made my point.

I thought for sure I'd convinced him but when I looked into his shifting eyes, he shook his head regretfully.

"I cannot," he said, his voice hoarse with need. "Please, my Lady, do not ask this of me."

"Call me Charlotte," I said, frowning at him. "I don't want to be 'your Lady' when you're making love to me. I just want to be *yours.*"

His eyes flashed at my challenge and I felt him surge against me, his cock swelling against my clit. He was close to that edge—I knew it. The line he didn't want to cross...except I knew that deep down, he really *did* want to cross it. I just had to show him how.

I leaned forward and kissed him again, darting my tongue into his mouth and threading my fingers into his thick, blue-black hair to pull him close. I rubbed my open pussy against him hard, letting my wetness envelope him completely.

This time, Kristoff kissed me back. His tongue met mine, stroking and seeking and his big hands came up to cup and knead my ass, pulling me even closer. When I finally came up for air, there was a wild look in his eyes and I knew I was close to getting through to him.

I got off his lap and crawled sinuously over to the silvery fur rug that was placed before the fireplace. The fire had burned down some now but I could still see myself in the three-panel viewer placed to one side of it. I supposed it was something the Empress could use to check her appearance before she went out on matters of State. Tonight it would serve a different purpose.

I positioned myself on my hands and knees and spread my thighs, opening my pussy for him wantonly. In the viewer I saw a blonde girl with over generous curves doing the same, her hair was tousled and her eyes were filled with firelight and need. Her breasts hung down like ripe fruit, her nipples dark and full with desire, almost brushing the soft fur of the rug.

I couldn't believe how eagerly, how shamelessly she offered herself. No—how shamelessly *I* offered *myself*. But the *need* was in me—on me—riding me mercilessly, urging me to give myself to the man I loved. The man I wanted to spend the rest of my life with. The man I wanted to breed me.

"Kristoff," I murmured, looking over my shoulder at him and spreading my thighs a little wider. "*Fuck* me."

"Charlotte," he grated in a deep, agonized voice. "Don't do this—you don't know what you're asking."

"Yes," I said. "I do." Lowering myself, I raised my ass higher in the air, spreading my thighs so that my pussy spread too, opening to show him my aching clit, inviting him in. "Fuck me," I repeated. "*Breed* me."

An animalistic growl broke from Kristoff's throat—the sound of a man who has been pushed too far—pushed to the breaking point.

"As my Lady wishes," he snarled and then he was behind me, his huge frame looming over mine, overwhelming me with his sheer, muscular bulk. His hands were suddenly all over me, stroking and caressing, sliding over my back and sides, reaching beneath me to cup my breasts, rolling my nipples between his fingers almost harshly until I gasped and cried at the sharp sparks of pleasure/pain his actions sent through my body. I knew he was making up for not being able to touch me before and I reveled in his rough caresses, arching like a cat under his hands, begging for more.

"Kristoff," I moaned, writhing beneath him. "*Please*."

"Is this what you want, Charlotte?" he growled in my ear and I felt the thick club of his sex rubbing hard against my open folds. "Is this what you *need*? To feel me deep inside you? Filling you? *Fucking you?*"

"Yes," I moaned wantonly. "Yes, *please!*"

"Such a good little female," he snarled in my ear as he fit the head of his cock to my entrance. "So good to open your sweet pussy for my shaft."

His words made me moan breathlessly with desire for I heard in his voice that same note of command—of dominance—that had been there when he licked and tasted my pussy so ruthlessly in the Pleasure House. I might be the Goddess-Empress and rule over the whole galaxy but in the bedroom, it was Kristoff who ruled. Who owned me completely.

I liked it that way.

With another animalistic growl, he pressed forward hard, burying himself in my open, unresisting pussy in a single thrust. Both of us were already so wet with my juices that he slid into me easily, despite his size, though I could feel his thickness stretching me deliciously wide. I gave a soft cry when I felt him bottom out inside me, the head of his cock giving the mouth of my womb a deep, hard kiss. God, it felt so *good* to give myself to him this way. So *right* to be so open for him.

"Please," I cried breathlessly. "Kristoff, *please!*"

He knew what I was asking for and this time he didn't hesitate to give it to me. I watched in the viewer as the huge alien warrior with the golden skin bent over the blonde girl and gave her his cock, thrusting deep and hard inside her, filling her to the limit as she moaned and cried and pressed back against him, tilting her hips back to offer him more—to give herself completely.

"Kristoff...*Kristoff!*" With every deep, punishing thrust I called his name—I couldn't help myself. I was delirious with lust—with the need to breed that was finally, *finally* being satiated. I moaned and begged shamelessly and gripped handfuls of the silver fur carpet, pressing back against him, learning his rhythm and joining it without hesitation.

His big hands bracketed my pelvis and I felt his fingers digging into my flesh, holding on to me as I bucked against him, while he thrust deep and hard and long inside me.

He was close and so was I—so damn close I could taste it. My orgasm was hovering like a storm cloud ready to break. I knew the pleasure would be as sharp and jagged as lightning when it came—and as drenching as a hot summer rain.

And then Kristoff stopped.

At first I couldn't believe it. I was so close...*so close.* But when I turned my head to look at him in the viewer, I saw it was true—he had stilled his relentless thrusting. And then, to my immense disappointment, he actually pulled out.

"*No*," I moaned—I couldn't help it. I was so close to the edge—so close to having the man I wanted forever. He couldn't stop now—he *couldn't*. "Kristoff," I begged him shamelessly. "Don't stop—I need you. I want you—*only* you. *Please.*"

"I think you're misunderstanding me, Charlotte." His voice was still low and rough with need. "I'm not stopping. Not when I'm so close to claiming you and making you mine."

Big hands flipped me over and suddenly I could feel the soft fur rubbing my bare back and ass and Kristoff was kneeling over me.

"What...?" I began, hardly able to form a coherent thought I wanted him so badly.

"If we're going to do this," he murmured, stroking a strand of hair out of my eyes. "If we're really going this far, then I want to do it face to face." He cupped my cheek and kissed me fiercely before pulling back to study my face. "I want to look in your eyes when I come inside you," he growled softly. "When I fill you with my seed and make you mine."

"God, *yes*," I breathed, opening my thighs to him. "Yes, I want that too!"

"Good." And then he was pressing himself inside me again, surging forward to open me completely in one hard thrust.

I moaned and locked my ankles around his hips, tilting my pelvis back to give him better access. This new position made me feel even more open—even more vulnerable and taken.

The pleasure began to build again like storm clouds coalescing overhead. I closed my eyes tight and concentrated hard on letting it build, on letting it come as I gave myself to Kristoff's deep, hard thrusts completely.

"No, Charlotte." The note of command was back in his voice. "Look at me," he demanded and my eyes fluttered open to see that he was staring at me intently. "Look at me while I *fuck* you," he growled. "While I claim you and come in you."

"All...all right," I stammered. Looking into his eyes while he thrust deep inside me was almost unbearably intimate but I wanted to do it—wanted to give myself completely in the way he demanded.

"That's good," he rumbled approvingly. Suddenly he reached between us and I felt the broad pad of his thumb slipping over the button of my clit. "Look at me, Charlotte," he repeated, never stopping his hard, deep thrusts inside me. "Look at me and tell me who you belong to."

"You!" I gasped as I felt the cloud above me break and the pleasure forked through me like summer lightning. "You, Kristoff— I belong to *you!*"

"That's right—you're *mine*," he growled. "Mine and mine alone *forever.*"

The possessive words spoken in that deep, hungry growl pushed me even higher. I felt my inner muscles clenching around his thick, invading shaft and then Kristoff allowed my orgasm to trigger his own and I felt an entirely different sensation. It was a hot, wet pulsing as spurt after spurt of his seed filled me, marking me, making me his forever.

I loved it.

"Yes...Kristoff, *yes*," I moaned, reaching for him. He'd been leaning over me, looking into my eyes. Now he crushed me to him, his hips pressing hard as though he wanted to get as deeply into me as he could while he filled me with his seed and claimed me.

I felt something surge inside me, some bone-and-blood-deep connection that filled me with a sense of power—the same power I had felt when I was Invested as the True Incarnation. The same surge I'd felt when Kristoff first went on his knees and made his vow to me.

The power of the Goddess, whispered a voice in my head. *She is here...she sees...she knows.*

And then a feeling of *rightness* suffused me—a feeling that came from outside myself and engulfed me completely, like an ocean.

The Goddess, I thought deliriously. *The Goddess approves...*

And I knew it was true. No matter what the Council of Wisdom or the priests and priestesses in the temple might say, the Goddess approved of my choice. Royal blood or not, Kristoff was worthy to be my Consort and the only man in my life forever.

Kristoff

I don't know how many time we made love that night. I honestly lost count—lost myself in the pleasure of giving my Lady pleasure. Especially since after the first time, I knew she could feel my pleasure the way I could feel hers. I knew because I could *feel* her feeling it.

Had there ever been a bond so deep? So intense? I didn't see how there could be. I had already bonded myself to Charlotte when I gave her my vow of loyalty, obedience, and protection. And now she had bonded herself to me by giving herself fully and without reservation to be filled with my shaft and seed. We had bound ourselves with a double cord and the results were immediately apparent.

Now the connection between us was a two-way street. Not only could I feel Charlotte's emotions, she could feel mine as well. If I had pain or pleasure, she felt it as I had felt hers before. I could even catch her thoughts at times, as she could catch mine.

"*I love you,*" I told her as we were drifting in a contented daze on the sleeping platform. She was curled in my arms, her back to my chest, her head resting on my arm. I wasn't certain if I had spoken the words aloud or not but it didn't matter—she heard them.

"*I love you too. And not just because of the blood I gave you. That was only the start of it. It's so much more than that. A connection so deep it's…well, I can't explain it. But it's wonderful.*"

"I feel it too," I whispered aloud, drawing her warm, curvy body closer to mine. "Our spirits are joined now."

She gave a soft laugh. "That's not surprising considering how often our bodies were joined in the past couple of hours."

She pressed back against me, rubbing her soft, warm bottom against my shaft. Despite the number of times we had made love, it rose, obedient to my Lady's summons.

"Charlotte," I murmured. "You'll wear me out. Even an Imperial Guard has his limits."

"I want you in me one more time," she said softly. "I want to fall asleep with you inside me. Can...could we do that?"

I felt a surge of love for her so deep it nearly overwhelmed me.

"We can," I told her. I liked the idea of being so intimately connected while we rested. Of falling asleep joined in that way.

Gently, I lifted her leg and pressed my shaft forward. She tilted her hips back, opening herself for me. I found her sweet heat and slid home with perfect ease, cradled in her delicious, tight warmth.

"Mmm..." Charlotte sighed contentedly and pressed back against me, taking me deeper. I felt her pleasure at being so completely filled and opened and I cupped her breasts, massaging them gently as I pleasured her very, very slowly.

Tomorrow I knew we would have to deal with the Council and decide what to do and say but just for tonight I wanted to forget there was anything in the way of our being together.

Tonight I just wanted to love her and know that she loved me.

"I do love you, Kristoff. So much..." I heard through our link and then we drifted into silence.

Chapter Thirty-two

Charlotte

Someone pounding on the door woke me up. I looked around blearily and realized that Kristoff was already alert, up on one elbow. He was also still hard inside me. Wow—how had he managed to stay hard all night like that?

The pounding came again and he withdrew, making me give a stifled little moan. I missed him the moment he was gone.

"Who is it?" Kristoff demanded, his voice deep and protective.

"It's me, Captain Verrai." The voice was vaguely familiar. I thought it might be the Guard who had warned us that the Trials of Ascension had been moved up. What was his name again? Something with a T…

"T'zorin?" Kristoff got out of bed and pulled on the bottom half of his uniform. He looked incredible in the short leather kilt with his bare, muscular chest.

Mine, I couldn't help thinking. *He's all mine now…and I'm his.*

It was a happy thought, shattered the next minute when I heard the other guard calling through the door.

"Captain, the Council of Wisdom is demanding that the Empress appear before them right now to tell who she has chosen as her Consort."

Crap! I sat bolt upright in bed, clutching the heavy, gold satin sheet to my chest as though the entire Council had suddenly appeared in my bedroom to glare at me accusingly. What were we going to do? I had foolishly assumed I would have some time—at least a day or so—to make some kind of a plan. Now, here I was, summoned to a Council meeting with no idea of what I would do or say.

Kristoff walked into the other room and I heard him conferring in low voices with T'zorin.

"You can go to the Council Chamber and try to delay some if you want, Captain," the other guard was saying. "I will escort the Goddess-Empress there when she is ready."

"No," Kristoff said at once. "I thank you for your offer, T'zorin but this is not a meeting which can be avoided or stalled."

My heart sank into my shoes. If Kristoff thought I had to go, then I had to go. But what was I going to say? I knew what I *wanted* to say, but I didn't think Kristoff would go along with it at all.

"Tell the honor guard we will be going to the Council Chamber very shortly," Kristoff told him. When he came back into the bedroom, his handsome face had a grim cast to it. "Come, my Lady—it's time to get you ready to meet the Council."

"All right." I lifted my chin and got up quickly. "Do I have time for a shower?"

"You'll have to," Kristoff said. "We must do the best we can to wash my scent off you. It won't be easy since you're completely covered in it—inside and out."

I blushed but held my ground.

"Why should we wash it off?" I asked, putting my hands on my hips. "Why don't I just tell the Council this is my decision and declare you my Consort."

He sighed. "Charlotte, we've been over this. It will look like you're committing blasphemy if you choose a non-Royal as your Consort."

"No—it will look like I'm making a new rule—the first one of my time as the Goddess-Empress. Which is that the Empress gets to pick her own mate and the Council has no say in her private life."

I liked the sound of that but Kristoff was already shaking his head.

"Do you know what that would do to the balance of power between the Royals and everyone else? If the Goddess-Empress is allowed to take a commoner bond-mate, the other Royals will be allowed to mate with them as well. It will mix and muddy the Royal bloodlines which have been carefully protected for centuries."

"Protected why? Just so the Royals can feel special?" I asked. "This isn't the Star Bellied Sneeches, Kristoff. I don't give a damn about upholding a law that basically keeps the Majoran people from having class equality."

"You'd better not let the Council hear you say that," he said grimly. "Or any of the leading Royals—you might as well paste a target on your back. My Lady, for your own protection, I beg you not to name me your Consort. If you have to say anything, tell the Council that you don't feel drawn to any of the candidates and you choose not to have a Consort."

"I thought you said they wouldn't like that either," I said, frowning.

"They won't. But it's better than naming a non-Royal as your Consort. Now come—we must get you ready to go."

He had me showered, dressed in another rich, royal looking gown—in shimmering gold trimmed with rubies this time—and on the way to the Council Room before I knew it.

I wished I had more time to argue my case for making him my Consort—I didn't like lying and I wanted to be upfront with the Council of Wisdom and let them know they didn't own me and couldn't dictate my life. But Kristoff seemed to think this would put me in an insane amount of danger and since he was the head of my security, I decided to listen to him

Soon I was standing in front of the assembled Council, who were sitting on their raised, semicircular platform, looking down on me again. I felt like a kid being called to the principal's office—not a good feeling.

Off to one side were the three candidates from the night before—the five year old boy, wriggling to be loose of his mother's arms, the old grandpa with gray hair who was asleep in a chair someone had pulled up for him, and Morbain, grinning like a cat who'd gotten into the cream.

Well, I would soon wipe that grin off his face, I thought with some satisfaction. Standing beside the little group of candidates was someone else I hadn't expected to see—Dr. Churika. She was dressed in a long gray robe and had her usual disapproving expression on her face when she looked at me. Clearly, she still didn't think much of me. That was okay—I didn't much like her either. Her bedside manner sucked.

"Now then, this meeting of the Council of Wisdom with the True Incarnation will come to order," Tannus said, banging on his podium with the fist-sized crystal he used for a gavel.

He had a smirky expression on his face. Clearly he and Morbain thought they had this in the bag. I would be more than happy to disabuse them of that notion.

"Let it be known that the Council of Wisdom has summoned the True Incarnation for the purpose of –" he began but Kristoff interrupted him.

"The Goddess-Empress is here as a courtesy to you, Head Councilor," he said, stepping forward with a frown. "But you should not get into the habit of summoning her at your whim. When all is said and done, the *Empress* has authority over the Council of Wisdom and not the other way around, as you are well aware."

Tannus frowned. "And the *Council* is in good standing with the Majoran Royal peerage, as *you* are aware, Captain Verrai. Therefore don't make threats you can't carry through with."

"No one is making a threat here, Councilor Tannus," I said, thinking it was high time I spoke up for myself. "Kristoff is simply letting you know that from now on if you want a meeting with me, you *ask* for one. Don't just have a meeting and expect me to show up."

He glared at me and seemed about to speak but Morbain stepped forward, stroking his long mustache.

"Now, now – there's no need for enmity between the Empress and the Council. It's simply been twelve hours since the Culling Ceremony – the traditional time limit for an Empress to announce her Consort following the Culling. Myself and the other, ah, *candidates* are assembled that you may choose between us." He smirked at me and said in a lower voice. "Just trying to put you out of your misery, my dear. I don't know how you've held out this long but by now you must be in absolute *agony* to have your, ah, *Royal needs* met. I stand ready to service you when you finally admit what you feel for me."

Kristoff growled possessively and stepped forward, his hand on the hilt of his sword but I put a hand on his bicep.

"It's all right," I said in a low voice. And then, lifting my chin, I addressed the Council. "I am happy to let the Council of Wisdom know who I would choose as my Consort," I said.

I saw Tannus and Morbain exchange a look of smug satisfaction.

"Very well, True Incarnation," Tannus said importantly. "Be so kind as to let us know which of these fine candidates will stand at your side during your Coronation ceremony tonight."

"None of them," I said clearly, looking Tannus in the eyes. "I choose *not* to take a Consort."

"What?" Tannus exploded. "But this is most irregular!"

"You cannot choose *not* to have a Consort," Morbain protested.

I ignored him and spoke to the head of the Council.

"What's *most irregular* is the way you tried to rig the Culling Ceremony last night," I said, barely hanging on to my temper. "You tried your best to give me no choice as to who I would share my life and my throne with. As a consequence, I reject every candidate you so *generously* offered."

"You cannot choose another Royal," Tannus said quickly. "The Council has ruled very firmly on that issue."

"I didn't say I was going to choose another Royal," I said, lifting my chin. "I said I wasn't choosing one of your candidates. I will rule alone, the way the previous Goddess-Empress and Sundalla the 887th both did after their Consorts died."

"Sundalla the 887th?" Morbain's eyes narrowed. "*Now* I know why the True Incarnation wants no Consort! She has formed a bond with this...this *commoner*." He gestured at Kristoff with disgust, who glared back at him.

"I never said—" I began, but Morbain was already shouting at Tannus.

"Head Councilor, I insist that a test be made to see if this little slut has bonded herself to another male—a *commoner* male—without the Council's permission!"

"How dare you speak so of my Lady?" Kristoff surged forward, putting a dagger blade to Morbain's throat. "The Goddess-Empress will not be thus spoken of in my presence on pain of death."

"She's not the Goddess-Empress until the coronation," Tannus said, raising his voice importantly. "And she will not be crowned unless the Council determines she is worthy. Dr. Churika, make the test."

The older woman came forward, frowning at me. She had a long, sharp pin in one hand and I wondered if she was intending to do some kind of a blood test.

Kristoff stepped between us, glaring at her.

"You will not pierce my Lady's flesh, Churika. Especially not on the orders of these two vipers." He glared at Tannus, whose eyebrows were extra-bushy with indignation and Morbain who was still puffed up with wounded pride.

"Very well," Churika said calmly. "Then I'll pierce yours, Captain Verrai."

Quick as a snake, she sank the long sharp pin at least two inches deep into the big muscle of Kristoff's upper arm.

"Ouch!" I gasped and put a hand to my own upper arm. I couldn't help it—I felt his pain. I knew Kristoff felt it too, though he stood there stoically, still blocking the way between me and the doctor.

"See? Do you see that?" Morbain shouted excitedly. "She felt his pain! The True Incarnation has allowed herself to be bonded by a lowly Guard! She has broken our most sacred rule and allowed her Royal blood to mix with that of a commoner!"

"*Why* is it a sacred rule?" I demanded, raising my voice to be heard above the babble. "So the Royals can keep feeling superior to everyone else in the Majoran Empire? Well I refuse to perpetuate this lopsided system and feed your fantasy of superiority! And I refuse to allow the Council of Wisdom to dictate to me and tell me who to spend the rest of my life with!"

"Blasphemy! Heresy!" Tannus bugled, his eyebrows working frantically. "The True Incarnation rejects the wisdom of the Council openly!"

"Because it's *not* wisdom—it's you and Morbain trying to rule through me!" I shouted back at him. "I'm not going to let you set up a puppet regime with me as the puppet!"

"Then maybe it's time for a change of regime." Morbain was

grinning evilly. "Maybe it's time that the reign of the Goddess-Empresses came to an end and someone *else* of Royal blood stepped in and took control of the Empire."

"You cannot do that," Kristoff growled at him. "To even speak of deposing the Goddess-Empress is to sign your own death warrant. As Captain of the Imperial Guards, I am within my rights to kill you here and now for having even uttered those words."

Morbain turned pale and backed up a step. "I'm only saying what everyone in this room and on the Council is thinking," he said self-righteously.

Unexpectedly, one of the Councilors spoke up. "Untrue—not all of the Council feel that way." It was the young Councilor—the one with brownish-tan skin and matching brown eyes. "And what's more, I want it known right now that I and the majority of the Council had *nothing* to do with choosing the Culling Ceremony candidates—Tannus and his subcommittee were the ones that deemed them appropriate although at least two of them clearly are not." He nodded his head at me. "My apologies, your Majesty. I should have spoken up sooner."

"How *dare* you, Minchin?" Tannus rounded on the youngest Councilor. "You can tender your resignation to this Council immediately!"

"Councilors, *please!* The issue isn't the Council of Wisdom's extremely *impartial* and *fair* choice of candidates for the Culling Ceremony," Morbain said loudly. "It's whether this little *slut* allowed herself to be bonded by a commoner—and Dr. Churika here has just proved that she has."

I looked in his eyes and suddenly knew he had planned this. *He* was the one who had left that scroll about Sundalla the 887th and her Guard for me to find. It was a safeguard—another way to depose me. If all his other plots failed, he could always claim that I had wrongfully joined myself to a commoner. I would have thought that I had played right into his hands but I had been falling in love with Kristoff long before I found the pornographic history scroll and began to draw parallels between that long ago Empress and her Guard and myself and Kristoff.

Speaking of Kristoff, his face was nearly white with fury at

Morbain's inflammatory words.

"I have warned you about speaking slanderously against my Lady, the Goddess-Empress. Now you die!" He surged forward again, only to be met by four of the Guards who were apparently loyal to either Morbain or Tannus blocking the way. "Stand back," he growled at them. "Don't make me kill you, Brothers. This male's insolence and blasphemy must be answered for."

"I'm afraid you won't have much luck convincing my personal guards to let you kill me," Morbain remarked, grinning nastily from behind the safety of the four armed warriors. "You see, these four were hand-picked by me—all of them are members of the Male Liberation Movement. We are tired of the tyranny of females and it ends here and now—today, along with the dynasty of the Goddess-Empresses!"

"You will never take my Lady's rightful place on the throne, Morbain," Kristoff snarled. "I'll kill you with my own hands before I allow it."

"Let's just take care of that then, shall we?" Morbain said. "Dr. Churika?"

I looked around for the little doctor, realizing I had lost track of her. To my horror, she was on Kristoff's other side and she had one of those futuristic hypodermic things in her hand.

"Kristoff—watch out!" I gasped as she darted forward. He looked but on the wrong side and Churika had a clear shot at him. At the last moment, I was able to push her away from him but not before she jabbed the hypodermic with it's hundreds of tiny needles into his thigh. I slapped it away, hoping against hope that I'd gotten it out of him before it could deliver its payload.

At first I thought I'd succeeded but then he staggered.

"My Lady…Charlotte," he murmured, his voice hoarse.

"Kristoff!" I felt like crying. "What did you give him?" I demanded, glaring at the Denarin doctor. "Whatever it was, I want the antidote *right now!*"

"I merely gave him a sedative, child." She gave me a condescending look. "The two of you appeared to be getting entirely too excited."

"How…could you?" Kristoff looked at her, his sword sagging.

Clearly he was fighting for consciousness, trying his best to fight off the sedative she'd given him. I was pretty sure he hadn't gotten a full dose but it was plainly enough to put him out of commission, at least for a while. "My old mistress...trusted you," he said to the doctor. "How could you...side with Morbain?"

"Sundalla the 999th never tried to change the entire order of the galaxy." She frowned at him sternly. "And we're not going to change it now. Morbain..." She turned to him. "You cannot depose the Goddess-Empress. No, Tannus," she went on when the Head Councilor would have interrupted her. "And don't start about how the Royals are all behind you. The common people are behind this girl." She gestured at me disdainfully. "The vids of the Trials of Ascendancy have spread like wildfire among them and the Majoran people as a whole *like* having an Empress. You'll never get enough support for a male dominated rule, no matter what you and Morbain think. You'll only plunge the galaxy into civil war and I will *not* allow that. I promised Sundalla the 999th that I would help to keep peace in the palace and the galaxy and I intend to keep my word."

Wow...I looked at her, surprised. Maybe she wasn't so bad after all. But her next words chased that idea right out of my mind.

"The old ways *must* be upheld no matter what!" She looked at me. "Which means you *must* choose one of the candidates from the Culling Ceremony. Since he is the only one of the correct age, it will have to be Morbain."

"What? No!" I exclaimed. "I wouldn't choose him if he was the last man in the entire galaxy! Besides, I'm already bonded to Kristoff."

"I warned you about that." She shook her head, looking sorrowfully at Kristoff, who was still barely on his feet. "I'm afraid that bond will have to be broken."

"You can't do that," I protested. "I thought nothing could break a bond once it was established!"

"Nothing can—except death." Dr. Churika looked up at Tannus. "Head Councilor, it is my professional medical opinion that Captain Kristoff Verrai must be put to death in order to nullify the bond between himself and the ascending Goddess-Empress, in order to clear the way for a proper bonding for her."

"No!" I gasped, grabbing Kristoff's arm. "No, you *can't*."

"The Council agrees that this is a sound decision," Tannus said, frowning.

"No it doesn't!" the younger Councilor, the one Tannus had called Minchin said. "We haven't even voted on the issue! You cannot keep speaking for the entire Council, Tannus!"

"A Council *you* are no longer on, Minchin," Tannus hissed. "As of right now I relieve you of your duties. You are dismissed from the Council of Wisdom and banished from Femme One."

"Aren't you overstepping your authority, Tannus?" The other councilor's eyes flashed. "Only the Empress may banish someone. Or are you taking over the Empress's duties in the same way you and Morbain are trying to usurp her power?"

"She has no power here—nor will she ever have," Tannus snarled. "Nor do you, Minchin. I order you to leave and I want the True Incarnation placed under house arrest in the Royal apartments until her bond can be broken so that she can form a more proper union."

"No!" I shouted and Kristoff glared at him.

"You'll never take Charlotte from me," he growled, lifting his sword and stepping in front of me. "You're going to crown her here and now as is her right as the True Incarnation."

I felt a surge of relief—he was shaking off the effects of the sedative! Now we would get out of here and—

Suddenly a big, hard hand closed around my upper arm and I felt something cold and sharp pressing against my throat.

"I have a better idea," a new voice said, right beside me. "Why don't *I* take the Empress off your hands so none of you have to worry about her anymore?"

Chapter Thirty-three

Kristoff

I felt Charlotte's surge of fear through our bond—it cut through the drug Churika had given me like a knife. Turning to confront this new threat, I saw with confusion that it was none other than T'zorin standing there.

He had a knife to Charlotte's throat.

"T'zorin," I growled. "What are you doing? Unhand the Empress at once!"

"Allow me to introduce myself," he said smoothly, ignoring my order. "I am *not* the Imperial Guard known as T'zorin, though I *am* making use of his body."

"Then who are you?" Tannus said, frowning.

"And how dare you lay hands on the Goddess-Empress?" Councilor Minchin demanded.

T'zorin—or the thing using his body—gave all of us a cold smile. "Count Doloroso, the last of the Assimilated at your service," he said, nodding his head in a brief approximation of a bow. "Your old Empress, Sundalla the 999th thought she had wiped out my entire race on the Last Day but she was wrong! I alone remained to carry on and repopulate my race and so I shall. You see, this female is not just the exulted Goddess-Empress—she is also a *La-ti-zal*. A female with bloodlines powerful enough to carry the first of a new race—the Organic Assimilated. A race I myself will start, beginning with her."

"You *dare!*" I lunged at him but he wrapped an arm around Charlotte and dug his knife into her neck, making a nick in her pale flesh. I felt both her fear and the sharp pain of the blade as it bit into her throat.

"I don't think so, Captain Verrai. Stay back!" He smiled at me mockingly and I felt sick—Charlotte's friend, Zoe had warned me that this bastard might still be at large. How could I have ignored her warning? How could I have just assumed that T'zorin's story of being attacked by pirates was true? I had thought that Morbain and Tannus represented the greatest dangers to my Lady's life but I had let the deadliest threat of all slip right past me, unnoticed.

"Let her go," I said, my voice coming out hoarse and rough. The last of the sedation had left my system now—my adrenaline was surging. But there was nothing I could do while the male who had been T'zorin still held a knife to Charlotte's throat.

"I don't think so," T'zorin/Doloroso said. "In fact, I think it's a bit too crowded in here for my taste. I'm going to take the Empress here on a little walk to someplace much more *exclusive*. Then we can discuss my demands."

"If you hurt her," I snarled. "If you so much as *touch* her—"

"Don't worry, Captain." He gave me a malevolent smile. "I'll take very good care of your lady." He raised his voice. "Now everyone clear out of my way or I'll slit her throat!"

"Do it," Charlotte gasped, looking at me with wide, frightened eyes. "He means it. I can feel it!"

I knew she was talking about what she called her "touch-sense." She had seen into Doloroso's mind and knew that he was serious in his threat to kill her if we didn't make way for him. But surely he knew if he killed her, he would lose his bargaining chip and be killed instantly himself. He didn't fear his own death—why?

I had no time to answer the question. As much as I hated it, I had to give in to the bastard's demands—at least for now.

"Move back," I said to the honor guard, who were still staring at the male they'd known as T'zorin in surprise and dismay. I couldn't blame them for letting him through to get close to Charlotte—I had let him as well, because it had never occurred to me that one of my most trusted guards could be a threat.

"That's the way." T'zorin—no, Doloroso, I reminded myself—began backing away, taking Charlotte with him. I followed, though at a distance. I didn't intend to let him leave the palace with her, no matter what he said. And once he was out of the Council Chamber, the way would open up some. I could get a sharpshooter with a tightly collimated blaster beam to pick him off the moment he took the knife from Charlotte's throat.

"Be calm," I sent to her through our link. *"I wont' let him hurt you, sweetheart!"*

"I'm trying." I could feel the desperate panic trying to break free inside her but she was doing her best to keep it at bay. Even with a knife at her throat she refused to cry or let herself become hysterical. Gods, how I loved and admired her!

Doloroso backed away, out of the Council Chamber door. I and most of the rest of the Council as well as Morbain and his own guards followed at a safe distance. Strangely, Doloroso didn't try to dissuade us from following. I had expected more threats but he simply dragged Charlotte away, keeping a firm grip on her and never letting his knife blade waver from her throat, even for an instant.

It wasn't until he backed down the small, side corridor that led to the Chambers of the Trials of Ascendancy that I began to have an inkling of what he had in mind.

And by then it was too late.

Charlotte

"Grab the knob, my dear. Open the door at once!" the person who was calling himself Count Doloroso snarled in my ear.

We were standing in front of the large door that led to the Garden of Death—the same place the hapless Eucilla had met her end. The place filled with poison gas and flora and fauna—well, poison to anyone but me, that was.

"No," I said, fear rushing through me. "No, I'm not going to let you poison everyone in the palace."

"Who said anything about poisoning the palace?" he purred in my ear. "There are probably other *La-ti-zals* here, especially among the Royalty. I don't want to kill any of my future brides. No, my dear—I simply want a nice safe place where we can stay unmolested while we wait for that foolish 'Council of Wisdom' to meet my demands."

Through the touch of his skin to mine, I knew it was true. But I still didn't like the idea of opening what amounted to a gas chamber and letting a terrorist inside. I wanted to refuse again but Doloroso dug his knife into my throat, letting the knife just pierce my skin for the second time.

"You know, my dear, I only need you for your womb," he remarked in a horribly conversational tone. "Everything else is unnecessary. Including your pretty eyes, your sweet little tongue, your dainty fingers and toes...I could cut any or all of those away from your lovely body and still have a perfectly serviceable vessel for the first of the Organic Assimilated."

I felt cold all over.

"All right," I whispered, groping for the knob. "I...I'll open it."

"*Charlotte – what are you doing?*" Kristoff's message came through the two-way link we now shared as the door to the Garden of Death swung open. He and the rest of the Council of Wisdom and Morbain were still following at a safe distance, trying to keep sight of me without antagonizing Doloroso.

"*I...I'm sorry, I couldn't help it,*" I sent back through the link, feeling sick and numb. "*He...he said he'd cut out my eyes and tongue if I didn't let him in!*"

"*Bastard!*" Kristoff's rage and fear for me were huge – filling me until I could scarcely breathe. "*I'll kill him! Hold tight, Charlotte! I won't let him take you!*"

I hoped he could follow through on his promise because now Doloroso was dragging me into the deadly Garden, his knife still at my throat. I looked around as well as I could, seeing the lovely flowering tropical plants, the curly golden bench, the trickling blue stream and the golden gravel path. If only I could get free of him for just a minute this place would kill him – if only he wasn't touching my skin the Garden of Death would take care of him for me!

When we were just inside the entrance he relaxed his grip on my arm. But before I could make a break for it, he locked one large, muscular elbow around my throat instead. I wasn't sure what happened to the knife but I didn't feel it at my neck anymore. Not that it did me any good – Doloroso – or the body he was inhabiting – was almost as tall and big as Kristen, and probably about a hundred times stronger than me. Ma*j*oran warriors are no joke.

Knife or no knife I was stuck.

"Let me go," I whispered in a choked voice, looking at Kristoff who was staring desperately at me through the invisible barrier that kept the poison gas inside the Garden. Behind him stood Tannus and Morbain and the rest of the Council of Wisdom. Some of them looked appalled but Tannus and Morbain didn't look too upset about the fact that I was now a hostage in a domestic terror situation at all.

"I don't think so, my dear," Doloroso purred in my ear. "I know perfectly well that the only reason this entire place isn't poisoning and attacking me is the fact that I have direct skin-to-skin contact with you." He nodded at the jewel colored attack-chipmunks who were watching him warily. "The minute I let you go I'd be nothing but poisoned bait for those little fellows. So, in the interest of staying alive..."

Instead of finishing his sentence, he produced something that looked like a small aerosol can. It was black with a silver cap and reminded me of my adopted mom's favorite brand of hairspray.

What in the world? I wondered, staring at it as well as I could over the arm locked around my throat. *Why does he have a bottle of Tresseme extra strength hold and what's he going to do with it?*

But of course it wasn't hairspray. As it turned out, it was some kind of glue. Doloroso sprayed it over one large palm and then grabbed my hand and held it tight. After a moment, I couldn't have let go of his hand even if I wanted to. We were stuck together.

"Now then. All safe and sound." He sounded extremely pleased with himself as he sheathed his knife and stood back, holding my hand which was glued fast to his.

"Let her go!" Kristoff was standing right on the other side of the invisible barrier now. The one that kept the poison in and any kind of darts or bullets or blaster shots out, I remembered ruefully. So there was no way they could bring in any kind of sniper to pick Doloroso off while he stood there. No wonder he felt safe enough to put away his knife—he no longer needed it.

"Not until my demands are met," Doloroso said smoothly, giving him a maddening smile. "And maybe not even then. Or maybe I'll return her to you after she's born the first of the Organic

Assimilated from her exulted womb."

"You bastard," Kristoff swore thickly. "Charlotte is *mine*. My fated mate and my love. If you think for a moment I'll allow you to keep her, to hurt her—"

"I'm afraid you have no choice," Doloroso said loftily. "As you can see, my dear Captain Verrai, *I* hold all the cards here and you have none. My skin-to-skin contact with the Empress protects me in this very deadly room. You don't *dare* attempt to enter—anyone who tries will die almost instantly, as we all saw in the case of the hapless Eucilla." He made a *tsking* sound. "Such a shame. Now then, for my first demand, I'll want every *La-ti-zal* in all of the Majoran system rounded up and put aboard my ship. Next—"

But he never got to name his other demands. Without warning, Kristoff drew his sword and ran through the barrier, into the Garden of Death.

Chapter Thirty-four

Charlotte

"Kristoff—*no!*" I screamed. He hadn't even given me any warning through our new bond. Maybe he was afraid I would try to stop him—if so, he was right, I would have.

Doloroso was clearly caught off guard. Obviously he hadn't expected anyone to be willing to dare the Garden of Death to save me. Hadn't he been at the Trials of Ascendancy when Kristoff had come in to help me drag Eucilla out?

Actually, no—I didn't think he had. I vaguely remembered him running up afterwards saying he'd been caught at the far end of the hall where he couldn't see the action. If he had, he would have known that Kristoff would come for me, even into a room that meant certain death for him if he didn't get out in time.

Doloroso fumbled for his knife but Kristoff was already in action. I saw the silver sweep of his sword blade coming down in a chopping motion.

The next thing I knew, the hand I was holding no longer had an arm attached to it.

Doloroso shrieked—a high, breathless sound as his severed stump started spouting blood everywhere. He sucked in his breath to scream again but the only sound that came out was a wracking cough. Nevertheless, he pulled out his knife with his remaining hand and waved it at Kristoff, who was still circling warily with his sword.

"The Empress! Help the Captain save the Goddess-Empress!" I heard someone shout outside the Garden's door. Looking up, I saw a crowd of Imperial Guards—my honor guard—surging forward. People were trying to get out of their way but unfortunately, not everyone could.

Morbain was one of the hapless few who was swept into the

lovely, deadly garden. He squealed like a pig and tried to get out again but he was bowled over by one of the guards and went crashing face-first into a large, flowering bush. The same one, in fact, that Eucilla had fallen into, I remembered numbly. At once the tiny, jewel-toned *terlings* swarmed over him, nipping and scratching. Morbain screamed and fishtailed, trying to get up, to get away from the little creatures but they were *everywhere,* covering him like a colorful, living patchwork blanket.

All around me, people were shouting and fighting and I still had a bloody, disembodied hand glued to my own. But I had eyes only for Kristoff. He was still squaring off against Doloroso, who had dropped his knife and held something else in his hand. Both of them were coughing steadily and I could see the marks of the poisonous leaves and flowers on the skin of their exposed arms and legs but neither one seemed to be paying any attention to it.

"A bomb—he's got a nano-lacerater bomb!" I heard one of the other guards shout in a choked voice. "Be careful, Captain Verrai!"

"That's right—be careful, Captain," Doloroso grated in a hoarse, strangled voice. "I *do* have a bomb. Not a very big one—but big enough to blow a hole in exactly one person here." He looked at me, his eyes wild and angry. "If I can't have this lovely *La-ti-zal,* no one can!"

With that, he dived straight at me.

I watched him come, feeling frozen in place, frozen in time. Everything seemed to be happening in slow motion—I was even able to see his bloody thumb pressing down on what I supposed must be the trigger mechanism of the small bomb.

"*No!*" Kristoff roared and launched himself at me.

Or, I *thought* he was aimed at me—but then I saw he was actually targeting the bomb instead. I watched with horror as he bore the maniacally laughing Doloroso to the ground and dived on top of the bomb, planning the golden breastplate of his uniform directly over the other man's clenched fist.

There was a muffled *bang*—more of a pop really—and then Doloroso was screaming again and Kristoff…

Kristoff wasn't moving.

He lay face down on the poison grass and didn't so much as

twitch when I ran over to shake his shoulder.

"Kristoff," I tried, sending through our new link. "Kristoff, please be all right! Please come back to me!"

Nothing.

Tears were pouring down my cheeks and I was shaking him, trying to roll him over but I couldn't manage—I still had the damn grisly hand glued to my own and Kristoff was too big, too heavy.

Dead weight, whispered a hateful little voice in my brain.

No—shut up! I told it fiercely. He's not dead. He's just knocked out or something.

"Your Majesty, can we help?" Suddenly two of the other guards who had rushed in were at my side. They were just beginning to wheeze from the poison air. I realized that the whole conflict, from the time that Kristoff had dashed into the Garden of Death and cut off Doloroso's hand to the time he had dived onto the bomb, had taken barely a minute or two. How could that be when it seemed so much longer? A lifetime at least.

"Grab him," I ordered, gesturing to Kristoff's inert form. "Drag him out of here. And you two," I pointed to two other guards. "You get Doloroso—I mean T'zorin," I said when I saw their confused looks. "Get him out of here and get him medical attention. Do *not* let him die!"

I didn't know why but I knew that was important. An inner sense I hadn't had before I was Invested as the True Incarnation was whispering inside me. This imposter who had found his way into my inner circle needed to be stopped and part of that was keeping him tied to the body he had hijacked.

"Help! Mercy! They are eating me alive!" The weak voice came from the bushes to one side of the door. Looking up as the first two guards dragged Kristoff out of the garden, I saw it was Morbain, still struggling under the furry blanket of angry *terlings*.

For a moment I was tempted to leave him there. But my oath came back to haunt me. First, do no harm...

"You help Prince Morbain," I told the last guard who was staggering by now. "And then all of you get out and seek medical attention. *Now!*"

I rushed out the door as I finished delivering my last order and went to crouch beside Kristoff, who was laid out, still face down, on the ground. Doloroso, his other hand now a pulpy red mess, was being dragged away screaming and swearing and bleeding profusely everywhere.

I paid him absolutely no attention. Instead I knelt by Kristoff and motioned to the guards, who were at the end of their strength.

"Turn him over, please."

I tried to keep my voice calm and collected but I could hear the edge of hysteria threatening to take over, just under the surface.

No, I told myself. *No, I have to keep control. I have to do this – have to save Kristoff. I can't do that if I lose my head. Keep it together, Charlotte!*

"I'm here, your Majesty! I brought my kit!"

I looked up to see the young female Majoran doctor rushing to my side.

"Oh, thank goodness!" I held out a hand to her – it happened to be the one with Doloroso's still glued to it.

She recoiled. "Your Majesty – what – ?"

"It's glued on," I said quickly. "It's not important right now. I mean it's awful, but what matters is Kristoff. He just fell on a bomb to save me. Help me!"

"Right away, your Majesty!" She knelt beside me, her long blue hair pulled back in a hasty ponytail at the nape of her neck, her long white robe getting dirty, though she didn't seem to notice or care.

At the end of their strength, the guards turned Kristoff over and I saw...nothing.

His face was slack and unresponsive but though the center of his golden breastplate was splattered with blood, the metal wasn't broken or corroded in any way.

"Oh, thank God," I whispered. "He must just be unconscious."

But when I looked at the Majoran doctor, she had a grim expression on her pretty features.

"You say he fell on a bomb, your Majesty?"

"Yes," I said. "It was...one of the guards called it some kind of...um..."

"A nano-lacerater, your Majesty," one of the guards who had helped drag Kristoff out said in a hoarse voice. "Nasty piece of work, those are."

"Help me get his breastplate off," the Majoran doctor snapped.

"I know how it works!" I tried to help but Doloroso's disembodied hand, still glued to mine, impeded my progress.

"Here, your Majesty." Reaching into her kit, the doctor took out a small aerosol can, like the one Doloroso had used in the first place, and sprayed it to the place where my hand was gripped by the dead one. It slid off at once, as though she'd greased my hand with baby oil.

"Thank you!" I shoved the awful thing away and wiped my slippery hand on my rich gold gown, heedless of the bloody smear I left on the priceless fabric. It was good to be free of the damn thing—I felt a momentary sense of relief, quickly quenched when I looked at Kristoff's slack face.

"Hurry!" Quickly I helped the doctor lift the heavy top of the golden breastplate. It felt like I was having a flashback to the first time I had ever seen Kristoff, when he lay on the ER gurney, out cold after delivering his strange message. But I hadn't known then what he would mean to me—hadn't loved him so much it felt my heart might break trying to contain all the emotion I felt for him.

"There. That's their entry point."

The Majoran doctor was pointing to a bloody, ragged hole in the white undershirt garment that Kristoff wore under his breastplate.

"What entry point? What are you talking about? How could anything get in? His breastplate was fine! There wasn't a crack in it." I protested, hearing that edge of hysteria in my voice again.

But I couldn't help remembering how it had been fine before, too, back on Earth when the nanos had gotten to him. Then he had needed a transfusion of my blood to make it through—here I didn't have any ready to go. No pre-drawn bags to hang. What was I going to do?

"A bomb like this is filled with lacerating nanobots," the doctor explained. "They're small enough to go through almost any substance without harming it. And they do—because they're programmed to wait until they find flesh to start doing damage. Once they start, well…" Grabbing the ragged edges of the hole in Kristoff's blood-splattered white shirt, she ripped it completely apart, baring his chest.

A sound like a strangled gasp was torn from my throat. There was a hole in Kristoff's chest—a hole that went all the way down to where his heart should be.

I say *should* be because it wasn't there.

I'd seen enough patients lying open on the OR table to know what someone's insides should look like. I knew the cardiac muscle with its elegant, fleshy curves. Your heart is as big as your fist so Kristoff's should have been large and visible but there was nothing.

Nothing but a bloody hole and a mass of mangled flesh.

A blood transfusion wouldn't save him this time. Not even if I gave him every drop in my body—which I gladly would have done. It was too late.

"I'm so sorry, your Majesty," the doctor said in a quiet voice. "But this…is not fixable. Not even with the latest technology. The nanobots must have been programmed to target the heart."

"I…I know," I said numbly. "I can see that."

"He performed his duty to the last, your Majesty." The doctor took my hand and squeezed it hard. I wished absently that I knew her name. "He took the blast that was meant for you. And he probably saved everyone in the palace. If the bomb had gone wild, it could have penetrated the barrier which guards the door to the Garden of Death. The whole palace would have been flooded with poisonous gas—tens of thousands who live and work here would have died."

I knew she was trying to make me feel better—to see what a hero Kristoff was. But all I could think was that it was all my fault. That if I hadn't turned out to be the Goddess-Empress and he hadn't come to save and protect me, he would still be safe.

He would still be alive.

"It should have been me," I whispered. And then the tears came pouring down my cheeks. Hot and wet and so painful I felt like my own heart was shredding in my chest as they came. Gone, he was gone and it was all because of me!

"He's gone," I heard a familiar voice say, echoing my words.

"Truly? A pity. He was a good guard. Sundalla the 999th's favorite, by all accounts."

"Well, at least this leaves the True Incarnation free to form another bond," the first voice said. "It's all to the best—much less trouble this way."

I looked up and saw who was talking. Head Councilor Tannus stood by, watching my agony with smug satisfaction. Beside him was Doctor Churika, a neutral expression on her face. If she was sorry for the awful death Kristoff had suffered on my behalf, her demeanor certainly didn't show it.

Rage suddenly filled me at their callus unconcern and at Tannus's actual *enjoyment* of my pain. There's a German word for that—for being made happy when someone else is hurt. I couldn't think of it then but I could certainly tell he was experiencing it. He thought he would get his own way now with Kristoff out of the picture, that he could pick my consort and rule through him, bypassing me except as a figure head.

No. Hell, no!

I stood on trembling legs, my rage so absolute I could barely see.

"You think you've won," I said to Tannus, my voice shaking with fury. "You think with Kristoff out of the way you can do anything you want."

He smirked at me. "Well, the death of Captain Verrai is, of course, most unfortunate. But now that he's gone, I think it would be best if you allow yourself to be guided by the Council in the matter of choosing a consort—"

"I don't want a Consort—*Kristoff* was my Consort! My fated mate—the man I was supposed to be with the rest of my life!" I shouted at him. "Don't you understand?" My voice dropped almost to a whisper. "When we joined—when we *bonded*—I felt her presence and her power. I felt the Goddess of Mercy's approval. Kristoff and I were *meant* for each other."

As I spoke, I felt a tingling run through me. A tingling that became a rush of power. It was the same power I'd felt when Kristoff gave me his vow, and when he had bonded me to him so beautifully the night before.

The Goddess, I thought, feeling light-headed and giddy. *The Goddess – she's here! Right here!*

"Yes, Child, I am with you," whispered a voice inside me. A strong, feminine, powerful voice that seemed to be made of pure sunlight—golden and perfect and unbreakable. I remembered Zoe saying the Goddess was real. I had felt her power before, but I hadn't really internalized the idea. Now it came home to me with a shock of recognition so deep it was like a blow to my heart. She *was* real and somehow, she had always been inside me. Waiting, like a seed waiting to grow and blossom. Waiting until I was ready to acknowledge and receive her.

Well, I was ready now.

"If you're here, Goddess," I said in a low voice. "If you're with me and I truly am your chosen vessel then *help me!*"

"Who is she talking to?" Tannus asked nobody in particular.

"Watch out!" Churika looked alarmed. "She's *glowing!*"

I looked down at myself and saw that it was true. There was a light shining out of my skin—a golden glow that suffused my entire body. There were actual beams of it shooting out of my fingertips and my scalp was tingling like it was shooting out of my hair as well.

I studied my hands and knew what to do.

Stooping, I knelt by Kristoff's still and silent form. Pressing my glowing hands to the hole in his chest, I poured all my will to live...all my desire...all my faith...all my hope...all my *love* into him. It was as though I was funneling a river of healing and life and power directly into his body.

"Live," I whispered to him. "Be healed...be whole...be mine again. I love you, Kristoff, come back to me!"

I'm not sure exactly what happened at that point. I wasn't myself—not fully, anyway. It was as though the Goddess took over my body and I was nothing but power and light and love for a moment.

I know from talking to Zoe and Leah—who had just gotten to the palace and saw the very last bit of it—that it looked like some kind of supernova had happened at the end of the small corridor where the Trials of Ascension were held. Zoe told me later it was like a huge, beautiful, completely silent explosion of golden light radiating out from the center where Kristoff and I were joined.

And then the light faded and I felt him moving under my hands. He coughed and stirred and looked up at me, his rainbow eyes confused.

"My Lady...Charlotte?" he asked, his voice slightly hoarse. It was as though he was just getting over a bad cold instead of coming back from the dead.

"Kristoff!" I explored his chest with trembling fingers. It was whole and strong again, without a mark on it. What was more, I could feel the strong, steady beat of a heart beneath his ribs.

"Charlotte?" He still looked confused. "What happened? I had the strangest dream. I was looking down on you from above—you were weeping but I couldn't reach you to comfort you."

"It was a nightmare," I whispered, beginning to cry again. "It was a nightmare but now it's over. Oh, Kristoff, it's over! And I love you so much!"

"I love you too, Charlotte." He wrapped me in strong, living arms and we clung to each other, not caring about the rest of the world for a while. Kristoff was back with me—nothing else mattered.

At last I came back to myself—well mostly, I was still glowing a little bit—and pulled back from Kristoff.

"I'm still not sure I understand," he said. "The last thing I remember was trying to keep you safe from Doloroso."

"You saved my life and the lives of everyone in the palace," I told him. "You're a hero—*my* hero. And you're also my Consort."

"Charlotte, no—you can't—"

"Oh yes I can," I told him. "Just watch me."

The Majoran doctor who had been crouched beside us, shielding her eyes from my light display, looked up at me wonderingly as I rose to stand in front of the Council and everyone else.

"He...he's alive," she whispered, looking at me wonderingly.

"My Goddess—you brought him back to life!"

"I'm not the Goddess," I told her, knowing it was true. "I'm just a vessel for her. A conduit for her to express her wisdom and patience and love...*and* her justice."

I glared at Tannus who looked like he didn't know whether to be confused or outraged but was definitely leaning towards outraged. He had completely missed the miraculous part about Kristoff being brought back to life. Instead of being awed by the miracle that had just occurred right in front of his eyes, he was angry that his plans for galactic domination had now taken a turn for the worse.

A greedy, petty man. I would deal with him later but I had other business first.

"People of Femme One," I shouted, raising my voice to be heard above the murmuring crowd. The news of what had happened in the Council Chamber must have spread like wildfire because the narrow corridor of the Trials of Ascension and the huge main hallway outside were now packed with people, both Royals and commoners alike.

"People of Femme One," I said again and somehow my voice carried over all of them with an echo of the Goddess's power and a hush fell over the crowd. "I stand before you as your new Goddess-Empress, Sundalla the 1000th," I said.

At my words, there was a rattling at the door of the first Trial— the Trial of the Orb and Scepter, I remembered. Suddenly it burst open and both of the golden, bejeweled implements flew over the heads of the crowd to land in my hands. They trembled in my grasp, like dogs that couldn't wait to get back to their master.

There was a gasp from everyone assembled. I raised the scepter high, letting the light reflect off the massive ruby at its head as I cradled the diamond-studded Orb in my other arm.

"I am the Goddess-Empress," I said, letting my words roll over all of them. "And I choose as my Consort, Captain Kristoff Verrai of the Imperial Guard."

There was an uneasy murmur at this and Tannus started to say something but I cut him off with a glare.

"Kristoff is *not* of Royal blood," I said. "But that does not matter to me or to the Goddess of Mercy. He has protected me with his life, sacrificed for me, and loved me as I love him. This is my first decree as Goddess-Empress—I am abolishing the law against Royal to commoner joinings. From now on, everyone is free to love and join with whomever they feel drawn to."

The murmuring got louder but it wasn't all unhappy. I saw several people rush to be together—Royals and commoners who had been kept apart by the foolish, classist law and would now be able to be together openly instead of hiding their love.

But not everyone was happy. Tannus, in particular, couldn't keep silent one more instant.

"I must protest this ridiculous and improper ruling!" he sputtered loudly. "As Head of the Council of Wisdom, I absolutely cannot approve such a preposterous, illegal—"

"Tannus!" I interrupted him, my voice still rippling with the aftereffects of the Goddess's power. "This isn't just my idea—it is the will of the Goddess of Mercy herself. You have seen what she can do." I gestured to Kristoff, who had gotten to his feet and was standing behind me, as steady as a wall. "Do you really want to pit yourself against her power and authority?"

He lifted his chin, his eyes narrowing.

"I don't believe the Goddess has anything to do with this—any of it!"

"Are you mad?" Doctor Churika frowned and backed away from him a step. "Didn't you see—Verrai's heart was *pulped.* He was *dead* and she brought him back!"

"I don't think he was really hurt at all." Tannus crossed his arms over his skinny chest stubbornly. "I think they cooked the whole plot up between the two of them so that they could be together. Which I will *still* oppose. The Empress must have a *Royal* consort and if she cannot choose properly for herself then I and the Council will choose for her."

"Councilor Tannus, your days of choosing anything but the method of your own death are over," my mouth said. I had the feeling of the Goddess filling me again—less pervasive this time but she was most definitely there and she was working through me to do what was necessary.

"Wh-what?" Tannus looked at me uncertainly. "How dare you speak to me like that, young lady?"

"It is not Charlotte of Earth who speaks but I, the one true Goddess," my voice said. *"Now, Tannus—choose the method of your death. Your life is forfeit as a consequence of your plotting and deception."*

Suddenly the door to the second Trial of Ascension swung open—the Trial of Flame and Scale. I heard a deep, echoing snort and a puff of dark gray smoke wafted from the entrance.

There were cries of fear and the people standing near the door shifted back, scrambling to get clear of it.

I could see why they were afraid—a dinner plate-sized eye as brilliant as pure, melted gold was looking out of the doorway. There was another snort and more hot smoke drifted out into the hall.

"Wha...what is—"

Tannus didn't get to finish his question because at that moment, there were panicked cries from the area around the Garden of Death—whose door was still standing open. I really needed to shut it—it wasn't safe.

Before I could make a move towards it, I saw a massive snake slithering out of it. The snake was a vivid, shimmering cobalt blue with a hood like a King Cobra's but probably three times as wide. In fact, everything about it was huge—except for the coloring and the hood, it reminded me of a giant python or anaconda. It slithered towards us—or rather, towards Tannus—and reared up in front of him so that its head was raised as high as his. Then it stayed there, swaying back and forth, almost as though it was trying to hypnotize him.

"A heartburst," I heard someone say—maybe the Majoran doctor who had tried to help me with Kristoff. "That's a heartburst, but I've never heard of one getting so big before."

Dr. Churika had moved far away from Tannus now—in fact, everyone had. He was in his own little circle of Hell, trapped between the immense snake and the Fire Drake which waited just on the other side of the door of the Flame and Scale chamber.

"I...I'm sorry," he said in a high, nervous voice, his bushy eyebrows working like wooly caterpillars on his forehead. "I never…I didn't mean…"

"Do not lie in your final moments on the mortal plane," the Goddess said through me. ***"Choose."***

Slowly, the massive heartburst snake wove its way towards him. Tannus backed up a step and then another and another. Slowly, he was being herded towards the dragon's door.

He didn't seem to realize that, though, until he was right at the doorway and another gush of hot smoke puffed out to envelope him.

"What? No!" he gasped, spinning around to see the huge golden eye. He tried to back away but he only succeeded in stepping on the trailing tail of the heartburst.

The giant snake hissed angrily and struck, its three-inch fangs sinking deep into the Head Councilor's neck. He wailed and stumbled blindly forward, straight into the doorway of the second Trial and the waiting jaws of the dragon.

The heartburst let go just in time as the Fire Drake snapped, its massive, razor-sharp teeth clicking shut around the Head Councilor. We heard him wail in terror and pain and then he was gone—a single mouthful for the immense Fire Drake.

With a hiss, the heartburst snake turned and headed back towards the Garden of Death.

I watched it go and felt the Goddess withdraw—though not all the way. I still had unfinished business here.

I was able to move and speak for myself again, so I walked over and shut the door to the Garden of Death firmly, making sure it was locked. Then I went to the door of the second Trial and shut it firmly too, closing away the Fire Drake until it should be needed again, hopefully many years in the future when I was ready to pass the throne on to my successor.

When that was done and the area was secure, I turned to face everyone again.

"Now—let all my faithful guards come forward," I said, motioning to my honor guard, the handpicked group that Kristoff had chosen who had remained loyal to me and had come rushing in to the deadly garden to save me. The Goddess was no longer speaking through me but I still felt her power — and she was the one who was giving me the words to say.

Silently, they shuffled forward. Many of them were scarred and cut by the poisonous plants and flowers and all of them were choking and coughing, having inhaled too much of the poison air in the garden.

"Your courage is beyond praise," I told them. I gave the golden scepter and orb to Kristoff to hold and turned back to them, holding out my hands. "Come to me and the Goddess will heal you through me."

One by one they came and I touched them and felt the healing power flow through me and my hands glowed with golden light. The marks and wounds faded from their skin and they stood upright, no longer coughing and choking. It was the most amazing thing — I watched it as though it was someone else doing it. And in fact it *was* — the Goddess was working through me in the most wonderful way. It made my doctor's heart sing with joy and I suddenly understood where my passion for healing had come from in the first place.

Then I heard a croaking voice say, "What about me?"

I looked up and saw a horrible sight.

Prince Morbain was hobbling forward although how he could move at all was beyond me. His face was horribly scarred and disfigured both from contact with the deadly leaves he had fallen into and from the angry *terlings* which had bitten and scratched him everywhere.

The vicious little creatures had chewed off his lips and earlobes and most of his nose, making his face look like a bloody skull. His formerly fine and rich clothes hung in tatters on his tall frame and somehow half of his luxurious mustache had gotten either ripped or burned or bitten off, giving him a gruesome, lopsided look. His feet must have gotten into the acid stream because his shoes were mostly eaten away and it looked like he was missing several toes. For that matter, his fingers weren't looking too good either — the *terlings* had really done a number on him!

He was what Zoe would have called "a complete fucking mess."

"What about me?" he croaked again. "I also went into the Garden of Death! And I am of Royal blood! You should have healed me first—before all these *commoners*." He jerked his head at my honor guard who stood around me, eyeing him impassively.

I looked at Kristoff who looked back at me frowning.

"He tried again and again to have you killed or to usurp your power. If it was up to me, he would die for his treachery. But the final decision must be yours, my Lady," he sent through our bond. *"I don't believe the bastard deserves to be healed but I know how compassionate you are."*

First do no harm, I told myself. With a sigh, I placed my glowing hands gently on Morbain's shoulders.

He reacted with a gasp and tried to shake off my grip. But he couldn't—again I felt the Goddess's energy flow through me and again she spoke, using my mouth as her own.

"For the sins you have committed against your own mother, Sundalla the 999th and for the attempts you have made against my new scion, Sundalla the 1000th, I condemn you," the Goddess boomed. *"You shall carry the wounds and pain of your time in the Garden of Death with you for the rest of your immortal life, Morbain. Never healing, never scarring—always fresh and weeping—your wounds will serve as a reminder to those that come after. This is your punishment from which you may not escape, even into death."*

Then she left me again with a great rush. I took a staggering step back into Kristoff's waiting arms, breathing hard. The Goddess was so immense it was hard to hold her all inside me. I felt like an overfull water balloon about to burst when she used me for her purposes.

"Gods," Kristoff murmured, trying to juggle the scepter and orb and hold me up at the same time. "Did you just curse him to an immortal life of pain and torment?"

"Not me," I whispered, feeling incredibly weary. "The Goddess. She did it."

"No!" Morbain staggered back, looking down at his bitten, burned, and maimed hands and arms. *"No, this cannot be!"* Turning, he fled in a shambling run. The people around him parted, making way as though he was infected with some horrible disease that might be catching.

I watched him go, feeling relieved and also very, very tired. Being the vessel of the Goddess was hard work.

"Is there anything else?" I murmured to Kristoff, as much as to myself.

"Doloroso—whatever happened to him? Did he die?" he asked.

"No and he needs to stay alive." I took a deep breath. "As long as he's locked in the form he's currently in, his ship won't generate another Doloroso for us to worry about."

"What?" Kristoff frowned and shook his head. "What do you mean?"

"His ship—it keeps a record—a backup copy, if you will, of his twisted personality. And whenever he dies in one form, it generates another to take his place—that's how the Assimilation works. We can't let that happen—Doloroso needs to stay alive and his ship needs to be quarantined and locked away forever."

"How do you know this?" he asked me.

I shook my head. The knowledge was just *there*, like a nugget of wisdom inside my brain. I had an idea that it was something my predecessor, Sundalla the 999th might have known and now her wisdom was being passed on to me.

"The Goddess, I suppose," I said. "Or maybe your old mistress knew."

"Ah yes, the Goddess." Kristoff gave me a quizzical expression. "Is she...gone?"

"I have a feeling she'll never be completely gone," I said thoughtfully. "I'm her conduit into the mortal world. I connect her to her creations and sometimes she needs a deeper connection than others." I thought of how I had felt her presence and her pleasure at the moment of our bonding the night before and how incredibly intense it had been. "You might see her again," I told Kristoff. "But don't worry—she likes you. Likes you a *lot*."

He smiled and drew me closer, still holding the scepter and Orb in one hand. It occurred to me that they weren't supposed to be able to tolerate anyone's touch but mine but clearly they approved of Kristoff too. Well, that was as it should be. He wasn't only going to be my Consort and husband, he was going to be my number one advisor in this role of awesome and immense responsibility I suddenly found myself thrust into.

And as for my other "advisors" the Council of Wisdom...well, I would deal with them later. But sufficient to say they were going to have a *lot* less power in the future.

"I'm glad the Goddess likes me since I *love* you," Kristoff murmured, and claimed my mouth in a kiss. There was a roar of approval from the gathered crowd and then two familiar faces were trying to get through the ring my honor guard had formed around me.

"Charlotte! Charlotte!" It was Leah and Zoe, both of them dressed beautifully and both out of breath from pushing and shoving their way through the packed hall.

"Leah! Zoe!" I nodded at my honor guard. "It's all right—these are my two closest friends."

They shrugged and stepped aside and then I was caught in the middle of a joyful, three-way reunion with all of us laughing and hugging and kissing and crying until I didn't know what to do with myself.

I looked around the hall filled with my new people, Royal and common alike. I looked at my best friends from Earth, my loyal guards, and of course, at my wonderful Kristoff. A feeling of joy filled me just as the Goddess had—an emotion almost too huge to contain.

I was home. Though I hadn't known it, this was where I had been headed all my life. This was why I could never click with my adopted family or feel a connection to anyone except my other two friends who were both *La-ti-zals* and had been meant to leave Earth too. It was because this place—this time—and the Goddess had been calling me.

Home. I was home and I knew I would never leave it again.

Epilogue

"So I heard you cleaned house around here." Zoe settled more comfortably on her golden cushion and nibbled another *peri-teri* fruit. It looked oddly like a miniature taco with a brownish-tan crust that split in half to reveal an inside that was dark brown with red and yellow splotches like meat with sauce and cheese. Despite its odd outward appearance, the *peri-teri* was delicious. It tasted like a cross between a watermelon, a strawberry, a peach, and buttered popcorn. Weird but addictively yummy.

I popped another fruit in my own mouth, savoring the crunch of the shell and the sweet, juicy texture of the fruit as I chewed before I answered.

"Yes, I touched everyone in the Council of Wisdom."

"You *touched* them?" Leah frowned at me. "What do you mean?"

I rapidly explained about my touch-sense and how I'd hidden it from them, along with my lack of sexual interest back when we lived on Earth.

"It's amazing your *La-ti-zal* powers developed before you even left Earth's atmosphere," Zoe remarked. "But then, I guess you are the grand-mamma of all *La-ti-zals*. And here I thought it was *my* fault you and Leah turned out to be special too—but I guess the blame for that would have to fall on *your* shoulders, Charlotte."

"Who's blaming who?" Leah asked, comfortably. "I'm *happy* I'm a *La-ti-zal*—I never would have gotten together with Grav otherwise."

"Yeah, I doubt I would have bonded with Sarden if I hadn't been one either." Zoe nodded thoughtfully. "I just wish we would have been more upfront with each other about what was going on with us. I wish I would have known I wasn't the only one who didn't much care for sex."

"Me too," Leah murmured. "I felt like such a *freak!*"

"Well, we're all making up missed time for that by enjoying sex *plenty* now." I thought of the delicious way Kristoff had made love to me for hours the night before after the grand Coronation ceremony and a shiver of pleasure ran down my spine.

"True." Zoe sighed happily. "So what did you see when you 'touched' the Council of Wisdom?"

"I saw which ones were loyal and which were with Tannus and Morbain." I shrugged. "The disloyal ones were locked away for committing treason — that was Kristoff's idea, not mine." As he was still head of my security, I believed him when he said they were still a threat.

"And what about Doloroso?" Zoe asked with a shudder. "Is he finally gone completely?"

"He's gone," I assured her. "We locked him in a stasis chamber — the same kind he had in his own ship — to make sure he can never die and spawn another version of himself. We never have to worry about him again."

After donning protective suits, some of my most trusted guards had been able to infiltrate the ship and rescue the others that Doloroso had stored in his stasis booths as "spare" hosts. They and several Grubbian merchants, which had also been found, were now living their own lives and the ship had been sealed and quarantined.

Morbain, also, had been confined to his quarters. He'd been cleaned up and treated as much as possible by the Majoran doctor I liked, whose name was Lanarra. But it didn't matter what she did, he kept on bleeding through his bandages and his cuts and burns and bites refused to heal. He was a truly horrible and miserable sight.

Just thinking of him made me shiver. I was glad the Goddess had been the one to punish him and not me, although most of the Royal Court didn't seem to know that. I got a great deal of respect everywhere I went and Kristoff declared that my safety should be secured for years to come. Not that it stopped him from being ever vigilant and watchful. Even being my Consort couldn't make him give up his duties as Captain of the Imperial Guards, always careful and protective, making sure his lady was secure.

"So you weeded out the baddies in the Council," Leah said. "What happened to the rest?"

"They're still the Council of Wisdom," I said. "But they don't have nearly as much power as they did. They can't dictate to the Empress or make major decisions without consulting me."

I had put the youngest Councilor—Minchin—who had spoken out against Tannus, in charge. My working relationship with the Council was now much more respectful and amicable than it had been under the old Head Councilor.

Kristoff had pointed out that the rest of the Council was probably afraid I would feed them to the Fire Drake but I didn't really believe they thought that. I had done some research and apparently having the Goddess manifest in the Empress was a fairly rare occurrence. I was incredibly grateful that she had chosen to come to me at the time she did. Without her, Kristoff would be dead and I would probably be joined to Morbain while he and Tannus ruled the galaxy through me.

"What about the doctor you told us about?" Zoe asked, breaking my train of thought. "You know—the one with the awful bedside manner?"

"Who—Doctor Churika?" I sighed. "I didn't have the heart to lock her away. I banished her from Femme One instead and sent her home. Lanara's my new Royal healer and she's teaching me everything she knows." I smiled happily.

Zoe grinned and popped another *peri-teri* into her mouth.

"Leave it to you to continue your medical training even now that you're queen of the universe."

"*Empress* of the *galaxy*," I corrected her automatically. "And you know I love to learn."

"I know." Leah frowned. "But you're not worried Churika will turn against you again? Maybe you should have locked her up along with the bad Council members."

"I thought about it, but I think she was just trying to keep the old order going—not actually overthrow the throne." I shook my head. "I just couldn't lock her away. She's Denarin, you know so she would have had two mates to miss her, not just one."

"That's hard to wrap your head around." Leah shivered. "I

can't imagine having *two* seven-foot-tall aliens to keep happy in the sack, not just one."

"Actually, according to Kristoff they have a really equitable relationship." I remembered the pair of mis-matched Denarins I had met when he first took me to see Dr. Churika on her home planet. The ones who had needed a Pure One to help them break the tie that had somehow mistakenly grown between them.

"Oh?" Leah asked. "How so?"

"They usually bond as boys and grow up together—there's one Alpha who works outside the home and the Beta usually stays home to help with everything around the house," I said. "That means the woman they find to bond with can choose what she wants to do—work outside or be a stay at home mom."

"Wow—that's great!" Zoe said enthusiastically. "It really does sound ideal—if you don't mind being split in two by two guys at once."

"Zoe!" Leah smacked her on the arm and our friend winced and grinned unrepentantly, her curly red hair bouncing.

"Well, it's *true.*"

"Look, all this is interesting…" Leah's face had gone suddenly serious. "But what I want to know is what are you going to do about the Alien Mate Index? You know—how the Commercians have set up shop on Earth and are basically *selling* Earth girls? It's awful! Now that you're Empress, Charlotte, you *have* to stop it."

"You sound like you have a personal stake in it, or something," Zoe said, frowning. "What gives, Leah—why are you so upset?"

"Well, remember how you told me being a *La-ti-zal* could be catching?" Leah nibbled her lower lip anxiously.

"Yeah, so?" Zoe frowned.

"I, uh, was just worried that I might have given it to someone else. Before I left Earth the second time with Grav."

"What? Who?" Zoe demanded.

"Well, promise you won't be mad at me…" Leah ducked her head. "It was your friend—you know the one from your law office that you recommended to me because she did really cheap divorce papers?"

"What?" Zoe exploded. "You made Rylee a *La-ti-zal*? Do you know what you've done?"

"I know, I *know*." Leah looked like she might cry. "Look, I'm not even sure I gave it to her, all right? It's just that our drinks got switched at Starbucks and she drank after me. Would that be enough to get it? I mean, I hope not but—"

"Guys, come on," I interrupted her. "You're both acting like being a *La-ti-zal* is some awful disease when it's actually pretty wonderful. Without it, none of us would be where we are today—or with the men we're with."

"That's true, I guess," Zoe said grudgingly. "It's just that I really *liked* Rylee and I *don't* like the idea of some alien jerk just buying her and taking her away from Earth."

"You mean like Sarden did with you?" Leah asked quietly.

"Shut up—that's different," Zoe said crossly. She looked at me. "Leah is right—you have to shut the Commercians and their damn Alien Mate Index down!"

It was on the tip of my tongue to say, *of course—I'll make it the first order of business.* But when I opened my mouth to say it, I heard a soft but powerful voice inside.

No, my child... there is more to come.

I closed my mouth and shook my head.

"No," I said. "I can't close it."

"What?" Leah and Zoe both exclaimed and Zoe demanded, "Why not?"

"The Goddess doesn't want me to." I looked at them apologetically. "That's not to say we can't regulate it some—put the guys who go there looking for a wife through a screening process and make sure the girls who get taken really want to go—something like that. But I can't shut it down completely."

"But—" Zoe began.

"Think of all the other *La-ti-zals* who could be on Earth right now," I said, before she could really get going. "Living lives of quiet desperation. Wondering, like we did, why they don't have any sexual urges or feelings. Wondering why they feel like they don't fit in—why they don't belong. Can you really condemn them to never find love and a rewarding life outside of our home planet?"

"I...never thought of it that way," Leah admitted.

"I didn't either until the Goddess showed me," I said. "Although I *did* give a pair of Denarins the coordinates to Earth. Only *after* I touched them and could tell that they wouldn't hurt a female, though."

"You what?" Zoe still looked upset. "Why would you do that?"

I shrugged. "They were stuck in some kind of a wrong bonding—remember I told you they come in pairs, one Alpha and one Beta? Well, these two were both Alphas and they were miserable together. They just needed the touch of a Pure One to help break their bond and then they swore to let her go."

"In the meantime some poor girl on Earth is going to think she's going crazy when she gets sucked through the bathroom mirror or the toaster or her yogurt spoon and winds up naked on those damn greedy Commercians' space station," Zoe grumbled. "Well all I can say is it better not be my friend, Rylee!"

"If it makes you feel any better, Grav and I can go check up on her," Leah said, patting her hand placatingly. "I'm overdue for a visit with my mom anyway."

"Yeah, well—okay." Zoe sighed and pointed at me. "And you better put some regulations and a damn good screening process into effect!"

"Now who's acting like the queen of the universe?" I said dryly. "Yes, Zoe, I'll see to it, I promise."

"Good." She sighed and settled more comfortably on the cushions of the gold brocade couch. "As long as Rylee and all the other girls like her are okay, I'm fine with a little interstellar adventure."

"I'm sure she will be," I said, smiling. "Don't worry about your friend, Zoe—she'll be just fine."

But would she?

* * *

Author's Note--if you have enjoyed Descended, please take a moment to leave a short review. Good reviews are worth their weight in gold--they help readers decide to take a chance on a new book. Also, they give me the warm fuzzies. :)

Thanks for being such an awesome reader! :) Evangeline

Want more Alien Mate Index?

Of course you do! And don't worry, book 4, **Severed**, is on the way in a couple of months. (And yes, I'm going to write more Kindred too.) For now, here's a blurb to get you interested.

Hugs to you all, Evangeline

.

Sneak Peek at
Alien Mate Index
#4: Severed

coming Fall of 2016

Rylee Hale is having a hard time. As a new business owner just starting out on her own, she's struggling to attract new clients to her paralegal business.

Then she attracts two that are way more than she can handle.

Drace and Lucian are Denarins—a race of the Twelve Peoples where two males bond together in order to join with a single female. An Alpha and a Beta make the perfect pair to attract and care for a woman in every detail of her life.

But what happens when two Alphas get wrongfully bonded? That's the dilemma Lucian and Drace are in and only a Pure One from Earth can help them. When they see Rylee helping a couple with their divorce in the AMI viewscreen, they decide she's exactly the female they need to break the bond between them.

Nobody asked Rylee what she thought about being abducted from her life on Earth and caught in the middle of a conflict between two huge, muscular alien males, but she's a smart girl — she can handle herself. But what will happen when the bond between Drace and Lucian starts spilling into her personal life? And once she gets a taste of being bonded to two sexy men who want to please her in every way, will she be able to stand by and watch them be...Severed?

Also by Evangeline Anderson

You can find links to all of the following books at my website: **www.EvangelineAnderson.com**

Brides of the Kindred series

Claimed (Also available in Audio and Print format)

Hunted (Also available in Audio and Print format)

Sought (Also Available in Audio and Print format)

Found   (Also Available in Audio and Print format)

Revealed (Also available in Print)

Pursued (Also available in Print)

Exiled   (Also available in Print)

Shadowed   (Also available in Print)

Chained

Divided

Devoured (Also available in Print)

Enhanced

Cursed

Enslaved

Targeted

Forgotten

Switched (Also available in Print)

Brides of the Kindred #18: Coming Fall of 2016

Mastering the Mistress (Brides of the Kindred Novella)

Born to Darkness series

Crimson Debt (Also available in Audio)

Scarlet Heat   (Also available in Audio)

Ruby Shadows (Also available in Audio)

Cardinal Sins (Coming Soon)

Alien Mate Index series

Abducted (Also available in Print)

Protected (Also available in Print)

Descended (Also available in Print)

The Institute series

The Institute: Daddy Issues

The Institute: Mishka's Spanking

Compendiums

Brides of the Kindred Volume One

    Contains Claimed, Hunted, Sought and Found

Born to Darkness Box Set

    Contains Crimson Debt, Scarlet Heat, and Ruby Shadows

Stand Alone Novels

Purity (Also available in Audio)

Stress Relief

The Last Man on Earth

Anyone U Want

Shadow Dreams

Mastering the Mistress

YA Novels

The Academy

About the Author

Evangeline Anderson is the New York Times and USA Today Best Selling Author of the Brides of the Kindred, Alien Mate Index, and Born to Darkness series. She is thirty-something and lives in Florida with a husband, a son, and two cats. She had been writing erotic fiction for her own gratification for a number of years before it occurred to her to try and get paid for it. To her delight, she found that it was actually possible to get money for having a dirty mind and she has been writing paranormal and Sci-fi erotica steadily ever since.

Find her online at her website: www.EvangelineAnderson.com

Come visit for some free reads. Or, to be the first to find out about new books, join her newsletter.

Newsletter – www.EvangelineAnderson.com

Website – www.EvangelineAnderson.com

FaceBook – facebook.com/pages/Evangeline-Anderson-Appreciation-
Page/170314539700701

Twitter – twitter.com/EvangelineA

Pinterest – pinterest.com/vangiekitty/

Goodreads – goodreads.com/user/show/2227318-evangeline-anderson

Instagram – instagram.com/evangeline_anderson_author/

Audio book newsletter – www.EvangelineAnderson.com

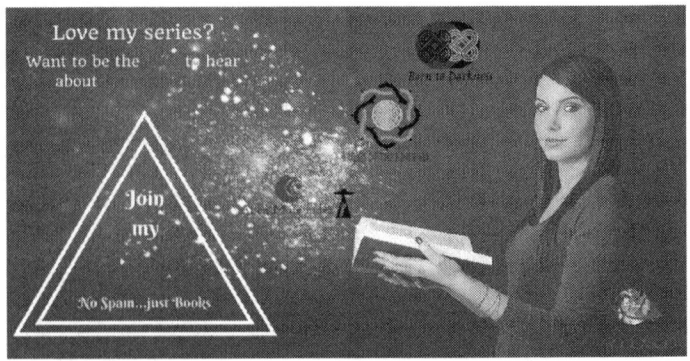

Join my newsletter at
www.EvangelineAnderson.com

Or if you love audiobooks, I have quite a few of those too...

Join my audiobook newsletter at
www.EvangelineAnderson.com

34745302R00224

Made in the USA
Middletown, DE
02 September 2016